* * *

Battle for Intus

Book Two of the Battles of the Republic

* * *

By James Rosone
and
Brandon Ellis

* * *

Illustration © Tom Edwards
Tom EdwardsDesign.com

* * *

Published in conjunction with Front Line Publishing, Inc.

# Table of Contents


Chapter 1: The Running Gunfight
Chapter 2: Briefing at Kita
Chapter 3: Game Point
Chapter 4: Storm Warning
Chapter 5: Pieces of the Past
Chapter 6: Doubts and Duties
Chapter 7: The Mysterious Sphere
Chapter 8: It's Not What it Appears
Chapter 9: Midnight Maintenance
Chapter 10: Wolfpack's Flight
Chapter 11: Hot Drop
Chapter 12: Ford's Watch
Chapter 13: Friendly Fire
Chapter 14: Test Site
Chapter 15: Subduing the Beast
Chapter 16: Night Thoughts
Chapter 17: Squadron Trust
Chapter 18: High Maintenance
Chapter 19: Whisper Point
Chapter 20: No Rest for Love
Chapter 21: Interview with a Zodark
Chapter 22: Second Thoughts
Chapter 23: Cracks in the Core
Chapter 24: The Wounded Bird
Chapter 25: Euphoria
Chapter 26: Learning Curve
Chapter 27: Valley of Doubt
Chapter 28: Duty and Instinct
Chapter 29: Orders Are Orders
Chapter 30 When a Plan Comes Together
Chapter 31: Micro-fissures
Chapter 32: Empty Cup
Chapter 33: Hit and Run
Chapter 34: Locus of Control
Chapter 35: Ready to Fly
Chapter 36: Edge of Darkness

Chapter 37: Burden of Command
Chapter 38: Codeword Athena
Chapter 39: Digital Hunt
Chapter 40: Ion Fire
Chapter 41: Cyber Strike
Chapter 42: Behind Enemy Lines
Chapter 43: Open Fire
Chapter 44: The Right Call
Chapter 45: Quiet Confessions
Chapter 46: Beyond the Pod
Chapter 47: Honor Among Heroes
Chapter 48: Clear Skies
Chapter 49: The Stage is Set
Abbreviation Key

# Chapter 1:
# The Running Gunfight

**Year 2097**
**Moon XF752 Orbit**
**RNS** *Poseidon*

Rhom shouted over the rising noise of alerts. "Zodark cruisers splitting! They're accelerating hard, trying to sweep around our flank. They're angling for the *Australia*!"

Lee grimaced. "They're trying to box us in. Not today. Bring primaries to bear. Target the lead cruiser and fire at will."

The *Poseidon's* 16-inch and 36-inch magrail turrets roared to life, hurling kinetic slugs at blinding speeds. One slug ripped straight through the nearest cruiser, followed by an internal explosion tearing it in half.

"Lucky shot," Rhom said, no doubt shocked his gun crews had scored such a hit with their first volley.

"My compliments to your crew," Lee replied, just as surprised as Rhom. *Maybe some luck is breaking our way after all...*

"*Thunder* scoring hits on a second cruiser," Sato said. "*Atlantis* is shifting to support—firing now!"

The combined barrage from *Thunder* and *Atlantis* smashed through another Zodark cruiser's armor. A fireball replaced it a moment later.

"Two down!" Rhom called.

The celebration was short-lived.

"*Oceanus* has taken a glancing hit. Plasma strike on her mid-section," Sato reported.

A thundering ripple across space signaled the *Australia's* response. Her twelve massive 36-inch magrail turrets—six per side—opened up, flinging projectiles cracking across the void with devastating force. One round clipped a Zodark battleship's prow—its forward plating peeled back, spewing debris and flashing with arcs of electricity.

"They're adjusting formation. Zodark battleship turning to bring broadsides," Rhom said.

"*Argo's* been hit," Sato called out. "Port side—looks like Deck 5 took a full plasma burn. They're still in the fight."

Lee scanned the tactical overlay. "Have *Oceanus* and *Stockholm* shift port to cover the *Australia's* flank. We need to keep them from closing the trap."

The starfield burned bright as another round of magrail salvos erupted from *Poseidon*, *Thunder*, and *Atlantis*. The darkness of space was alive with fire trails, detonations, and expanding clouds of shrapnel.

Zodark laser fire lanced back—white-hot, disciplined beams burning into hull plating. A near-miss skimmed *Thunder's* ventral hull, the weapon's heat sparking flames along its lower decks.

"Sir," Rhom said, "remaining cruisers are adjusting again. Not breaking off."

"They're stalling for time," Lee muttered. "That second frigate must've already radioed for help."

After they'd burst through the stargate not long ago, the situation had rapidly escalated into a full-scale engagement. Their arrival had placed them directly in the midst of a Zodark gas mining operation—where four bulbous mining vessels had been tethered to a collection array glowing with processed gases. When they'd first engaged, the *Poseidon's* turbo-lasers had struck one of the miners, causing it to erupt in a brilliant fireball. However, Lee's tactical decision to attack the mining site alerted nearby Zodark forces, who responded with overwhelming numbers—two battleships, four cruisers, and additional reinforcements arriving.

As the Republic ships found themselves outgunned, they formed a defensive perimeter, with the RNS *Australia*, commanded by Captain Eamon Roberts, serving as their main firepower. The man was also the Deputy Joint Task Force Commander—the ranking Republic officer in theater.

Initially, the *Poseidon* had scored a critical hit on the lead Zodark cruiser with its magrail turrets, splitting it in half, while the *Thunder* and *Atlantis's* combined firepower had destroyed a second cruiser. Despite these early successes, Republic ships began taking damage, with *Oceanus* suffering a plasma strike and *Argo* experiencing significant hull damage on Deck 5.

The Zodark forces employed encirclement tactics, attempting to isolate and destroy the *Australia*. Lee had ordered *Oceanus* and *Stockholm* to protect their flagship's flank, while continuing to engage the enemy. The Republic ships had inflicted significant damage on a Zodark battleship, but Lee had recognized the enemy was stalling for time as additional reinforcements approached.

With communication delays hampering coordination and no word from the Primord frigate with their rendezvous coordinates, the Republic squadron had found themselves in a desperate holding action against superior numbers.

At the moment, the gas miners had gone dark—either shutting down systems or preparing to self-destruct. One floated dead, spinning slowly in the wreckage of its sister vessel.

Sato glanced at her Qpad. "We've got less than ten minutes until we're potentially overwhelmed. Still no word from the Primords."

Lee stared at the hell unfolding outside their hull. Even with the hits they'd landed, the enemy force hadn't blinked.

"Then we hold. We hold the line until they get here. No one breaks formation. No one runs."

The *Poseidon's* next salvo streaked through the black.

"New contacts," Rodriguez called from comms. "Enemy strike wings launching. Fighters and bombers."

"Visuals coming up," Sato confirmed.

On screen, swarms of small Zodark starfighters—sleek, batlike vessels with emerald ion drives—poured out from the hangar bays of the battleships. Heavier bombers followed, each with torpedo pods and underwing payloads.

"Thirty-six fighters. Twelve bombers. They're forming up fast," Rhom said.

"They're going for a coordinated strike," Lee replied. "We're about to get hit hard."

He looked toward Sato. "Alert all ships—brace for incoming."

A priority comm beeped through from the *Australia*. Roberts's haggard face appeared on the tactical screen.

"Commander Lee, what the hell are you waiting for with those probes? We need intel from this sector now. Launch everything we've got—the more eyes out there, the better."

"Aye, sir," Lee acknowledged. "Baldry, deploy all reconnaissance probes, maximum spread pattern."

Ensign Jace Baldry punched in commands on the sensor console. "Launching probes now, sir. Deploying in five-second intervals."

On the tactical display, small blue dots burst from the *Poseidon*'s launch tubes, streaking outward in all directions. Almost immediately, several winked out as Zodark point defenses caught them.

"Four probes down already, sir," Baldry reported, eyes dead set on his station's interface. "Six more advancing deeper into the sector. Trajectory calculations complete—they'll reach about six million kilometers in seventeen minutes."

"How many made it past their front line?" Lee asked.

"Nine total still operational, sir. Three more just went dark—Zodarks are picking them off."

The trap had been sprung—and now, the full hammer of the Zodark war machine was descending.

Before the strike wings could fully break formation, a new blip appeared on the sensor feed.

"Unknown contact—friendly IFF!" Rhom yelled out. "It's Primord. A frigate just jumped in—right into the middle of the fight."

The vessel broadcast across encrypted channels, delivering the jump coordinates.

Rodriguez's voice rose. "Transmission confirmed. Data received—coordinates relayed to the squadron."

Roberts's tone sliced through the battle noise. "All ships—break contact immediately. Prepare for emergency FTL. We're jumping to the new coordinates now."

"Reynolds," Lee said. "Calculate jump path and spool engines—get us the hell out of here."

"Jump solution plotted. Spooling now—ten seconds," Reynolds replied.

"Witkowski, prep local jammers and launch flares. Make us a hard target in case they try to hit us during spool."

"On it, Captain," replied the EWO, Lieutenant Jakub Witkowski.

The space around the Poseidon flared with defensive countermeasures. Plasma bolts raced toward them, narrowly missing as the ship's frame vibrated under the intensity.

"Five seconds."

Through the main monitor, the rest of the squadron pivoted. *Thunder* and *Oceanus* had formed a rear shield with the *Australia*, while *Atlantis* and *Argo* covered the right flank.

"Two seconds."

The Ark-Fold FTL drive screamed to life.

"Wait!" Baldry's voice rang to life. "Sir, we're getting an upload from Probe Seven! It found something near the third planetary body."

"Reynolds, hold jump," Lee ordered.

"Holding at T-minus one, sir. Drives still hot."

"How long for the full upload?" Lee demanded.

Baldry's kept his gaze locked on the data streaming across his monitor. "Eighteen seconds for complete data transfer. Eighteen percent... thirty-six percent..."

Rhom grabbed at his leg, something Lee caught out of the corner of his eye. "Captain, enemy fighters closing!"

"Forty-three percent... sixty..."

Multiple impacts rocked the hull as Zodark energy weapons found their mark.

"Damage to starboard, section three, upper gun deck," Sato reported.

"Eighty-nine percent..."

The bridge lights flashed on and off repeatedly as another hit landed.

"Complete!" Baldry said. "Upload received."

"Jump now!" Lee commanded.

The *Poseidon*—and the rest of the battered Republic task force—vanished in streaks of light, leaving nothing behind but shockwaves and a sky full of fire.

Silence returned to the bridge.

Lee slumped slightly in his chair, exhaling for what felt like the first time in minutes.

No one said anything at first—the air filled with the soft hum of systems stabilizing and the quiet rustle of relieved breathing.

Rhom spoke first. "Close call, everyone."

Sato sat back, rubbing her temple. "If that Primord ship had shown up even a minute later…"

"We might not be here," Lee finished her sentence for her.

Rodriguez nodded. "Those bombers could very well have been our death."

Lee looked around at his crew—exhausted, burned out…but alive. He let himself feel the weight of everything they'd survived. The pressure in his chest finally began to ease.

"That was our welcome to Rass," he said.

"Think the rest of the mission is going to be easier, sir?" Reynolds asked.

Lee smiled. "Not a damn chance."

**Chapter 2:**
**Briefing at Kita**

**Year 2097**
**Stavros Naval Shipyard, orbiting Helios Forge**
**Primord system of Kita**

A week had passed since Lee's narrow escape. The memory of those final seconds still played in his mind every so often—jumping out just in time. Many of his ships had taken major hits before that transition. It was a miracle they hadn't lost anyone.

In the interim, he and his damaged squadron, along with the *Australia*, had traveled back toward Kita for repairs. Now, as the Republic recon task force burst out of the FTL bubble, the usual discomfort of the transition hit Lee. As the Ark-Fold FTL drives disengaged and the MPD thrusters kicked online, his stomach churned, and a brief dizziness took hold. The disorientation slowly faded as they returned to normal space.

In spite of years flying through the void, he'd never quite acclimated to the sensation of FTL exits. Sometimes, it was even painful. He once described it to a civilian reporter who'd never experienced FTL travel as the experience feeling like growing pains—and all over the body—for a split second, then gone, and the gone part was just odd, and something he really couldn't describe.

As the starfield stabilized, so did planet Kita. She was an emerald jewel of a world. Before her was an absolutely giant structure coming into view—the Stavros Naval Shipyard.

It sprawled outward from the planet's orbit. It was full of docks and repair bays. Its incredible size boggled the mind—twice the size of Earth's New York City. Two hundred berths stretched out—each was capable of holding vessels from frigates to orbital assault ships.

Repair drones swarmed around the shipyard. Worker ships moved around damaged vessels. Sparks from welding torches lit up the docks, accompanied by the blue flare of plasma cutters slicing through twisted metal. Tethered Primord technicians in EVA suits floated between hull breaches.

"Rodriguez, request docking permission for the fleet," Lee said.

"Aye, sir." Lieutenant Rodriguez interacted with her console. A moment later, her voice rang out. "Permission granted, Captain. We're receiving individual berth assignments now."

The main viewscreen displayed a holographic overlay of the shipyard. Primord symbols pulsed beside each dock. A translation holo-program kicked in to convert the Primord script to Republic Standard.

"*Poseidon* is cleared for Berth Xy-9," Rodriguez said.

Lee nodded. Damage assessment data scrolled across a secondary display. Another ship, the *Argo*'s, magrail barrels one and three were red. It meant they needed to be fixed. He studied the detailed breakdown of the frigate's injuries.

"*Argo*'s starboard hull is breached in three sections," he muttered, more to Sato than the bridge crew. "Primary reactor off-line, life support systems running on auxiliary power. That last volley nearly gutted her."

The screen highlighted the vessel's wounds—tears in the exterior plating, exposed power capacitors sparking into the void.

*They were lucky to make it back at all*, Lee thought.

"Take us in, helm," Lee said. "Nice and easy. Let's not add any more scratches to our paintwork, all right?"

As the *Poseidon* glided toward its berth, the rest of his fleet moved to their own docking points. The massive repair clamps of Xy-9 reached out to embrace his ship like the arms of a metal giant. The docking rings engaged with a *thunk*.

"Docking complete, Captain," Rodriguez reported. "All systems nominal."

Lee nodded just as Rodriguez's console beeped.

"Sir, priority message from Captain Eamon Roberts on the RNS *Australia*. He's requesting your immediate presence for a briefing. Commander Sato is to accompany you."

"Understood," Lee said. "Rhom, you have the bridge. Once repairs are underway, the crew can begin rotating for shore leave."

"Aye-aye, Captain."

Lee tapped his comm. "Engineering, this is the captain."

After a moment, Chief Engineer Boyd MacGregor's thick tone filled the bridge. "MacGregor here, sir. What can I do for you?"

"Chief, I need you to oversee the repair process. Keep a detailed log of all work done and materials used."

"Aye, Captain. I'll be on it. Any particular systems you want prioritized?"

"Focus on the hull breaches and weapons systems. The usual. We need to be combat-ready as soon as possible."

"Right, Cap. I'll have the crew swarming over her right away."

"Good. And, Mac, try not to antagonize the Primord engineers this time."

A chuckle came through the comm. "Oh, all right, Captain, but where's the fun in that?" He sighed. "But don't you worry a lick. I'll play nice with them ones."

"See that you do," Lee directed. "We need their expertise."

"Understood, sir," MacGregor replied. "Though I still say our systems are more resilient than theirs. Especially with those Altairian Gen-II Arkanorian Reactors we're running. Each one generates sixteen hundred megawatts. That's an obscene amount of power."

"It's impressive," Lee agreed.

"Impressive? It's revolutionary, sir. Those damn things power the ship's two Cyclone MPD thrusters for interplanetary travel and two Ark-Fold FTL drives for interstellar jumps. I mean, impressive, no? These Ark-Fold drives cut FTL travel times from two light-years per month to one light-year per day. That means the old six-month haul from Earth to New Eden is now just six days. Obviously, that's a new type of ball game right there."

"When you put it that way, Mac, I see why you're still excited about them. Now, just get us back in fighting shape."

"Aye, Cap. We'll have the old girl purring like subatomic strings vibrating in eleven dimensions."

*What the hell does that mean?* "Excellent. Keep me updated on your progress."

"Will do, sir. MacGregor out."

Lee faced Sato. "Commander, shall we?"

"After you, Captain." Sato motioned toward the bridge's exit.

Lee addressed the bridge crew once more. "As you were. Rhom, you have the conn."

"Aye, sir. I've got the conn," Rhom replied.

Lee and Sato strode off the bridge and down the corridor. The lift doors opened, closing quietly behind them.

"Hangar deck," Lee told the elevator. The lift whirred to life, taking them downward.

Sato cleared her throat. "Captain, if I may speak freely?"

Lee kept his eyes still on the lift's display. "Of course, XO. What's on your mind?"

Sato hesitated. "Been reviewing our recent engagement reports, sir. Casualty rates for human forces compared to our allies… they're disproportionate."

"Go on."

"It's just… I understand the importance of our mission, sir—abolishing slavery across the galaxy, expanding human influence, gaining access to advanced technologies, medicines, and scientific knowledge." Sato's voice lowered slightly. "But, I can't help but notice we're often at the forefront of the most dangerous operations."

"Are you suggesting our allies are holding back?"

"Not exactly, sir," Sato replied. "More that… well, humans seem to be assigned to the most aggressive maneuvers. Our tactics are often more… direct than those of

the Primords or any other species we know of in the Galactic
Empire.”

"You're not wrong. Humans have a reputation for
being effective shock troops.”

"I acknowledge that, sir,” Sato replied. “But at what
cost? Sometimes it feels like we're…” She trailed off,
searching for the right words.

"Like we're what, Commander?” Lee asked.

"Like we're being used as cannon fodder. Our allies
benefit from our aggression. You know, our willingness to
take risks. Are we truly equal partners in this alliance?”

The lift slowed to a stop. Neither officer moved to exit.

Lee turned to fully face Sato. “Those are dangerous
thoughts, Commander. But I'd be lying if I said they haven't
crossed my mind as well. We're in a… challenging situation.
Humanity's still proving itself on the galactic stage. Our
aggression, our adaptability—they're assets our allies need.
Thing is, you're right to question if the cost is too high.”

Sato nodded. “I appreciate your understanding, sir.
Don't mean to sound disloyal or ungrateful for our allies'
support. It's just…”

"It's a heavy burden to bear,” Lee finished for her.
"And it's our job to make sure that burden is worth it—that
the sacrifices we make lead to a better future for humanity and
our allies alike.”

The lift doors opened, showing a busy hangar.

"Keep thinking critically,” Lee said. “But remember,
we have a duty to perform. We can question the larger picture,
but we can't let it compromise our mission or the safety of our
crew.”

"Understood, Captain. Thanks for listening.”

As they stepped out into the hangar, Lee added quietly,
"And, Sato? These conversations stay between us.
Understood?”

"Of course, Captain.”

On the hangar deck, crew members and maintenance
personnel scurried about. They prepped shuttles and
performed checks on crafts. Lee and Sato made their way past

them and to the personnel transfer tube connecting *Poseidon* to the shipyard proper.

As they stepped through, the *Poseidon*'s stuffy corridors gave way to the natural architecture of the Primord facility. Living plants grew from the metallic floor. Their leaves swayed in an unseen breeze. A weird impression of being observed overtook Lee as they passed a cluster of fernlike flora. The fronds turned, tracking their movement.

Lee shook his head. "I swear those plants have eyes."

"Second that," Sato said.

Holodisplays lined the walls and showed real-time data of every ship docked in the facility. Automated repair drones zipped through specially designed conduits, ferrying tools and materials to where they were needed most.

The Primords' technological prowess was evident in every aspect of the shipyard's operations. Lee made a mental note to have his engineering team study their methods closely. Maybe they could come up with something as clever as the Prims. With Mac and his crew, Lee figured they could.

As they walked the corridors, the plant life continued to react to their presence. A vine-covered arch they passed under rustled as if greeting them. A cluster of purple flowers brightened as they neared, only to dim once they'd moved on. For a few seconds, Lee walked backwards to observe. And, yes, when another person closed in on the purple flowers, the flowers lit up, only to dim back down once the individual walked on by. To Lee, it was remarkable. If he had time, he'd love to read a peer-reviewed article on what the heck that was about, and why it brightened in the presence of a human.

Five minutes passed, and Lee and Sato arrived at the briefing room—a big chamber with a large holoscreen in the center. There sat Captain Eamon Roberts. As the task force commander aboard the RNS *Australia*, a *Ryan*-class battleship, Roberts served as Lee's direct superior and critical link to the higher Fleet Command. His ship was docked at the shipyard as well.

Lee snapped to attention, saluting. "Captain Roberts, Captain Ripley Willis Lee reporting as ordered."

"At ease, Captain," Roberts said. "I've reviewed your after-action report and the combat vids. Interesting job."

"Thank you, sir. We sustained heavy damage, but the crew performed admirably under extreme tactical pressure."

Roberts's expression remained stern. "Your after-action documentation lacks specific detail regarding evasive pattern selection during your FTL exit from the battle. The tactical analysis section is incomplete. I expect more thorough documentation in future reports, Captain Lee."

Lee stiffened slightly. "Understood, sir. I'll ensure all subsequent reports include comprehensive tactical breakdowns with full pattern nomenclature and response metrics."

Before they could continue, the door slid open. A towering Primord male entered. He drew everyone's attention. Lee looked up at the newcomer. The Primord's giant elongated nose and oversized pointed ears made him unique even among his own kind.

"I am Admiral Dhorsar," the Prim said, raising his arm in the customary Primord greeting. "Please, be seated."

Lee and Sato sat on chairs seemingly grown from roots straight out of the floor. The seats swiveled smoothly, which was odd considering their organic appearance. The meeting table before them glittered like a nebula trapped in crystal.

Captain Roberts started the meeting. "Let's begin. The data from your surviving probe has given a… somber picture."

A holographic display powered on, showing a view of the Rass system. Admiral Dhorsar gestured, and the image zoomed in on planet Rass.

"As you can see," Dhorsar said, his translated voice carrying a little distortion, "the Zodarks have established a defensive network."

The holo highlighted rings of massive asteroids near Rass, floating at various strategic points in the system. Each rock bristled with weaponry.

Roberts chimed in. "We're looking at approximately seventy-eight of these platforms. They're significantly smaller than moons but large enough to house substantial firepower."

Lee took in the images on the screen. "Those aren't natural formations. What kind of armaments are we dealing with?"

Dhorsar manipulated the hologram, zooming in on one of the asteroids. "Each platform is equipped with high-yield laser cannons and torpedo tubes. The firepower is… considerable."

Sato spoke up. "Any weak points we can exploit?"

"That's where it gets interesting," Roberts replied. "Intel suggests there are six hub platforms, each controlling thirteen others. Take out a hub, and you neutralize its subordinate platforms."

"Sounds like a priority target," Lee said. "Threat assessment?"

Dhorsar's features twisted into what Lee assumed was a grimace. "The hubs are heavily fortified. Our scans indicate thick rock shielding, possibly reinforced. A sustained bombardment would be… inefficient."

"Not to mention it would telegraph our intentions," Lee added. "How many Zodark personnel are we looking at inside these hubs?"

Roberts shook his head. "Unknown. We're still analyzing the data, but it's clear they're manned facilities. Understand, this is the first time we've encountered such defensive platforms. We're still analyzing to find their weaknesses before we even attempt an all-out assault."

Sato leaned back in her organic chair, which adjusted to her posture. "The density of these asteroids is remarkable. Do the scans show they're far more compact than natural formations? I know they're reinforced, but is that really rock material or armor?"

"It's real rock," Roberts said. "The Zodarks have engineered these to be incredibly robust too. Our standard mining equipment would be ineffective. And look at the control systems embedded throughout. They're listed under the largest of the asteroids on the image there. They've essentially turned these asteroids into massive maneuverable space stations."

The holo zoomed in on the biggest asteroid. It displayed numerous sophisticated systems. Gravitational field manipulators littered the surface. This allowed control over the asteroid's movement. An inertial dampening grid crisscrossed the interior to stabilize the rock during maneuvers as well. Spatial displacement engines sat nestled deep within the rock, while a communication array sprawled across one hemisphere. Plasma containment fields glowed in a few places above the rock's surface. They were there to channel immense energies to power the rock, and everything else inside.

"The defensive capabilities are equally impressive," Dhorsar said. "Point-defense systems, torpedoes, and what appear to be gravity manipulators."

Lee scratched his chin. "They could theoretically defend an entire planet with just a handful of these stations."

"And they have seventy-eight of them," Robert said. "That's precisely why we need to understand them better, Lee. These aren't just weapons. They're incredible feats of engineering—like worlds in themselves, really. Now, to Rass itself..."

The hologram shifted to the scarred surface of Rass. Its terrain was marred by mining operations and industrial complexes. Deserts stretched between scattered mountains. The occasional rivers and lakes came into view. Roughly forty percent of the planet's surface remained covered by oceans, though even these appeared lifeless.

Networks of buildings and facilities dotted the crimson landscape. When the hologram zeroed in on a specific region, Lee's stomach turned. Images of enslaved Primords toiling in harsh conditions moved across the holo. Emaciated figures, their skin hanging loosely on skeletal frames, strained under backbreaking work. Some tossed massive stones into metal crates. Others hauled buckets overflowing with glimmering dust. In deep pits, Primords chiseled at rock faces. They worked these people practically to death.

*Who'd want to live under those conditions?* Lee mused. *No one, and it's why we fight.*

Heavily armed Zodark guards patrolled the area. In one of the vids, a group of Primords struggled to push an enormous hovercart filled with ore. Their feet slipped in the loose soil as they fought against the weight. Nearby, others were forced to sift through piles of what appeared to be toxic waste with their bare hands. They searched for something Lee couldn't quite make out while their skin peeled.

Although Lee maintained a stoic exterior, his inner fury blazed like never before. The injustice of it all—the subjugation, the cruelty, the disregard for life.

*These damn Zodarks need to be stopped*, he thought. *It's as simple as that.*

Lee read the population estimates—1,200,000 Primords enslaved on Rass. They were outnumbered by 50,000,000 Zodark occupiers.

"Captain Lee, the intelligence we've gathered is invaluable," Captain Roberts said. "We're still extrapolating information from our task force's data from all the probes that survived long enough to transmit info, but it's already showing a clearer view of the situation planetside."

Lee nodded, forcing himself to focus on Roberts's words.

"Now," Roberts continued, "We have a new mission for you and Commander Sato. To be clear, all our missions have changed not a little, but a lot after the intel we've gathered. Why? Because we need more intel from the glimpse of information we received in the Rass system."

Lee straightened in his chair, all attention on the man.

"Your task force will join a Primord squadron patrolling the space lanes between Rass and Intus," Roberts said. "Primary objectives are twofold: disrupt Zodark supply convoys and gather additional intelligence on enemy movements and capabilities there. This will give us additional valuable intel that'll help us strike at the Zodarks' core in the Rass system."

"Understood," Lee said. "What level of engagement are we authorized for?"

"You have clearance for offensive operations against supply ships and light escorts. Avoid prolonged engagements with heavy capital ships."

Lee nodded. "Rules of engagement for civilian traffic?"

"Standard protocol. Detain and search if suspicious, but no unprovoked attacks."

"What about our sensor profile?" Lee asked. "Will we be running silent or maintaining open comms with the Primord squadron?"

"Maintain encrypted comms with your Primord allies. Emissions control is at your discretion based on tactical situations."

"Understood. Any specific intelligence targets we should prioritize?"

"Focus on ship movements, convoy patterns, and any signs of new weapon systems. We're particularly interested in their long-range sensor capabilities."

Sato perked up. "What about extraction protocols if we're compromised, sir?"

"Emergency rendezvous coordinates will be transmitted to your nav computer. The Primords have designated safe harbors if needed."

"Copy that," Sato said. "Duration of the operation?"

"Initial deployment is for two months, with the possibility of extension based on results."

Lee said, "And our rules for engaging Zodark military installations?"

"Observe and report only, unless directly threatened. Your fleet won't be big enough for a full-scale assault. In other words, I know you'd succeed in whatever engagement you conduct, but I don't want the risk. If you need to defend yourself, of course, you do what you must in order to survive and get the intel back to us."

The briefing concluded with a detailed overview of their operational areas. Lee studied the holomap as it highlighted three key regions.

"Sector 2 will serve as Forward Operating Station Bulwark," Captain Roberts explained. "I'll be assuming direct tactical command of this operation from my flagship, the *Australia*. The FOB will consist of my *Ryan*-class battleship and Primord retrofitted transports they've turned into expeditionary bases. Mobile supply depots, munitions bunkers, and fuel stores.

"To be clear, Captain Lee, as your Deputy Joint Task Force Commander, I'll be overseeing the entire Sector 2 campaign. Under my direct command will be five Primord battleships, six cruisers, four frigates, and six corvettes. Your mission remains intelligence gathering and convoy disruption along the specified routes.

"For this operation, I'm assigning you operational control of the *Bolt* and *Scimitar* frigates, along with the *Polaris*, *Horizon*, and *Cobalt* corvettes. You'll report directly to me at 0800 and 2000 hours daily with full situation reports. Any engagement with enemy forces must be documented with complete tactical breakdowns. Additionally, again I've tasked Commander Jay Tulip—JT—as Red Team and Lee, for a second time, you're Blue Team."

Lee kept his expression neutral. "Understood, sir. I'll ensure all vessels under my command maintain strict reporting protocols and adhere to the mission parameters you've established."

"Good." Roberts stood. "Any other questions?" After a moment of silence, he nodded. "Everyone, dismissed."

## Chapter 3:
## Game Point

**Year 2097**
**Forward Operating Base Oteren**
**Planet Intus**

The rec hall was quiet today as Lieutenant Naomi Love gripped her paddle, her focus on the small white ball. Any opportunity for action, any action, was always a plus for her. She served, sending the ping-pong ball across the table.

"Weeks of this," she said as she returned a volley. "Starting to feel like we're on an extended vacation."

Chief Brian Ford laughed. "Careful what you wish for, Lieutenant. Boredom's better than bullets any day."

Love smirked. "Says the man who can disassemble an Osprey blindfolded. At least you've got projects."

"True." Ford backhanded the ball.

Love hit a tricky shot.

Ford swung his paddle and missed the ball. "Point, you."

Several months had passed since the Intus invasion. In a fierce orbital battle, Earthers and Primords had clashed with the Zodark fleet. Deaths on both sides mounted. Some ops Love had been in terrorized her nightly dreams. Both sides bled. In the end, the Zodarks broke. As the enemy fled, they abandoned a large ground force.

To Love, Zodarks had a different emotional capacity to *not* care, even for their own when it came to failure. War was the ultimate test, and it defined who they were. She couldn't verify any of this, but from what she'd observed during the Intus campaign, it appeared to be the case. War was their life. It had to be if they marched across star systems to enslave others not of their own ilk. Across the galaxy, she imagined there were a lot more species out there, and they all, including humans, thought differently. There was no doubt in her mind. That was just how it was, and a warlike group like the Zodarks valued life in a completely different way than Earthers.

For the past two weeks, Lieutenant Love and Chief Ford had found themselves in an unexpected lull. In that time, they'd gotten closer as comrades, as close as an officer and a non-commissioned officer could professionally be. Sometimes, Love let the formalities relax, like today. Other times, they gave each other advice as equals, which Love tolerated, but they both understood the fundamental truth, that she was his superior, the one he took orders from, and they maintained that boundary.

With their Osprey—the *Jack*—grounded, they'd spent a lot of time waiting around, and impatiently. This calm was deceiving, though. In that time, the planet transformed even more. It seemed like every week, more buildings went up, erected by the Prims, who were doing their best to bring back cities the way they'd had them before Zodarks had taken over.

In the last few months, Earthers had expanded as well. They'd established a network of bases and firebases. New Primord military installations sprouted like steel jungles too.

Still, peace remained elusive. Allied forces combed the mountains and forests, rooting out pockets of Zodark resistance. They even uncovered and destroyed a hidden underwater base. It proved the enemy was everywhere. As Intus healed, the forests growing back where they were once charred by battle, it was clear that the war here, though changed from the initial engagements, was far from over.

Through the holowindow, large supply ships hovered nearby. Their side thrusters kept them steady as they lowered CHUs into place—rectangular, containerized housing units that soldiers called "Chews." The crews arranged them in perfect rows, creating another temporary residential block for the expanding base.

At three different positions around the perimeter, Love spotted the unmistakable profiles of M88 Howitzers. These weren't standard artillery—they were the Republic's latest heavy hitters. Each could launch a 240mm projectile carrying one hundred sixty pounds of high-explosives, smoke, or white phosphorus up to eight hundred kilometers. The projectiles used specialized glide tech, letting them loiter above units for twenty-four hours before power depletion. Once infantry tagged a target, the AI-assisted warheads struck damn hard, and damn fast.

Beyond the housing zone, the base sprawled across the landscape with multiple runways and parking ramps filled with military craft—P-97 Orions, Reaper ground assault ships, Ospreys, and various transport vessels. Behind the flight line, hangars and maintenance facilities stretched rows upon rows of additional CHUs, each housing sixteen soldiers with their own bathroom and shower facilities.

"Looks like we're getting more neighbors." Love nodded toward the window.

Ford glanced over his shoulder. "Yeah. Still, can't wait till we get more proper buildings up. As usual, the Republic will make this base something badass when it's finished."

"Heard anything from Coop lately?" Love asked.

"Last I heard, he's still up there on the *Gallipoli*, circling this mudball we call home."

"Poor guy. Breathing recycled air while we've got all this." She motioned toward the holowindow. Outside it was a blue sky. A Primord city with skyscrapers was being built in the distance. A forest a hundred meters away jutted toward the sun.

"Don't forget the ocean," Ford said. "Nothing beats a swim after a long day."

Love was about to serve, then stopped midswing. "You're still going in there? After that… thing they spotted?"

"You mean our friendly neighborhood sea monster? Come on, that's just scuttlebutt."

"Scuttlebutt with teeth, apparently," Love said, her serve more aggressive than before. "I haven't dipped a toe in since I heard about it."

"Your loss." Ford slammed a return shot. "Though I gotta admit, the description's pretty damn wild. What was it again? A squid-dragon hybrid?"

Love snorted. She kept the volley alive. "Something like that. Octopus with wings and a snout, if you believe the stories."

"Sounds like someone's been hitting the bottle a bit too hard." Ford laughed. "Can you imagine that thing flopping around on the beach?"

"Hell, no." Love missed a return as the image struck her mind. "Worst. Creature. Design. Ever. You know, sometimes I wonder if Coop's got the right idea up there. At least he's doing something."

"Oh, the *Gallipoli*, where personal space goes to die, and the phrase 'cabin fever' takes on a whole new meaning?"

Love held the ping-pong ball. "Fair enough. Still, gotta be nice to have a clear purpose. Up there, it's all about readiness, vigilance. Down here…" Love gestured at their surroundings.

Beyond the window, the constant sounds of construction equipment filled the air. Cranes swung CHUs into position while teams of Synths moved about, connecting power and water lines. They were transforming this area from a bunch of temporary structures into a permanent installation.

"Down here, we wait," Ford finished for her. He set his paddle on the table. "Falls on us to be ready at a moment's notice. 'Tis the nature of our work."

"You're right, of course. It's just…"

"Frustrating?"

"Yep. Frustrating." She paused, letting the silence grow awkward before she suddenly declared, "Serve!"

Ford hit it over the net. "You know, if you're that bored, I could always use a hand running maintenance checks on *Jack*."

"I'm pretty sure my bird's in better shape than half the fleet already."

"Flattery will get you everywhere. But there's always room for improvement." He slammed a forehand too fast for Love to return.

"Nice shot, Chief."

"What's the score?"

"You a lot, me not much."

"My serve." Ford served the ball. "Ever run into any Altairians?"

Love softly hit the ball back, tricking Ford for a point as he reached for the ball but missed. "Ha! Caught you off guard."

"Good one. But, seriously, you ever see one of those Altairians in person?"

"Just on vids and images." Their form came to mind. Standing at five and a half feet tall, they had a striking resemblance to humans with their bipedal look. However, their features set them apart. Hands with six fingers and a thumb. White skin as tough as leather. Their heads were crowned with short, thin snow-white hair while the rest of their bodies were hairless. Perhaps most unsettling were their eyes—coal black, devoid of any iris or color. They were one of a handful of species in the alliance with humans, called the Galactic Empire.

Ford lobbed the ball high, forcing Love to backpedal. "Same. Caught a glimpse of a Tully once, though. Talk about a sight."

"Tully?" Love grunted, lunging to return the shot.

"Yeah, you know, the Yeti-looking fellas." Ford's paddle connected with a *thwack*. "All fur, muscle, actually kind of a semi-cute dog face, but nose more flattened than a dog's snout."

Love sent the ball back. "Sounds like someone I dated once."

"Yetis," Ford said, "did you know they're pretty dang important to some Native American tribes?"

"Seriously? You gonna talk this junk now?"

"Anything to take you off your game." The volley kept going. "Anyway, fascinating stuff. In certain Salish traditions, they're known as Sasquatch. Considered guardian spirits of the forest, or something like that."

The ball whizzed past Love's ear, her attention on the new topic at hand. She retrieved it, tossing it back to Ford. "You're boring me. You're right; it's taking me off my game."

Ford continued, "Some believe they possess supernatural abilities, like the power to turn invisible or paralyze humans with a single glance."

"Really?"

"Yeah." Ford served.

"No, really? You believe that?"

"I think—"

Love smacked a hard hit across the net, cutting Ford off mid-sentence. "Not interesting, or interested. See my face? Yeah, bored again." She tried to withhold a smile but couldn't.

"Ha! See, you like it. Deep down, you're all over this info, aren't you?"

She shook her head.

Ford shrugged. "There's even a tribe in Northern California that considers them a separate race of humans, driven into hiding by warfare."

"Warfare? What?"

Love's paddle connected with a crack, the ball barely skimming over the net, Ford missing. "Game point."

Ford sighed. "I thought you weren't keeping score."

"All to keep you off your game." She gave a wry smile while tapping the top of her head. "I've been keeping track."

"Yep, and my serve. Game point. You get this, you win."

Ford was good at everything, especially ping-pong. She could have sworn he was letting her win, but who cared? This was just another thing to do while they awaited their next mission.

Love bounced the ball once, twice, then served. Ford's return was lightning-fast, but Love deflected it. The volley intensified, neither willing to concede.

Back and forth they went, the hollow pop of ball against paddle resounding through the recreation hall. With a grunt, Ford swung hard—too hard. The ball soared over the table, beyond Love's reach, and clattered to the floor behind her.

Ford set his paddle down. "Well, you got me, Lieutenant."

Love grinned, wiping her brow. "Good game, Chief."

"Yeah, good one."

She knew she'd won, but Ford had let her. The man usually came out on top in everything, whether it was mechanics, trivia, or sports.

A tinge of envy sparked in her. She'd worked hard her entire life to be the best, to prove herself. Here was Ford making it all look effortless. What was his story? She knew next to nothing about his childhood, his past. The man was an enigma, always ready with a solution or a fascinating bit of knowledge but never revealing much about himself.

You read about these types in books, watched them on soap operas or in movies, and here was one right in front of her, showing her that authors, screenwriters, and directors could get some personalities right.

"Best two out of three?" Love asked.

Ford smiled. "You sure, Lieutenant?"

"If you don't take it easy on me, I'm sure."

"All right. Just too restless, huh?"

Love hesitated, the ball resting in her palm. "Just want to play another. I can ask someone else if you want."

Ford's expression softened. "You know, sometimes it's OK to just… breathe. Have you been talking to your counselor?"

She opened her mouth to respond, but the words caught in her throat. Instead, she served again, the ball flying past Ford.

"Hey, I wasn't even ready. But seriously, just, take some time to have a chat with someone other than me."

"We're at war, Chief. The enemy could be anywhere, anytime. If we're not ready—"

"You know that's not what I'm talking about."

"What are you talking about, then?" she asked, but she already knew. He was referring to her reluctance to see a psychologist about Jack's death. He believed discussing her feelings and what Jack's passing meant to her would help her heal. It was the same old advice—talk it out and you'll feel better. She'd heard it all before. Couldn't be further from the truth.

Love forced a grin. "Well, that just changed the mood."

"I overstepped. We all cope in our own ways."

The rec room's intercom crackled to life. "Attention, all personnel. This is a general quarters announcement. All command staff, Delta operators, and designated support teams report to Briefing Room Alpha at once. Battalion XOs, company COs, and platoon leaders are to attend. S-2 and S-4 representatives required. Logistics and comms chiefs, have your latest SITREPs ready. Repeat, all specified personnel to Briefing Room Alpha at once. That is all."

After the message repeated a second time, Ford faced Love. "Looks like you got your wish, Lieutenant."

Love nodded. "Looks like I did. You ready? Ah, stupid question. Of course you are."

"And you?" Ford asked.

"I'm raring to go. In fact, chomping at the bit. I'm always prepared, and this is what I'm made for. I was built for this."

"Any more clichés you want to use?" Ford asked.

"Nope. Let's do this," she said, heading for the rec hall's exit and toward the corridor leading to Briefing Room A. Finally, there was something to do and, more importantly, perhaps some Zodarks to weed out of their holes.

**Chapter 4:**
**Storm Warning**

**Year 2097**
**FOB Oteren**
**Planet Intus**

Tension floated in the air of the dimly lit briefing room. Love sat straight in her chair. A holo displayed at the front—a map highlighting the dangerous terrain controlled by the Zodark insurgency.

The room fell silent as Commander Rhett Granger cleared his throat. His gaze swept across the group of Republic Army soldiers, pilots, and support personnel.

"Ladies and gentlemen," Granger said, "what you're about to hear is classified. Our mission is high-risk, with potentially severe consequences if we fail."

The holographic display sputtered before zooming in on a specific region. The terrain materialized—rugged mountains, dense forests, and winding valleys. Granger's hand passed through the hologram, showing a particular area.

"This is our drop zone," he said. He traced the outline of a clearing only slightly visible through the thick canopy. "It's deep in Zodark-controlled territory, heavily fortified and notoriously difficult to access."

The map shifted. It showed layers of topographical data. Steep cliffs and narrow passes appeared.

"The terrain is treacherous," Granger continued, manipulating the hologram to showcase different angles. "These forests limit visibility and will complicate our air-support capabilities."

He zoomed in on a few jagged peaks. "The mountainous landscape provides numerous ambush points. Intelligence suggests the Zodarks are using cave systems as hideouts."

A new layer appeared on the map, highlighting weather patterns. Dark clouds swirled over the region.

"To complicate matters further, we're looking at a significant storm system moving in." Granger's brow furrowed. "It'll make navigation challenging, but it might also provide us with some much-needed cover."

The hologram changed again. Red lines and pulsing dots littered across the terrain. Love leaned forward, her eyes narrowing as she studied the new information.

"Now, let's get into the nitty-gritty," Granger said. "Our intel on Zodark movements and fortifications is extensive but time-sensitive."

He pointed to a cluster of red dots near the drop zone. The hologram zoomed in yet again, showing anti-aircraft batteries. "These are our primary concerns for the initial insertion. They're heavily guarded and will need to be neutralized quickly."

Next, Granger pointed at a portion of the map with a bunch of interconnected lines. "These represent known patrol routes. They're regular but not entirely predictable. We'll need to time our movements carefully to avoid detection."

The hologram pulsed. Several new markers appeared, scattered across the region. "These are supply caches. Securing them is a secondary objective, but it could significantly hinder Zodark operations in the area." Granger hesitated for a moment, his attention back on the group before him. "I won't sugarcoat this. The terrain is against us, the weather's unpredictable, and we're dropping right into the hornet's nest. But the intelligence we could gather, the blow we could strike to Zodark operations—it's worth the risk."

Granger's expression darkened as he continued, "Before we dive into the specifics of our mission, let's review the current situation with the Zodark insurgency. After our joint operation with the Primords to liberate Intus, the Zodarks were forced to retreat. However, they left behind a significant number of well-trained and highly motivated troops. And, for the last few months, we've been thinning their herd, and doing a damn good job."

The hologram changed to show red hot spots across the planet's surface. "These areas represent known Zodark strongholds. Their insurgency has been particularly active in the past two months, disrupting Primord reconstruction efforts."

Granger zoomed in on one region. "Here, they've sabotaged critical infrastructure, including power plants and water purification facilities. This has left thousands without basic necessities and hampered our ability to stabilize the region."

The image shifted to a destroyed Primord settlement. "The Zodarks have also been targeting newly liberated Primord communities. Their tactics are brutal—designed to instill fear and undermine confidence in our protection. We've seen a spike in civilian casualties, particularly among former Primord slaves who are trying to rebuild their lives."

He then highlighted several key locations. "The insurgency has also been hitting our supply lines hard. They're using their knowledge of the terrain to stage hit-and-run attacks, disrupting our logistics and making it difficult to maintain a consistent military presence in outlying areas." He straightened his lips in a hard line. "Look. The Zodark insurgency is not just a military problem—it's threatening the very stability of Intus. Every day they remain active, they're eroding the trust we've built with the Primords and undermining our efforts to help this planet recover from decades of Zodark oppression. That's why this mission is so critical. We need to strike at the heart of their operations and show both our allies and our enemies that we'll not allow the Zodarks to reclaim any part of this world." He looked around the room, meeting each person's gaze. "Any questions?"

Love raised her hand. "Sir, what's our extraction plan if things go south? That terrain doesn't leave much room for error."

Granger nodded. "A valid concern, Lieutenant Love. We'll have a rapid response team on standby, but given the hostile environment, extraction windows will be narrow."

He manipulated the hologram once more. "These are our designated extraction points. They're spread out to give us options, but each comes with its own risks. We'll need to be adaptable."

Another hand went up. "What about communication? That storm's going to play hell with our signals."

"Good point," Granger said. He zoomed in on a particular area of the map. "We've identified natural formations that should provide some shielding from the electromagnetic interference. We'll be setting up relay points here, here, and here." Three spots on the map brightened blue.

The questions continued, each one adding another layer of complexity to the already daunting mission. Love listened, doing her best to memorize each detail, every probable pitfall, and every slim advantage they might have.

"Any more questions?" Granger asked. When no one answered, he continued, "All right, people, let's break this down. We're dividing into teams for a multipronged assault against the Zodark insurgency. Delta Force will be conducting a series of high-value target extractions, while Army soldiers provide overwatch and secure exfil routes. Lieutenant Love, you'll be lead pilot, Wolfpack Actual. Your Osprey will spearhead the insertion of our main strike team. Your crew, including Ford, will assist in coordinating logistics during the drop and provide on-site support as needed."

Granger scanned the room. "We'll have Orion fighters providing top cover throughout the AO, with Reaper drones for real-time ISR. S-2 will be feeding intel updates to your team leaders as the situation develops. Expect frequent SITREPs and be prepared to adapt to changing battlefield conditions. Got it?

"Now, this operation kicks off at 0500 hours tomorrow. I want everyone locked and loaded, ready to dance. We'll be pushing the Zodarks back to whatever hell they crawled out of. Detailed mission packets will be distributed through your secure channels within the hour. Study them, know them, live them. Any complications, you report up the chain immediately. Clear?"

A chorus of "Yes, sir!" echoed through the room.

Granger crossed his arms. "Now, we've lost good men and women getting us this far. Their sacrifices won't be in vain. Stay focused, stay alert, and we'll make it through this. Dismissed."

As the room cleared, Love recalled a few recent missions. She'd flown more sorties in the past several months than most pilots flew in a year, besides the last two weeks, when it'd been quiet. Her last drop had been difficult—setting down troops on a narrow mountain ledge, the Osprey's nose angled precariously over a sheer drop.

Love looked at Ford as they prepared to leave. "I'm heading back to my quarters," she said. "Need to rest up and run through some scenarios."

Ford nodded. "Smart move. I'm off to the rec center for a game of chess with the boys. Then it's lights out for me."

"Good luck. See you on the flight line with Lieutenant Green and Corporal Williams."

Second Lieutenant Caleb Green and Lance Corporal Tyrell Williams had been important members of Lieutenant Love's Osprey crew. In fact, without them, she might have crashed and burned too many times to count. Their teamwork had been honed well together, especially through so many missions. Love's copilot, Green, had proven himself an incredible officer, assisting with navigation, communications, and aircraft systems management. His quick decision-making was more than a plus during their most dangerous missions.

Williams worked with Ford in the back of the Osprey. He helped troops get in and out safely, controlled the ramp, and provided cover fire. Together, they kept their weapons ready to protect soldiers leaving the ship.

"Aye, Lieutenant. See you tomorrow," Ford said.

Love strode down the corridors of Forward Operating Base Oteren. As she passed by the holowindows, the Intus terrain spread outward before her. It was all a bizarre group of colors and shapes, still foreign despite her months stationed here. Twisted trees with bright green leaves swayed in the breeze. In the distance, strange creatures loped across open fields, their six legs moving them at a fast pace.

A flash of movement drew her attention to a flock of birdlike creatures soaring overhead. Their wings glittered with an almost metallic shine, refracting the light of Intus's twin suns as the bright glowing balls fell over the horizon. For a few moments, Love watched the sunset.

Her gaze drifted farther, to the horizon where the towering spires of Intus's newest Primord city development jutted into the sky. The Primord architecture was quite different from the natural landscape—all straight lines and shining surfaces. Construction drones whirred around the half-finished structures.

Once a thriving Primord world, Intus had fallen to the Zodarks and their allies long ago, its people enslaved. Now, liberated by the combined forces of the Primords and Earthers, Intus was experiencing a renaissance. The Primords were reclaiming their world, rebuilding with a freakish speed.

When Love reached the area where her CHU was located, she stepped outside the main building. The moment she exited, heat and humidity hit her like a wall of water. Sweat seeped from her pores. Her uniform clung to her skin within seconds. She quickened her pace, more than happy to escape the sweltering conditions.

Reaching her CHU, she punched in the access code and practically dove inside, shutting the door behind her. The stress of the planet outside faded away in an instant, replaced by the greatest thing in the world—cool air.

Her CHU was a step above standard. While some poor saps were sweating it out with only fans in the heat, Love lived in a bit of luxury. The small containerized housing unit was actually comfortable. It was large enough for the essentials but a far cry from the hellfire conditions others endured on this overly hot planet.

A twin-sized bed occupied one wall, its covers neatly tucked. A desk sat opposite, its surface clear, save for a few datapads. A small built-in closet housed her uniforms and personal items. The bathroom was little more than a closet itself, with a tiny sink and shower stall.

Love moved to her desk. She pulled open a drawer, grabbing the worn edge of a photograph and carefully extracting it. Jack's face smiled up at her, frozen in time. It sent an ache through her chest.

She held the photo to the light, the memory of that day flooding back. The Rhea system, the Blue Horizon Meridian transport vessel, the Zodark laser slamming into the ship. The explosion. Jack's weight in her arms as they huddled in the escape capsule, his life slipping away.

Love pressed her lips to the photograph, then carefully placed it next to her boots, a reminder to transfer it to the transport's dashboard tomorrow. It was a small ritual, a protection of sorts, to keep her and her crew safe at all times.

Pushing the memories aside, Love busied herself with a simple dinner. The rations were bland but filling, much different from the meals she and Jack had once shared. As she ate, she flicked on the small holovision. The chatter of a popular drama filled the room.

As the episode played on, she stared at the photo by her boots. Tomorrow would bring new challenges, new dangers. But for tonight, in this small room on Intus, she allowed herself a moment of peace.

# Chapter 5:
## Pieces of the Past

**Year 2097**
**FOB Oteren**
**Planet Intus**

The chessboard made him focus. It was a silent battlefield of strategy. Studying it with his forehead wrinkled in concentration, Brian Ford was oblivious to those watching around him. Across the table, Lance Corporal Tyrell Williams glanced at Ford, watching the master at his work.

Ford moved his queen diagonally across the board to what looked like a harmless spot.

"Interesting move there, Chief," Williams said, scratching his chin.

"You've got a strong defense set up. Opens up some options for me while maintaining pressure on your king's flank. Just letting you know."

Williams shook his head. "You're probably ten moves ahead already, scheming behind that friendly facade."

"All I'm doing is enjoying the game. Your last move was quite clever, by the way. Forcing my bishop back really limited my options on the queenside."

"Killing me with kindness. I see how it is." Williams used his rook to capture one of Ford's pawns. "For someone who talks so much, we don't really know anything about you besides your wild theories and your reputation as a miracle worker in the hangar."

Ford shrugged. He slid his bishop across the board, putting Williams's king in check. "Just focusing on the game, Corporal. Your move."

Williams furrowed his brow, examining the board like a biologist looking under a microscope. After a moment, he moved his king out of danger. "Where'd you learn to play chess like this?"

Ford's hand paused over a pawn. His usual smile faltered for a moment. "My father taught me," he said. "He was… particular about how I learned."

"Particular… how?"

"He believed in excellence. Anything less was unacceptable." The happy, concentrated mood at the table dissipated as Ford continued. "I remember sitting across from him, just like this, when I was seven. He'd set up these hard-ass scenarios, expecting me to solve them in minutes. Every mistake was…" He trailed off, his eyes distant.

Williams listened. "Sounds rough, Chief."

Ford nodded, moving a piece on the board. "There was this one time, I must've been nine or ten. We were playing, and I thought I had him cornered. I was so proud of myself. Then he found this brilliant escape. Turned the whole game around. I started crying. Couldn't help it. I'd tried so hard, you know? And he just… looked at me with all this horrible disappointment. Told me that tears were for the weak. Said I'd never amount to anything if I couldn't control my emotions. I mean, that's fine and all, until he took me out back with a metal clothes hanger and used it like a whip on my butt until I stopped shedding tears. He did that a lot. Don't know why, other than he was trying to teach me things."

Ford blinked, seeming to come back to the present. He glanced at the board, noticing Williams's last move. "Oh, nice play there. You've really improved your endgame."

"Thanks." Williams chuckled. "Your childhood sounds like it kinda sucked."

Ford's smile returned but didn't quite reach his eyes. "It is what it is. That's why I don't usually talk about my childhood. Tends to bring the mood down. I ain't gonna talk about my mother. That's when the mood really drops." He feigned a soft laugh.

"Hey, no judgment here. We've all got our baggage."

"Yeah, not one for dwelling on the past." With a fast decision and a quick motion, Ford slid his knight in an L shape over the board, setting up a trap. It would take Williams several turns to fully figure out what he'd done. "Checkmate in seven," Ford said.

Williams eyed the board. "Damn, Chief."

"My father… always said the endgame was where true masters really showed themselves."

"Well, if your dad saw you now…"

Ford's hands tensed on the edge of the table. "Overdose. I was eleven. Synth-heroin. Found him in the bathroom. Usual heartbreaking story."

"Dang, Ford. You're right, let's not talk about your childhood."

"Yeah, better not." Ford shook his head. He could still see him—slumped against the bathtub, needle still in his arm. His eyes… always the eyes in his memories. They were open, but there was nothing there. Ford had to tell his mom and watched her world crumble in an instant. At the time, it changed everything. His mom couldn't cope and started drinking. She became angrier than her father had ever been.

He had a similar backstory to Love, but he'd do his best not to tell her. Ford didn't want to create some weirdness between the two. And hopefully Williams wouldn't open his trap, but the guy was usually good at keeping his mouth shut when it came to private matters.

Ford motioned to the board. "Your move, by the way."

Williams moved his knight, a decent play delaying Ford's checkmate by a move. "Glad you made it out all right."

"Yeah. Feel incredibly lucky." He moved his bishop, continuing the assault on Williams's king. "Check."

Williams pushed a pawn out, blocking the check. "Well, maybe I should talk about your childhood, put you off your game more."

Ford countered, his queen sliding into position. "Left home when I was twelve. Couldn't take it anymore. Streets weren't much better, but at least I could choose when to run. Got better at chess by playing the masters in the parks."

"Twelve? What the hell? Man, that's bad."

"Survival was challenging. I managed. Snuck back home sometimes, when I got desperate enough. For food, mostly."

Williams made another move, his bishop taking one of Ford's pawns. "Crazy story."

Ford moved swiftly, his rook capturing Williams's bishop. "Tougher staying away, sometimes. Mom... she'd leave food outside. Sandwiches, canned goods. Things I could grab and run with."

"At least it sounds like she cared."

Ford giggled. "Maybe. Felt more like a trap, most days. Like she was trying to lure me back. I'd take the food, but I couldn't face her. The guilt, the shame... suffocating like hell."

Williams pushed his queen to stave off Ford's advance. "Life."

Ford's knight leapt across the board, putting Williams's king in check for the third time. "Yep. 'When you change the way you look at things, the things you look at change.' Wayne Dyer."

"Good words." As Williams contemplated his next move, a low rumble shook the recreation center. Both men glanced toward the holowindow, where dark clouds were rolling in, blanketing the usual view of the planet's many moons.

A flash of lightning illuminated the sky. Instead of a jagged bolt, it spread out in a weblike pattern, crackling across the clouds in shades of purple and green.

"That's... different," Williams said.

Ford frowned. "Ionic dispersion in the upper atmosphere. Creates some pretty spectacular light shows here on this planet. Where've you been? I've been down here as long as you and seen that plenty of times. Gonna be worse tomorrow, during our op."

Another rumble shook the base. The lightning flashed again, twisting into spiral shapes across the dark sky.

"Beautiful," Ford whispered. "No matter how many times I see it, it never gets old."

Williams moved another pawn. "Good, keep your attention on the storm while I pull out my secret weapon."

"Secret weapon? Ha! Still, great move, but I see one that could have been better. Anyway, I was fourteen when I stopped going home altogether. Built a car from scraps I found in junkyards. It was my ticket out. Checkmate," Ford said after moving a piece.

Williams grimaced. "Ford, how did you… I know you're damn good, but you made up that story to distract me."

"You think I'd need to make up a sad story to beat you?"

"No."

"Well, then…"

"Was it true? Your childhood?" Williams pressed.

"Yes, I truly had a childhood," Ford teased.

"You know what I mean. Did those things happen?"

"Maybe."

Williams smiled. "You're full of crap, then. Damn, Chief. You got me good."

"Did I?"

"Was it real? Any of it?"

"Could've been." Ford glanced at the clock. "We should get some shut-eye. Big day tomorrow."

They got up to leave, Ford walking toward a different exit than Williams.

"Where you going, Ford?"

"Got a date."

"What? With who?"

"With a hot little AT-70C Osprey Assault Transport—the *Jack*."

**Chapter 6:**
**Doubts and Duties**

**Year 2097**
**RNS *Gallipoli***
**Intus Orbit**

Blake "Coop" Cooper shoveled a forkful of mystery meat into his mouth. He grimaced at the taste. Bland. Needed salt. Heaps of it.

It was lunchtime, and RNS *Gallipoli*'s mess hall was crowded with pilots and crew members. Coop glanced down at his tray, eyeing the unappetizing mound of reconstituted potatoes and overcooked green beans.

*Great! How appetizing. What should I expect, suddenly a five-star chef?*

"I swear, they're trying to kill us with this slop." Coop poked at the meat with his fork.

Bear, a hulking figure who squeezed into the seat across from him, chuckled. "I like it. Remember that time on Intus when we had to eat those weird purple fruits? Now that was fantastic."

"It was OK," Coop said.

Bear shrugged. "Maybe you just don't like food."

Raven, sitting next to Coop, snorted. "You mean the ones that made your tongue swell up like a balloon, Bear? Yeah, good times."

Coop grinned, pushing his tray away. "I'll take my chances with the mystery meat, thanks."

Bear stretched his long arms, nearly knocking over Raven's drink. "How the hell do they expect me to fit in those new Orion drone pods? I swear, I'm gonna need a shoehorn to squeeze in there."

"Maybe they'll let you stick your head out the top," Raven said, ducking as Bear playfully swatted at him.

"They're the same size as the previous ones, Bear," Coop said.

"Not so sure about that."

Raven nodded. "Bear, hate to say it, but Coop's right."

Coop leaned in, lowering his voice. "You know who really needs to be squeezed out? Strike. Guy's got a stick so far up his butt, I'm surprised he can sit down straight."

Bear's smile faded. "C'mon, Coop. Strike's not that bad. Just doing his job."

"Yeah, his job of being a grade-A pain in our rears," Coop said. "You see him during the last briefing? Thought he was gonna pop a blood vessel over a minor formation change."

Raven rolled her eyes. "Here we go again. Cooper's daily 'Bash the Boss' session."

"Just sayin'," Coop continued, "the guy needs to lighten up. We're not fresh-faced cadets anymore."

"Look, I get it," Bear said. "Strike can be intense. But he's got our backs. Always. Remember that close call a few weeks back over the Liziopnin Sea, or however you say it? If it weren't for his quick thinking—"

"Yeah, yeah." Coop waved him off. "I know. But would it kill him to crack a smile once in a while?"

"Seriously? You care now if he smiles or not? C'mon, man. When we first met you, Coop, we could have said the same damn thing about you." Bear sat straighter. "You know, maybe if you stopped giving him reasons to frown…"

Coop clutched his chest in mock offense. "You wound me, Bear. Wound me! Here I thought my roguish good looks and charisma were all I needed with that… Strike."

"You're about as irresistible as this meat," Raven said.

The usual knot formed in Coop's stomach. He'd been covering it well, keeping up the confident facade. Lately, every time he climbed into his Orion fighter's drone pod, doubt crept in. The controls that had once felt like extensions of his own body now seemed odd, his decisions second-guessed at every turn.

He'd tried to compensate. Dialed back the cocky pilot act. Focused on being a team player. The results spoke for themselves. His performance in the Orion cockpit simulators had been mediocre at best, his once-legendary maneuvers today more likely to end in simulated fireballs than victory laps.

*What's gotten into me?*

Although he hadn't lost an Orion on his watch for quite a while, who knew? With his slow responses, it could happen again any day. The last thing he wanted to do was fail a mission because of this weird change in his flying style, his odd new lack of confidence, his suddenly doubtful mindset, or whatever was plaguing him.

Coop opened his mouth, half tempted to confide in his friends. It was interrupted by a crackle from the overhead speakers.

"Attention, Jolly Rogers Squadron. Report to Briefing Room C in fifteen minutes. Repeat, report to Briefing Room C in fifteen minutes, Jolly Rogers Squadron."

"That's us." Bear slumped forward, his forehead thudding against the table. "Every damn time. Right when I was about to hit the gym."

Raven gathered his tray. "Yeah, because you really need more muscle, Hercules. Any bigger and we'll have to strap you to the outside of the pod and give you the controls there. Hell, maybe we just give you a suite."

"I'd be up for that," Bear said.

Coop stood. "Come on, kids. Duty calls. Let's go see what fresh blood Strike has cooked up."

As they made their way out of the mess hall, Coop's mind had already shifted gears to the upcoming briefing. The corridor stretched before him. Bear and Raven flanked him.

As they rounded a corner, Coop spotted two people approaching. Beside Phantom, a lanky pilot with a shock of red hair, Ninja, walked with his usual lack of confidence. Even though the guy could pilot like an ace, he still carried himself like a rookie—the way Coop was feeling these days.

"Well, if it ain't the Three Musketeers," Phantom said. "Off to face the firing squad?"

"Nah," Coop replied, "just another day in paradise. You know how it is, Phantom. Some of us have to do real work around here."

"Real work? Is that what you call your performance lately, Cooper?"

"Hey, someone's gotta make this job look good," Coop shot back.

"Wasn't talking about it looking good."

As the group exchanged quips, a part of him hoped to catch a glimpse of Lieutenant Naomi Love somewhere in the corridor. Her presence always managed to both excite and unnerve him. He knew it was a foolish thought. She was stationed on Intus, down on the planet below.

*What am I thinking anyway? A woman like Naomi is way out of my league.*

She was smart, capable, with a strength seeming to radiate from her very being. And him? Just another hotshot pilot with more baggage than a long-haul transport, and losing confidence with every mission.

As they continued down the corridor, Coop's mind wandered. He thought about his past relationships—if you could even call them that. Brief flings, nothing lasting. Always keeping people at arm's length, never letting anyone get too close. It was easier that way, wasn't it? No risk of disappointment, no chance of letting someone down.

With Naomi Love, it felt different. She stirred something in him, a longing he couldn't quite pin down. In truth, it terrified him. What if he actually tried? What if he let her in, only to screw it up like he always did? She probably wasn't interested in him anyway. Chief Brian Ford had once told him that Love had been married before. Something about her husband dying in a crash. Or shot? Blown up? He couldn't remember. Just for that, he should stay away, but his mind wouldn't let him.

The group arrived at the briefing room, its reinforced doors sliding open. Coop stepped inside. The room was a semicircular amphitheater. Tiered seats faced a large holographic display at the front. Viewports lined one side, showing a beautiful view of planet Intus.

Strike stood at the front, his posture straight, eyes scanning the room as pilots filed in. Coop took his seat and glared at the holographic display. It showed a tactical map of a sector on Intus. Pulsing red markers indicated enemy positions. The holo shifted to a topographic map of a mountainous region.

"Here we go," Strike said. "Starting at 0430 tomorrow, we got a critical mission. Our objective is to provide close-air support for ground troops landing to engage with Zodark insurgents."

Coop felt a jolt of excitement course through him at the mention of CAS. To him, it was fun blasting Zodarks at every possible opportunity. He focused on the tactical overlay, taking in the terrain features and potential hot zones.

Strike zeroed in on a particularly rugged area. "The Wolfpack Osprey squadron, led by Lieutenant Naomi Love, will be inserting troops here. They start at 0500 tomorrow." A red marker blinked on the map, indicating the drop zone. "It's a hot LZ, surrounded by dense forest and riddled with enemy positions."

Coop's pulse quickened at the mention of Love's name. He bent forward slightly, studying the treacherous terrain around the drop zone. With Love in the picture, he needed to look good, so he needed to be at the top of his game.

"Our job is to keep the insurgents on their asses or running for their lives during insertion and extraction," Strike said. "I cannot stress this enough: precision is key. We're operating in close proximity to our own forces, so there's zero room for error. Zero!"

The holographic display switched, showcasing a rendering of the forest canopy. Strike manipulated the image, peeling back layers to reveal the network of ravines and hidden paths beneath. "Pay attention. This isn't your typical engagement. The forest is thick, providing ample cover for the enemy. Targets will be elusive and hard to spot. You'll need to rely heavily on your targeting systems."

Strike pulled up several thermal imaging scans. "These are recent recon passes. Study them. Memorize them. The insurgents are using the natural terrain to mask their movements. Your job is to flush them out without leveling the entire forest before the drop, understood? We weed out as much as we can before the Deltas and Army soldiers do the rest. But we'll be overlapping, so I cannot emphasize this enough—avoid collateral damage at all costs. We're here to protect our people and neutralize threats, not turn the place into a wasteland."

He brought up a bunch of icons on the map, each with a different color. "Blue markers are confirmed friendly positions. Green are potential Prim civilian areas. Red are known enemy strongholds. Anything unmarked is a potential hostile zone, but verify before engaging."

Strike continued, detailing extraction plans, communication protocols, and rules of engagement. With each passing minute, the intensity of the mission became more apparent. "This isn't just about firepower, people. It's about precision, timing, and coordination. One wrong move, one miscalculation, and we could be looking at friendly fire incidents or civilian casualties. The terrain is working against us. These ravines and caves provide perfect cover for the insurgents. They know every nook and cranny while we're flying blind. You'll need to rely on ground intel and each other."

The holographic screen changed, showing a time lapse of troop movements. "The insurgents are mobile, adaptive. They'll be changing positions constantly. What looks like a clear shot one second could be a disaster the next. The margin for error is microscopic. A few meters off, and you could be hitting friendlies instead of hostiles. To top it off, we're looking at potential atmospheric disturbances. Electrical storms could interfere with comms and targeting systems. Any questions?" When no one asked one, Strike ended the briefing. "You're dismissed."

As everyone rose to leave, doubt crept into Coop. With the storms heading in, the mission became more daunting— even for a pilot at his best.

## Chapter 7:
## The Mysterious Sphere



**Year 2097**
**RNS *Poseidon***
**Sector 2**

On *Poseidon*'s main display, swirling colors and geometric tear-shaped patterns moved over the screen. It was a visual of their FTL travel. Beside Lee, XO Sato sat at attention, her focus on her chair's holo.

"Status, XO," Lee said.

"All ships maintaining formation, Captain. The *Bolt*, *Cobalt*, *Polaris*, *Scimitar*, and *Horizon* are in perfect sync. Primord battleships holding position as well."

"Any details from Space Command about mission parameters?"

"Unchanged, sir. We're to conduct a thorough sweep of Sector 2, gather intel on Zodark movements, and engage only if necessary."

"Good. Any word from Captain Roberts?"

Sato shook her head. "No new communications, Captain. Last update was two hours ago."

Lee drummed his fingers on the armrest. "Keep an eye on our long-range comms. I want to know the moment anything comes through."

"Understood, sir. Permission to speak freely?"

"Granted."

Sato hesitated, then spoke. "The crew's been talking. There's concern about the Primord ships. Some worry their presence might attract unwanted attention like last time."

"Noted, XO. We need to trust our allies. We'll not have a repeat of the last operation. They'll be on their own patrols, and we'll need to assist them if necessary, and vice versa." The whirling patterns on the main holo shifted and coalesced, and Lee straightened in his chair. "Prepare for transition to normal space."

The bridge became a bedlam of activity as the fleet dropped out of FTL. The colors on the holographic screens gave way to the blackness of space, dotted by distant stars. They jumped to coordinates Echo-426 by Tango-114, approximately 750,000 kilometers from Forward Operating Station Bulwark, where Captain Roberts directed not only his battle group but several others throughout the sector. The challenge remained significant—Sector 2 covered vast operational terrain, and despite their relative proximity to FOB Bulwark, the *Australia* and its support vessels remained well beyond visual range. Even with advanced sensor suites, the sector's complex spatial topography meant vessels could operate for weeks without encountering allied patrols.

Sector 2 was a critical trade route. It was known for frequent Zodark activity due to its strategic location. The latest reports indicated increased Zodark patrols in the area. They were likely protecting supply lines or preparing for a major operation.

"We'll need to be extra vigilant here," Lee said. "Sato, coordinate with our squadron of vessels. I want constant communication."

"Yes, sir."

Lee opened a comm channel. "Captain Roberts, this is Captain Lee. We've entered the sector. Do you copy?"

A gravelly voice came through. "Loud and clear, Captain Lee. I want your fleet to patrol coordinates two-four-one by three-five-four. Maintain a maximum distance of two kilometers. Staggered diamond formation. It'll give you the best sensor coverage without sacrificing defensive capabilities."

"Agreed, Captain. Any particular areas of interest?"

"Focus on the outer edges of the last reported trade route. That's where we're most likely to catch Zodark ships trying to slip by unnoticed."

"Affirmative, sir. We'll keep our eyes peeled."

"If you encounter hostiles," Roberts said, "observe and report first. We don't want to tip our hand unless absolutely necessary, nor do we need a replay of the last mission's disaster. If engagement becomes unavoidable, focus on disabling their propulsion and comms. Standard procedure if you encounter civilian vessels. Verify their credentials and escort them out of the area if necessary. We can't risk civilians getting caught in a crossfire."

"Anything else we should be aware of?" Lee asked.

"Affirmative. Keep an eye out for any unusual energy signatures. Intel suggests the Zodarks might be testing new weapons technology in this sector."

"Noted. We'll recalibrate our sensors accordingly."

"Initial sweep should take about six hours. We'll reassess after that and adjust our strategy if needed. Any more questions?"

"Negative, Captain. We're moving into position now. Lee out." He faced his crew. "I want every sensor working overtime. Rhom, coordinate with Engineering. I want our reaction time cut by twenty percent."

"Aye, Captain." Rhom tapped commands into his console.

Lee focused on the main display, watching as the fleet spread out into their assigned positions.

"Captain," Sato said, "*Bolt* and *Cobalt* are ready for their scouting assignments."

"Send them out. Tell them to focus on these coordinates." He highlighted several areas on the tactical interface. "That's where I'd hide a convoy if I were the Zodarks."

On the bridge, officers called out sensor readings and status updates until tactical brightened like a forward operating base under fire. Rhom's voice burst through the noise of the bridge. "Contact! Multiple Zodark signatures detected! That was fast."

Lee's eyes narrowed. "Details, Rhom. What are we looking at?"

"Sir, it appears to be a lightly defended supply convoy. Six cargo vessels, two escort cruisers."

"Lieutenant Rodriguez, transmit immediate tactical data package to FOB Bulwark. Priority channel, security protocol Delta-One. Include full sensor readings, target composition, and defensive capabilities assessment," Lee ordered.

"Aye, Captain. Transmitting tactical data package to RNS *Australia* at Forward Operating Station Bulwark via encrypted channel. Priority flagged, sir," Rodriguez responded.

Moments later, Rodriguez nodded at her console. "Sir, response from Captain Roberts: 'Proceed with interdiction operation. Neutralize escort vessels and secure cargo ships for intelligence gathering. Australia standing by for situation reports. Authorization code Tango-Romeo-Eight-Four-Niner.'"

Lee evaluated options. "All ships, this is Captain Lee. Prepare for hit-and-run operation. I want maximum speed and surprise. Weapons hot, but hold fire until my command. Deploy Starfish pattern—spread out evenly in a circular formation to maximize coverage and create multiple angles of attack."

The tactical display changed as the allied ships shifted into formation. The RNS *Poseidon* took point, flanked by the frigates *Bolt* and *Cobalt*. The corvettes *Polaris*, *Scimitar*, and *Horizon* spread out.

The Zodark convoy crawled along the trade route ahead. Six cargo freighters, filled with supplies for the enemy's war effort.

"Distance to target?" Lee asked.

"Ten thousand kilometers and closing, sir," Reynolds replied.

Lee calculated the remaining time before they reached optimal firing range. The magrail guns had an effective range of eight thousand kilometers, and their Havoc-II missiles could reach targets up to fifteen thousand kilometers away.

"All ships, prepare for long-range engagement," Lee ordered. "Activate SW countermeasures immediately. Disperse any potential enemy laser fire." SW, or Sand-Water missiles, were defensive countermeasures that, when detonated, released clouds of sand and water particles into space to scatter and weaken incoming enemy laser fire.

The fleet complied.

"Enemy sensors have detected us," Rhom reported. "They're powering weapons."

"Tactical," Lee said, "prepare magrail batteries one and two. Target the lead Zodark cruiser."

"Aye, sir. Magrail batteries one and two charging."

"Frigates *Bolt* and *Cobalt*, lock missiles on the second cruiser," Lee ordered over the fleet comms. "Corvettes, stand by to engage the freighters. Aim for engine clusters—disable, don't destroy. We want those supplies."

Acknowledgments streamed in. The tension on the bridge thickened. The distance closed to eight thousand kilometers.

"Sir, we're entering optimal magrail range," Reynolds said.

Lee nodded. "Maintain distance at eight thousand kilometers. Begin firing sequence."

"SW countermeasures and jamming sequence deployed and activated," the EWO, electronic warfare officer, Lieutenant Witkowski reported.

"Excellent," Lee said. "Rhom, target the lead escort cruiser. Fire magrail guns on my mark."

"Magrail guns locked and ready," Rhom said, his fingers ready over the holocontrols.

Lee took a breath, eyes on the enemy icons moving across the tactical display. "Mark."

The *Poseidon* shuddered as twin twenty-four-inch magrail guns blasted forth projectile after projectile. Electromagnetic rails launched armor-piercing rounds through space at near-light speeds.

"Impact in eighty seconds," Sato said.

On the tactical display, the projectiles raced toward their target.

Rhom squinted at his station. "Enemy ships launching torpedoes. Multiple inbound signatures detected."

"Deploy countermeasures," Lee said. "Engage point-defense systems."

"Point-defense systems active," Witkowski replied. "Autocannons and laser clusters ready to intercept incoming torpedoes."

With this, eighteen 30mm quad-barrel point-defense guns, or PDGs, came online. They consisted of dual-barreled turrets, launching armor-piercing rounds tipped with devastation packages. Once the onboard sensors detected optimal range, the warheads burst apart, transforming each projectile into a cloud of hotter than hell metal fragments. This defensive curtain shredded incoming missiles and forced enemy fighters into evasive maneuvers.

Inside each turret hub, a three-person team worked with Synths, the humans providing oversight while the synthetic humanoids calculated firing solutions.

"Frigates, engage the second cruiser with missile salvos," Lee said.

The *Bolt* and *Cobalt* shot volleys of Havoc-II missiles. Trails of glowing gas marked their path as powerful engines propelled them quickly toward the target.

"Corvettes, engage the freighters now," Lee continued. "Target their engines from long range."

The *Polaris*, *Scimitar*, and *Horizon* adjusted their positions. Their long-range turbolasers acquired locks on the freighters' engine signatures.

Lee said to Rhom, "Monitor for any vessels attempting to escape."

"Aye, sir. Enemy laser fire incoming," Rhom said. "Our SW countermeasures are dispersing the beams effectively."

"Maintain SW countermeasures at full capacity," Lee ordered.

"SW dispersal pattern holding. Impact in ten seconds," Rhom said, referring to the magrail tungsten rounds.

On the display, the kinetic projectiles closed the final distance.

"Three... two... one... impact."

The lead Zodark cruiser convulsed as the rounds struck. The immense kinetic energy penetrated its armor, which buckled and failed under the assault. The projectiles tore through the hull, triggering a chain of explosions.

"Direct hit! Armor collapsing," Rhom said. "Severe structural damage detected."

"Prepare to fire another volley. Target their weapons systems."

"Magrail batteries recharging," Rhom responded.

"Sir," Sato said, "enemy torpedoes within interception range. PDGs, point-defense guns, engaging."

Autocannons and laser bursts sprang to life across the fleet. They unleashed streams of projectiles and beams, intercepting and destroying the incoming torpedoes.

Rhom faced Lee. "All torpedoes neutralized, sir."

"Outstanding."

The missiles from the *Bolt* and *Cobalt* continued their approach toward the second cruiser.

"Missile impacts in ten seconds." Rhom eyed his console, his focus dead set on the monitor.

"Enemy ships altering formation," Reynolds said. "They're beginning evasive maneuvers."

"Maintain pressure. Corvettes, status on the freighters?"

"Freighters' engines targeted," came the response from the *Polaris*. "Firing turbolasers now."

Beams of energy lanced across the expanse. They struck the freighters' propulsion systems from six thousand kilometers away. However, they did little damage.

"Frigates are engaging enemy escorts attempting to retreat," Sato said. "Additional missile impacts on Zodark cruiser in three... two... one..."

On the tactical screen, the Havoc-II missiles slammed into the second cruiser. The explosions tore across its hull, breaching compartments.

"Enemy cruiser has sustained critical damage," Rhom said. "Propulsion and weapon systems are off-line."

"Excellent work. *Polaris*," Lee said, "switch to missiles on the supply ship. Fire on my mark."

"Aye, Captain. Loading missiles now."

"Three… two… one… mark."

"Missiles away."

Lee turned to Rhom. "Let's finish off their combat capabilities. Fire magrails at any remaining operational targets."

"Targets acquired. Firing magrail guns."

Once more, the *Poseidon* unleashed its devastating kinetic projectiles.

"Enemy ships are launching another wave of torpedoes," Rhom said.

"Maintain countermeasures and PDG fire," Lee ordered.

"Countermeasures dispersed and jamming currently active," Witkowski noted.

Rhom nodded. "And, point-defense systems are engaging incoming torpedoes."

"All ships, continue sustained long-range fire. Do not allow the enemy any respite."

The fleet maintained their positions, exploiting their superior range and firepower. The *Poseidon* added her might—energy beams, missiles, and magrails crippling enemy vessels.

"Enemy fleet is in full retreat," Rhom said.

Sato read the data streaming on her holo. "Sir, damage report from all ships. All units report minimal damage. No casualties sustained."

"Great work, everyone," Lee said. "We've neutralized the convoy."

An alarm blared, reverberating off the walls. Red lights flashed in sync with the klaxons, coloring the command center. A blinking red icon appeared on the main holoscreen—a newly detected object.

"Captain, we're picking up a massive energy signature," Rhom said.

"Source?" Lee asked.

"Bearing zero-one-zero, range sixty-eight thousand kilometers. Energy readings are off the scale."

Lee stared at the main screen. "Visual confirmation?"

"Not yet, sir. Sensors are struggling to process the data."

Lee's gut tightened. "All ships, halt advancement. Maintain current positions and readiness."

The fleet began its deceleration process. Massive fusion engines at the rear of each ship flared to life. Blue-white exhaust fired in the opposite direction of travel. Maneuvering thrusters along the hulls fired in sequence, turning the ships to slow their approach. The ships' inertial dampeners fought against the forces to keep the crews steady.

As the fleet slowed, space seemed to expand around them. The streaking stars began to settle into points of light. Ships drifted slightly apart as their engines worked differently based on their size. The massive engines burned hot as they fought against momentum, their computers fine-tuning power levels.

"Sir, the energy signature is increasing exponentially," Rhom reported. "It appears to be some kind of… massive ship."

Lee pressed the fleet-wide channel. "Prepare for potential engagement."

"Wait," Sato said, scanning her holographic display projecting from her chair. "Visual contact established."

On the main viewscreen, a colossal object appeared. It looked like a massive celestial body, approximately 1,700 kilometers in diameter—roughly half the size of Earth's moon. Though it was irregular, jagged-looking, like a meteor, it showed an atmosphere, with clouds drifting across its surface. Patches of dense vegetation covered large areas, interspersed with blue lakes and rivers. Near the poles were glaciers. It had to be a meteor of some type, but with an atmosphere? It didn't make sense.

As the sensors gathered more data, the meteor's true nature revealed itself. Protruding from various points along its rocky exterior were unmistakable weapons systems—massive cannons embedded in mountainous ridges, the blue glow of an ion cannon array nestled between two large craters, laser turret installations dotting the surface like artificial volcanoes. At what appeared to be the equator, a series of torpedo tubes gaped like caverns, ready to unleash destruction. Defensive shield generators stood like monolithic spires at strategic points, while sensor arrays swept the surrounding space continuously. This was a heavily armed fortress disguised as a natural phenomenon, bristling with enough firepower to obliterate an entire fleet.

Now, though much larger, this was similar to the weapons platforms posing as meteors that had been discussed in the briefing with Captain Roberts at the Kita shipyard. Now, a giant one floated before them, however very far off, thousands of kilometers away.

"How did that get there?" Lee asked. "This can't be a coincidence."

*First we learn about their seventy-eight armed asteroids, and now we find this. Could this be related to their asteroid weapon stations?* Lee wondered. *But this is far larger than anything in their known arsenal.*

"Sato, run a comparison analysis between this object's energy signature and what we know about their asteroid platforms around the Rass system."

After a few moments of tapping on her holo projecting from her chair, she eyed Lee. "Scans indicate it's not of any known design," Sato said. "Energy readings are unprecedented. I've never… heck, even the Republic, sir, has never witnessed anything like this."

Deep down, Lee didn't buy it. To him, it stank too much of Zodark involvement to be anything innocent. That they had their hand in this, plus, the weaponized asteroids in the Rass system—well, Zodarks could be some tricky strategists sometimes.

"Rodriguez, establish immediate encrypted communication with Forward Operating Station Bulwark. Priority Alpha. Transmit full sensor data package with tactical assessment to Captain Roberts on RNS *Australia*," Lee commanded.

"Transmitting now, sir. Full spectral analysis, defensive capabilities assessment, and comparative sizing metrics included."

The bridge fell silent as they awaited a response, the massive armed celestial body looming on their viewscreen like a slumbering titan. Minutes stretched into what felt like hours.

Lee turned to Sato. "I need more information. Is that thing operational? Active? Or is it under construction?"

Before Sato could answer, Rodriguez interrupted. "Sir, response from Captain Roberts: 'Maintain observation distance. Approach with caution. Intelligence value of target supersedes all other mission parameters. Reinforcements en route.'"

Lee acknowledged the order, even as Sato's console beeped with new information.

"Sir," Sato reported, "I'm detecting energy signatures consistent with recent combat."

Lee's expression hardened. Someone had already encountered this monstrosity—and based on the lack of wreckage in the surrounding space, they hadn't survived to report it. He just hoped it wasn't civilians, or heck, any allies. Perhaps it was simply target practice, a training run to keep the giant weapons platform in top condition.

"Main drives to standby," he ordered. "We may need to move quickly if that thing decides we're worth its attention."

# Chapter 8:
## It's Not What it Appears

**Year 2097**
**RNS *Poseidon***
**Sector 2**

*Poseidon*'s viewscreen filled with the image of a huge, irregular shape floating in space. Lee stood, his eyes on the object.

"All ships, form up in discovery pattern," Lee ordered. "Maintain defensive posture. We don't know what we're dealing with here."

Acknowledgments echoed through the comm as the fleet moved into position. Lee turned to his science officer. "Lieutenant Conklin, what are we looking at?"

Lieutenant Brenda Conklin worked on her console's interface. "Sir, initial scans confirm it's approximately one thousand, seven hundred kilometers in diameter. And with a stable atmosphere. And it's breathable." Conklin's voice held a note of wonder. "Oxygen levels at twenty-three percent, nitrogen at seventy-seven percent. Carbon dioxide at eight hundred and two parts per million."

Lee studied the readouts on the holo. "That's higher than Earth standard."

"Indeed. It's likely contributing to the vegetation we're detecting." Conklin brought up a new set of images. "Large swaths of green, sir. And water. Lakes, rivers. Yet, the weapons, and the types—I'd say it's likely Zodark."

"My thoughts exactly. What about those structures?" Lee asked.

Conklin zoomed in on a section of the surface. "Alien in design. Unlike anything in our database, but we're not detecting life forms."

On the bridge's holodisplay, the buildings came into focus. Lee'd ordered probes to scan the meteor, and after a long journey taking twenty minutes, finally drones sent data to the *Poseidon*. The ship's science computers analyzed them, projecting the structures on the main holo. Most were smaller domes, but some were spires reaching 608 meters into the air. The images blinked repeatedly as the computers refined their calculations.

The science officer explained the process. "Our scanners measure the composition and volume of the detected buildings, even at vast distances from our probes. We factor in material density and structural engineering principles. The computers then extrapolate the dimensions, and we then perform deep scans, where it gives us an actual picture."

Red highlights appeared on specific portions of one of the structures. "These are key structural elements," Conklin continued. "Their size and placement indicate load-bearing capacity. We use this to confirm our height estimates."

Green markers outlined the base stones. "The depth and spread of these foundations support our projections for the spires' height and mass."

As the officer spoke, the outlines grew solid, showing how the city looked—that's if it was a city fused with a military installation. The bridge crew watched as the metropolis took shape before their eyes. Lee thought of New York, but twice its size and with alien formations and structures. Next, the weapons came into view, many showing on the screens, the types, the ammunition capacity, and the sizes.

"Energy readings?" Lee asked.

"Off the charts, Captain," Conklin reported.

As Conklin finished her report, Communications Officer Rodriguez spoke. "Sir, we're receiving a hail from the *Horizon*. It's Captain Lipun."

"Put him through, Rodriguez."

The viewscreen switched to show Lipun, his face bearing the marks of years in space with deep-set eyes missing nothing and a tight-lipped expression giving him a neutral disposition. "Captain Lee, our science officers have detected some anomalies regarding this object we're approaching."

"Go on, Captain," Lee said.

"Our scans indicate that deep within the object, there are multiple engines powering what appears to be a terraforming process. These engines are in pristine condition. However, we're unable to determine an exact age for either the meteor or the structures on its surface. It's… puzzling."

"We've encountered similar difficulties. Lieutenant Conklin?"

Conklin turned to face *Horizon*'s captain. "Sir, we're experiencing significant interference from energy emissions emanating from the object. Our chronometric sensors are unable to penetrate these fields, preventing us from obtaining accurate dating."

Lipun's science officer, visible in the background, chimed in. "We've also noted unusual cloud formations in the atmosphere. The particulate composition suggests artificial seeding, yet the distribution patterns are unlike any known terraforming techniques."

Conklin nodded. "Agreed. We've detected an internal heat source maintaining a stable surface temperature of approximately twenty-two degrees Celsius. This heat, combined with the engineered atmosphere, creates an environment highly suitable for colonization. For the Zodarks, they'd feel just fine down there."

Lee stroked his chin. "Yet there's no signs of inhabitants?"

"Correct, sir," Conklin confirmed. "We've found no evidence of waste accumulation, power grid remnants, or communication array debris typically associated with colonies or military bases. It's as if there was terraforming, but no one lived in the structures… ever."

Lipun nodded. "Our estimates say the site was started between nine hundred and twelve hundred Earth years ago, but the margin of error is significant due to the energy interference."

Regarding the briefing he'd had with Roberts at the Kita shipyard, these meteor weapons platforms were rather new, not old. So, this posed a conundrum. Were the Zodarks tricking them or was this something built long ago, and potentially by someone else other than the Zodarks? Thing was, Lee's crew had detected weapons activity not too long ago, and if Lee was a betting man, he'd put some money on the fact the Zodarks were attempting to cause confusion to lure them closer. "Captain Lipun, what do you propose?"

The captain raised his chin, his facade confident. "We should send probes to the surface to collect samples and conduct a more thorough investigation. There may be valuable technology or information to be gleaned."

Before Lee could respond, Commander Sato cleared her throat. "Captain, I agree."

Lee nodded. "Conklin, launch a dozen atmospheric probes and terrain-based drones."

"Aye, sir."

After an hour of waiting, with constant communication between his small battle group and his crew, Conklin called for Lee. Once he reached her station, she pointed to the incoming datastream.

"Captain, the probes are sending back remarkable information. The surface contains minerals we've never encountered before. The vegetation appears engineered at the molecular level—possibly designed to process atmospheric toxins. And the structures..."

Lee leaned closer, studying the readouts. "Any signs of weapons activation?"

"Negative, sir. All weapons systems appear dormant, though fully functional."

"Captain," Rhom said. "I'm losing telemetry from probe seven... eight... nine—"

The holographic display flickered as one by one, the probe signatures winked out.

"Sir," Conklin's voice rose. "All surface drones are being systematically neutralized. Energy weapons fire detected across the meteor's surface."

That's when the ship's proximity alarms blared. On the tactical display, a massive energy surge erupted from deep within the meteor's core, building rapidly as it traveled toward the surface.

"Energy buildup detected," Sato said. "Captain, if that's what I think it is—"

The energy reading climbed exponentially, the sensors' indicators flashing into the red zone.

"Sir," Conklin's voice had gone quiet, "if that thing detonates at this range, the blast radius will encompass our entire battle group. We don't have time to clear the danger zone."

Lee rushed back to the captain's chair. "Rodriguez, open fleet-wide channel." *We need to leave these coordinates, and now.*

## Chapter 9:
## Midnight Maintenance

**Year 2097**
**FOB Oteren**
**Planet Intus**

Brian Ford lay under the AT-70C Osprey's belly. He moved his flashlight beam across the exposed circuitry. Right now, the hangar was filled with the voices of crewmen preparing for tomorrow's upcoming mission. Engines revved, then died. Auto-wrenches buzzed. Synths stacked crates.

Outside, the moons hung in the sky. The clouds from before dissipated, slowing the wind to a nice breeze. The chatter of Intus-shriekers filled the air, drowning out the croaking sounds of their reptilian prey. Ford recalled his walk here after his chess game with Corporal Williams, when he'd nearly collided with one of those winged creatures.

The Intus-shriekers, though lazily named, gave out horrible shrieks some nights. Hell, every night. Ford was thankful for his soundproof quarters. Otherwise, he'd never get any sleep. These small beasts, with their translucent membrane wings and elongated snouts, were a menace up close. Ford shuddered, recalling their putrid odor. Physical contact with an Intus-shrieker left victims reeking of a noxious combination of sludge and the most revolting mucus imaginable. The stench could remain for days. It rivaled even a skunk's odor back on Earth.

Shaking off the unpleasant memory, Ford refocused on the task at hand, grateful he had dodged the Intus-shrieker on his way here.

Ford traced wires, checking connections. He scrunched up his nose as he spotted a frayed section near the landing gear. *How did I miss that on the last inspection twenty minutes ago?*

Private First Class Harbin stood nearby. He watched Ford work as if learning from a master. "Chief, you've been at this for hours. Shouldn't we call it a night?"

*Call it a night? This is more important than life itself. Gotta keep this Osprey in working order.* "Negative. Not finished yet. I'm glad I saw this." Ford grunted, not looking up from his work. "Hand me the nanosplicer, would you?"

Harbin rummaged through the toolbox, producing the device. "Here you go, Chief."

"That's it." Ford took the tool. Its tip hummed to life when he pressed it against the damaged wiring. Microscopic filaments shot out, weaving themselves into the frayed section.

"You figured it out?" Harbin asked, peering closer.

"Yep. Repairing the break at the molecular level. Stronger than new. Hand me the torque wrench."

Harbin complied. "Aye, sir."

Footsteps came closer to Ford, then stopped. "Is that you, Ford?"

Ford grimaced at Love's voice. "Shouldn't you be asleep, Lieutenant?"

"I had a hard time sleeping. Went for a walk outside on the tarmac, then saw some lights and noises in the bay here. I can't say I'm surprised to see you."

"Lieutenant, I suggest you take a sleeping agent and get some good shut-eye."

"I could say the same for you," Love retorted. "Regardless, I did, and no dice."

"Yeah," Ford said. "Sometimes they don't take effect for a while."

Love walked around to the ramp, her boots in clear view. "I'm afraid you're going to wear yourself out if you keep this up. Maybe it's time to take a breather and take your own advice? You know, get some sleep and get to this early in the morning."

Ford's shoulders tensed, but he didn't look up, continuing to adjust a bolt. "I'm fine. Just being thorough."

"Thorough is good. Obsessive isn't. When's the last time you took a nap?"

"Don't need one." Irritation crossed Ford's face. "With all due respect, I know what I'm doing."

"Never said you didn't. Even the best need rest. You've been at this for how long tonight?"

"Long," Harbin answered for him.

"I appreciate your initiative, Private, but I'll take it from here. I'll address this personally next time. Stand down," Ford said.

"Roger, sir."

Ford set down his tools, having finished the job. He crawled out from under the Osprey and wiped his hands on a rag. "There's always more to do. Can't afford mistakes out there."

"How many double checks have you done, and repairs on already repaired areas?"

Ford looked away, tossing the rag on the floor. "Understood."

Love nodded. "Mistakes happen when we're exhausted too. Come on, let's get some shut-eye. The Osprey will still be here in the morning."

Ford hesitated, torn between his drive to keep working and the logic of Love's words. He crouched down, his eyes fixed on the exposed wiring where a panel had once been. The removed panel now lay on the cement floor beneath the bird. Ford thought of improvements and adjustments. He glanced back at Love. "Just give me another hour."

Love grinned. "Not a chance, Chief. Consider it an order if you have to."

Ford moved under the Osprey and closed up the access panel. "Understood."

"Ford, you're gonna burn out at this rate. I bet Harbin over here has seen you triple-check every system."

Harbin gave her a nod, confirming her suspicions.

"Just being thorough. Besides, I have a blast doing this."

Across the hangar, a specialist and a corporal hefted crates onto a transport. Their banter drifted over, along with their good-natured ribbing.

As Ford walked toward the hangar's exit with Love, two Synths stood at attention by the bay's opening.

"749," Ford said, "I need a full fuel distribution analysis, pronto. And, 482, get on that targeting guidance system. Need another check, just in case."

The Synths' optics brightened in acknowledgment. "Affirmative, Chief Ford," 749 replied. "Commencing fuel distribution scan."

482 ambled toward the Osprey. "I'll initiate targeting guidance diagnostics. Estimated completion time—seven minutes."

Ford nodded, satisfied. He turned. Love was watching him, arms crossed.

"What?" he asked, feigning innocence. "Just delegating some tasks."

"Ford, I know you're trying to play this off, but—"

A sudden crash interrupted her, followed by a string of colorful curses from the specialist. "Corporal, you almost took off my foot!"

"All right, let's go, Ford," Love said. "Maybe you can talk me to sleep on the way to my quarters."

"Maybe."

"You're nervous," Love insisted. "I hear it in your voice."

"I'm fine," Ford said.

"You're not. What's going on?"

They walked on the idle airstrip toward their quarters. "Carl."

"Carl?" Love asked.

"Yeah. I haven't heard from him in a while."

"Could be he's busy?"

"Yeah." Who knew, though? In truth, Carl was the only family Ford had, and if he lost him for some reason or other, he didn't know if he could cope.

"I'll get a message to him, get any updates on his status in… where is he?"

"Carl owns Wenthrow Nanotech Refitters in Austin, Texas," Ford said. "Best place on Earth."

"Are you serious? Best place? Austin or the refitter joint?"

"Both."

"Oh boy, Ford. You definitely need some sleep."

Ford followed Love into the officers' lodging. The cool air was a nice respite from the humid night outside. The corridor lights were dimmed, at odds with Ford's restless mind.

"Get some rest, Ford," Love said, pausing at her door.

"Yes. You too."

As he entered his own quarters, exhaustion settled over Ford. He'd been running on caffeine and Neurostim pills for days, pushing his body to its limits. The Neurostim, a potent cognitive enhancer, kept his mind sharp, but even it had its limits.

He sat on the edge of his bed, rubbing his eyes. *Sleep. Right. Easier said than done.* Carl had taught him too well when he'd worked for the man. The problem was that Carl had instilled in him a perfectionism bordering on obsession, but it worked well for Ford. The chief could repair the Osprey with his eyes closed, but that didn't stop his mind from spinning with possibilities, improvements, and potential problems.

As he lay down, staring at the ceiling, Ford knew sleep wouldn't come easily. The caffeine still coursed through his veins. The lingering effects of the Neurostim kept his thoughts lit up with pressing potential issues with the *Jack*. He closed his eyes, trying to quiet his mind. Images of circuitry and schematics spun behind his eyelids.

*What if something goes wrong during the mission? What if I missed something important?* The Osprey's systems were complicated, interconnected. One small oversight could lead to catastrophe.

Ford's eyes snapped open. Sleep, it seemed, would have to wait. He had work to do.

## Chapter 10:
## Wolfpack's Flight

**Year 2097**
**FOB Oteren**
**In Flight to DZ Cragstone**
**Planet Intus**

Love's eyelids fluttered open. She blinked, trying to clear the fog from her vision as the room slowly came into focus.

*How long did I sleep? A few hours? Damn.*

She turned off her alarm and groaned. Pushing herself up, she swung her legs over the edge of the bed. Love's gaze drifted to her boots beside her bed, searching for Jack's photo. Her brow furrowed when she didn't see it. She distinctly remembered placing it next to her boots last night.

Her heart rate quickened as she scanned the floor. It was her good luck charm, the angelic presence to keep her, Ford, her copilot, and all the troops she transported as safe as possible. The boots were there, right where she'd left them, but no picture. A knot formed in her stomach as she dropped to her knees, peering under the bed.

*Where is it?*

Love stood and made her way to her desk. She yanked open drawers, rifling through papers and personal items. Nothing.

"This doesn't make sense," she said. "I know I took it out last night."

Had she dreamed taking out the photo? Was her exhausted mind playing tricks on her? She downed a Neurostim pill. It woke her immediately, her mind clearing away the haze.

She upended her laundry bag, shook out her flight suit—even checked inside her boots. She went to the bathroom, flinging open the medicine cabinet. Toothbrush, razor, painkillers—but still, no image of Jack. Love gripped the edges of the sink, staring at her wild-eyed reflection.

"Think," she told herself. "Where else could it be?"

Back in the main room, Love dropped to her hands and knees a second time. She peered under the desk, into every shadowy corner. The possibility that someone had entered her quarters while she slept came to mind.

Love sat back on her heels, running shaky hands through her hair. The room was a disaster. Clothes strewn about, drawers hanging open, personal items scattered across every surface. But the one thing she desperately needed remained absent.

She closed her eyes, trying to calm herself. The photo was like an anchor. It reminded her of why she fought, why she kept everyone as safe as possible under her watch. Without it, she felt adrift, untethered from the purpose that drove her. She wasn't religious, but she believed this was her protection from beyond the veil, and there was no better protection than that.

"Get a hold of yourself," she said. "Relax. It's gotta be here somewhere."

She glanced at the clock. Her heart skipped a beat. No time. She cursed under her breath. If she didn't leave now, she'd be late for preflight checks.

With a frustrated moan, Love ran her fingers through her hair one last time. The photo would have to wait. She snatched up her flight suit and hurriedly dressed. Love felt off-balance without Jack's picture, a fact troubling her more than she cared to admit. She recognized the need to wean herself off this emotional dependency, to trust in her own abilities without the constant reassurance of Jack's frozen smile.

After rushing down the corridor toward the hangar, she entered the giant space ten minutes later. Immediately, she sought out her Osprey, the *Jack*. There, working diligently on her ship, was Chief Brian Ford.

Love strode over. "Morning, Chief."

"Morning."

"Sleep well?" Love asked.

"Sure," Ford replied. "You?"

Love shrugged. "OK. Why you look like you haven't slept a wink?"

Ford put a tool in his toolbox. "You're speaking quickly. What's the matter?"

"You haven't seen my photo of Jack around, have you?"

"Your photo? It's right where you always keep it."

"What do you mean? I looked everywhere."

Ford gestured toward the cockpit. "On the dashboard of the Osprey. Where else would it be?"

"That's impossible. I took it with me after the last mission."

"You sure about that?" Ford asked.

"Of course I'm sure. I remember taking it back to my quarters."

"I can assure you, it's been there since I started my checks this morning."

Love shook her head. "That doesn't make any sense. I tore my room apart looking for it."

"Maybe you're remembering a different day?"

"I'm not losing my mind, Chief," Love said.

"Stress and fatigue can play tricks on anyone's memory."

Love ran a hand over her face. "I suppose that's possible. But I could've sworn…"

"Why don't you take a look for yourself?"

Love followed Ford up the ramp, into the troop bay, and to the cockpit.

"You sure you're all right?" Ford pressed.

Love nodded, but uncertainty nagged at her. "I'm fine, just… confused."

Love looked at the dash. There, taped securely, was Jack's photo. Her breath caught.

"It's… it's here," she muttered, reaching out to touch it. "But how? I could've sworn…"

"Maybe you need more rest," Ford said.

"You and I are on repeat with that suggestion."

"Seems so."

Love rubbed her temple. "Let's double up on stims."

Ford frowned but didn't argue. He handed her a canteen filled with a caffeine mixture. She drank a few sips, grimacing at the bitter taste.

"Thanks," she said. "That should keep me going. Where'd you get that, the swamp?"

"Worse. The mess hall. Anyway, just… be careful."

"Always am," Love replied, settling into the pilot's seat.

Ford hesitated, then turned to leave. "I'll finish prepping the troop bay."

"Roger."

As he exited, Second Lieutenant Caleb Green entered, taking his place in the copilot's seat.

"Mornin'," Green said, running through his preflight checks.

Love touched Jack's face on the photo with her fingertip. "Green. Ready for another day blasting the Zodarks?"

Green chuckled. "As ready as I'll ever be. Rumor has it the Deltas got some new tech. Something that'll give us an edge."

"Probably the same ol', same ol', just nice and polished."

The sound of boots on metal caught their attention. Love glanced back to see Ford and Corporal Williams preparing the troop bay.

"Incoming," Ford called out. "Deltas are boarding."

Love took a deep breath, pushing aside her earlier confusion. "All right, let's get this bird in the air."

The engines roared to life, vibrating through the Osprey's frame. Love tightened her grip on the controls, her focus laser-sharp thanks to the Neurostim pills, and maybe that mud Ford had tried to pass off as coffee.

"Preflight checks complete," Green said.

"Copy that," Love replied. "Troop bay secure?"

Ford's voice crackled over the intercom. "All secured. We're good to go."

Love turned her attention to the hangar bay doors. "Roger that. Preparing for takeoff."

The Osprey's ramp closed with a loud click.

"Control, this is Wolfpack Actual," Love said into her helmet's mic. "Requesting clearance for takeoff."

"Wolfpack Actual, you're cleared for takeoff," came the reply. "Winds are calm, visibility excellent. Storms on its way. Heads up, and good luck out there, Lieutenant."

Love eased the Osprey forward. The hangar bay fell away beneath them. As they ascended into the early-morning sky, adrenaline surged through Love.

"Wolfpack, this is Actual. Sound off," Love commanded.

One by one, the other Ospreys in her squadron reported in.

"Wolfpack Two, ready."

"Wolfpack Three, all systems go."

"Wolfpack Four, standing by."

"Wolfpack, this is Actual. We're heading to Waypoint DZ Cragstone. ETA forty-seven minutes. Maintain formation and stay alert."

As they climbed, the twin suns of Intus peeked over the horizon. It turned the sky into oranges, pinks, and purples. In the distance, mountain peaks reached toward the sky, their snowcapped summits quite different from the lush greenery blanketing their lower slopes. Mist clung to the valleys, slowly dissipating in the warmth of the rising suns.

"Wolfpack, maintain formation," Love said. "We've got a long flight ahead. Stay sharp and keep your eyes peeled for any anomalies."

The squadron of Ospreys sliced through the air. Below Love, the dense woodlands spread far and wide, broken by flowing rivers and massive lakes.

Love's eyes narrowed as she spotted a dark, roiling mass in the sky as they approached the mountains.

Ford's voice cut through the cockpit. "Lieutenant, the Deltas are getting antsy. They're seeing the storm on approach."

Love keyed her mic. "All units, prepare for extreme turbulence." *This drop just got a lot more interesting.* "Wolfpack, be advised. We've got a monster storm ahead. Looks like it'll reach the DZ same time we do."

As if on cue, the first raindrops splattered against the windshield while the comm erupted with chatter.

"Wolfpack Actual, this is Three. Confirm visual on that storm system. It's gigantic, over."

"Four to Actual. Please verify mission status. Those conditions look beyond operational parameters, over."

Love took a deep breath, her eyes on the black clouds ahead. Lightning illuminated the sky. Although it looked like they were flying straight into the jaws of disaster, Love knew this storm could work in their favor.

"Wolfpack, this is Actual," she said. "That storm's going to give us cover. The Zodarks won't be expecting a drop in these conditions."

Green nodded in agreement. "It'll mask our approach and jam their sensors. The Deltas can use the chaos to their advantage on the ground."

"Exactly," Love said. "We're going to give the Zodarks one nasty wake-up call."

"Actual, this is Two. Confirm go-no-go for current flight path through severe weather, over."

More lightning flashed in the distance. "Confirmed, Two," Love said. "Mission parameters unchanged. We're flying into hell."

# Chapter 11:
## Hot Drop

**Year 2097**
**DZ Cragstone**
**Planet Intus**

The Osprey bucked as a gust slammed into its side. Love maintained an iron grip on the stick, her gaze on the strobing flashes of lightning cutting through the dark clouds ahead. Hailstones battered the window, each impact resounding through the cockpit.

"Wind shear from port side," Green reported. He looked between the instrument panel and the storm enveloping them. "Adjusting thrusters to compensate."

"Good man," Love said. The altimeter wavered, numbers spinning as the Osprey fought to maintain altitude. She glanced at it, then back to the swirling maelstrom outside. "Hold her steady. We drop below twelve hundred meters, we're flirting with ground fire."

Green nodded, fingertips gliding over the interface. "Thrusters adjusted. Altitude holding at thirteen hundred meters. Crosswinds are fierce."

A bolt of lightning lit up the horizon, showing the mountain peaks they headed toward.

Static crackled in her helmet. "Wolfpack Actual, this is Wolfpack Two. Visibility's dropping fast. Requesting permission to adjust formation."

Love keyed the comm. "Negative, Wolfpack Two. Maintain tight echelon. We spread out, we're easy pickings. Those Orions, Reapers, and Raiders have been sweeping the area for the past thirty mikes. They're our eyes until we're clear of this soup."

"Copy that, Actual," Wolfpack Two replied. "Maintaining position. Just thought I'd ask."

A bead of sweat trickled down Love's temple. She ignored it. The Osprey shuddered as another gust hit them. "How are the systems holding up?"

"All systems nominal," Green answered. "Drives operating at ninety-eight percent. Airframe stress within acceptable parameters. Inertial dampeners compensating for atmospheric turbulence. VTOL systems primed for rapid deployment. Life support optimal. Troop bay secure, all harnesses engaged. ECM suite active and jamming enemy frequencies. Forward sensors degraded by storm interference but still functional. Hydraulics and landing gear pressurized and responsive. Fuel cells at eighty-nine percent capacity. No critical alerts on any subsystems. We're good."

"Great. Let's keep it that way." Love adjusted their heading slightly, steering them between two towering cloud formations. The turbulence lessened for a moment, a brief respite.

Another voice chimed in over the comms. "Wolfpack Actual, this is Wolfpack Three. Radar's picking up intermittent blips at our ten o'clock. Possibly atmospheric interference, but could be hostiles."

"Understood, Wolfpack Three. Stay sharp. Don't know what that could be. Weapons systems hot, but hold fire. We don't want them to know we're coming."

"Roger that," came the reply.

Green tapped the radar display. "I'm seeing them too. Signals are faint, could be nothing."

"Or it could be something," Love said. "Eyes open." She switched channels. "Ford, how's it looking back there?"

Ford's voice was calm. "Troops are strapped in and ready. Deltas are itching for action. Hull's taking a beating from the hail, but no breaches. We're golden, Lieutenant."

"Good to hear. Watch the port stabilizer."

"Already on it," Ford replied. "She's holding tight. You just keep us in the air."

"That's the plan."

Green scanned the dashboard. "Storm front's intensifying ahead. Recommend we ascend to fifteen hundred meters, try to get above the worst of it."

Love considered for a moment. "Negative. Higher altitude makes us more visible. We stay low and ride it out."

"Understood," Green said without hesitation.

The comms crackled again. "Wolfpack Actual, this is Wolfpack Four. Got a strong tailwind pushing us. Speed increasing by ten knots."

"Compensate as needed," Love ordered. "Stay tight. We don't need any stragglers."

"Copy, Actual."

Thunder boomed, so loud it seemed to originate from within the cockpit itself. The Osprey vibrated in response, the controls resisting for a moment before settling.

"That was close." Green tapped on the holo before him.

"Too close," Love agreed. She surveyed the dark skies. "Let's hope lightning doesn't decide we're a good target."

"Metal bird in a storm," Green said. "What could go wrong?"

Love chuckled. "Just another day in paradise."

A warning light blinked on her console. She tapped it. "Got a pressure drop in engine two."

"Compensating," Green said, turning a holodial. "Diverting power from auxiliary systems."

"Good catch." Love adjusted their pitch, leveling out the ride as much as possible. The mountains loomed closer, silhouetted against sporadic flashes of light.

"Wolfpack Actual, this is Orion Lead—Strike. Area ahead is clear of hostiles. Storm's playing havoc with our sensors, but we've got your six."

"Appreciate it, Strike," Love said. "Stay sharp."

"Roger that, Actual."

Green glanced over. "Holding steady at two hundred and twenty knots. Fuel consumption normal."

"How's your first storm run?" she asked.

Green shrugged. "I've had smoother flights, but nothing I can't handle."

"Good. Keep your head on straight, and we'll get through this."

Another burst of hail rattled against the cockpit. The sound was deafening, like a thousand bullets hitting at once. Love squinted, trying to peer through the onslaught.

"Visibility down to less than a kilometer," Green noted. "Switching to instruments."

"Already there," Love said. The HUD projected a wireframe of the terrain ahead, data scrolling rapidly.

"Ford," she called over the intercom. "Everything still secure back there?"

"All secured, Lieutenant," Ford confirmed. "Deltas are calm as ever. You'd think they were on a pleasure cruise."

"Good to know someone's enjoying the ride."

"Can't say the same for myself. Shouldn't have had that ham sandwich for breakfast," Ford said. "But I've got faith in your piloting."

Love smiled. "You keep getting lunch and breakfast mixed up. When we get back, I'll give you a lesson on daily meals, all right?"

"Copy that."

Green pointed at a new blip on the radar. "Unidentified contact at our three o'clock. Moving fast."

"Orion Lead, this is Wolfpack Actual," Love said into the mic. "We've got a possible incoming at our three. Can you confirm?"

"This is Coop. No visual contact, but LIDAR's painting a bogey. Profile matches Zodark *Vulture*-class scout. Unusual to encounter one in this AO. Haven't had a confirmed sighting in two months, over."

"Coop, Wolfpack Actual. This is Strike. Copy your last. Maintain current heading and continue to monitor. All units, be advised of possible hostile recon element in vicinity. *Vulture*-class, single count. Wolfpack Actual, confirm Coop's report, over."

"Wolfpack Actual. Can confirm Coop's SITREP. Sensors correlate. No additional contacts at this time, over." Love changed to her squadron's channel. "All units, stay alert. Prepare for possible engagement. ETA to DZ, eight minutes."

Green armed the weapons systems. "Guns hot. Missiles primed."

"Let's hope we don't need them," Love said. "But be ready."

The storm intensified. Wind howled around them, and the Osprey shook.

"Hold her together," Love whispered, coaxing the controls. She eyed Jack's picture for a millisecond, sending a prayer for everyone on the mission.

A bright light streaked past the cockpit, so close it left a residual glare.

Love followed it, whipping her head to port. "Whoa!"

"What the hell was that?" Green followed her gaze.

"That's incoming fire!" Love said. "Evasive maneuvers!"

She banked hard, the Osprey veering left. The engines growled, responding well.

"Coop, we are under attack!" Love shouted into the comms. "Engaging evasive actions."

"Copy, Actual. Moving to intercept," Coop said.

Green tracked the attacker on his display. "It's a Zodark fighter. Fast. Did the Zodarks bring in reinforcements without our knowledge?"

"No idea. Now, Coop, stay with me," Love said. She dove into a cloud bank, using the storm as cover.

The Osprey rattled as they pushed through the turbulent air. Love's focus narrowed.

"Hostile is circling around," Green warned. "He's persistent."

"Let him come," Love said through gritted teeth. "We'll be ready."

The comms buzzed with chatter as the other Ospreys adjusted their formations, pilots exchanging quick updates.

"Actual, this is Wolfpack Two." The pilot's voice boomed through her helmet. "We're moving to support."

"Affirmative, Wolfpack Two."

"I'm readying the weapons array," Ford said. "Give the word, Lieutenant."

"Wait for it," she said. The Zodark fighter appeared on their starboard side, edging closer.

"Now!" Love commanded.

Ford fired a burst from the side-mounted magrail gun. The rounds streaked toward the target, but the fighter rolled away at the last moment.

"Missed," Green said.

"I see that," Ford replied. "There's a first for everything. Next time, he's down."

"He's quick," Love said. She pulled the Osprey into a steep climb. The fighter pursued, closing the gap.

"Where are you, Coop?" Love veered starboard, the black cloud concealing her Osprey.

Coop's tone burst over the link. "Raven and I are closing on your six. ETA two mikes."

Love flicked a switch. "Deploying countermeasures."

The Zodark Vulture unleashed a barrage of lasers. Warning klaxons blared as the Osprey's armor took the salvo.

"Armor integrity at eighty-nine percent," Green said. "A few systems redlining. Diverting power to engines."

More chaff and flares erupted from the Osprey's tail, briefly disorienting the pursuing Vulture.

"Wolfpack Actual, this is Coop. Visual on bogey. Permission to engage, over."

"Coop, you are weapons free. Clear our six so we can make the drop," Love said. "Four minutes to DZ."

Coop crackled through the comm. "Copy that. Raven, form up on my wing."

"Roger, Coop. I've got your back," Raven responded, his fighter falling into formation, showing on the Osprey's interface.

The two starfighters screamed by Love's Osprey, afterburners blazing as they headed toward the Vulture.

"Fox Three!" Coop called out as he launched missiles.

The Vulture jinked hard, evading the initial wave, but Raven was ready.

"Guns, guns, guns!" Raven's cannons lit up the sky, peppering the Vulture's hull.

"This bastard's tough," Coop growled. "Love, we need to coordinate. Can you bring her around?"

"Affirmative, Coop. Executing Thach Weave. Green, redirect power to rear guns," Love ordered, swinging the Osprey into a sharp turn.

The Osprey's stern guns opened up, catching the Vulture in a crossfire between it and the Orions.

"Direct hit!" Green shouted. "Vulture's hull is breached!"

"Finishing the job," Coop said grimly. "Fox Two!"

A missile streaked from Coop's fighter, finding its mark. The Vulture exploded in a fireball.

"Splash one," Raven confirmed. "Skies are clear, Wolfpack Actual. You're clear to proceed to the DZ."

"Copy that, Coop, Raven. Great work," Love said. "All hands, prepare for combat drop. Three minutes. Green, give me a SITREP on our systems."

"Aye. Engines at eighty-four percent, hull integrity holding at eighty-six percent. We're banged up, but she'll fly."

"Roger that. Coop, Raven, provide high cover until the drop is complete."

"Wilco, Wolfpack Actual. We've got overwatch. Get those Deltas on the ground."

Two minutes until the drop.

"SIGINT is minimal, but something's off," Green said. "Possible EMCON from hostiles." The terrain below was pockmarked with deep shadows and sporadic flames, thick smoke billowing across the landscape. The aftermath of the Republic's pre-assault bombing runs was evident. "Reapers and Raiders did a number on the area about thirty mikes ago."

"Affirmative, Green. Maintain OPREC. Wolfpack, maintain high alert," Love said.

OPREC—operational security, meant keep your mouth shut and stay off comms unless absolutely necessary. Basic stuff, but stuff that could get you killed if you forgot it. Love had seen a few training vids of units getting wiped because someone couldn't resist running their mouth on an open channel.

"Thermals are degraded. Residual heat signatures from the pre-assault bombardment are masking potential tangos," Green said, fine-tuning the sensor array.

Love's eyes swept the darkened horizon. "Understood. Zodark forces may be employing thermal dampeners. Stay frosty."

Green adjusted the scanners. "Copy. Confirming BDA from earlier strikes. Their coordinated SEAD operation was successful. Multiple Zodark positions neutralized."

"Acknowledged," Love responded. "Prepare for potential triple-A as we approach the DZ." She patched into the troop bay. "Deltas, we may be looking at a compromised insertion point."

"Wilco," Ford said. "Updating threat assessment based on most recent intel from ground teams. Smoke's playing havoc with visual, but it should provide some cover for our insertion."

Love nodded. "Let's hope it works both ways. All hands, stand by for final approach. We're going in blind, but the element of surprise is on our side. Prepare for rapid deployment on my mark."

The Osprey squadron continued its descent towards the war-torn landscape, ready to insert Delta squads into the heart of the Zodark insurgency's territory.

On her cockpit display, she watched as Coop's Orion zeroed in on enemy positions. Beams of light and streaks of missiles rained down, targeting the weapons platforms.

"Taking out their eyes," Raven reported. "You've got a clear path in thirty seconds."

"Affirmative." The altimeter dipped for a second before Love corrected her course. "Green, status on the weapon systems?"

He was ahead of her. "Engaging weapon systems now."

Love's adrenaline surged. They were descending to the drop point. "Ford, get those magrails ready."

"On it." Ford's response was immediate. "Magrails online. Targeting weapon platforms. Williams and I are both opening fire."

The Osprey's magrail guns rushed to life, sending a hail of projectiles toward the ground. The recoil reverberated through the aircraft, a steady thump-thump-thump.

"Direct hits on enemy positions," Green confirmed, eyes glued to the targeting screen.

Love banked right, avoiding a fresh burst of anti-aircraft fire.

Coop's voice chimed in again. "Two platforms down, one to go. Raven, with me."

On the holo, the two Orions performed a synchronized dive. Their combined firepower lit up the jungle, obliterating the final weapons platform in a fiery mess.

"That's the last of them," Raven confirmed. "Thought you might enjoy the fireworks."

She smirked. "Just focus on keeping my soldiers safe."

"Yes, ma'am," Coop said.

Ahead, the dense canopy of the drop zone came into view, a dark mass dotted with the occasional glint of light. The designated clearing was just beyond.

"Prepare for drop," Love said. "Ford, get the Deltas ready."

"Already in position," Ford confirmed. "They're locked and loaded."

"Good. We're going in hot."

The Osprey tilted forward. The wind resistance increased, buffeting the aircraft as they continued to lower altitude. Zodark warrior blaster fire streaked past them, too close for comfort.

"Green, deploy countermeasures."

"Deploying chaff and flares," he responded. A bunch of pops sounded as metallic strips and bright flares launched.

"Descent at optimal speed." Love scanned for obstructions.

Suddenly, a sharp jolt rocked the Osprey. Alarms shrieked, and the aircraft lurched sideways.

"We've been hit!" Ford shouted.

"Damage report?" Love wrestled with the controls.

"Port engine compromised," Green read off. "Throttle response is sluggish."

The Osprey bucked against Love's commands. Through the canopy, she spotted movement on the ground. Tangos with four arms, all carrying weapons and rushing into the LZ, their blasters glinting.

"SITREP on altitude?" she asked.

"Maintaining, but systems are strained," Green said. "LZ approach is FUBAR."

The clearing below erupted with activity. Zodarks were deploying crew-served weapons with alarming speed, others establishing a defensive perimeter.

"All Wolfpack elements, this is Actual. LZ is hot, repeat, LZ is hot," Love transmitted. "Execute fallback protocol Delta."

"Wolfpack Two, solid copy."

"Three, roger that."

"Four, wilco."

A beam sizzled past their starboard side.

Love juked the stick, evading another blast. "We're taking fire. All elements, abort landing. Repeat, abort landing. Establish holding pattern at grid Papa Echo four-five-eight-two-three-four."

The Osprey groaned as Love pulled up. Below, more Zodarks emerged from the tree line, their weapons trained skyward.

Coop's voice crackled over the comm. "Wolfpack Actual, ISR confirms multiple triple-A emplacements in the AO. Recommend immediate egress."

"Copy that, Overwatch." Love banked hard to avoid another energy blast. "Wolfpack elements, maintain max standoff distance. Prep for hot insertion on my mark." She gritted her teeth, guiding the Osprey in a wide arc. "Coop, request fire mission on grid square. Danger close."

"Solid copy, Wolfpack Actual. Fire mission incoming. Stand by for BDA."

Love took a deep breath, surveying her squadron regrouping. The mission parameters had just shifted big-time. "Williams, Ford, prepare for suppressive fire as we circle back!" Her voice cut through the static of the intercom. "We can't afford to lose visibility on those Zodarks!"

"Copy that!" Williams responded.

The Osprey banked. Love pushed the aircraft. Wind howled past the cockpit, the terrain below a blur of shadow and firelight.

As they looped around, a flash erupted to her starboard side. An Osprey engulfed in flames spiraled downward, a trail of smoke trailing its descent.

"Damn it!" Love's heart clenched. "Green, SITREP!"

"We lost Wolfpack Three!"

"Copy that," she replied tightly. "Stay focused! We need to get our people on the ground."

Tracer fire arced across the sky. The Zodarks were relentless in their assault. Love weaved through the maelstrom, maneuvering past bursts of fire.

"Multiple hostiles, bearing two-seven-zero, range eight hundred meters," Green reported.

"Ford, Williams, weapons free on my mark," Love said. "Engage all hostiles in Sector Bravo. Fire for effect!"

The Osprey's side-mounted magrail guns blared. Explosions dotted the landscape where enemy positions had been moments before.

"Lieutenant, ammo's running low!" Ford said.

"Hold steady!" Love scanned between the instruments and the battlefield ahead. "Keep the pressure. Just a few more seconds until we clear."

The terrain ahead opened into a narrow valley. "There!" She pointed. "That's our spot."

"Looks tight," Green said.

"It'll have to do." She angled the Osprey downward, descent swift but controlled. "Wolfpack Actual to all elements, new LZ at grid Romeo Tango four-five-four-eight-seven-one. Prepare for immediate dust-off on my mark."

"Brace for landing!" Williams called out. The Osprey hurtled toward the earth, magrail cannons still blazing, as Love guided them into the battle.

The Osprey touched down with a jolt. Love kept the engines hot. "Deltas, move out!"

The ramp lowered, and soldiers poured into the fray, fanning out to secure the perimeter.

"Enemy forces closing in!" Green said. Red dots multiplied on the radar display.

"We're sitting ducks here." She keyed the intercom. "Williams, status on ammo?"

"Down to our last belts!"

"Make them count." She scanned the sky. "Any word from air support?"

"Negative," Green replied. "They're tied up elsewhere."

*Of course they are.* She clenched her teeth, frustration simmering.

An explosion rocked the left flank. Dirt and shrapnel rained down, pinging off the hull.

"Zodarks breaching the perimeter!" Ford's voice was strained.

"Wolfpack Actual to all elements," Love's voice sliced through the comm. "LZ is compromised. Execute immediate exfil. I say again, abort current DZ. All birds, lift off and stand by for new coordinates."

A chorus of "Roger, Actual" crackled through the comms.

"Zodarks breaching the perimeter!" Ford said. "They've got us zeroed!"

"Execute emergency extraction protocol," she commanded. "We are Oscar Mike in two mikes. Get our boots back on board!"

After Ford relayed the orders, the holodisplay showed the Deltas initiating a fighting withdrawal. They leapfrogged back to the Osprey, laying down suppressing fire.

"Green, prep for dust-off," Love said.

Green hesitated. "Ma'am, engines are redlining. We pushed them beyond operational parameters."

"No choice. Override safety protocols." She rerouted power. "We punch out hot or we don't punch out at all."

"Overriding now."

Love keyed the fleet-wide channel. "All Wolfpack elements, form up on me at rally point Echo. We're finding a new LZ, over."

Williams stumbled aboard, panting into his mic, his stressed tone coming through Love's helmet. "That's everyone!"

"Strap in!" Love shouted. She pulled back on the yoke, the Osprey lifting.

Blaster fire streaked past, too close. Alarms blared, the cockpit awash in flashing lights. The craft shuddered as they climbed. Love pushed it higher, eyes on the dark clouds.

"Two bogeys on our six!" Green's voice was grim.

"Deploy countermeasures!" She banked left, then right, zigzagging to throw off enemy aim. *Where the hell are these Vultures coming from?*

Flares burst behind them. Chaff scattered.

"Wolfpack elements, status report," Love ordered.

"Wolfpack Two, ammo critical, engines strained."

"Wolfpack Four here, similar situation. We're running on very little, Actual."

Green glanced at her. "Suggestions?"

She met his gaze, determination steeling her voice. "We push for rally point Echo. All elements, form up on me."

"That's deep in enemy territory," Green said.

"It's our best play." Love changed their heading. "If we can make it over the ridge, we can lose the Vultures in the canyon. Tight formation, people. We watch each other's six. Coop, where are you?"

Static came in response.

"Coop?"

There was no reply.

"Strike, this is Wolfpack Actual, we need cover ASAP."

Again, nothing came over the radio.

Love grimaced. "Wolfpack elements, can you establish comms with Strike or any Orion assets? Our long-range is dark."

After a moment of tense silence, the responses filtered in:

"Wolfpack Two, negative contact. Comms are scrambled beyond squad net."

"Four here. Can't punch through the interference."

Green's brow furrowed as he studied the communications panel. "Looks like we're being jammed. All frequencies outside our encrypted squad channel are saturated with noise."

"Damn it," Love muttered. She keyed her mic again. "All elements, be advised: we are EMCON Alpha. Maintain radio discipline and stick to squad freq only. Hostiles likely have ears on any other channels."

A series of clipped acknowledgments followed as the battered Osprey squadron pressed on, isolated from wider support and deep in enemy territory. The remaining Ospreys fell into formation behind Love's bird.

"Wolfpack Two, taking fire on our nine!"

"Four, providing cover. Ammo's almost gone!"

Behind them, the pursuing fighters gained ground. The Ospreys' engines sputtered in unison, each kilometer hard-fought. Love focused on the looming ridge ahead, willing her battered squadron to hold together just a little longer.

"Come on," Love whispered. "Just a bit farther."

The ridge stood ahead. She pushed the throttle to maximum, every muscle tense.

A warning light flashed. "Engine one is failing," Green said.

"Shut it down before it blows. We'll operate on one."

He complied. The Osprey lurched but held course.

They crested the ridge, the canyon yawning before them. Love dipped low, hugging the walls. The narrow passage forced the enemy to break formation.

Green exhaled. "Terrain's working in our favor."

"For now." She steered the twists and turns, the rocks a blur at their speed, the rest of the Ospreys in her squadron on her tail.

An impact rocked the rear of the aircraft. Sparks flew, systems blinking.

"Rear stabilizer blew!" Green's voice rose.

"I've got it." She compensated manually.

Ford spoke up, "Lieutenant, the men are secure, but we've taken damage. Something hit us, a stray Zodark fire, I don't know."

"Acknowledged."

The canyon opened into a wide expanse.

"Rally Point Echo in sight," Green confirmed.

"Prepare for emergency landing," Love said. "We're not going to stay airborne much longer."

Green spoke between gritted teeth. "Landing gear is compromised."

"Then we'll make do without." She scanned for a suitable spot. A stretch of flat terrain bordered by thick forest caught her eye.

"LZ in sight!" Love angled the descent, the other Ospreys following her lead.

# Chapter 12:
## Ford's Watch

**Year 2097**
**FOB Oteren**
**DZ Cragstone**
**Planet Intus**

As the Osprey rattled in the turbulent air, Brian Ford gripped the edge of his jump seat. The troop transport's interior buzzed with the straining engine vibrations and the chatter of soldiers preparing for combat. He scanned the troop bay, taking in the layout.

Two rows of jump seats lined the sides of the cabin, facing inward. Between them, a narrow aisle ran the length of the bay, cluttered with gear and the seated troops' armored legs. Overhead, exposed pipes, wiring, and support struts crisscrossed the ceiling. Red and white LED strips cast light everywhere.

The Deltas, clad in battlesuits, cradled their rifles. Most carried the M91 heavy blaster rifle, with a few specialists sporting heavier weapons. Visors obscured faces, shoulders set.

At the rear of the bay, a hydraulic ramp stood ready for rapid deployment. Tie-down points dotted the deck, securing various equipment cases and additional ammunition crates.

Across the bay, Corporal Tyrell Williams sat on his own jump seat beside the opposite magrail gun, hands resting lightly on the controls. Their gazes met for a brief moment. Ford gave a subtle nod. Williams returned it. No words needed; they'd been here before.

"LZ in sight!" crackled Lieutenant Love's voice over the comms.

Ford shifted in his seat. The five-point harness pressed into his shoulders and chest. They'd already aborted a few drops. For this one, with the damage done, they needed to let the soldiers loose here or abort the mission altogether and go home—something Ford knew none of the Deltas would agree upon.

Williams glanced over. "Ready for this, Chief?"

Ford smirked. "You know it."

Ford braced himself at his station, the magrail gun controls at the ready, feet planted on the textured metal deck. He ran a quick diagnostic on the weapon console—everything came back green on the small display panel.

"Looks like we've got a few visitors coming to the party." Williams peered through the narrow viewport.

"I see 'em," Ford said.

The Osprey jolted, dropping a few meters before stabilizing. Ford's stomach flipped, but he steadied himself, gripping the magrail handles. Outside, the landscape spread out—pointed rocks and swirling dust under a bruised sky. Flashes of enemy fire streaked upward, cutting through the haze.

Ford swung the magrail toward the left flank. His helmet's visor synced with the gun's targeting system, a digital overlay highlighting movement against the barren terrain. A Zodark warrior appeared in his sights. Ford's breath slowed. He lined up the crosshairs, exhaled, and squeezed the trigger.

The magrail spat a tungsten slug with ridiculous speed. The recoil hummed through his arms. In the distance, the Zodark staggered and fell. A plume of dust highlighted its fall. A grin wrinkled Ford's face.

"One down," he said.

On the other side of the Osprey, Williams engaged another target. "Got eyes on a sniper nest." A burst from his magrail, and debris exploded where the enemy had been.

"Nice shooting," Ford said.

The Osprey descended rapidly now. Evasive maneuvers tilted the deck. Ford's boots stayed planted, his body moving in sync with the bird. He continued firing in controlled bursts.

"Time to earn our keep," he called to Williams.

Their Osprey hit the ground hard. Metal screeched, and Ford's teeth rattled in his skull as they skidded to a halt. Through the open rear hatch, he caught glimpses of Wolfpack Two and Four touching down, their Deltas spilling out and securing the area.

"All stations, report!" Lieutenant Love's voice came through his helmet.

Ford ran a systems check on his station. "Rear guns operational, ma'am." The magrails had held up, though the ammo was low.

"Engines critical, but bird's still operational. Barely holding," Green replied from the cockpit.

Ford's jump seat creaked as he leaned forward, scanning the troop bay. Their Deltas were on their feet, gear rattling as they prepared to deploy.

"Let's move," Ford signaled.

He and Williams rushed to the rifle rack near the rear hatch. Ford grabbed his weapon, checking the chamber and magazine. Williams reached for his rifle but fumbled as the sling caught on the bracket.

"Seriously?" Ford said, irritation flaring. He slung his own rifle over his shoulder. "We're on the clock."

Williams cursed under his breath, scrambling to free the strap. "Got it, got it."

Outside, combat intensified. Muffled explosions and the staccato of gunfire seeped into the cabin. The ramp lowered, hydraulics hissing. Swirling dirt filled the bay.

Ford gave Williams a final glance before heading toward the ramp. "Stay sharp."

Stepping onto the metal ramp, Ford took the lead. Every nerve in his body was alert, senses sharpened by adrenaline. He raised his M87 assault rifle, his heart pounding. Lives depended on him, on his accuracy, on his ability to maintain his composure. He moved forward, boots clanking softly against the ramp.

He scanned the horizon through his rifle's sights. The HUD overlaid vital information: wind speed, elevation, potential threats. A faint rustle reached his ears, barely audible over the distant rumble of artillery.

"Left side, ten meters," Ford said, voice a whisper.

Williams adjusted his aim without a word, covering the designated sector.

Ford narrowed his eyes. The rustling grew louder—a subtle movement among the stunted shrubs. He held up a clenched fist, signaling a halt.

From the underbrush, a Zodark soldier emerged. The alien moved like a predator, unaware he was in Ford's sight.

Ford exhaled slowly, steadying his aim. He squeezed the trigger. Three bursts of gunfire shattered the stillness. The Zodark collapsed in a heap.

"Target down," Ford confirmed.

"Scanning for more," Williams replied.

They waited, but no additional movement caught their attention.

"Area clear—for now." Ford tapped his comm unit. "All units, proceed."

"Move out!" voices echoed.

Inside the Osprey, the Delta soldiers sprang into action. Boots thundered against the ramp as they disembarked. Ford stood aside, rifle ready, eyes never leaving the horizon.

"Move out! Double time!" the squad leader yelled through the helmet comms. "Go! Go!"

The Deltas rushed forward. They quickly disappeared into the thick undergrowth of the jungle edging the valley. The sounds of boots crushing leaves and branches cracking faded as the soldiers melted into the trees.

"Able Actual to gunner one, advancing on bearing zero-three-zero," a voice crackled in Ford's earpiece.

"Gunner one copies, Able Actual," Ford responded. "Maintain COMSEC."

"Wilco, out."

The comms erupted with controlled chatter.

"Able Seven to Able Actual, ridge is clear. No OPFOR in sight, over."

"Able Actual copies. Proceed to phase line Bravo, out."

"Charlie Two to Able Actual, requesting permission to advance, over."

"Negative, Charlie Two. Hold your position. Stand by for further info, out."

Ford took in the stream of information, mentally mapping each unit's position.

Williams crouched. "All teams are on the move."

Ford nodded. "Stay alert. This area's too quiet."

He turned just in time to see more Deltas exiting the Osprey, one of them stumbling on the ramp, nearly tripping. The soldier caught himself, but a piece of equipment—a flash-bang grenade—tumbled from his battlesuit, clattering onto the metal surface.

"What the hell?" Ford snapped.

The soldier scrambled to retrieve the grenade. "It slipped."

Ford glared at the ramp. A discarded ammo clip lay near the edge, barely visible. It must have been dropped by one of the first soldiers out.

"Watch your footing," Ford said. "And secure your gear!"

The soldier secured the grenade. "On it."

Ford hadn't noticed the ammo clip until now. A small detail, easily overlooked—but not excusable. If the soldier had fallen under fire, the consequences could have been dire.

Williams gave him a sidelong glance. "Take it easy. It was a slip up."

"Slip ups get people killed." *These are Deltas. They don't mess up like this. There's no excuse.*

He surveyed the area a second time, frustration gnawing at him. Ford prided himself on catching every detail, anticipating every variable. Missing something, even something so trivial, was unacceptable.

"Chief, all units are proceeding as planned," Williams said.

Ford pressed his comm. "Alpha Team, status report."

"Alpha One here. Advancing to Objective One. No contact yet."

Williams stepped closer. "You're wound tight. Maybe ease up a bit."

Ford shot him a hard look. "Affirmative."

A distant explosion lit up the sky. A plume of smoke rose against the dark clouds.

Ford's brain swirled with thoughts. The stumble on the ramp replayed in his mind—a minor incident, yet it might be emblematic of larger concerns.

The wind picked up. Static crackled in his earpiece. "Interference on the comms."

"Could be the storm," Williams said.

"Or continued enemy jamming." Ford's attention snagged on a flash of movement in the distance. "Hold on." He raised his rifle, peering through the scope. The thermal imaging picked up a vague heat signature behind a rock formation.

"Possible contact at three o'clock," Ford said.

Williams followed his line of sight. "I see it."

They watched for a moment. The heat signature disappeared.

"Could be an animal," Williams said.

"Or a scout." Ford toggled the comm. "Alpha Team, be advised. Potential enemy scout spotted east of your position."

"Able Actual copies," the team leader responded. "We'll keep eyes on it."

Ford lowered his rifle, unease settling in his gut. The variables were stacking up—interference, unseen threats, minor mishaps.

"The comms are getting worse," Williams said. "If we lose contact—"

"We won't."

A burst of static cut through his earpiece, followed by garbled voices.

"—repeat, under heavy fire—"

"Say again?" Ford pressed a hand to his helmet. "Alpha Team, report!"

No clear response came. The static intensified, then ceased.

Williams wrapped his knuckles on his helmet. "I'm not getting anything."

Ford's frustration spiked. "We need to reestablish communication." He moved swiftly back into the Osprey's cabin, accessing the external console. He pressed several buttons on the controls, attempting to boost the signal.

"Come on," he muttered.

Error codes flashed across the screen. Signal jamming was confirmed.

"Enemy's disrupting our comms," Williams said.

"Working on a workaround." After a moment, Ford straightened his lips in concentration. "Got it." The console indicated a secured channel. "Stand by for traffic. Initiating ECCM." Ford continued to work on the interface. "Tango Sierra. Crypto established. Alpha One, this is Ford. SITREP, over."

The radio came to life. "Ford, Alpha One. Taking heavy contact, but advancing. OPFOR in retreat. AO nearly secured. Clear to RTB for fuel and maintenance, over."

"Alpha One, copy. Maintain scheduled comms for duration of op. QRF on standby at FOB Oteren for contingencies. Confirm final exfil timeline, over."

"Ford, Alpha One. Wilco on comms. Estimate seventy-two hours until exfil required. Will advise if timeline changes, over."

"Alpha One, solid copy. We'll be wheels up on your word. Ford out."

Lieutenant Love's voice burst through. "Ford, Williams, secure for takeoff. Departing in three-zero seconds."

"Roger," Ford replied, locking his harness.

The Osprey's remaining engine reached full pitch. With a lurch, the craft lifted, the other Ospreys following.

As they climbed, the battlefield was laid out below. The Deltas pushed forward through the dense jungle, wisps of smoke marking enemy positions they'd overrun. The mountain valley's steep walls gradually shrank from view as the Osprey banked hard, setting a course for Oteren.

Ford's thoughts lingered on the men they'd just dropped off. The Osprey would return soon enough for extraction, and he silently hoped that when that time came, all of these Deltas would be accounted for and alive.

## Chapter 13:
## Friendly Fire

**Year 2097**
**Mission Cragstone Vanguard**
**RNS *Gallipoli***

The dim glow of the screens colored Coop's face as he manipulated his Orion pod's controls. Around him, other pilots were synced with their drones. His Orion fighter soared through Intus's skies, fresh from helping Lieutenant Naomi Love's Osprey during a troop drop.

The holographic display erupted with a swarm of red markers—enemy positions scattered across the terrain below. Coop scanned for patterns on the ground. He tapped into Raven's channel.

"Multiple hostiles at grid nine-charlie. Think you can keep up?"

He heard a chuckle. "Try me."

Coop plotted a course, punching commands over the interface. "Let's split the formation. You take the high road, I'll skim the treetops."

"Copy that. On your lead."

They flew apart. Their drones sliced through the thick plumes of smoke rising from the battlefield. Flak peppered the air, black blossoms rocking the drones but failing to deter their path.

On Coop's HUD, a cluster of enemy anti-aircraft units blinked. Coop tagged them, the targets highlighting across his display.

"Raven, priority on those AA units. Marked them for you."

"Targets acquired. Engaging now."

Raven's Orion peeled farther off, unleashing a barrage silencing the ground fire. He weaved between bursts of shrapnel, heading toward a looming threat ahead—a massive cannon turret nestled among craggy outcrops.

"There she is," Coop said.

"Visual on the turret," Raven replied.

"Let's make it go away."

"On your wing."

They executed a coordinated ingress, dropping altitude to exploit the smoke cover. Coop's HUD flashed as the forward-looking infrared system engaged. The enemy turret's infrared signature lit up as it tracked, its capacitors charging for imminent discharge. Coop's targeting reticle pulsed red as the fire control system achieved a solid lock. He trimmed his attitude, adjusting for maximum probability of kill.

"Fox Two," he muttered, thumb hovering over the weapon release button on the control stick.

His Orion released two Joint Advanced Tactical Missiles. The missiles streaked toward the turret. His tactical monitor tracked their progress before the turret erupted in an explosion, a fiery bloom sending debris outward. Coop grinned.

"Scratch one turret."

"Bull's-eye," Raven said.

Coop's holographic display flashed with new intel—a fortified weapons platform came into focus, full of defenses. He zoomed in on the screen, the close-up image showing a lot of armor and a lot of armament.

"Got another target," Coop said.

"You thinking what I'm thinking?" Raven asked.

"Unfortunately."

The platform was a big threat, but his drone was running low on munitions. Fatigue tugged at the edges of his mind. It reminded him he'd been going at this pace for a little too long. Sleep would be good when he had a few hours off.

Ground comms crackled to life in his ear. "We're pinned down! Direct fire on the west side!"

Another voice cut in. "Need air support now! Enemy reinforcements moving in!"

Gunfire and explosions resounded through the transmissions.

"Mortar team here! Request suppression on enemy artillery at sector four!"

"Bravo team taking heavy casualties! We can't hold!"

The desperation in their voices was almost too much, and Coop had heard it all before. "Strike, Coop. Tally hostile triple-A site at grid MB four-four-eight five-one-four. Engaging to neutralize immediate threat to ground elements."

"Coop, Strike. Roger that. Be advised, friendlies at four-five-one five-one-two. Maintain situational awareness. Good hunting."

"Raven, we need to take out that platform," Coop said. "Our guys are getting hammered."

"Understood. You lead, I'll cover."

Coop steadied himself. "Switching to magrail guns."

"Roger that."

They dove toward the platform. Enemy fire intensified. Blaster rounds cut past them. Alarms blared as an energy beam grazed the drone's fuselage.

"Armor integrity at eighty-eight percent," the system alerted.

Coop ignored it. His focus homed in on the platform. He squeezed the trigger, magrail guns unleashing a load of tungsten rounds. Sparks flew as the projectiles slammed into the armor.

"Partial damage," Raven said.

Coop adjusted his approach, skimming a bit too close to the terrain. "Need a better angle." The platform grew larger, its guns training on his drone.

"Coop, watch out!"

A laser beam seared past. The drone shook as systems overloaded.

"Controls are sluggish," Coop said.

"Pull back! You're too exposed!"

"Not yet."

He lined up for another attack. Ground voices pressed in.

"Hostiles breaching our perimeter!"

"Air support, where are you?"

Coop's heart pounded. He armed his last countermeasure—the SM-97 Starbursts.

"Deploying Starbursts," he declared.

"Those are for countermeasures," Raven said.

"They'll blind their sensors. Might give us an opening."

"Your call."

He launched the missiles. The sky lit up as the Starbursts detonated, a firework of flares. He hoped this would overwhelm enemy targeting sensors.

Coop banked left, then straightened. "Sierra Hotel. Weapons free."

With the enemy's aim disrupted, Coop let loose another volley from the magrail guns. This time, rounds found their mark, penetrating exposed sections of the platform.

"Critical hit!" Raven said.

The platform convulsed in a string of explosions, secondary eruptions blasting through its structure.

"Ground teams, the platform is down," Coop transmitted.

"Copy that! We see it—great work!"

Coop's drone pod's interface blinked with new information. Enemy icons lit up on the display. New red markers appeared. Ground chatter filled his ears again, voices overlapping.

"Enemy armor advancing at sector seven!"

"Need immediate support at grid five-delta!"

Coop's vision blurred for a moment. He shook his head, trying to focus.

*Why am I so out of it?*

"Coop, you getting this?" Raven's voice blurted through the noise.

"Yeah, I've got it." Coop keyed in coordinates. The battlefield spread out below. Nothing but smoke and flashes. He squinted at the numbers.

"Targets at grid eight-bravo," a ground troop shouted. "They're hammering us hard!"

Coop glanced at the map. "Copy that. Adjusting course."

"Wait," Raven interjected. "Eight-bravo? I thought they said five-delta."

Coop frowned. "They're all over the place. Let's hit them at eight-bravo first."

"Affirmative," Raven said. Hesitation colored his tone.

Alerts stacked up on Coop's display. His head throbbed, and he stifled a yawn. He punched in the sequence to arm his missiles, eyes on the highlighted zone.

"Coop, we need to prioritize," Raven said. "What's the plan?"

"I'm on it," Coop replied. "Cover me from ground fire. I'll take out their artillery."

"Roger that. Moving into position."

Raven's drone veered off, its guns spitting fire at enemy emplacements. Coop descended, lining up his shot. Another weapon platform loomed.

"Firing now," Coop muttered. Doubt hit him—was this the right target? The right grid? *Did they give me the right coordinates?*

He hesitated, seconds slipping away. Then, pushing aside the uncertainty, he launched the missile.

A warning flashed on his screen. Heat signatures— moving into the strike zone. His heart lurched as figures materialized on the HUD.

"Ground team, hold position!" he yelled into the comm. "You're moving into a hot zone!"

Static answered him, then fragmented voices.

"Say again, air support?"

"Get out of there!" Coop shouted. "Missile inbound on your location!"

"Negative, we're advancing on enemy lines!"

Panic surged. "Abort! Fall back now!"

He watched as the missile closed in. Time seemed to slow, the seconds stretching into a hellish eternity.

The explosion erupted, a blinding flash consuming the figures on his screen. Debris and smoke billowed upward, blotting out the scene below.

Silence filled his headset. Coop's breath caught in his throat. His hands gripped the controls.

"Ground team, report status," Raven called out.

"Two KIA, multiple wounded!" came the reply. "Possible friendly fire from air support, but systems are malfunctioning. We can't confirm!"

Coop's world tilted. The words hammered into him—possible friendly fire. His missile. But was it really his mistake?

"God," he whispered. "What's happening?"

The voices over the comm mixed together.

"Command, we need immediate evac!"

"Stay low and hold your positions!"

Coop barely heard them. Confusion and guilt crashed over him. A tidal wave of conflicting emotions threatened to drown him where he sat. His gaze fixed on the smoking crater—the spot where allied soldiers had stood moments before.

"Coop." Raven's voice was softer now. "Talk to me. What happened?"

He couldn't find the words. His throat tightened, mind racing back over the sequence of events. The conflicting coordinates, the hesitation, the launch. Something wasn't adding up.

"Coop, we need to keep moving," Raven pressed. "Others are depending on us."

He swallowed hard. "I… I screwed up."

"We'll sort it out later. Right now, we have to stay in the fight."

Coop's hands trembled on the controls. Every instinct screamed at him to disengage, to retreat from the horror he'd caused.

"Air support, this is Ground Team Alpha," a new voice came in. "We need cover at grid six-charlie. Can you assist?"

Coop stared at the new marker blinking on his screen. His voice failed him.

"Coop," Raven said. "They need us."

"I can't," he murmured. "I can't…"

"Listen to me," Raven replied. "Right now, those guys are out there, and we're their only support."

Gunfire and explosions transmitted through the open comms.

"Taking heavy fire at six-charlie!"

"Enemy infantry closing in!"

Coop squeezed his eyes shut, his mistake pressing down hard. Finally, he opened his eyes. "Copy that, Ground Team Alpha. Moving to provide support."

"Appreciate it, air support."

He adjusted his course, fingers steadier now. Still, the shadow of his possible screw-up stayed with him like a lump of spoiled food in his stomach.

"Raven, form up on me," he said.

"Right behind you."

They flew in tandem. The battlefield unfolded before him. Flames dotted the landscape, smoke trails winding upward.

"Targets ahead," Raven said.

"Engaging with caution," Coop replied.

They opened fire. The bursts drove back the enemy forces. The ground team advanced, their movement more confident with the support overhead.

"Good effect on target," Ground Team Alpha reported. "Thanks for the assist."

"Anytime," Coop said.

While they circled back, his gaze drifted to the site of the earlier strike. The smoke had thinned, revealing scorched earth and twisted metal.

"Coop, focus," Raven reminded him.

"I'm trying."

"One moment at a time. We'll get through this."

He nodded, though Raven couldn't see it. The comms crackled.

"Enemy armor detected north of your position," a voice warned.

"Understood," Coop said. "Moving to intercept."

They pressed on. The battle was far from over. Each movement was heavier than the last, each decision heavy with the mistake hanging over him.

"Coop," Raven said, "you're a damn good pilot. The finest. Keep going. We have more people to save."

He didn't reply. Words felt hollow. He'd killed his own men. People sacrificing to save not only others of his species but all subjugated species out there.

As they engaged the next target, it all seemed like a dream. Weapons fire lashed out from his drone. Perfect hit.

"Vehicle neutralized," he confirmed.

"Roger that," Raven said.

The comms remained active. Republic ground forces were gaining ground, the tide slowly turning.

For Coop, the battle had shifted inward. Doubt gnawed at him, questions without answers swirling in his mind. He steadied the drone for a moment, unfocused. How could he ever focus after this?

"Coop, you still with me?" Raven asked.

"Yeah," he lied.

The HUD streamed with new data, but it all seemed distant.

"Air support, regroup at Waypoint Bravo," Strike ordered.

"Roger," Raven said.

Coop set the coordinates, his movements automatic.

"Take a breather when we get done," Raven said. "You've been at it for over twenty hours."

"Maybe."

Two soldiers gone. Because of him.

He stared ahead, the horizon on the screen nothing but a blur.

## Chapter 14:
## Test Site

**Year 2097**
**RNS *Poseidon***
**Sector 2**

Lee wanted out of this part of the sector, away from this asteroid, and as soon as humanly possible. When the energy spiked inside the meteor, it quickly died. And it all happened after their surface probes were blown out of existence.

He'd been in space long enough to trust his instincts—most times. Right now, every nerve ending told him to get *Poseidon* away from this chunk of rock. Whatever trick was buried in that asteroid made his skin crawl. They came, they gathered intel for the Republic and Primords at the particular anomaly to study, and now it was time to exit the scene.

He punched the comm. "Engineering. MacGregor, we need those coolant systems operational. Let's go. We're on the clock."

"Cap, I pushed these coolant systems way past redline getting us through that last fight," Mac's voice crackled over the comm. "Something was up with them, and I finally figured out what. We're fixin' them now. Yet the primary loops are still running hot. Secondary backup's barely keeping up. You move this ship now, we'll fry every cooling rod from deck three to Engineering."

"We don't have time for—"

"With respect, sir," Mac said, "I bypassed three safety protocols just to get us here. These readings are critical. Push these systems again before they rebalance, we'll be floating dead in space while our core melts down. And I don't mean that figuratively."

Lee looked at the asteroid looming on the main viewer. "Mac…"

"Captain, you want this ship to hold together or not? Two more minutes. Gettin' it handled."

Lee exhaled, fighting the urge to override his engineer's caution. "Two minutes, Mac. Not a second more."

"Aye, sir. Engineering out."

Lee leaned back, his gaze locked on that ancient rock while an unseen clock ticked away in his mind.

Conklin faced Lee from her station on the bridge. "Captain, you need to see this immediately."

Lee crossed the distance to her station. Arrays of data and images flooded several interfaces at her science station—analyses of the meteor's composition, scans from both their team and the other ships in the squadron.

"Something doesn't add up," Conklin said.

"Go on."

She tapped a sequence, highlighting mineral deposits and isotopic ratios from some core samples one of the probes took before a cannon disintegrated it. Just before it went out of commission, it sent information back to the *Poseidon*. "The materials are ancient, but the arrangement—the construction—it's too… perfect. Natural formations don't exhibit this kind of uniformity."

"What are you suggesting?"

"It's a facade."

A knot formed in Lee's stomach. "Explain."

"We've identified traces of engineered alloys beneath the surface, masked by layers of asteroid debris. The configuration kinda… well… yeah, it doesn't kinda, it suggests a massive energy core at the meteor's heart, which we know, but it's not just a weapon's array, a weapon's platform."

"You mean, it's an engine, and a colony as well? I think I've gathered that already, Conklin."

"Negative, sir. I don't think it's either one of those. I think it's a warhead." Conklin's voice dropped. "Captain, I believe this entire meteor is a disguised bomb."

Alarm surged through him. "How certain are you?"

"Highly. The energy readings are consistent with a dormant weapon. And it was starting to activate before it shut off, but now it's starting again, but this time, more active."

Since they'd arrived, they'd moved closer to the meteor, so at the moment, Lee wasted no time. "All stations on the bridge, this is the captain. Initiate emergency protocols. Prepare for immediate evacuation from current position." Lee commed Mac. "We have to leave immediately. Where are we with this?"

"A minute," MacGregor replied.

"It's been more than two minutes since we last talked."

"My apologies, sir. And… wait a moment. Yes, being told it's done. Good to go, Cap."

Lee clicked the comm off. Around him, officers moved fast.

"Reynolds," Lee said, "plot an exit trajectory away from the meteor. Vector two-three-seven mark six. Maximum thrust."

Reynolds tapped on the navigation console. "Vector two-three-seven mark six set. Engines primed."

"Engage full reverse thrust. Divert all available power to engines." Along with what Captain Eamon Roberts of the RNS *Aussie* had briefed him about—the weaponized asteroid platforms created by the Zodarks and situated throughout the Rass system—this new celestial body might be another type of platform, another weapon created by the enemy—a massive bomb. Whatever the reason for its presence in this sector, they could investigate that later. Perhaps it was a lure, a trap, which Lee was beginning to suspect, especially with no sign of inhabitants on that big rock. The Zodarks were constantly developing new methods to eliminate Earth forces and their allies, and Lee knew they'd stop at nothing to achieve that goal.

"Aye, sir. Engaging now." The *Poseidon* lurched as the engines surged, propelling the ship backwards.

"Rodriguez, when are those reinforcements from Bulwark due to arrive?" Lee asked.

Rodriguez typed on her console, and read the data scrolling on her monitor. "Sir, they're due here in nine minutes." Lee strode to his captain's chair and tapped his comm panel. "All hands, general quarters, general quarters.

All hands, man your battle stations. This is not a drill. Repeat, this is not a drill."

He waited, letting the alert klaxons sound before opening the channel fleet-wide. "Attention all ships. Immediate retreat. All ships to follow our vector at maximum speed. We have detected a critical anomaly. The meteor is possibly a high-yield explosive device. I say again, execute immediate withdrawal. Maintain comm silence unless absolutely necessary. Initiate evasive pattern Omega Six. Acknowledge with encrypted burst transmission."

"Message acknowledged by all ships, Captain," Rodriguez told Lee.

"Engineering," Lee said.

"Mac here."

"Redirect all nonessential power to propulsion. We need every bit of thrust."

"I already got the message. We shut down secondary systems."

"Sir," Conklin blurted out while monitoring her interface, "the energy core is becoming more active."

"How long until safe distance?" Lee asked.

Reynolds glanced at his readings. "At current acceleration, six minutes."

"Not good enough. Push the engines beyond the safety threshold if you have to."

Reynolds nodded and overrode the engine safeties. The ship groaned as the thrust intensified.

"Captain, incoming transmission from *Horizon*," Rodriguez said.

"Put it through."

A holographic image of Captain Lupin materialized. "Captain Lee, our long-range scanners are detecting anomalous readings beyond the meteor's vicinity."

"Can you pinpoint the source?" Lee asked.

"Negative. The signals are erratic, possibly masked. Be on high alert for potential ambush."

"Understood. We'll deploy scout drones on our retreat vector."

"Advisable. We are also detecting unusual radiation spikes consistent with weapons charging. Origin unknown, but they are definitely artificial."

"Noted. We'll keep our sensors at maximum and weapons hot. Any other tactical concerns?"

"Yes. The meteor's energy signature is interfering with our sensors. There might be more radiation spikes than we can currently detect."

"Agreed. We'll stay at battle stations throughout our withdrawal. Stay in close contact."

"Affirmative. Out."

"Captain, new readings indicate an exponential rise in energy emissions." Conklin's eyes widened at her console.

Lee's mind flashed again to Captain Roberts's briefing about the Zodark asteroid platforms. *This meteor-like object…* He cut his own thoughts off. "This weapon's platform was more than just that. A facade. This entire structure is going to blow. Time to critical?"

"Impossible to determine, but it's accelerating fast."

Lee cursed himself for not seeing it sooner. The Zodarks had somehow, and recently, perfected turning asteroids into weapons. This wasn't just a simple trap—it was a full military installation disguised as an abandoned outpost, or heck, a fake long-lost colony or military installation, on top of a damn meteor half the size of Earth's moon.

"Prepare for potential shock wave impact. Mac, status of the engines?" Lee asked.

"Holding, but they're nearing the redline. Crank it up more and we'll be scattering engine parts across ten star systems."

"Keep them there," Lee said. "Don't exceed."

"Captain…" Conklin twisted in her chair to face him. "This whole setup. I think… well… that it's more than a trap. It's a test site. They're probably gathering data on how we respond, how our ships perform under stress. The energy readings, they're being transmitted somewhere else. Perhaps off-site. Long range, maybe from another sector altogether. Every move we make—they're studying us."

Lee's blood ran cold. "So we're not the target. We're the guinea pigs."

"Exactly. Think about it. They're willing to sacrifice an entire weaponized meteor just to analyze our tactical responses, our ship capabilities, our emergency protocols. The real weapon is probably something much bigger or in more abundance, and this is just their dress rehearsal. They want to know exactly how we'll react when they deploy the actual thing, or things."

"You're sure?" Lee asked.

"I mean, it's just a theory, but why go through all this trouble and create something so elaborate just to blow up a small squadron like ours? There's got to be a bigger reason, a bigger picture."

"And now they know precisely how long it takes us to detect the threat, how our sensors handle the energy spikes, our evacuation speeds…" Lee curled his fingers into fists. "We just gave them a complete combat analysis of our fleet's capabilities."

*Perfect. We're not just in danger—we're helping them refine their weapons.*

"All ships report they are following our lead," Rodriguez relayed.

"Maintain formation. No one gets left behind. And transmit everything we've learned about this installation to FOB Bulwark. They'll send to Space Command. They need to know the Zodarks are expanding their asteroid weapon program beyond their defensive networks."

Sato leaned closer to Lee. "Distance now at thirty-eight thousand kilometers and increasing. Just a little more and it should do. We may be out of radiation potential or EMP reach, I believe, but I'm not entirely sure. It's the debris and fragments I worry about from a meteor that size exploding."

A sudden flare from the viewscreen caught everyone's attention. The meteor brightened, veins of light crisscrossing its surface like a net.

Conklin analyzed the data. "The outer shell is disintegrating. It's shedding mass to reduce inertia before detonation."

"Options?"

"We have to keep moving," Conklin said.

"Mac, give me everything you've got," Lee ordered.

"Rerouting life support reserves to engines," Mac said.

"MacGregor, any way to boost our speed further?"

The chief engineer hesitated. "There's the emergency surge capacitors, but they're meant for short bursts. Prolonged use could overload the drive. Another push and we'll be writing our names in the stars with our own disintegrating hull."

"Engage them." *We have no idea how large of an eruption this will be.*

"Aye, sir."

The *Poseidon* lurched again, the stars on the viewscreen stretching as their velocity sped up.

"Distance?"

"Fifty-one thousand kilometers," Reynolds said.

Lee turned to Conklin. "Will that be enough?"

Conklin checked her calculations. "Negative. The more distance we put between us and that thing, the better our chances."

*No truer words were ever spoken.*

"Captain, sensor readings from the meteor are off the scale," Rhom said. "Can we pick up our pace?"

"Negative." Lee activated the ship-wide channel. "All hands, brace for possible impact." He switched off the link and eyed Reynolds. "Maintain course. Do not deviate."

"Yes, Captain."

Lee's thoughts ran like a racehorse. They had waltzed right into a trap. No time for regret. Survival was all that mattered now.

"Hold steady," he said. "Distance?"

"Seventy-three thousand kilometers and climbing," Reynolds replied.

A flash erupted from the meteor, eclipsing the surrounding stars. The bridge flooded with a white light. Lee shielded his eyes, the automatic dimmers on all screens going into action.

"Brace for impact!" Lee shouted.

The ship lurched as a shock wave slammed into them. Consoles blinked, and the overhead lights dimmed. Sparks flew from a panel to Lee's left.

"Damage report!" Lee demanded.

Sato viewed her chair's holo. "Multiple systems failing, Captain. The port-side magrail cannon is overheating and at risk of fusion collapse. Our aft sensor array is off-line, leaving us blind to anything behind us. Armor integrity holding. Emergency solar fields are holding, but they're draining power fast."

Sato's expression tightened as she read off more data. "Captain, *Horizon* has a critical situation in Engineering. They are reporting that the containment field in reactor two is fluctuating. If it fails, they'll have to eject the core and lose the reactor. Their engineering reports indicate they're attempting to stabilize, but they're preparing for emergency ejection."

She looked up from the holo, her face pale. "And, sir, the *Polaris*… they're reporting a cascade failure in their main reactor core. They're minutes away from a potential core breach."

"Rodriguez, get me Captain Bayes," Lee said.

The comms officer shook her head. "No response from the *Polaris*, sir."

Before Lee could respond, alarms blared anew.

"Incoming objects!" Rhom shouted from tactical. "Debris from the explosion—no, wait. They're reading as hostile signatures."

"On screen."

The viewscreen shifted to reveal dark shapes emerging from the cloud of debris—the unmistakable silhouettes of Zodark Vultures.

"Damn it!" Lee said. "Where did they come from?"

Sato glared at her holoscreen. "I don't know, but they used the explosion to mask their approach. There's nearly sixty of them, fifty-eight to be exact."

"Tactical, target those Vultures. EWO, engage all point-defense systems. Launch countermeasure package Alpha, SW missiles."

"Aye-aye, Captain!" Rhom responded. "Activating PDGs."

"Point-defense grid online," Witkowski replied. "Launching countermeasures."

The *Poseidon*'s missile bays lit up, releasing a swarm of decoys and chaff. The space around the ship shimmered as the countermeasures diffused incoming enemy fire. All the while, bus-sized fragments from the asteroid zipped past the fleet—luckily, none hitting a ship.

Lee punched the all-fleet channel. "To all vessels: This is a free-fire zone. Weapons free, defensive measures authorized. Protect yourselves and your fellow ships."

"Multiple bogies, bearing zero-two-four!"

"Reynolds, execute evasive pattern Charlie Two," Lee said. "Get us out of their firing solution."

"Executing Charlie Two, sir," Reynolds acknowledged.

The ship shuddered as impacts rattled its hull.

"Engineering to Bridge!" MacGregor's voice crackled over the comm. "Got a mess down here, Captain! Coolant leak, and the starboard power coupling's gone haywire. My people are on it, but I need those medics standing by!"

"Comms, alert medical. All emergency response teams, deploy," Lee said.

"Aye, sir. Dispatching now," Rodriguez replied.

"Tactical, concentrate all forward batteries on the lead Vultures. Fire at will!"

"Weapons hot, engaging targets," Rhom responded.

The *Poseidon*'s magrail cannons thundered, blasting out at the enemy formation. Several Vultures disintegrated under the onslaught.

"Direct hits confirmed, Captain," Rhom reported. "But we've got more inbound."

"Steady as she goes."

"*Polaris* is responding!" Rodriguez said. "They're firing on the Vultures flanking us."

On the viewscreen, missiles expelled from the wounded *Polaris*, striking several Vultures, all of which disintegrated into clouds of debris.

Just then, bright streaks of energy lanced through space, cutting across the starfield from a direction Lee hadn't anticipated. Dozens of Zodark Vultures erupted.

*What the…* Lee thought.

"Sir," Rodriguez said, her voice rising slightly, which was uncanny for the usually calm communication officer. "Detecting Republic IFF signals. The *Hydra* and *Argo* are closing fast—they've brought friends."

On the main viewport, two Republic heavy cruisers appeared, and bore down on the Vulture formation, weapons ablaze. Flanking them were two Primord battleships. They did more than beat up the Zodark forces—they tore through them.

"The reinforcements from Bulwark," Lee said, looking at his watch. "And, right on time."

The holo showed the ships advancing at combat speed. Their firepower created a wall of hell, chewing through the Zodark formation. The Primord vessels cut wide arcs through the enemy ranks, their weapons batteries firing in coordinated salvos leaving nowhere for the Vultures to hide.

"Sir, the Vultures are breaking formation," Rhom reported. "They're attempting to regroup."

"Not if our friends have anything to say about it," Lee said.

As if on cue, the Republic cruisers launched a spread of missiles spiraling outward in hunting patterns, seeking the fleeing Zodark craft. The explosions lit up space, each one letting Lee know that the hostiles were being eliminated.

"The *Argo* is hailing us," Rodriguez said.

"Put them through."

Captain Liza Horn appeared on screen. "Captain Lee. Looks like we arrived just in time for the party."

"Your timing is impeccable, Captain Horn. I owe you one."

Horn grinned. "Consider it repayment for your endless hard work and dedication. The Primord battle group commander sends his regards as well."

On the tactical display, the remaining Vultures fell into full retreat. They scattered in all directions as the Republic and Primord ships continued their assault. What had been a swarm of nearly sixty enemy craft was now reduced to less than a handful of fleeing vessels.

"Sir, the Vultures are abandoning the engagement," Rhom confirmed.

Lee nodded, watching as the last of the Zodark ships flew off into the distance, pursued by a final volley from their allies claiming three more before they could escape.

"Damage report," Lee said.

"All critical systems functional. Engineering reports they've contained the coolant leak. The *Polaris* is stabilizing their core, and *Horizon* has managed to secure their nacelle," Sato reported.

Lee exhaled slowly, the tension of the last few minutes releasing. They'd survived the explosion and the ambush—barely—but there would be questions to answer. What exactly was that meteor-weapon? Why had the Zodarks positioned it here? And most importantly, what were they planning to do with the data they'd collected?

"Wait," Sato said. "One of the Vultures is adrift. Minimal power readings."

"On screen."

The image showed a Zodark fighter, its hull scarred and engines sputtering. Around it, the expanse of stars stretched into infinity. Just beyond the Vulture, the Republic corvette RNS *Scimitar* caught the light of a distant sun. Unlike its allies, the *Scimitar* appeared pristine, its hull barely touched by the recent conflict.

"An opportunity," Lee mused. "Rhom, can we capture it?"

"Possible, sir. We can use a shuttle to tow it in. It's only a kilometer from us."

"Do it. I want that ship in our hangar for inspection."

"Aye, Captain."

Minutes later, a shuttle deployed, flying carefully to latch onto the disabled Vulture. Lee watched as they brought it closer.

"Sir, shuttle reports successful capture," Rodriguez said.

"Excellent."

Baldry faced Lee. "Captain, I'm detecting a life sign on that Vulture."

"A surviving Zodark?"

"Seems so."

Lee tapped the comm. "Hangar deck, this is Captain Lee. Be advised, you've got a live one coming in. Secure the area and have security teams there on standby."

"Acknowledged," the crew chief replied.

On the bridge's main screen, the shuttle guided the captured Vulture into the hangar bay. It touched down. Deck hands swarmed the area, with a small security detail of two Army regulars forming a protective perimeter around the Vulture.

Lee crossed his arms. "Get me more boots on the ground, ASAP. I want a full tactical team down there yesterday. And tell them to hold off on cracking that bird open until we've got proper backup."

"Aye, sir," Rodriguez responded, relaying the orders.

Suddenly, the Vulture's hatch exploded outward. A blur of blue skin and flashing metal erupted from the opening. The Zodark warrior, a towering beast with its muscles rippling, burst onto the deck.

Two of its arms wielded a sword while another clutched a blaster. With lightning speed, it lashed out at the nearest trooper, disabling him with a one-handed hammer blow. A second soldier raised his weapon, only to be sent flying by a powerful kick.

Chaos engulfed the hangar as klaxons sounded and personnel scattered.

"Where's our backup?" Lee demanded.

"Two minutes out, sir," Rodriguez said.

"We need to contain this *now*."

The bridge crew scrambled to respond as the Zodark continued its rampage, the next few minutes promising to be a dangerous game of cat and mouse in the bowels of the *Poseidon*, the alien's weapon blasting everything in sight.

"Bridge, this is Chief Hanzlik! The Zodark's loose in the hangar! It's taking down our men—stuns aren't working!"

Lee's grip tightened on the armrest. "Casualties?"

"Several wounded! It's a nightmare down here! Send more troops."

Without another word, Lee walked into his office next to the bridge. A moment later, he emerged with an SXR-30 Raptor stun rifle in hand.

"Captain, perhaps you should remain on the bridge," Sato said.

Lee shot her a steely glance. "I'm not sitting by while that thing tears up my ship."

She nodded. "Aye, sir."

Lee checked the rifle's magazine, ensuring it was loaded. Slinging it over his shoulder, he headed toward the exit. "Sato, you have the bridge."

## Chapter 15:
## Subduing the Beast

**Year 2097**
**RNS *Poseidon***
**In Orbit Above Jita**
**Rass Star System**

The hangar bay of the RNS *Poseidon* erupted into chaos, the air thick with smoke from damaged conduits and the sharp tang of burning electronics. Shouts reverberated off the reinforced bulkheads as Republic forces moved to contain the threat at the center of the storm—a towering Zodark warrior. The creature stood three meters tall, its leathery blue skin glistening with sweat, muscles rippling with raw power. Its four arms flexed with lethal intent, two of them wielding swords that slashed through the air, keeping its attackers at bay. A discarded enemy blaster lay near a toppled console, its charge spent, but the Zodark's sheer strength made it no less deadly.

Lee burst through the hangar's main doorway, his boots slamming against the scorched deck. His pulse pounded, but his grip on his rifle was steady as he took in the scene. He wasn't here to fight, but he had to make sure his people could neutralize this threat before this Zodark was able to escape his hangar deck. The Zodark had already sent a handful of deckhands sprawling, their bodies slumped against crates, and now it turned its three-eyed glare on the Republic forces closing in.

Master Chief Petty Officer Jeff Hanzlik, the highest-ranking Master-at-Arms aboard *Poseidon*, led the response. His team of Republic Navy MAs, armed with SXR-30 Raptor stun rifles, formed a tight perimeter around the Zodark. The sleek, matte-black rifles were loaded with 30-round magazines of electrical stun darts, designed to incapacitate with high-voltage charges that disrupted neural pathways. Supporting the MAs were Republic Army soldiers, the ship's embarked muscle, their own SXR-30s raised and ready. The soldiers followed Hanzlik's lead, their faces set with determination despite the alien's imposing presence.

"Spread out—don't let it close the distance!" Hanzlik barked, his voice a gravelly command that cut through the chaos. He aimed his SXR-30, tracking the Zodark's movements. "Target the torso, concentrated fire!"

The Zodark moved with terrifying agility for its size, ducking and weaving as the first volley of stun darts hissed through the air. The electrical darts sparked with blue energy as they flew, trailing thin vapor lines, but the creature's leathery skin and quick reflexes made it a difficult target. Several darts missed, embedding into the deck or nearby crates with sharp cracks, their charges dissipating harmlessly. The Zodark roared, a guttural sound that echoed through the hangar, and slashed its swords in a wide arc, forcing the nearest MA to leap back.

One of the Army soldiers, a corporal, stepped too close while trying to get a clear shot. The Zodark lunged, one of its lower arms lashing out with claw-tipped fingers. The blow sent the corporal crashing to the deck, his SXR-30 skittering out of reach. The alien raised a sword, its three eyes glinting with predatory focus, but Hanzlik reacted instantly.

"Fire, now!" he shouted, squeezing the trigger.

The MAs and Army soldiers unleashed a barrage of stun darts, the SXR-30s humming with each shot. The Zodark twisted, dodging several darts, but this time its luck ran out. A half-dozen darts struck true, embedding into its leathery torso and upper arms with soft thuds. Blue arcs of electricity crackled across its skin as the darts discharged their high-voltage payloads, sending jolts through the creature's nervous system. The Zodark staggered, its movements slowing as the electrical charges disrupted its muscle control, but it still refused to fall, roaring in defiance.

"Keep it up!" Hanzlik ordered, reloading his SXR-30 with a fresh magazine. "Hit the joints—immobilize it!"

The team adjusted their aim, targeting the Zodark's elbows and knees. Another volley of darts found their mark, sinking into the creature's leathery skin. The electrical charges intensified, arcs of energy leaping between the darts as they overloaded the Zodark's decentralized nervous system. Its four limbs spasmed, the swords slipping from its grasp and clattering to the deck. The creature's knees buckled, its massive frame swaying as the cumulative effect of the charges took hold.

One final dart, fired by Hanzlik himself, struck the Zodark square in the chest. The electrical surge coursed through its body, and with a choked screech, the alien collapsed backward onto the hangar floor, the impact sending a tremor through the deck. Its chest heaved with labored breaths, but its three eyes fluttered shut, the beast finally knocked out by the relentless barrage of electrical stun darts.

Silence fell over the hangar, broken only by the hiss of steam from damaged conduits and the groans of the injured. The Zodark lay still, subdued at last.

Master Chief Petty Officer Jeff Hanzlik lowered his SXR-30 Raptor stun rifle, his sharp eyes scanning the alien to ensure it was truly down. Around him, Republic Navy Master-at-Arms personnel and Army soldiers held their positions, their weapons still trained on the creature, breathing heavy from the adrenaline of the fight.

Seeing the beast was down, Lee stepped closer, his boots crunching over debris—a shattered crate, a stray stun dart casing. The air was thick with the acrid scent of burnt circuits, and a thin haze of smoke lingered from a damaged conduit overhead, its exposed wiring sparking faintly. Medics rushed into the bay, their red-and-white kits slung over their shoulders, moving with practiced urgency. Two of them knelt beside the injured corporal who'd been swatted aside by the Zodark, his arm bent at an unnatural angle. Another medic helped a dazed deckhand to his feet, pressing a compress to a gash on the man's forehead.

"Get them to the Medbay now!" Lee ordered, his voice calm but firm. The medics nodded, supporting the injured as they shuffled toward the bay's exit, their boots leaving faint blood smears on the deck.

Lee turned to the fallen Zodark, its massive frame still intimidating even in unconsciousness. Three meters tall, four muscular arms, leathery skin taut over bulging muscles—it was a warrior built for battle. Capturing it alive was a stroke of luck, one they couldn't afford to waste. He tapped his comm, the small device clipped to his uniform humming to life. "Lee to Sato."

Commander Noriko Sato's voice came through, steady despite the tension of the recent battle. "Sato here, Captain. Status?"

"We've got a live Zodark," Lee said, his tone clipped. "Subdued in the hangar bay. It put up a hell of a fight—some injuries, but no fatalities. I need you to report this to Captain Roberts immediately. Relay what happened and request guidance on next steps."

"Understood, sir," Sato replied. "I'll get on a secure channel with Roberts now. Any immediate concerns?"

"Just get it done," Lee said. "We're moving the prisoner to the brig. I'll update you once it's secure."

"Copy that. Sato out."

As Sato handled the report, Lee turned to Hanzlik, who was already coordinating the transfer. "Master Chief, let's get this thing locked down. Maximum security protocols."

"Aye, aye, Captain," Hanzlik replied, his gravelly voice steady. He gestured to his MA team and the Army soldiers. "You heard the Captain—let's get this bastard moved to the brig, ASAP!"

Four MAs and a pair of Army soldiers stepped forward, hauling a reinforced hover sled into position beside the Zodark. The sled's anti-grav unit hummed softly, lifting it a few inches off the deck. With a collective grunt, they rolled the alien's massive frame onto the sled, its limbs splaying awkwardly, each clawed hand still twitching faintly from the electrical charges. Hanzlik slapped translucent cuffs made of reinforced polymer onto the Zodark's wrists and ankles, the material shimmering as it adapted to the alien's physiology, locking tight with a magnetic click.

"Let's move!" Hanzlik ordered, taking point as the team guided the sled toward the hangar's exit. Lee followed, his eyes scanning the surroundings as they moved through the *Poseidon*'s corridors.

The ship was still reeling from the battle that had led to the Zodark's capture. Though the *Poseidon* hadn't taken heavy damage, the signs of strain were everywhere. A technician knelt by a wall panel in the corridor, her toolkit open, a diagnostic scanner beeping as she traced a flickering power conduit. Sparks flared briefly, and she muttered a curse under her breath, tightening a connection. Further down, a pair of engineers ran diagnostics on a door mechanism, its servos whining as they recalibrated the alignment. The overhead lights flickered once, then steadied, casting stark shadows on the bulkheads, where a faint dent marked a near-miss from enemy fire.

"Clear the passage!" Hanzlik shouted as they approached a junction. Two crew members—a young ensign and a petty officer—froze midstride, their eyes widening at the sight of the Zodark. The alien's blue skin gleamed under the corridor lights, its four arms draped limply, each ending in clawed fingertips that scraped the edge of the sled. The crew members pressed themselves against the wall, giving the group a wide berth as they passed.

The ship's intercom crackled to life, a voice announcing, "All nonessential personnel, remain at your stations." A klaxon sounded in the distance, a low wail signaling ongoing security protocols. Another technician darted past, a tablet in hand, her screen flashing with alerts about a minor coolant leak on Deck 3.

They reached the brig after a tense few minutes, the heavy doors looming ahead—panels of reinforced metal interlaced with energy conduits. Hanzlik pressed his palm against the scanner, the device glowing green as it verified his identity. With a low rumble, the doors parted, revealing a corridor lined with cells, each sealed behind thick transparent barriers of high-density composite. Soft, pulsating lights traced the edges of the cells, and the air was cooler here, carrying a faint hum of electrical fields.

"Far end," Hanzlik directed, guiding the sled into an empty cell. The flooring inside shifted to a reinforced grid, designed to anchor the most dangerous prisoners. The team lowered the sled, letting the Zodark's weight settle onto the grid with a dull thud. Hanzlik unlatched the cuffs from the sled, transferring them to the cell's built-in restraints—heavy alloy chains that descended from the walls. He secured each of the Zodark's four limbs, the magnetic seals locking with a sharp click. The chains retracted slightly, pulling taut to limit movement.

Lee stood just outside the transparent barrier, watching as the Zodark's massive form was splayed out, its chest rising and falling with deep, steady breaths. Even unconscious, the alien exuded an unsettling aura of latent power. The barrier sealed shut with a hiss, its surface shimmering as the energy field activated, ensuring the prisoner wouldn't escape.

"Prisoner secure, Captain," Hanzlik reported, stepping back to join Lee. "Not going anywhere."

"Good work, Master Chief," Lee said, his gaze lingering on the Zodark for a moment longer. They'd captured a live enemy—a rare opportunity. Lee was curious to see what Captain Roberts would have to say about this.

*******

Lee strode out of the brig, the heavy doors rumbling shut behind him with a metallic clang, the locking mechanism ensuring nothing could leave that wasn't supposed to. His boots echoed in the corridor as he made his way toward the bridge, the weight of the recent skirmish still pressing on his shoulders. The *Poseidon* hummed around him, its systems stabilizing after the battle, but the signs of strain lingered. A technician jogged past, a tablet in hand, muttering about a pressure variance in the aft thrusters. The ship had taken a beating, but it was holding together—Lee expected nothing less from his crew.

He stepped onto the bridge, the command center buzzing with quiet efficiency. Officers manned their stations, screens glowing with tactical readouts and damage reports. Sato stood near the central console, her sharp eyes scanning a holographic display of the sector. She glanced up as Lee approached, her expression a mix of focus and lingering tension from the battle.

"Prisoner's secure in the brig," Lee said, his voice steady as he took his place at the captain's chair. "Hanzlik's got it locked down tight. Any word from Roberts?"

Sato nodded, tapping a command into her console. "Just came through, sir. Secure message, text only—no video. He's got orders for us."

Lee's brow furrowed, but he gestured for her to proceed. Sato pulled up the message, her fingers swift on the controls, and the text appeared on the main viewscreen:

> From: Captain Eamon Roberts, RNS *Australia*
> To: Commander Ripley Willis Lee, RNS *Poseidon*
> Priority: Immediate
> Message: Zodark capture confirmed. Well done. Rendezvous at coordinates 773-228-459, Sector 2, ASAP. Republic shuttle dispatched with specialized Republic Intelligence team to handle prisoner and exploit captured Vulture starfighter. Team will assume custody upon arrival. Do not deviate. Acknowledge receipt and compliance.
> End Transmission

Lee read the message, his jaw tightening slightly. He exchanged a glance with Sato, who mirrored his frustration with a subtle frown. The coordinates weren't far—a few hours at most—but they were off their current patrol route, pulling them away from their mission to scout Zodark activity in the sector. Lee understood the necessity; capturing a live Zodark was a rare opportunity, and Republic Intelligence needed to handle it. But that didn't make the detour any less irritating.

"Great," Sato muttered, her tone dry as she plotted the new course on the navigation console. "We take a prisoner, and now we're playing taxi service for some intel team. I thought we were supposed to be hunting Zodark ships, not running errands."

Lee leaned back in his chair, crossing his arms. "What did we expect, Sato? We nabbed a live one—now we deal with the consequences. Roberts isn't wrong to send a team. That Zodark and its Vulture could give us intel we can't afford to miss." He sighed, rubbing the back of his neck. "Doesn't mean I have to like it. Pass the coordinates along to the rest of our scout team and let's move. I'd like to get us back on mission as soon as possible."

Sato gave a curt nod as she tapped on the controls as she relayed the acknowledgment to Roberts and passed along the change of plans to the other ships of their patrol. "Message sent, sir. Course laid in for 773-228-459. ETA three hours at standard cruising speed."

The *Poseidon*'s engines thrummed with a deeper pitch as the vessel accelerated, the stars on the viewscreen elongating slightly as they shifted course.

The bridge settled into a focused rhythm, officers monitoring systems and scanning for threats. Lee's mind churned as he stared at the coordinates on the screen. A specialized Republic Intelligence team meant professionals— interrogators, tech experts, maybe even a xeno-specialist. He hoped they were as good. The sooner they took custody of the Zodark and the Vulture, the sooner *Poseidon* could return to the fight.

Three hours later, the *Poseidon* dropped out of its high-speed cruise, the stars snapping back into sharp points on the viewscreen. "Approaching coordinates 773-228-459," Lieutenant Reynolds reported from the navigation station. "Sensors picking up a Republic shuttle, IFF confirmed. They're hailing us, sir."

Lee straightened in his chair, his earlier annoyance giving way to a sense of anticipation. "On screen," he ordered.

The viewscreen flickered, displaying the shuttle—a sleek, angular craft with the Republic's insignia etched on its hull, its engines glowing faintly as it held position. The intelligence team was here, ready to take over the next phase of this operation. Lee stood, adjusting his uniform. It was time to meet them.

# Chapter 16:
## Night Thoughts

**Year 2097**
**RNS *Gallipoli***
**Intus Orbit**

Coop lay on his bunk, staring at the metal gridwork of the ceiling above. He shifted onto his side, then onto his back again.

Fragments of the day's mission replayed in his mind. Lines of code, targeting grids, the sudden flash on the horizon—all jumbled together in a knot he couldn't untangle. He squeezed his eyes shut, but the darkness only made things worse, bringing back more recent memories he wanted to forget. On his HUD, icons had blinked out—friendly markers vanishing one by one. Deltas. His own people. Dead. And it was his fault.

A bitter taste rose in his throat. How could he have misread the coordinates? The missile—the JATM—had arced beautifully, perfectly, lethally. Guilt pressed down on Coop, wanting to tighten its grip around his neck.

Coop contemplated the aftermath of his mistake. What he'd done—firing on his own people—it all felt like it was going to crush him. He knew what lay ahead—a series of evaluations and inquiries dissecting every moment of the mission.

He'd be grounded immediately, his wings clipped while the incident was investigated. The thought of facing a board of inquiry made his stomach ache. He'd have to relive those terrible moments again and again, explaining to stern-faced officers how he'd misidentified friendly troops as hostiles.

Bile rose and he swallowed it down. *Why me? I was just trying to save them, not kill them!*

Psychological evaluations would be extensive. Probing. They'd question his judgment, his mental state, and his fitness for duty. Flight simulators would recreate the scenario, forcing him to confront his fatal error… over and over and over again.

The JAG office would get involved, of course. There might even be talk of a court-martial. Perhaps worst of all was the knowledge he'd have to face the families of those he'd killed. How could he possibly explain? How could he ever ask for forgiveness?

New training would surely follow—enhanced friend-or-foe identification protocols, stricter weapons release procedures. Would any amount of training erase the doubt now planted in his mind? Could he ever trust himself in the cockpit again?

Footsteps shuffled outside the barracks, followed by the low murmur of voices. Laughs echoed, conversations about tomorrow's drills, someone's bad hand at poker. Life went on around him, oblivious to the turmoil twisting inside. He just wanted to curl up and die.

Coop sat up, swinging his legs over the edge of the bunk. The cool air of the barracks chilled the sweat on his brow.

"Can't sleep either, huh?"

Coop looked down to see Raven leaning his shoulder against the doorway, yawning.

"Something like that," Coop said.

Raven gave a half grin. "Long day. Try to get some rest."

"Yeah. Will do."

As Raven's footsteps faded, someone else filled the doorway. Tall, confident, that usual stride—Strike.

"Coop," Strike said. "Walk with me."

Without a word, Coop hopped off the bunk. The two men moved through the *Gallipoli*'s corridors, the clang of their boots the only sound between them.

They entered Strike's office, a tight space cluttered with flight manuals, charts, and models of Orion fighters. Various generations of the starfighter were displayed on a shelf along the back wall. Strike closed the door after they stepped inside.

"Have a seat."

Coop remained standing. "I'd rather stand." His insides wanted to be on his outsides. What had recently happened ate at every fiber in his being, making him numb.

Strike nodded, settling into his own chair. He studied Coop for a moment before speaking. "I wanted to talk to you about today's mission."

Coop bit at his inner cheek. "I screwed up."

"Listen—"

"I fired on our own men. The Deltas… I saw their markers disappear. I heard their calls. And I—"

"Coop," Strike interrupted. "You didn't."

Confusion smacked Coop across the face. The skin around his nose crinkled. "What do you mean?"

Strike rested his elbows on the desk. "Received intel from Republic Command. Our systems were compromised during the mission. The Zodarks launched a coordinated cyberattack on our communication and targeting arrays."

"A cyberattack?"

"Yes. They infiltrated our network protocols, manipulated data streams. What you saw—what you heard—well… wasn't real. They injected false Delta chatter, fabricated coordinates. Wanted you to believe you were firing on friendlies. Wanted you to think you killed your own people. Happened to a few other pilots as well."

Coop shook his head slowly, trying to process the information. "The icons on my HUD… the comms traffic—it… wasn't real?"

"Correct," Strike said. "Our cybersecurity team is working to patch the vulnerabilities. We're implementing new safeguards to prevent future intrusions."

A cold sensation settled in Coop's chest. It spread outward. Not a shiver, but deeper somehow. "So the missile… it didn't hit our guys?"

"No," Strike said. "There were no Deltas in that grid square. You engaged some trees and rocks instead. Nothing more."

"You're serious?"

"Affirmative."

"This isn't a joke?"

"I can assure you with absolute certainty, Lieutenant, that this isn't a joke. The gravity of this situation precludes any form of levity. We may not see eye to eye, but I trust you can recognize the seriousness of my demeanor and understand this would be highly inappropriate timing for any attempt at humor."

Coop's tension eased. "Understood. How'd they bypass our multilayered authentication? Encryption protocols should have prevented this. I mean, I know they've breached our systems before, but spoofing friendly fire? That's a new tactic. When was the last time they managed to infiltrate our networks this deeply?"

"A few times, three years ago."

"And our secured comms—how'd they manage to inject false chatter without triggering alarms?"

Strike tapped a few commands onto a pad on his desktop, bringing up a holographic display of code fragments and network pathways. "They've developed advanced electronic warfare methods of spoofing—methods we've only theorized about. They were a step ahead."

"So, we're operating with compromised data while they manipulate our systems."

"Actually, our cybersecurity team has already developed a patch for this. Within the next twenty-four hours, the Orions will have updated encryption, heuristic scanners, the works. The Primords and the Altairians apparently contributed to the fix—it went all the way to the top. But as soon as they finish these updates, it will be a nonissue."

"What safeguards do we have against *future* attacks, sir? They could overlay hostile indicators on actual friendly positions. In that scenario, I could actually…" He trailed off.

"I'd suggest a change of thinking," Strike said. "That's exactly what they want—to make us doubt ourselves, hesitate when decisions matter most."

"It's already difficult as is to distinguish between real and false data in combat conditions."

Strike stood. "I understand your concerns, Lieutenant. We've all faced similar challenges. Our training and protocols are designed to help us navigate these situations."

Coop's eyes dropped to the floor. The blue-gray pattern of the deck plates seemed to blur. "I'm concerned about my ability to perform effectively given these new variables, sir."

"Look," Strike said, softening his tone, "your piloting skills are exemplary, particularly with the Orion drone. However, maintaining psychological resilience is equally important. We need to adapt to these new threats."

"Understood," Coop said.

Strike circled the desk. "Lieutenant, this situation affects the entire squadron. We face these challenges as a unit."

"Sir, the complexity of the issue concerns me."

"Acknowledged, Lieutenant."

Coop looked up. "What's our next course of action, sir?"

"Adapt our strategies, enhance our training, and maintain tactical superiority. Mutual vigilance is critical. Our cyber teams are on this."

"Captain, I'd like to contribute beyond flight duties. Perhaps I could assist the cybersecurity team in analyzing the breach."

"Potential merit in that suggestion, Lieutenant. I'll consult with Lieutenant Bigsby about integrating you into their operations. Don't entertain optimistic outcomes on that front, Coop."

"Aye, sir."

"All right, well, get some rest first," Strike said. "You've had a long day."

"Rest hasn't been easy to come by."

Strike gave a fast nod. "Try. And that's an order."

Coop gave a half-hearted salute. "Yes, sir."

As he turned to leave, Strike called after him. "And, Coop?"

He glanced back. "Yeah?"

"Don't beat yourself up over this. The fault lies with the enemy, not you."

"I'll try to remember that."

The corridor outside felt chillier than before, the lights dimmer. As Coop walked, his thoughts were a tangled mess of relief along with lingering doubt.

He wandered into the mess hall, now nearly empty save for a few late-night stragglers nursing cups of coffee. He poured himself a mug, the bitter aroma offering a small distraction. Taking a seat by the viewport, he stared out into the star-speckled void.

The vastness of space had always brought him solace—a reminder of the bigger picture, of possibilities beyond the confines of the ship. But tonight, it felt different. The stars seemed out there, but lost in the dark.

"You processing some heavy intel, airman?" someone asked.

Coop turned to see Bear. He sat in the seat across from him. "Couldn't steal a scrum of sleep either?" Bear said.

"Nah." Coop sipped his coffee.

"Heard about the glitch today. Nasty business."

"Yeah," Coop murmured. "Spoofing. Not a glitch."

"Same, same." Bear shrugged. "You OK?"

"Fine."

"You're a lousy liar." Bear chuckled. "But I won't press."

"Ever think about how… you know… how easy it is for things to go crazy sideways out there?" Coop asked.

"All the time," Bear said. "Part of the job description. Nothing goes right. The only thing an experienced drone operator can do is use his squadron, his lucky charms, and blast as many Zodarks before they blast you. Make sense?"

"Yeah, but this…" Coop motioned vaguely. "Being spoofed, manipulated. Makes you wonder what else we're blind to."

"Can't control everything, Coop. Can only control how we respond."

"Sounds like something out of a self-help holo." Coop smirked.

"Hey, maybe I missed my calling," Bear said. "But seriously, don't let them mess with your head. That's the Zodarks' game."

Coop nodded, gazing back out at the stars. "Easier said than done."

"True enough." Bear stood. "Get some rest, man. Tomorrow's a new day."

"Thanks." Coop watched Bear head toward the exit.

Left alone, Coop finished his coffee. His mind drifted to thoughts of home. Memories of his father's stern words, his strict nature, chasing him out of the house when he came home with a bad grade, the constant push to be better, to be flawless. All that sat on his shoulders on a daily basis.

Coop remembered his mother's forced smile, persisting even as his father berated him. He thought of the delicious meals she'd prepare, followed by tense dinners where silence reigned and eye contact was avoided. Now, years later, anger welled up inside him—a desire to confront his father for the pain he'd caused, for making both Coop and his mother feel so alienated, so dumb, so unwanted. It was a unique kind of loneliness, he realized, to feel isolated even when surrounded by family.

When he made it back to his bunk, he pulled out the small, worn journal—Presley Paul Cooper's war diary. Thumbing through the pages, he stopped at a passage: "In the chaos of battle, doubt is the enemy's ally. Trust in your training, trust in your squadron, and above all, trust in yourself. Faith and God is a notch above all that, as well. Mix that together, and you've got a bag of miracles."

Coop's ancestor had faced uncertainties too, in a different time, against different enemies. The tools and tactics might have changed, but the core remained the same.

Closing the book, Coop lay on his pillow. Perhaps this time, sleep might find him.

**Chapter 17:**
**Squadron Trust**

**Year 2097**
**RNS *Gallipoli***
**Intus Orbit**

At 0600 hours, Coop stepped into the briefing room. Pilots milled about, voices low. Before he could take a seat, Bear and Raven intercepted him.

"Coop," Bear said. "You doing better?"

"Affirmative."

Raven nodded. "Was worried when we heard about the EW attack with the false chatter. Kinda relieved, too. Don't know how to feel, honestly. Still, you holding up?"

"Sure. Ready for whatever comes next, fellas." *Can we change the subject?* "Let's grab our seats."

"Coop." Bear gave him a direct stare. "Remember, we're in this together. All of us. Don't carry nothing alone, all right?"

"Like I said last night, you need to become a motivational coach or something," Coop replied.

"And prevent myself from killing Zodark pricks?" Bear teased. "Never."

Coop grinned. "True."

They settled into their usual spots as the rest of the squadron filed in. Conversations hushed.

Strike strode to the front. Without preamble, he activated the holodisplay. "We've got a new development some of you are already aware of."

Graphics blinked to life. Schematics, data streams, and code scrolled in midair.

"Yesterday's mission was compromised by a sophisticated cyberattack," Strike said. "The enemy infiltrated our flight systems and comm links, injecting false data."

Murmurs rippled through the pilots.

"While we have always dealt with electronic warfare, this latest attack was able to manipulate sensor readings and comms," Strike continued. "In short, the Zodarks' EW measures were more advanced than we anticipated."

Coop's muscles tightened. The memory of the false Delta chatter and misleading HUD data flashed in his mind.

Strike zoomed in on a rotating model of their standard Orion fighter. "They exploited vulnerabilities in our communication and targeting subsystems, creating phantom friendly and hostile signatures in certain areas of the map, along with false chatter. Meaning, where those signatures were showing on some pilots' HUDs, well, there was actually nothing there."

Across the way, Phantom rested his hands on the seat in front of him. "So they're trying to make us think we're engaging hostiles or accidentally firing on friendlies when we're actually targeting nothing at all?"

"Precisely," Strike confirmed. "You might hit a pond, kill some fish, but other than that, you're not hitting any legitimate targets or friendlies. We caught it this time before any real damage was done. For anything, right now, I believe their attempt was to simply confuse our pilots and create doubt. I don't know what elaborate scheme they're attempting with this, though."

"What's to stop them from trying a second time and potentially succeeding with all our comms and holos?" Bear asked. "Totally having us fire at ghosts. Or, eventually, at our own allied troops?"

Strike's expression hardened. "That's where these new protocols come in. Our cybersecurity teams, in coordination with our Primord and Altairian allies, have already developed a solution to this problem that is currently being implemented."

The holodisplay shifted to a list of tactical updates. Technical jargon scrolled alongside visual aids.

"First," Strike continued, "we're rolling out a software overhaul. All fighters will receive an update to patch existing security gaps."

Coop scanned the information. Enhanced encryption, adaptive firewalls, AI threat detection.

"Second, we're switching to new encrypted communication channels," Strike said. "It'll make intercepts significantly more challenging."

A pilot near the front raised a hand. "Won't that affect sync times with the drones?"

"Minimal latency increase," Strike said. "Engineering assures us it won't impact operational efficiency."

Bear exchanged a glance with Coop. "Sounds like they've been busy," Bear whispered. "Hopefully they get overtime pay. None of 'em probably slept a wink last night."

"Third," Strike continued, "manual overrides. In the event of a system compromise, you must be prepared to fly without AI assistance."

"Old-school," Raven said.

"Consider it a chance to hone your skills," Strike challenged. "Training sims start at 1800 tonight."

"Looks like sleep's off the agenda," Raven said under his breath.

"Look, everyone, adaptability is our greatest asset," Strike said. "The enemy evolves—we must stay a step ahead. This is asymmetrical warfare. I need every one of you operating at peak tactical efficiency. Anticipate. Adapt. Overcome."

Coop's mind went to the last mission, the moment his controls had faltered. Doubt kept creeping in.

"Cooper." Strike's voice resounded in the room.

He snapped to attention. "Sir?"

"You'll need to debrief with tech support about the glitch," Strike said. "Provide any insights you have."

"Understood."

Strike's gaze lingered a moment before moving on. "Now for our primary objective."

The holodisplay changed to a terrain map of the conflict zone. Icons indicated hot spots and potential enemy positions.

"Intel suggests the Zodark forces on Intus are receiving external support," Strike said. "We have reason to believe it's connected to the recent cyberattacks, though we're still actively tracking the source."

He zoomed in on a particular region. "Our mission tomorrow is to investigate a suspected ground convoy. SIGINT has picked up unusual electromagnetic signatures in this area, consistent with a Zodark jamming unit, likely protecting some sort of air defense cluster."

"Primord involvement, sir?" a lieutenant asked.

"Negative. We've confirmed with our Primord allies that they have no operations in this sector. These signatures suggest something… different."

Strike continued, "Primary objective is recon and intel gathering. We need to confirm the nature and composition of this convoy without alerting them to our presence."

He highlighted a bunch of waypoints. "Coop, Raven, Bear, and Phantom, you'll be piloting our Orion drones for this operation. Avoid detection and try to gather some detailed intelligence we can use." Strike then outlined the roles of the rest of the squadron. Reapers would be on standby for close-air support if needed. Two Orions were assigned to high-altitude surveillance, maintaining a broader view of the operation area. A pair of aircraft would provide electronic warfare support, ready to jam enemy communications or counter any unexpected threats.

"Sir," Raven asked, "given the nature of the recent cyberattack, how reliable are our sensors?"

"Good question," Strike said. "Look, the Republic isn't the only one who knows how to use electronic warfare to spoof or deceive an adversary. This recent incident caught us by surprise, but with help from our Primord allies and our own EW wizards, they have created a patch that should help prevent this from happening again. That said, no plan survives contact with the enemy and its incumbent upon us to remain vigilant and monitor your systems. Trust your instincts. If something doesn't feel right, report it immediately. Any further questions?"

Silence settled over the room.

"Good," he said. "Thoroughly familiarize yourselves with the new protocols. Dismissed."

As pilots began to rise, Raven motioned to both Bear and Coop. "Can we talk?" The man looked a little distraught.

"Sure, what's up?" Coop asked.

"Not here," Raven said.

Raven led them to the maintenance hangar. The space, usually busy, was relatively quiet at this hour. They found a secluded corner behind a partially dismantled B-99 Raider engine.

Raven glanced around before speaking in a low tone. "Guys, the Zodarks' level of access to our data… it's unprecedented."

"You thinking what I'm thinking?" Bear asked.

"Yeah," Raven continued. "There might be a mole in Republic Command. It's the only way they could have gotten past our security so easily. I mean, what happened, that's unheard of."

Coop frowned, rubbing his temples. Raven and Bear had always been slightly conspiratorial, but this was a different level. "I think you're taking this a bit too far."

Raven shot Coop a look. "Seriously?"

"They're an advanced species. Like us, Zodarks can meddle in other species' technology. Back on Earth, nations did this for a hundred years or more."

"Not this in depth. I've never heard of this happening, have you?" Bear asked.

"Negative, but like I said, I think Raven's taking this too far."

"Honestly, Coop, I'm not."

Bear wrinkled his brow. "Coop's got a point, too. Are you a cybersecurity expert all of a sudden, Raven?"

"Not an expert, but I've got more background in this than you might think. At the Academy, I specialized in advanced cyber warfare alongside my pilot training."

"You never mentioned that before," Bear said.

"He *has*," Coop replied. "Before being stationed on the *Gallipoli*, he wouldn't shut up about all the *knowledge* he has."

"Well, I can't shut up now either." Raven shrugged. "What the Zodarks did… it's advanced. It's nearly impossible without inside help."

Coop leaned against the engine, his skepticism wavering. "Explain."

"Look," Raven continued, lowering his voice further, "our systems have multiple layers of security. Firewalls, encryption, air-gapped networks. To break through all that, inject false data, and manipulate our comms in real time? That requires intimate knowledge of our protocols, network architecture, and encryption keys."

Coop shook his head. "Look, Raven, I realize you may know a thing or two more about cybersecurity than I do, but let's walk this dog for a moment, shall we?" he said. "Why would any Earther *want* to work with the Zodarks? I mean, they're vicious four-armed beasts with a penchant for enslaving other species. And even if someone were sufficiently sadistic to want to cooperate with them, how would they do that? What, is there some website I don't know about? WorkwiththeZodarks.com? And even if they did manage to make contact, how are they going to communicate? Do *you* speak Zodark? It just doesn't track."

Raven's face was red after being publicly called out. An awkward pause hung in the room. "I concede the points you've made, Coop, but something still doesn't sit right with me. From my estimation, the Zodarks would need access to our most secure databases to accomplish what they've done, maybe even source code for our flight software. That's not information that's stored in a remotely accessible location."

Coop sighed heavily. "I'm sorry. I just don't see it, man." He pushed himself to stand. "Look, I get that this whole situation was seriously messed up. But right now, I need to rest before training at 1800. My head's killing me."

"Get some shut-eye, Coop," Bear said. "We'll keep this between us for now."

With a nod, Coop excused himself and headed back to the barracks. Inside his room, he moved to his locker. From the top shelf, he retrieved the worn leather journal. Presley Paul Cooper's legacy. Like always, he needed it like it was his control stick in his Orion's pod.

He went through the pages until a passage greeted him:

*- April 15, 1944 — Over occupied France*

*-*

*Today, our squadron faced our toughest mission yet. We were escorting bombers to a factory deep in enemy territory when we were ambushed by a group of Focke-Wulf 190s. The sky erupted.*

*In the middle of the dogfight, I lost sight of my wingman, Norm. When I spotted him again, he was being tailed by two enemy fighters, and his Mustang was trailing smoke. Every instinct told me to*

*break formation
and help him, but
our orders were
clear. We had to
protect the
bombers at all
costs. For a split
second, I
hesitated.*

*Then I
heard Bucky's
voice crackle
over the radio:
'Pres, I've got
the bombers. Go
get our boy!'*

*I peeled
away from the
formation. I
trusted Bucky
with my life, and
I knew he'd keep
his word. As I
closed in on
Norm's pursuers,
I saw the rest of
our squadron
tightening their
coverage around
the bombers.*

*It was a
brutal fight, but
we managed to
drive off the 190s
and get Norm
safely back to
base. His plane
was shot to hell,*

*but he walked away with barely a scratch.*

*Later, when the brass questioned our deviation from the mission plan, every single pilot in the squadron backed up our decision. We stood united, and they couldn't argue with our results, that all bombers had returned safely and we'd shot down seven enemy fighters.*

*That day taught me an invaluable lesson: in the heat of battle, it's the trust between wingmen that keeps you alive. Orders are important, but the bonds forged in combat are what truly win wars. Your squad is your family in the sky, and that*

*bond is*
*unbreakable.*

Coop sat back, pondering the words. Even if he didn't agree with Raven and Bear all the time, at least on a mission, he knew he could trust them.

He closed the journal. Later, he had training. Tomorrow, though, was going to be a big day.

## Chapter 18:
## High Maintenance

**Year 2097**
**FOB Oteren**
**Planet Intus**

The hangar reverberated with the constant noise of repair operations. Amidst it all, Ford stood apart. His focus was trained on the Osprey before him. The craft shined under his care, every panel polished, every bolt tightened to perfection.

He pressed his gloved hand along the underside of the ship, fingers probing for any imperfection. Every noise in the hangar bay faded into the background. This was Ford's domain—a place where perfection wasn't just valued, it was life-saving.

A faint glint appeared. Squinting, he spotted a screw protruding ever so slightly from the access panel near the port thruster. "Who the hell installed this panel?"

A mechanic, eyes wide beneath his grease-smudged cap, crawled out from under the craft's retractable landing gear assembly. "That was me, Chief."

Ford stared. "You call this secured? Might as well hand the enemy our playbook."

"Sorry, sir. I'll fix it right away."

"Sorry doesn't cut it," Ford said. "If this bird loses a panel midflight, it's on you. On all of us."

The surrounding crew exchanged uneasy glances. Conversations hushed, and the clang of metal on metal seemed louder amidst the sudden quiet.

Ford turned away, not waiting for a response. He moved to the starboard side, looking for any discrepancies. Observing a smudge on the canopy glass, he grabbed a rag and wiped it clean.

"Double-check all your work," Ford said. "I want these ships mission-ready. No exceptions."

A mechanic muttered under his breath, "What does he think we're doing? Twiddling our thumbs?"

Ford's head snapped up. "What was that?"

The man shifted uncomfortably. "Nothing, Chief."

"Then get back to work. And if you think this is too much, there's the door. I could write you up for insubordination, and that goes in your permanent record. You want to risk a demotion or even a court-martial over this? Now, are we clear?"

"Yes, sir. My apologies."

Ford rounded on the mechanic. "Did I ask for your damn apology? In this outfit, we don't apologize, we fix our mistakes and do better. You think 'sorry' is gonna patch up a busted troop transport or save anything? Now square yourself away and get back to work. And if I hear another smart word outta you, you'll be scrubbing latrines with your toothbrush."

Ford pointed to a crate left unattended. "Equipment doesn't store itself, people. Secure that, or it'll become shrapnel at the first hard turn."

Ford moved on, his pace quickening. "Hydraulic lines need pressure testing. Calibration reports should've been to me an hour ago. We're not running a daycare—this is the Republic military. Act like it."

To Ford, results mattered more than feelings these days. Their labor stood between survival and oblivion for many.

A figure stepped into his path. Lance Corporal Tyrell Williams stood at attention. "Chief, with your permission, I'd like to offer an observation."

Ford kept a fast stride. "Make it quick, Lance Corporal."

Williams fell in beside him. "Sir, the crew's been under a lot of pressure lately."

"They need to be, Williams."

"Understood, sir. My worry is that this relentless schedule might compromise our ability to maintain equipment properly."

"Are any of them out there fighting for their lives, searching for Zodark warriors, helping their brothers and sisters who are dying, losing limbs, anything like that?"

"Negative, sir."

"Then I want no complaints."

"Sir, if—"

Ford stopped short. He gave Williams a hard look. "You think I care about their comfort when sloppy work gets soldiers killed?"

"No, Chief. I'm just worried that excessive strain might lead to the very mistakes we're trying to prevent."

"They need to toughen up. The enemy isn't giving us second chances."

"You're right, sir. I only meant to suggest that a balanced approach might yield better results."

"I lead by example," Ford said. "If they can't keep up, that's on them."

"Acknowledged, sir. The team is committed to meeting your standards."

A clatter reverberated as a wrench slipped from a mechanic's hand, skittering across the floor. Ford's attention flicked to the source. "Secure your tools! Or do I need to give a lesson on basic protocols?"

"Sir," Williams said. "I can assure you the team is giving their utmost in these demanding conditions."

"Their best isn't good enough until this hangar runs flawlessly." Ford's gaze moved to the next task at hand. He walked to another Osprey, its final diagnostic still pending.

Ford's mind flashed to the Delta squads he'd helped deploy. He was exhausted, needing rest, but the Deltas and Army soldiers out there had it far worse. They needed more than just a break; they needed perfection from him and his team. Every mechanical failure, every overlooked detail could mean death for those soldiers. He'd seen too many not come back. As the one in charge, the burden of getting everything right fell squarely on his shoulders. That was fine. Good. Because no one would, or could, run this hangar as well as him, he thought. The Republic was counting on him, and he couldn't let them down. No, he couldn't rest, not when the lives of soldiers were at stake. He had to keep pushing, keep working, get it right every single time.

Ford went to the maintenance access panel and activated the external interface. The displays on the portable diagnostic unit came to life. Data scrolled across the monitors. He noted the readouts, listening to the subtle sounds of the ship's systems powering up remotely.

A stutter in the power grid caught his attention. He tapped a few commands on the display. "Fuel intake manifold's lagging by half a percent," he muttered to himself before turning to another worker. "Jones! Run a bypass on the fuel regulators. I want that lag eliminated."

Jones glanced up, fatigue all over his features. "On it, Chief."

Heavy boots struck the metal flooring nearby. Commander Rhett Granger headed toward Ford.

"Chief Ford."

"Commander."

"Need a moment of your time."

"Yes, sir." Ford followed Granger a few steps away.

"Need your help with something sensitive," Granger said.

Ford waited, thinking it a little out of place as Granger hesitated for a second.

"It's about Lieutenant Love. Medical flagged some concerning patterns in her last psych eval."

"Sir, if you're suggesting she's unfit—"

Granger shook his head. "I'm suggesting she needs someone watching her six who isn't obligated to report every observation to Medical. Someone who understands combat stress. Someone who understands her."

"You're asking me to monitor her? Off the record?"

"I'm asking you to make sure we don't lose another good officer because the system's too rigid to let them process grief their own way. Can you do that, Chief?"

Ford had seen it before—good soldiers benched because they couldn't check the right boxes on a standardized assessment. And Love, well, she was different than most, a pilot better than most. She flew like her life, and her crew's life, depended on it because, in many ways, it did. Sitting in the cockpit, flying that Osprey, was where she processed every damn thing.

"I'll keep an eye on her, sir."

"Good man." Granger nodded before turning on his heel and exiting the hangar as swiftly as he'd arrived.

Ford stood there, the conversation processing in his head. He already felt responsible for Love since Jack's death—they'd been close, as close as a non-commissioned officer and an officer could ever be, and deep down in his own mind, to a dead ghost, Ford had promised Jack he'd look after her if anything happened. Now it was official, albeit off the books.

Williams headed in his direction. "Everything all right?"

"Yeah, just some additional responsibilities."

"Anything I should know about?"

Ford shook his head. "Command stuff. Nothing that affects our maintenance schedule."

"If you say so."

Ford would need to be subtle with this as Love was perceptive, and the last thing she needed was to feel like she was being babysat. He'd keep her flying, keep her focused. Sometimes the best therapy was staying in the fight, not being pulled from it.

"Gotta get back to work," Ford said.

Ford walked to *Jack*, Lieutenant Love's Osprey. The massive transport craft had become an extension of the Lieutenant herself. Ford understood that—machines were more reliable than people sometimes. They broke in predictable ways, and if you knew what you were doing, you could always fix them.

People were messier. Love had been pushing herself hard since losing Jack, flying longer missions, volunteering for the most dangerous runs. On the surface, she maintained the cool professionalism expected of an officer, but Ford had caught glimpses—the slight tremor in her hands during pre-flight checks, the way she sometimes stared into nothing during mission briefings before snapping back to attention.

He'd watch over her, not just because Granger asked, but because it was what Jack would have wanted. He'd make sure she stayed mission-ready, keep her from crossing the line between dedication and recklessness. More importantly, he'd make sure the brass saw her as the exceptional pilot she was, not as a liability.

He straightened his shoulders, pushing aside his worries for the moment. *Back to work*, he told himself. *The machines won't fix themselves, and every second counts in keeping our forces battle-ready.*

"Jones!" he yelled. "Get over here, pronto!"

**Chapter 19:**
**Whisper Point**

**Year 2097**
**FOB Oteren**
**Planet Intus**

Lieutenant Naomi Love sat on a worn crate in the hangar bay. She was on her break. Her comrades, Williams and Ford, were among the mechanics here, busy as heck with their tasks. Part of Love felt guilty for not helping, but mostly she was tired. She decided to relax there, just watching, just taking a breather. It was a good place to unwind, staying close to the action without having to actually do anything.

Ford stood near *Jack*'s open hatch. "Double-check the hydraulics," Ford barked. "I want those magrails calibrated yesterday."

A young technician flinched under his critical tone. "On it, Chief!"

Ford's usual calm had been replaced with a weird edge. He snapped at another crew member. "That's the wrong torque setting. Do it again."

Love frowned. The pressure was getting to everyone, but Ford's intensity stood out. The guy demanded perfection—an impossibility for anyone. Any deviation drew his ire, and since perfection was impossible, his anger was seeping everywhere. She'd watched as the once friendly, funny man had turned cold over the last several months—but why?

Rising from the crate, Love walked around equipment and personnel and toward Ford. She needed to tell the guy to ease up. Before long, Ford might burst a blood vessel or something worse. Tools clanked and technical jargon pierced the air as she made her way toward him.

In stride, she touched the fuselage of an adjacent Osprey. "How's she holding up?" Love asked a mechanic inspecting the landing gear.

"Solid, Lieutenant. She'll fly well."

"Good to hear."

Near the comms station, a voice caught her ear. Love stepped closer, saying, "Repeat that last transmission."

An operator leaned forward, pressing a hand to his earpiece. "Lima Company sustained heavy casualties. Medevac requested at grid two-six-charlie. Immediate extraction required."

Without hesitation, Love stepped even closer to the operator. People needed help, and she needed a purpose right now. Being idle, doing nothing, was not a purpose. Getting men and women home safely was what she did best, and it was a mission she could throw herself into with all her heart, with everything she's got. "I'll take the medevac."

The operator glanced up. "Lieutenant Love, the area's hot. Command estimates heavy enemy presence."

"That's fine. Prep my bird."

Commander Granger approached. "Lieutenant, you volunteering for this op?"

"Affirmative, sir. *Jack* is mission-ready."

"Intel reports active Zodark patrols. LZ might be compromised."

"I can handle it."

"Of all pilots, I know you can. Departure in twenty mikes. Mission brief will be uploaded to your HUD. Mission brief will be uploaded to your HUD. Here's what ya' got. Assigning a comprehensive medical team to this op. Two combat medics skilled in emergency care, one flight nurse, an emergency physician, and two medical technicians to assist with patient care and equipment."

"Understood, sir," Love said.

"Bring our people home, Lieutenant."

"Will do."

As Granger walked away, Love heard footsteps behind her. She turned to see Ford, his expression neutral but his eyes showing concern. "Permission to speak freely?"

"Granted, Chief."

"Are you certain about taking this medevac mission? You've been on continuous ops for the past seventy hours."

"Those wounded don't have the luxury of waiting, Ford. I'm fit for duty."

"With respect, Lieutenant, fatigue affects judgment. Are you sure you're at your best?"

"I appreciate your concern, Chief, but I know my limits. I'm good to go," Love replied.

Ford looked down for an instant. It was clear he thought otherwise. "Understood. If you're proceeding, I'll need to run a final systems check on the weapons. You're pushing the *Jack* hard these days."

"I appreciate the extra attention you're giving her, Chief."

"Just doing my job, Lieutenant. Somebody's got to make sure this bird stays in the air."

"Good. I need my crew at peak efficiency."

"Which means you need to trust me when I say you should grab some rack time before wheels up. It's critical for mission readiness. Even a five-minute power nap can do wonders."

"I'll manage."

"Will you, ma'am?" Ford's tone became heavy. "The success of this mission depends on your performance. A compromised pilot puts everyone at risk." A moment passed between them in silence. Ford stepped back, straightening.

Love's expression hardened. "You're exceeding your authority, Chief. Fall back in line. And I'll rest when the mission's complete."

Ford gave a crisp nod, his eyes conveying what his words couldn't. "Clear skies." He turned, disappearing into the flurry of activity on the hangar deck.

Frustration simmered beneath Love's skin as she made her way toward *Jack*.

"Lieutenant Love."

She turned to see Williams approaching, datapad in hand. "Chief Ford and I are about to perform the final checks together. Estimated time to completion is eight minutes."

"Very well. Proceed with urgency. We're on a tight schedule."

"Aye, Lieutenant."

As Williams moved to the Osprey, a group of medical personnel strode toward Love. They were dressed in combat fatigues with medical insignias, each carrying specialized gear.

A woman led the group. Love read the name on her tactical vest: "ITO." The woman saluted. "Major Emiko Ito, emergency physician, reporting for duty, Lieutenant."

The woman behind her, balancing a portable vital signs monitor, spoke next. "Flight Lieutenant Riley Shae, flight nurse, ma'am."

Two individuals hefting large trauma kits tailed them. The man introduced himself first. "Staff Sergeant Barney Abbot, combat medic." The woman beside him followed. "Staff Sergeant Poppy Huntley, also combat medic." Finally, two more personnel pushing collapsible medical tables followed: Corporal Daniel Huff and Corporal Emily Ash, medical technicians.

There were more medical personnel than Granger mentioned. Love nodded to them. "Welcome aboard, team. Get your gear stowed and tables set up in the troop bay."

The team moved into the Osprey's interior. Major Ito began assessing the medical equipment right away. "Corporal Huff, run a check on the oxygen supply. Corporal Ash, prep the trauma kits."

Staff Sergeant Abbot secured the collapsible stretchers. "We're setting up for multiple casualties. Any intel on the number of wounded?"

Love shook her head. "Not yet. Prepare for worst-case scenario."

Flight Lieutenant Shae was calibrating the vital signs monitors. "All monitoring equipment is online, ma'am."

Staff Sergeant Huntley said, "IV fluids secured and ready for rapid infusion if needed."

Huff and Ash pulled out the collapsible medical tables and locked them into place beside the main one. Huntley and Abbot unpacked their trauma kits, laying out supplies in nice rows, while Shae and Ito handled the bigger equipment—ventilators, cardiac monitors, and diagnostic tools.

The troop bay, usually meant for sixty-four soldiers, now looked like a dang good med unit. They'd used every bit of wall space for supplies. IV bags hung from ceiling hooks, and monitors were powered on, ready. What had been empty space minutes ago was now prepped for whatever casualties came their way.

"Major Ito," Love said, "how long until you're fully set up?"

Ito looked up from her work. "Five minutes, Lieutenant. We'll be ready before preflight is complete."

"Good." Love walked into the cockpit. It welcomed her with the soft glow of instrument panels. Sliding into the pilot's seat, she began the preflight sequence.

*Focus*, she told herself. She could feel her exhaustion starting to surface, but she shook it off.

She initiated the systems check, going over the controls. Every switch, every gauge responded as expected.

A sharp rap on the cockpit doorway caught Love's attention. Corporal Williams stood there with the datapad.

"Go ahead, Corporal."

"Just finished the weapons check, ma'am. The magrails and missiles are locked and loaded. Blaster cannons are primed. Countermeasure systems are green."

"Excellent."

Williams grinned. "This'll be a good flight. I can feel it."

Before Love could respond, Lieutenant Green, her copilot, squeezed past Williams into the cockpit. "All systems are go on my end."

Love nodded, hiding a yawn. "Let's hope that feeling of yours is right, Williams."

Green shot her a concerned look but said nothing.

"Lieutenant, fuel levels are at max capacity," Ford's voice crackled over the intercom.

"Roger that. Loadout secured?"

"Affirmative. Medical supplies are stowed, and stretcher positions are prepped."

"Copy. Gear up and stand by for departure."

"Standing by."

Love took a deep breath. Through the open hangar bay door, the forward operating base spread wide, personnel working and moving about on the tarmac. Mechanics prepped ships while others drove along in MJ-50 cargo tractors, towing equipment and supplies. The day waned. In the distance, plumes of smoke rose from ongoing battles, dark against the orange-tinted sky. The twin suns hung low on the horizon, resembling two massive fires descending into the landscape. Love glanced at the Osprey's dash clock: 1847 hours. Sunset was approaching rapidly.

Lieutenant Green said, "Lieutenant, engines spooled and ready for takeoff."

"Copy that. Let's get clearance and get airborne. What's the latest on our LZ?"

Green consulted his display. "LZ Whisper Point is still hot, ma'am. Enemy activity reported within three klicks. We're looking at a hot insert and extract."

Nothing unusual.

"Understood. We'll hug the weeds on our approach. Keep an eye on those terrain-following systems. I don't want any surprises in this fading light."

"Affirmative, Lieutenant. Terrain-following radar engaged and functioning nominally."

Love keyed her comm. "Tower, this is Wolfpack Actual, requesting immediate clearance for takeoff on heading four-nine-zero."

After a brief pause, the tower responded. "Wolfpack Actual, you're cleared for takeoff on heading four-nine-zero. Winds light and variable. Godspeed."

"Roger that, Tower. Wolfpack Actual rolling," Love replied, easing the throttle forward, feeling the subtle shift as the Osprey lifted off the deck. Guiding the craft out of the hangar, she adjusted her heading toward the coordinates uploaded to her nav system.

Behind her, the hangar shrank until it was just another point among the sea of lights on the base. She pushed the engines, the whir turning into a steady roar.

"Williams, status update."

"All systems operational. Navigational data confirmed. ETA to Whisper Point is twenty-five minutes at current speed."

"Keep an eye on the scanners for any unfriendlies."

"Will do."

Behind Love, in the troop bay, the medical team continued their preparations. From the cockpit, Major Ito briefed her team on potential scenarios. "Given the combat situation, expect blast injuries, gunshot wounds, and possible crush injuries."

"We've got universal donor blood ready if needed," Huntley said.

Ash's tone rang out: "Trauma kits are prepped and easily accessible, Major."

"Life support systems are all a go," Shae reported.

Love adjusted the controls as she scanned the instrument panel. Exhaustion tugged at the edges of her consciousness. Nonetheless, she shoved it aside. There would be time to rest later.

For now, she flew.

**Chapter 20:**
**No Rest for Love**

**Year 2097**
**In Flight to LZ Whisper Point**
**Planet Intus**

The steady thrum of *Jack*'s engines resonated through the cockpit, settling Love's nerves. She gripped the control stick and looked out at the horizon ahead. Intus unfurled below, its terrain cloaked in dusk's dim.

"Altitude holding steady at fifteen hundred meters," Green said from the copilot seat.

"Copy that," Love said. She double-checked the flight plan displayed on her HUD. The LZ was fifteen minutes out, a straight line disrupted only by the unpredictable Intus weather patterns.

Williams's voice came over the comms. "All good back here."

"Ford here. Magrails calibrated for atmospheric conditions. Cooling systems are optimal for sustained fire if needed."

"Excellent," Williams said. "How's the energy draw looking?"

"We're running at alpha level," Ford confirmed. "Power cells are fully charged. Ready for extended engagement. Backup units are also registering top-tier. We're REDCON-1 status across all boards, and it ain't changing."

"Good to hear," Williams said.

Love glanced sideways at Green. "Keep an eye on that storm front to the west. Don't want any surprises."

"Monitoring it. Winds are stable for now."

Love nodded, returning her focus ahead. Each passing second stretched for far too long. They needed to get these injured troops home, and if she could, she'd push this ship to its maximum speed. Yet best to remain calm, ready.

"ETA to LZ is ten minutes," Green said.

"Roger."

Minutes ticked by. At the seven-minute mark, Love opened a channel: "This is Wolfpack Actual to Ground Command. Approaching LZ Whisper Point. Requesting situation update."

"Copy, Wolfpack Actual," a voice crackled back. "LZ Whisper Point is secure at this time. Be advised, possible enemy activity reported in the vicinity. Skirmishes earlier have stirred up some unwanted attention."

"Understood, Ground Command. Maintaining alert status." Love adjusted their approach vector. She took a steadying breath. Images flickered in her mind—wounded soldiers, faces full of pain. Medevac missions carried a different type of stress.

"How's the weather looking?" Love asked.

"Wind speeds increasing slightly but within safe parameters," Green reported.

"Good. Continue keeping an eye on those scanners."

"Will do."

The terrain below grew more treacherous as they neared LZ Whisper Point. Jagged rocks and sparse, wind-beaten vegetation dotted the landscape. The ground rose and gained a good bit of elevation with each passing instant. In the distance, a massive stone spire jutted from the earth. It looked like an arrow, its tip penetrating high into the sky. The formation's sharp point explained half of this area's name, though the origin of "Whisper" remained a mystery to Love.

"Five minutes out," Green said.

"Time to earn our keep." Love pressed on her comm link to the troop bay. "Williams, Ford, get ready for deployment. We're on final approach."

"Roger that, Lieutenant," Ford said.

Love glanced back into the cabin, where the medical team was making final preparations. Major Emiko Ito, the emergency physician, was double-checking equipment with Flight Lieutenant Riley Shae, the flight nurse. Staff Sergeants Barney Abbot and Poppy Huntley organized their trauma kits, while Corporals Daniel Huff and Emily Ash made sure the collapsible medical tables were secure.

"Major Ito," Love said, "we're on final approach. You ready?"

Ito looked up. "We're set, Lieutenant."

As they descended, the landing zone came into view—a cleared space with infrared strobes, visible only through night vision devices or a Republic HUD screen. Figures moved below, some lying prone on stretchers, others standing by.

"Touchdown in thirty seconds," Green said.

"Bringing us in smooth."

"Yes, ma'am."

The Osprey's landing gear extended. Love eased back on the throttle, guiding *Jack* onto the ground. The moment the ramp lowered, the sounds of the battlefield rushed in—distant gunfire, shouted orders, far-off explosions.

Williams and Ford moved swiftly and descended the ramp to assist. Love leaned forward in her seat, eyes on the cockpit monitors. Even through the digital display, the reality of the situation hit her hard.

*******


Soldiers lay on bloodied stretchers, some missing limbs, bandages soaked through. As the med team moved out of the Osprey and into the clearing, Ito gave orders. "Shae! We've got an arterial bleed here! Move!"

Flight Lieutenant Shae rushed forward, applying pressure to the wound with gauze with one hand while she pulled out a tourniquet with the other. As soon as she had the tourniquet tightened, she grabbed a portable vital signs monitor. "BP's dangerously low, Major!"

Major Ito didn't have time to respond. Staff Sergeant Abbot knelt beside a soldier with a chest wound. "Huntley, I need that thoracic kit now!"

Staff Sergeant Huntley sprinted over with the trauma kit. "On it! Huff, prep the defibrillator!"

Corporal Huff scrambled to set up the equipment. "Ready in ten seconds!"

A Delta sergeant, face contorted in agony, let out a bloodcurdling scream as they lifted him. "Easy there," Ford said, helping to carry the weight.

"Got you," Williams added, taking the other side.

Nearby, Primord soldiers stood in stoic silence, their injured comrades receiving minimal attention. The contrast was jarring—their detachment a bit strange compared to human responses and reactions.

Major Ito hit her comm button. "Lieutenant Love, we've got eight critical, five stable," she reported, mentally triaging the order she would help the patients in. "Two might not make it to base."

"Understood. Get them loaded ASAP. We'll be wheels up in three."

Ito moved over to the soldier who had just had the defibrillator used on him. She looked up at the EKG monitor. "He's still in V-tach," Ito explained. "Push one milligram epi and continue compressions."

The soldier had been hit by a Zodark blaster, burning his left arm clean off at the elbow and apparently disrupting his heart's electrical signals. Ito ran through her mental checklist of any other contributing factors to the man's irregular heart rhythm.

"Let's get an IV of normal saline on him before we shock again," she directed. The soldier's body was going into shock, and the fluids might help turn it around.

The pilot, Lieutenant Love, interrupted Major Ito's thoughts. "Ito, we've got incoming hostiles. We need to go now!"

Major Ito shook her head. "Give me two minutes," she pleaded. "We can't move this one yet!"

"You've got one minute, then we're taking off, ready or not!" Love replied.

Outside the Osprey, gunfire erupted.

*Crap!"* thought Ito. *I need to get this guy stabilized.*

"CPR cycle is almost up," said Ito. "Everyone clear!"

The patient's heart rhythm was still in ventricular tachycardia, so she initiated another shock.

"Damn it, he's still in v-tach," said Ito. "Shae, push lidocaine and let's get oxygen on him."

The Osprey's bay filled with pained cries and monitors beeping. Ito could hear the sounds of battle outside getting closer.

"Ramp up! We're out of time!" Love ordered, powering up the engines.

The last of the medical team made it inside.

"All aboard," said the crew chief, Ford.

The Osprey lifted off the ground, and Major Ito's pulse quickened. Saving this soldier's life would be a little harder on the move, even if all the tables and beds were secured.

"Let's see if third time's the charm," said Ito. "Everyone, clear!"

After verifying that no one was touching the patient or the gurney the man was laying on, she initiated another shock.

"Yes!" Ito exclaimed. "We've got normal sinus rhythm."

The soldier came to with a start, letting out a horrified shout as he saw his missing arm for the first time. His cry was loud and agonizing enough that Ito was sure the pilot could hear it up in the front.

"It's all right, soldier," Lieutenant Shae reassured. "We're going to take care of you."

"Make sure we get his pain level under control," Ito directed. "I'm headed over to the next patient."

As Major Ito traversed across the back of the Osprey, assisted by her magnetic boots, she could catch a glimpse of dark clouds outside.

*Last thing we need!* thought Ito.

She moved over to a patient that had a weak and thready pulse, rapid breathing, and pale, clammy skin. He was clearly dealing with hypovolemic shock after significant blood loss. The medics already had saline running wide open through an IV.

"Lets get some oxygen on him and run some plasma," Ito ordered.

"Yes, ma'am," replied Staff Sergeant Poppy Huntley.

Ito's comm came to life. "ETA to base is eighteen minutes," said the co-pilot.

"Let's make it fifteen," Lieutenant Love replied. She felt the Osprey pick up speed, its engines whirring louder.

Major Ito moved on to a patient with a fifth degree burn on their leg. The charred white skin and exposed bone on the would have made the average person sick to their stomach, not to mention the distinct smell of burning flesh. However, Ito only saw a series of actions to be performed. The team had already elevated the patient's affected area above the level of the heart, started an IV, and sprayed the wound with a disinfecting solution.

"If we're going to save your leg, I need to get this nanite foam on your wound quickly," Ito explained. "I'm not going to lie to you—I've heard it is quite uncomfortable. Right now, you're not feeling any pain because your burn killed the nerves, but we're about to bring them back to life. I'm going to give you some meds on board to help with that, but don't try to be a hero. If you need more, just signal."

"OK, Doc," the young man replied, his voice shaking.

*I've got to make sure he doesn't go into shock*, Ito thought to herself.

She jumped to another patient while she waited for the pain meds to kick in. The soldier in question had had a compound fracture to his fibula and tibia after being thrown by a Zodark. His bones were exposed through the skin on his shin.

*Still, it could have been a lot worse*, she thought. The patient, although in a very serious condition, had been given pain medication and an IV. As long as he didn't develop compartment syndrome, he should recover quite well.

"Help me set the leg," Major Ito directed.

Staff Sergeant Barney Abbot quickly complied. They moved so swiftly that the patient didn't even really have time to react.

"Use the nanite sutures, and this one should be just fine," said Ito.

Major Ito returned to her burn patient and applied the nanite foam. The young soldier groaned in discomfort and tapped the side of the bed.

"I've got you, soldier," said Lieutenant Shae as she pushed more pain meds.

"Twelve minutes from base," the co-pilot announced.

"Turbulence ahead," warned Lieutenant Love.

Ito cursed under her breath. Her team was functioning like a well-oiled machine, but having their supplies slosh around could really put a kink in things. The view outside the windows grew progressively darker as they flew closer to whatever storm was about to disrupt their world.

"Major, we could use a hand over here!" said Staff Sergeant Huntley.

The soldier in question had apparently gotten too close to the claws of Zodark soldier—his midsection had huge gashes on it. Huntley and Corporal Huff had done their best to control the bleeding, but it was clear that the patient was crashing.

*What I wouldn't give for a stable floor and an operating table*, thought Ito. She was sure he had some internal bleeding, and the IV fluids weren't enough to remedy the shock his body was going through.

"Thank God for nanites," she muttered.

The Osprey shuddered as it was buffeted by heavy winds. The sky outside was nearly black now.

"Am I going to die?" asked the soldier before her. Ito noted how he looked too young in her mind to be here.

"Not if I have anything to do about it," she replied.

She struggled to keep her hands steady enough with all the turbulence to administer the nanite gel where it was needed most, but she did not let on just how difficult the procedure was. Ito watched his vitals pensively, breathing a bit easier when she observed his pulse and blood pressure stabilizing.

"I've got to move on to other patients, soldier, but you're in good hands," said Major Ito.

The young man grabbed her arm before she could rush off. He practically had tears in his eyes as he whispered, "Thanks, Doc."

She smiled briefly at him, putting her hand on his before replying, "No problem, soldier. Hang in there."

Then she was off yet again, to another patient.

"Four minutes out," co-pilot Green called over the increasing roar of the storm. "Base has emergency medical teams standing by."

"Almost there, people," said Love. "Hold on!"

Some of the supplies were magnetically attached to the tables, but even with secured medical supply bags, some of their gear started to slosh around. Major Ito grabbed at some gauze before it flew onto the floor.

*Sure hope our pilots know what they're doing*, thought Ito.

The next few minutes were fraught with tension. The first patient Ito had helped, the one who had gone into v-tach, was destabilizing again. She focused all her attention on keeping him alive despite the insane conditions. Then, suddenly, the Osprey touched down on a landing pad with a jolt.

"Medical teams are standing by, Major Ito," said her pilot, Lieutenant Love as the back hatch opened.

Ito and her team rushed forward with gurneys and equipment, prioritizing the most critical of the group to head to Medbay first. The crew of the Osprey helped them to move the more stable patients, which Ito noted with appreciation.

Love stood back, watching as each soldier was carefully moved. Major Ito looked up at Love as she coordinated with the base medical team. "Thanks for the quick extraction, Lieutenant."

"No problem."

*******


As the flurry of activity moved away from the Osprey, a strange emptiness fell onto Love. The adrenaline driving her was fading, or was that simply sleepiness pushing through?

Love exited the Osprey, stepping out into the rain. The droplets pelted her helmet. She opened her visor and took a deep breath, letting the warm air fill her lungs. Tilting her head back, she let the warm rain drops smack against her face.

The rest was short-lived. Her comm came to life with Commander Granger's voice.

"Lieutenant Love, we've got another situation. Can you and your team handle another medevac mission? Same medical crew."

"Yes, sir. We're on it. Send the intel to my HUD."

"Affirmative."

Love spotted Ford, Williams and Ito heading toward the hangar bay, helping guide a stretcher.

"Ford!" she called out, jogging after them. "I need your help."

Ford looked up, handing his end of the stretcher to another medic. "What you need, Lieutenant?"

"Energizer pills. We're heading out on another op."

Ford's brow furrowed. "Another mission? Now?"

"No time. We've got wounded out there."

Ford reached into his pocket and handed her a small bottle of pills. "At least let me get you some coffee."

Love nodded. Ford disappeared momentarily and returned with a mug. She downed the pills quickly, then took a sip. "It's cold." She drank it anyway.

"Lieutenant," Ford started, concern evident in his voice, "I—"

"We've got to go." She sprinted back toward *Jack*, its ramp lowered, waiting.

## Chapter 21:
## Interview with a Zodark

**Year 2097**
**RNS *Poseidon***
**In Orbit Above Jita**
**Rass Star System**

Captain Ripley Willis Lee stood in the hangar bay of the RNS *Poseidon*, arms crossed, his gaze fixed on the Republic shuttle that had just touched down. The craft's engines whined as they powered down, a faint hum reverberating through the deck. The shuttle was a sleek, angular design, its hull emblazoned with the Republic's insignia—a stark contrast to the scorched panels and scattered debris still littering the bay from the earlier skirmish. The air carried a faint tang of coolant and burnt metal, but the space was operational again, thanks to the crew's swift repairs.

The shuttle's rear ramp descended with a hydraulic hiss, and Lee straightened, his sharp eyes taking in the team as they emerged. He'd expected professionals, but he was modestly impressed by what he saw. Two distinct groups disembarked, each moving with purpose, their gear and equipment slung over shoulders or rolling on compact carts. The first group—three men in crisp Republic Intelligence uniforms, their kits marked with interrogation tools and medical supplies—exuded a quiet intensity. The second group, a five-man technical intelligence (TechInt) team, carried cases of diagnostic gear, quantum forensic rigs, and air-gapped analysis units, their faces lit with barely concealed excitement as they spotted the captured Zodark Vulture starfighter across the bay.

The Vulture sat in a cordoned-off section, its dark green hull absorbing the light, its aggressive geometry still inspiring a flicker of dread despite its damaged state. The starfighter had taken hits during the battle—a scorched wing, a cracked cockpit canopy—but it was largely intact, a prize that could yield critical intelligence if exploited properly.

The lead officer of the intelligence team approached Lee, his stride confident, his Republic Army uniform bearing the rank of Major. He was a tall man with a lean build, his dark hair cropped short, and his piercing gray eyes assessing Lee with a professional sharpness. He extended a hand, his grip firm as they shook.

"Commander Lee, I'm Major Daniel Voss, Det-5, Republic Intelligence," the officer said, his voice steady and authoritative. "I'm the commanding officer of this detachment. We're here to handle the Zodark prisoner and exploit the Vulture. Appreciate you getting us here quickly."

"Major Voss," Lee replied, nodding. "Welcome aboard the *Poseidon*. You made good time."

Voss gestured to the two men behind him, both looked to be in their thirties, their faces set with quiet determination. "This is my interrogation team. Mr. Marcus Hale, lead interrogator, and his partner Dr. Malik Reza, our resident xeno-behavioral psychologist specializing in Zodark physiology and culture. They make for a hell of a tiger team." Hale was broad-shouldered, his jaw set like he'd seen his share of tough assignments, while Reza carried a tablet with Sumerian glyphs on the screen. Reza struck Lee as being the analytical type, already calculating the challenge ahead.

Voss then nodded to the five-man TechInt team, who were already gravitating toward the Vulture, their gear carts parked beside them. "And this is my TechInt crew, led by Captain Ethan Chen, he's my chief analysts and engineer. That's Lieutenant Ryan Keller, Sergeant Nathan Brooks, Corporal David Lin, and Corporal James Patel. They'll handle the Vulture—air-gapped analysis, of course. We're not taking any chances with Zodark tech."

Lee took in the team. Voss's crew was clearly prepared to work immediately; their equipment was organized and their focus sharp. He respected that kind of efficiency, even if he was still annoyed at the detour. Across the bay, he caught Captain Chen whispering to Keller, his voice tinged with excitement. "Look at that Vulture—damaged, but not bad. If the nav and comms systems are still functional, we're in business. I can't believe our luck."

"Hope like hell it doesn't blow up in our faces," Keller muttered back, half-joking, as he adjusted a diagnostic scanner on his cart. "We'll need to assess the threat level to us and the ship before we crack it open."

Voss turned back to Lee, his tone brisk. "Commander, we'll need a place to stow our gear and a secure workspace for the TechInt team—preferably near the Vulture, with isolated systems for their analysis. My interrogators also need to see the prisoner ASAP to begin their assessment. Do you have a place we can we set up?"

Lee uncrossed his arms, gesturing toward the bay's exit. "I'll have my crew set you up. There's a secure compartment near the brig for your interrogation team to store gear and work—close enough to access the prisoner. For the TechInt team, we'll clear a section of the hangar bay here, near the Vulture. We've got portable barriers to give your people some privacy and isolated power units to keep everything air-gapped. My engineers will ensure your systems stay disconnected from the ship's network."

Voss nodded, satisfied. "Appreciate it, Commander."

Lee continued, his tone firm but not unkind. "One thing you should know, Major—we're still on patrol. The *Poseidon* has a mission to scout Zodark activity in this sector, and until I get orders to return to Primord or Republic space, I'm continuing that mission. You'll have what you need, but I can't afford distractions."

Voss met Lee's gaze, his expression unwavering. "Understood, Commander. We won't interfere with your mission. My team operates independently—all we need is a place to work, a steady comm link to our backend support and higher headquarters, and time. If we obtain any actionable intel, you'll be the first to know. We'll share everything that can help your operation."
******

The secure compartment adjacent to the brig hummed with quiet intensity, its sterile walls reflecting the soft glow of medical consoles and a holoscreen feed. The air was cool, tinged with the faint antiseptic scent of the ship's filtration system. Beyond the thick transparent barrier, the Zodark pilot, who they had managed to identify as Zar'Qui based on his identification, sat restrained in his cell, alloy chains anchoring his four muscular arms to the reinforced grid floor. His leathery blue skin glistened under the overhead lights, and his three eyes tracked every movement with predatory focus. The Zodark's chest rose and fell steadily, but his silence carried the weight of defiance.

In the adjacent command room, Commander Ripley Lee stood beside Major Daniel Voss, eyes glued to the holoscreen feed. Lee's jaw was set, but his gaze betrayed fascination—a captain accustomed to battle, now witnessing a different kind of warfare. Voss, tall and lean, monitored a separate tablet, cross-referencing incoming data from the TechInt team in the hangar bay.

Marcus Hale stood before the barrier, adjusting a small earpiece linked to the Altairian universal translator mounted on the wall. His broad shoulders were relaxed, and a disarming smile played on his lips, as if he were about to chat with an old friend. Beside him, Dr. Malik Reza calibrated a console, his lean frame rigid, his dark eyes fixed on the biometric readouts streaming from sensors embedded in Zar'Qui's restraints. The console's interface displayed heart rate, neural activity, and blood chemistry, each spike a clue to the Zodark's state of mind.

Hale glanced at Reza, his voice low. "Ready to dance, Doctor?"

Reza's lips barely moved, his tone icy. "Keep him talking. I'll handle the pressure." He tapped a command, and a faint hiss signaled the release of Neuroplex-4, a happy drug, into the cell's ventilation. The compound, designed to lower inhibitions and boost suggestibility, dispersed as a fine mist, invisible but potent.

The Zodark's nostrils flared, his head tilting slightly as the drug took effect. His three eyes narrowed, but a subtle looseness crept into his posture, his chained arms relaxing a fraction.

The display in the command room showed Hale and Reza at work, their voices clear through the secure link. "They're good," Lee said, almost to himself. "Like watching a surgeon and a chess master at once."

Voss nodded, his gray eyes flicking to Lee. "Hale's the scalpel, Reza's the hammer. They'll crack him, but it'll take time. Zodarks don't break easily." He tapped his tablet. "Chen's team is pulling data from the Vulture now—flight logs, mostly. We'll use it to verify whatever this pilot says."

Lee's comm beeped, and he activated it. "Lee to Bridge. Sato, I need you to set up a secure channel to Captain Roberts and our Primord liaison. As Voss and his team work, I'll send them regular updates on what they're uncovering and how we might be able to use it."

"Understood, sir," Sato replied. "That's a good idea. I think Roberts will like that. I'll make sure the reports are sent as I receive them."

Lee returned his attention to the brig and the drama unfolding as he watched with rapt attention as the lead interrogator, Hale, began his dance.

Marcus Hale stood before the barrier, his broad shoulders relaxed, a warm smile softening his rugged features. His earpiece, linked to the Altairian universal translator, hummed faintly. Beside him, Dr. Malik Reza monitored a console, his lean frame taut, his dark eyes scanning biometric readouts—heart rate, neural activity, blood chemistry. The console's sensors, embedded in Zar'Qui's restraints, provided a window into the Zodark's physiology, but the team needed a baseline to distinguish truth from deception.

Hale's voice was easy, almost conversational, as he began. "Zar'Qui, I'm Marcus. That's Dr. Reza. You holding up all right in there? The brig's not exactly cozy, but if you need water, medical attention, anything like that, just say the word." His tone was genuine, inviting trust, his eyes studying Zar'Qui's reaction.

Zar'Qui's middle eye narrowed, his voice a low growl through the translator. "Your concern is wasted, human. I need nothing from you." His posture remained rigid, but a faint twitch in his lower left arm betrayed a flicker of discomfort—perhaps from the restraints or the lingering effects of the stun darts.

Reza's console registered the response. After noting the heart rate and neural activity, he must have determined that Zar'Qui was speaking the truth or was at least neutral because he nodded ever so slightly to Hale, who continued, undeterred.

"Fair enough," Hale said, his smile unwavering. "Must be tough, though, being away from your clan. The D'Shawni, right? I hear they're a proud bunch. You got family back home? Siblings, maybe, or young ones waiting for you?" His question was soft, probing without pressure, designed to elicit a response Zar'Qui wouldn't feel compelled to lie about.

Zar'Qui's three eyes flickered. "I have… offspring. Four. They are strong, like their mother." His voice carried a trace of pride. The Zodark's physiology relaxed a bit as he spoke of something personal. Reza studied his console and nodded to Hale once again.

In the adjacent command room, Commander Lee watched the holoscreen feed, arms crossed, his sharp eyes tracking the interplay. Beside him, Voss monitored a tablet, cross-referencing data from the TechInt team dissecting the Vulture starfighter in the hangar bay. Lee's jaw was set, but his expression held a quiet awe at the interrogators' craft—a chess game played with words and drugs, not weapons.

"Huh, so this is how it's done," Lee murmured. "Start easy, then go hard?"

Voss nodded, his gray eyes flicking to the tablet. "Something like that. Right now, Hale is establishing the baselines for Reza's bag of tricks. They're a deadly duo once they get going. Hale sets the traps. Reza springs them. Give them some time—they'll paint you a picture."

"Yeah, of what?" asked Lee quizzically.

"Don't know. Sometimes it's a picture of what's happening in the grand scheme of things, other times, it's just a snapshot of what just happened. The more they can keep the prisoner talking, the more they can extract. The more we piece it all together with information from other prisoners, signals intelligence and other data points, we begin to gain an understanding of what's happening around us," Voss casually explained. "Then when we pair all that information together with some of our AIs… let's just say they are powerful tools if you know how to use them."

"I'll bet," commented Lee as he watched Hale continue his craft. "And Chen's team? How do they fit into this?"

"Two-fold—they help to verify the prisoner information by comparing it against whatever electronic information they are able to retrieve, while also unlocking further digital insights into how the Zodark Empire and its military operate," Voss explained. "If we're lucky, they'll uncover the flight logs, locations, and possibly other warships the fighter's mothership was in contact with or near. Who knows? They might uncover a pending operation in Rass or even Intus we aren't aware of yet. We'll see, though—it takes time and careful practice to navigate your way through alien technology and electronics." He held a hand up to forestall Lee from asking another question before turning up the volume to listen to the interrogator's next question.

Lee had been half-listening to Hale continue to talk to the Zodark about his children while Voss had answered his questions, but it did seem that the conversation was about to turn.

Hale casually commented, "I always wanted to be a pilot—to see the stars the way you are able to. I hear it feels like you could reach out and touch the cosmos with your hand," he regaled whimsically.

Zar'Qui smiled slightly, nodding along.
*******


The subtle hiss of pressurized vapor passed unnoticed beneath the ambient hum of the chamber's filtration system.

Dr. Malik Reza watched the atmospheric readout spike by half a percent—just enough to signify the next dose of Neuroplex-4 had begun circulating.

He adjusted the feed, then glanced at the biometric overlays hovering above the interrogation table. Zar'Qui, bound and seated, barely twitched—but Reza wasn't watching for gross movements. He was watching for micro-tells.

The middle eye twitch came first. Then a half-degree slump of the shoulders.

*Good*, thought Dr. Reza. The added dose of N4 was taking hold.

Opposite the room, Hale leaned casually against the wall console, arms crossed, tone warm and conversational. He was in the groove now—building rapport, seeding suggestion, all without a single raised voice.

"Congratulations," Hale said smoothly. "Four children—that's a handful. I'll bet they're proud of their dad, flying a Vulture out there."

Zar'Qui lifted his chin, puffing his chest ever so slightly. "They are, as I am of my father and grandfathers before me. Service to the Empire brings honor to our family name, our tribe, and our clan."

On Reza's console, neural activity spiked in the honesty quadrant—baseline confirmed. *The truth, at least in this Zodark's mind.*

Hale kept going, relaxed but deliberate. "I always wanted to be a pilot, you know. Always imagined what it'd be like—slicing through the stars, the whole galaxy at your fingertips."

Zar'Qui tilted his head slightly, curious.

"I mean," Hale went on, "we've got pilots in the Republic, sure, but you..." He gestured, smiling. "You've danced between dreadnoughts, haven't you? Woven through an armada, ships bristling with weapons, with comrades at your side. That's not something many of us get to see. That's... glorious."

Reza saw the shift—posture softening, pride swelling. The N4's euphoric whisper was now inside Zar'Qui's bloodstream, tinkering gently with inhibition pathways, dulling the survival instinct, amplifying emotional resonance. It didn't make a subject spill secrets—it made them *want* to share.

*A dangerous thing, euphoria.*

"You are right to be jealous, Hale," Zar'Qui replied, voice rising with pride. "The sight of a sea of warships—shaped by flame and fury—is awe inspiring. Your kind has no idea the force about to be unleashed upon you."

Reza noted the phrasing: future-tense confidence, not speculation…certainty.

He tapped a marker into the interrogation log. This would be another useful string to pull later.

To Reza, pharmacological interrogation wasn't some crude shortcut—it was science as leverage. Every subject had a threshold. Some required pain. Others just needed to feel heard. He could deliver both.

His fingers hovered near a separate control on the console—Pyroxin-K, the fire drug. It was a different tool—the stick to N4's carrot. Hale hadn't asked for it yet.

*Not now*, thought Reza. *Not while Zar'Qui was still basking in his own ego.*

Reza allowed himself the faintest smile.

The dance was just beginning.

<h1 style="text-align:center">Chapter 22:<br>Second Thoughts</h1>

**Year 2097**
**RNS *Gallipoli***
**Intus Orbit**

Mission parameters flashed across Coop's pod simulator screen. On Intus below, his Orion drone soared into the dusky skies. The horizon dimmed with the last remnants of daylight.

"Coop, you good?" Raven's voice crackled in his helmet.

"All good," Coop replied. "Bear, you with us?"

"Right on your wing," Bear affirmed. "Let's keep it tight."

They curled their starfighters around the Forward Operating Base Oteren, lights twinkling on the complex like stars fallen to earth. His HUD indicators caught a silhouette descending onto a pad—the *Jack*. Lieutenant Naomi Love's Osprey settled smoothly.

"Hold formation," Coop said, pulling his attention back to the mission.

"Eyes on the prize, Coop," Raven teased.

Coop smirked despite himself. "Just making sure our favorite pilot sticks the landing."

"She always does," Bear chimed in. "Now, about that convoy…"

"Affirmative," Coop said. "Let's review the operation parameters. Our primary objective is to gather intel on the convoy's composition, cargo, and destination without being detected. This information is crucial for upcoming operations against Zodark supply lines. Right now, with our systems just updated after the last security breach, it's absolutely critical not to get shot down and if you do, you better make sure you hit the self-destruct on your drone before you lose contact with it. The last thing we want is for any Zodark scum to get their hands on our latest drone tech. They've already spoofed us once, and our countermeasures are barely in place. If they captured one of our drones now, they might be able to reverse engineer our newest security protocols and system architecture. It could give them the edge to develop undetectable infiltration methods. Next time, we might not even know they're spoofing our systems until it's too late. If there's even a hint of detection, we abort immediately. The intel's valuable, but not at the cost of giving the Zodarks a roadmap to bypass our latest defenses. We can't afford to let them leapfrog our security again."

"Got it, Coop. Maintaining low altitude and reduced velocity," Raven said. "Standard approach protocol."

Coop adjusted his heading, the drone responding well. They dipped lower, the canopy of trees brushing beneath. The twilight made shadows move in awkward ways, the landscape a vista of dark shapes and fading light.

"Hostile detection system active at zero-nine-zero degrees," Raven noted.

"Acknowledged," Coop said. "Initiating countermeasures. Stand by." Coop tapped a bunch of commands, and from his drone, a cluster of decoy signals burst forth, scattering like seeds on the wind. "Decoys away."

Bear's voice carried a note of satisfaction. "That should effectively obscure our presence."

"Maintain current altitude," Coop said. "Avoid providing clear targeting opportunities."

"Confirmed," Raven said. "Observing significant signal interference on monitoring systems."

Coop assessed his display. The hostile detection sweeps now showed considerable electronic noise, concealing their actual positions. "This should provide adequate cover."

"And potentially divert their analysis resources," Bear said.

They continued, maintaining their course. "Be advised," Coop said. "Detecting anomalous readings."

"Please clarify," Raven replied.

"Intercepting data transmissions from the target. However, they're exhibiting unusual characteristics. Not matching known protocols," Coop explained.

Bear sounded unconcerned. "Could be insignificant. Possible environmental interference."

"Possibly." Coop remained alert.

"Conducting supplementary scan," Raven said. "Confirming anomalous transmissions. Potential countermeasures from the target."

"Or more complex defenses," Coop replied. He banked hard, easily avoiding a jutting rock face. A mountain range filled his view.

"Your tone's a bit different, Coop. Are you considering mission abort?" Bear asked.

Bear knew him well—Coop's subtle tells, his change in vocal pitch, and what they meant. "Just evaluating all scenarios," Coop replied. He guided them toward a narrow pass between the peaks.

"Coop," Bear pressed, "we've operated under more severe conditions. The mission objectives remain paramount. We're fine."

Coop maneuvered his starfighter drone through a narrow mountain passage. The jagged walls of rock were mere meters from his wingtips. The corridor twisted and turned, which meant split-second vector changes.

On his heads-up display, Coop tracked the icons representing Raven's and Bear's Orion fighters. They followed his lead, adapting to the challenging terrain. The mountain's heart seemed to constrict around them, and the passage narrowed further as they progressed.

Shadows crossed Coop's screens as the peaks above intermittently blocked the sunlight. The drone's sensors showed a real-time holomap of the corridor, highlighting obstacles and the safest flight paths in subtle outlines on Coop's HUD. Adrenaline hit him as they emerged from the mountain's grip, the sky opening up before them.

"Well, that was fun. Anyway, I concur with Bear," Raven said. "Recommend adhering to established protocol."

Coop's brain spun. Memories of the last mission surfaced—the confusion, the pseudo-friendly fire, the nagging suspicion of internal sabotage.

"Consider the discrepancies from our last engagement," Coop said. "These anomalies may indicate more significant issues."

"Negative. Command just provided clarification on that matter. We are good to go," Bear said.

"Really? Did they provide satisfactory explanations?" Coop asked. "Or merely downplay the incidents?"

"Coop, what's the deal? Are you going to question everything now? We gotta focus on the mission objectives," Bear replied.

Coop hesitated, his finger over the throttle. "I'm just saying we should exercise caution. This could be a strategic misdirection, fellas."

"Look, Coop, you're overanalyzing the situation. Looking for things that aren't there," Bear said.

"Coop, we need your decision," Raven responded. "Do we proceed with the operation?"

The convoy's position shifted slightly on Coop's HUD. The sensor readings wavered, the equipment struggling to lock onto the target as if they were trying to hold on to smoke.

They approached low at Mach 4 at 4,900 kilometers per hour. They were 816 kilometers away from their target—a distance they could cover in about ten minutes if they maintained their current velocity.

The ground rushed by in a continuous emerald smudge. Clearings, lakes, and outcroppings streaked by in the blink of an eye. Coop searched for any sign of a trap or unexpected resistance. The sheer speed of their approach left little room for error.

"Affirmative," Coop said at last. "If we detect anything out of the norm or if it feels like our systems are compromised, we abort."

"Acknowledged," Raven confirmed.

Bear's tone lightened. "Excellent."

They advanced. Still, Coop couldn't shake the unease. He'd looked over the readouts, seeking patterns, inconsistencies—anything to confirm his suspicions, or perhaps challenge them. Maybe he was wrong. But… wait… "Detecting a spike in data transmission."

"Likely insignificant," Bear replied.

"The pattern seems too uniform for random interference," Coop said.

Raven responded, "Possible encrypted communication between convoy units."

Coop scrunched his face, the lines around his nose wrinkling. "But, Raven, they could be coordination of unknown elements."

"What's your reasoning?" Bear challenged. "Our presence remains undetected."

"Unless it doesn't," Coop said.

Bear sighed. "What-if, what-if. If you can't make a decision because we are seeing ghosts where there aren't any. Maybe you need to hand off control to someone else."

"No, you're right. I think I'm just being overly cautious," Coop admitted.

They skimmed over treetops, the foliage whizzing beneath them. In the distance, the skeleton of a new Primord city rose against the horizon. Half-finished structures reached skyward, surrounded by drones flying about, helping with the construction effort. Enormous cranes pivoted. Fleets of compact stratolayers flew between the rising structures. From what little Coop knew, the stratolayers were agile single-pilot shuttles. Each was flown by a skilled architectural engineer. Some ferried essential materials, while others examined the emerging edifices. The stratolayers, about the size of ground vehicles, moved well as they navigated the partially completed buildings. Their pilots guided them through narrow gaps and around protruding beams.

"Look, we've got decoys up," Raven said. "Our signatures are masked."

Coop took a breath, weighing his options. The mission clock ticked, each second a reminder of their dwindling window. Were they being fed incorrect information and lured into danger, or was everything as it should be? "We continue the operation. But we'll adjust our approach vector to maintain unpredictability."

They needed to get closer for clearer scans. At the same time, proximity increased the risk of detection. Something wasn't right. The sensor readings were fluctuating. The data was distorted.

*This doesn't make sense*, Coop thought. *It's like they knew we were coming.*

He cycled through different scanning frequencies, but the interference remained.

"Agreed," Bear said. "Let's complete the objective."

Coop changed his drone's course a little, the others following suit.

"Maintain communication discipline," he ordered. "Radio silence unless absolutely critical."

"Understood," Raven confirmed.

As silence took over, Coop remained locked on his HUD, every anomaly a potential threat.

Three minutes later, the convoy came into the sensors' visual range. On Coop's screen, a line of armored vehicles trundled along a narrow valley path. These looked like Primord vehicles, but that was the point, as intel had pointed out. These were Zodarks driving these things, moving who knew what to who knew where.

The vehicles resembled Earther assault and supply transports with an alien twist. Their shapes were more rounded, almost bulbous, reflecting the Primords' love for organic, flowing designs. Heavily armored personnel carriers led the way, their dome-like turrets swiveling. Behind them lumbered supply trucks, their bloated forms hinting at vast cargo holds within.

Interspersed among these were smaller, faster vehicles—probably scouts or command units. Their podlike shapes seemed almost out of place among their bulkier counterparts.

"Visual on target," Coop said.

"Copy visual," Raven and Bear echoed.

Coop's pulse quickened. "Initiating scan." Data streamed in, but the readings remained erratic. "Still getting interference."

"Could be some kind of electromagnetic anomaly," Raven suggested. "Gotta get closer."

"Or intentional jamming," Coop replied.

Bear's impatience bled through. "Do we have enough to report back?"

"Not yet," Coop said. "Need clearer intel."

Coop surveyed his holographic display. He manipulated his Orion's sensor arrays. Each touch initiated a different scanning protocol. One activated a deep-penetrating infrared sweep, while another initiated a multispectral analysis of the convoy's emissions.

"Careful," Raven warned. "Don't tip our hand."

Coop nodded. "I know."

He pulled up a secondary display, fingers sliding across a particle density readout. A twist of his wrist fine-tuned the resonance detectors, searching for any odd energy signatures betraying the convoy's true nature.

The more he tried to clarify the data, the more it seemed to run from him. Unease settled deeper in his gut as he cycled through different frequency bands, each giving only static or garbled data.

"Coop, time's up," Bear said. "We need to move closer or bug out."

Recent intelligence briefings showed a new Zodark capability—the potential to hack into, and hijack, Republic drone technology, a feat that could compromise the Republic's entire tactical advantage on Intus.

The Orion drones were equipped with entanglement communication systems, a technology they had thought unbreakable until now. They'd thought wrong. He grimaced. One wrong decision could create a security nightmare.

*Am I overthinking this?* Coop thought.

"We show ourselves at this low altitude, they can knock us down," Coop said. He hesitated once more, torn between the necessity of the mission and the instinct to retreat.

"Coop?" Raven said.

As Coop debated in his mind, on his HUD, the convoy's blips scattered. Vehicles veered off the main path, disappearing under the dense forest canopy.

"They're breaking formation," Coop said. He pushed the controls forward. The data feeds blinked. Troop numbers and logistical details faded quickly.

"What's happening?" Raven's voice cut in.

"They're breaking formation," Coop repeated. "Losing their signals."

Troop numbers, vehicle types, and details they'd barely begun to catalog faded from the screens.

"Damn it," Coop muttered. "We've got almost nothing. The intel we managed to gather is minimal at best."

He manipulated the sensors, trying to recapture the fleeing signals. However, the forest seemed to swallow their targets whole, leaving them with little more than small amounts of the important information they'd come for.

Bear grunted, the sound laced with frustration. "Increase sensor range. We can't lose them now. We hesitated."

Coop toggled the controls to amplify the drone's scanners. The visuals blurred. Static crept in. "It's no use. They're slipping out of range."

"How can they just vanish?" Raven asked.

"Maybe they've got underground facilities," Coop said. "Where the hell did they go?"

Their targets had slipped away, carrying off the info they'd been tasked to obtain.

This should have been a straightforward operation—a quick, stealthy op to gather data without alerting the enemy. They should have been in and out before anyone had known they were there. Coop knew that if he hadn't second-guessed himself, if he'd trusted his equipment and training, they'd have secured valuable intel.

*Why am I being like this? Why hesitate?* Coop asked himself. He didn't know. Fear? He wanted to stare in a mirror and yell at himself. He'd blown a routine reconnaissance into a major issue. And all because of his growing paranoia about potential Zodark electronic warfare attacks.

"Circle back," Coop said. "Maybe we can catch a trace."

They banked their drones, performing a wide sweep over the area. The forest stretched everywhere, shadows melding into one another as dusk settled in.

"Still nothing," Raven reported after a few minutes.

"We're wasting time," Bear said. "Command will want our Orions back."

"All right. Form up and head back to base," Coop said.

They ascended. The flight back was somber. Failure felt heavy in Coop's drone pod, almost blanketing him. The intel they'd failed to gather could have shown crucial weaknesses in Zodark supply lines. Now, those vulnerabilities would remain hidden. This would potentially cost lives in future missions.

As they approached FOB Oteren, the base spread out wide across the Intus landscape. Their drones homed in on the landing zone, guided by the base's beacon.

"Proceeding to landing sequence," Coop said.

One by one, the Orion drones touched down on the tarmac, their engines powering down. Coop deactivated his control interface, and the holographic displays faded away.

The pod's door slid open with a hiss. He removed his helmet, stepping out onto the simulation chamber's raised platform.

Exhaustion seeped into Coop's muscles. More than that, a growing frustration twisted inside him. He replayed the mission in his mind—the hesitation, the lost opportunity.

"What's wrong with me?" he said to himself in a whisper, rubbing his temples.

Bear headed toward him. "You all right?"

"Fine."

Raven joined them. "We did what we could."

"Hardly," Coop snapped. He took a breath. "Sorry. I just… we had them, and then—"

"Hey, things happen," Bear interrupted. "Come on, debriefing's in five. We're the last team to return. They're waiting for us."
*******

They walked toward the debriefing room. Crew members moved past them, discussing routines and repairs, oblivious to Coop's inner hell. He wanted to pull his hair out.

Reaching the debriefing room, they filed in along with several other squadron leaders and their teams. The large space quickly filled with pilots, all standing at attention. Strike took his position at the front, hands clasped behind his back. "At ease."

Coop stood between Bear and Raven, his posture rigid, aware of the squadron leaders flanking his team.

"Today's operation was a multipronged reconnaissance effort, targeting several key Zodark supply routes. Intelligence gathered from these convoys is vital to our ongoing strategic planning." Strike paused, scanning the room. "I'm pleased to report that several teams achieved their primary objectives, securing valuable data on enemy movements and capabilities."

His gaze then locked onto Coop. "However, not all units met with equal success. Lieutenant Cooper?"

Although the other pilots maintained their professional demeanor, Coop could feel their sideways glances.

"Sir," Coop said.

"There was a window of opportunity to gather the necessary intel. It required prompt action. Hesitation in the field cost us dearly."

"Understood, sir."

"You froze, Cooper. That's not just about you anymore. Every second you waste second-guessing yourself puts a target on all our backs. We drill, we train, we prepare for a reason. When it's go time, you act. Anything less, not acceptable."

"Aye, sir."

To Coop's surprise, Strike's expression lightened a little. "Trust your judgment, Lieutenant. You've demonstrated skill in the past. We need that decisiveness."

Coop nodded. "I will, sir."

Strike addressed the room. "That goes for all of you. Dismissed."

As the group dispersed, Strike spoke up again. "One moment. The following pilots stay behind: Cooper, Bear, Raven, Phantom, Ninja, and Ajax." Strike waited until the others had left. "At 0600 hours tomorrow, you'll commence training on the AS-90 Reaper drones. Since the battle for Intus is now more of a ground campaign supporting the Army, the need for more pilots flying ground attack drones is needed, and our squadron is going to provide some pilots for it. I decided to assign the six of you to this mission, to support our Army brothers slogging it out with the Zodarks."

Coop's pulse quickened. The Reapers were top-tier attack drones, reserved for specialized missions.

"We have a covert operation in development," Strike said. "You'll be trained and prepped as the primary team."

Bear kept a professional demeanor. "Understood, sir."

"What's the mission parameters?" Raven asked.

"Details will be provided during training," Strike replied. "For now, focus on familiarizing yourselves with the Reaper systems." He glanced at his datapad. "Report to Simulation Room Alpha at 0600 sharp. Dismissed."

The pilots nodded in unison. "Yes, sir."

As they exited the room, they headed down several corridors toward their barracks. While Coop walked, the echo of Strike's words followed him.

*Trust your judgment.*

He clenched his fists. Tomorrow was another day—a new opportunity. The path ahead was uncertain, but for the first time in a while, he felt some hope. That he could do this with confidence—and he promised himself he would.

**Chapter 23:**
**Cracks in the Core**

**Sector 3**
**Moon Kaelus, Zhoraan Orbit**
**Rass System**
**RNS** *Poseidon*

The air inside Hangar Bay 4 was thick with the acrid scent of overheated electronics and bitter, reheated coffee. Major Daniel Voss maneuvered past armored isolation containers, diagnostic equipment, and bundles of thick data cables sprawled across the deck like mechanical veins. At the hangar's heart stood the captured Zodark Vulture, its sleek hull still exuding menace, even immobilized and inert.

Detachment 5's best minds clustered around the alien starfighter, each Republic Army tech analyst and intelligence specialist deeply immersed in their work. They'd been at this relentlessly for days, and fatigue showed clearly in their weary postures and shadowed eyes.

Voss approached Captain Ethan Chen, who stood focused, hunched over a glowing terminal, his eyes tracking complex lines of alien code. Chen didn't even glance up at Voss's arrival.

"Captain Chen," Voss announced calmly, leaning in slightly to draw the man's attention without startling him.

Chen blinked hard, breaking his concentration. He straightened, stretching his shoulders. "Major Voss. Didn't see you there. Sorry—it's been a long couple of days."

"Understandable," Voss replied with a knowing nod. "What's your status here? Have we extracted anything actionable yet?"

Chen gestured toward the alien craft. "We have, but it wasn't easy. The Zodarks weren't amateurs. They layered multiple security countermeasures into the fighter's system— viral payloads, recursive firewalls, even physical data traps. We had to pull the entire data core out and move it into an isolated sandbox network—fully air-gapped from the

*Poseidon*'s systems. Took two full days just to safely breach the initial encryption."

"But you got through," Voss prompted.

Chen's tired expression turned into a cautious, satisfied grin. "We did, sir. Once inside, we recovered comprehensive flight logs from the Vulture's onboard navigational core. They confirm multiple recent rendezvous points in the Rass system between this fighter and its mothership, a Zodark cruiser designated Za'rath. Our analysts are pinpointing the exact coordinates, but we've already identified at least four confirmed staging locations."

Voss inhaled slowly, letting the implications settle in. The significance of these staging points was enormous. They now had real targets—clear opportunities to strike back against the Zodark offensive.

"What else?" Voss asked, his voice tight with anticipation. "Fleet composition? Order of battle?"

Chen's fingers tapped the console rapidly, bringing up a cascade of data visualizations. "Better than we'd dared to hope. The fighter logged passive sensor sweeps of Zodark fleet assets operating in close proximity. Confirmed numbers include forty-two frigates, thirty-seven cruisers, thirty-one battleships, a single star carrier—the first hard evidence of one encountered by Republic forces—and three Orbot battleships. It's an unprecedented intelligence coup."

Voss stared at the screen, momentarily stunned by the magnitude of the intel. It felt as if they'd just been handed the keys to the enemy's war chest. Detachment 5 had justified every ounce of faith placed in their expertise.

"Outstanding, Captain Chen," Voss finally replied, genuine admiration in his tone. "Your team just changed the strategic calculus. Keep digging—I want every byte you can extract. No stone unturned."

"Understood, sir. We're only scratching the surface so far," Chen assured him, energy renewed by Voss's evident excitement.

Voss stepped toward his workstation at the hangar's edge, his mind already organizing the critical points of his forthcoming intelligence report. This data would reshape battle plans, strengthen alliances with the Primords, and give their reconnaissance mission the strategic initiative it desperately needed.

Sliding into his chair, Voss keyed open a secure comm line. A calm automated voice prompted, "Please state recipient."

"Commander Lee. Priority channel," Voss stated crisply. "I need to speak with him immediately."

*******

**RNS *Poseidon***
**Commander's Ready Room**

Commander Ripley Lee leaned forward at his workstation, swiftly punching in his command code as the priority channel indicator flashed urgently. The screen cleared, revealing Major Daniel Voss, his face barely concealing restrained excitement.

"Commander Lee," Voss began, getting straight to the point. "We've cracked open the Zodark fighter's data core. It's been a goldmine."

Lee sat upright, his attention razor-sharp. "Tell me."

Voss took a deep breath, organizing his thoughts. "Captain Chen's team has recovered extensive navigational data from the Vulture. We've positively identified several staging points within the Rass system, locations frequently visited by the Zodark cruiser Za'rath, the ship this fighter was operating from. We can't say with certainty, but these coordinates could be Zodark staging points or possible logistic bases."

Lee felt his pulse quicken, adrenaline surging through his veins at the implications of this news. He'd risked straying from his primary mission when they had captured this Zodark pilot—and now that gamble had paid dividends beyond anything he'd hoped. He felt a sense of vindication swell in his chest.

"There's more," Voss continued eagerly. "We were able to a confirm a breakdown of warships from passive sensor sweeps of the captured Vulture. This is by no means a list of the enemy fleet, just the vessels the Vulture was in contact with. Its substantial—forty-two Zodark frigates, thirty-seven cruisers, thirty-one battleships, a star carrier—this is the first confirmed Republic sighting in Rass—and three Orbot battleships. It's the clearest intelligence picture we've ever had of their fleet disposition in the Rass system."

Lee's mind raced with the news. This was beyond anything he thought they would find. With such precise fleet intelligence, Republic and Primord planners could finally move from reactive posturing to proactive strikes.

"Major, this is outstanding work," Lee said firmly, his tone professional but energized. "Give my complements to Captain Chen and your entire team. Keep at it, who knows what else we might find. I'd like you to keep me updated as new intel emerges. Who knows, we might be able to put some of it to good use."

"Of course, Commander. You'll have them," Voss confirmed, nodding crisply. "We're barely scratching the surface here. I'll let you know when we find something more."

"Good," Lee replied, ending the call and switching immediately to a separate secure channel. Lieutenant Commander Sato's calm features appeared on the comm screen, ready as always.

"Sir?"

"Sato, it looks like Det-5 hit the jackpot." Lee quickly relayed the findings from Voss's team, laying out the captured navigational data and detailed enemy fleet composition. Sato's eyes widened slightly—the closest she ever came to outright astonishment.

"This changes the entire dynamic of our mission, sir," she responded quietly. "How do you want to proceed?"

Lee didn't hesitate. "Prepare a full intel summation. Make sure Captain Roberts and our Primord allies receive priority copies. Flag it urgent—recommend immediate planning sessions to discuss strategic implications."

"Yes, sir. I'll get it out right away," Sato said with a resolute nod.

"Outstanding. Let's keep pressing forward. We'll maintain our current recon posture until new orders come through."

"Understood, Commander."

As the screen faded back to standby mode, Lee allowed himself a brief, private moment of triumph. Capturing the Zodark had seemed reckless—an impulsive gamble made on intuition alone. But now that gamble appeared to have paid off.

Looking at the tablet on his desk, Lee sighed. Before him sat the true burden of command—an endless mountain of paperwork awaiting his review and signature.

*Back to the grind...*

**Chapter 24:**
**The Wounded Bird**

**Year 2097**
**LZ Silverwater**
**Planet Intus**

Naomi Love tightened her grip on the controls of the Osprey AT-70C as it lifted off from LZ Silverwater. The river below reflected everything erupting around them. Pointed rocks and vegetation blurred beneath the aircraft. Inside the cockpit, the muffled sounds of shouted orders and pained groans seeped through her helmet. She glanced at the status displays—everything operational—but her gut told her this was going to be a rough extraction.

Love took a deep breath. The engines roared as she pushed the throttle forward. The distant rattle of gunfire echoed—they were still in the hot zone.

Her comm crackled. "Lieutenant Love, this is Lima Six. Suppressing Zodark positions east of your vector. Airspace is tight. Push it to the max!"

"Copy that, Lima Six," Love replied. She glanced at the terrain ahead—a bunch of canyons and ridges. Perfect for an ambush. She banked the Osprey hard left, skimming the tips of twisted metal protruding from the ground—remnants of battles long past.

From the displays on the dash, Love intermittently eyed the screen showing the cabin, though keeping her attention on the main holo before her to keep track of their flight. In the back, the medical team was fast at work, moving together with the automaticity that only comes from extensive training.

Love's helmet filled with the sound of rushing air and distant explosions. She wished she could make the ride smoother. Every bump could mean life or death for the men and women behind her.

Love cut through the comms. "Gunner stations, report!"

Corporal Williams responded first. "Starboard magrail locked and loaded. Acquiring targets."

Ford's voice followed. "Port side ready. Visual confirmed on enemy emplacements."

"Engage at will," Love commanded.

"Engaging now!"

The Osprey shuddered as the .50-cal magrails unleashed a torrent of fire. Tracers arced toward the ground, and distant bursts signaled direct hits.

"Target neutralized," Williams reported.

"Multiple hostiles at three o'clock," Ford said. "Adjusting fire."

Love focused on the horizon, but her peripheral vision caught flashes from the ground. The Zodarks were retaliating. Her console lit up with warning indicators.

"Incoming anti-aircraft fire!" she said.

She pulled the stick back, ascending as a streak of energy sliced through the space they'd just vacated. Klaxons blared.

"Deploying countermeasures," she announced.

Flares burst from the Osprey's sides, decoying the heat-seeking missiles spiraling up toward them. Love rolled the aircraft, weaving between the fiery trails.

Major Ito yelled, "We need more stability back here!"

"Doing what I can, Major," Love replied. "All that life-saving you're doing back there won't count for much if I don't get us out of here in one piece."

"Ford, Williams, suppress those AA units!" Love ordered.

"Roger that!" Ford swung the magrail toward the source of the enemy fire. "Firing!"

The Osprey's guns thundered, shells raining down on the Zodark positions. Explosions blossomed below as munitions found their marks.

"Direct hit on AA unit!" Williams confirmed.

"Good work," Love acknowledged. She scanned the instrument panel—a new warning flashed. "We've got a radar lock."

She dove the Osprey toward a canyon, hugging the terrain to break the lock. The sudden descent caused a lurch.

"Watch the g's!" Ito yelled. "Patient stability is compromised!"

"Sorry, Major," Love replied, leveling out as they entered the canyon.

A missile streaked above them, failing to adjust to their rapid change in altitude.

Love guided the Osprey through the canyon's twists, the walls rising on either side. The sensors beeped—more signals ahead.

"Enemy drones converging," she informed the crew.

"Adjusting targeting parameters," Ford said. "Switching to autotracking. Engaging drones."

Williams joined in. "Firing on drones at nine o'clock!"

The magrails blazed, cutting down the machines darting toward them. Metal fragments hailed down as drones exploded midair.

"All drones neutralized," Ford reported.

"Nice shooting," Love said.

Another alert flashed—a Zodark fighter inbound.

"Zodark fighter on our six!" she warned.

"I can't get an angle on it," Williams said.

Love gritted her teeth. "Hold tight."

She pulled back on the yoke, propelling the Osprey upward and looping over. The sudden maneuver caught the fighter off guard.

"Fighter overshot us," Ford said.

"Bringing us around," Love replied. She aligned the Osprey's nose toward the enemy aircraft.

"Weapon systems locked," the onboard AI announced.

"Firing missiles," Love said.

A pair of smart missiles shot forward, their trails curving as they went after the fighter. The Zodark pilot tried to evade, but the missiles adjusted course.

"Impact in three… two… one," Ford counted.

A flash marked the fighter's demise.

"Target eliminated," Williams said.

Relief was fleeting. An alarm sounded—a damaged rotor. A slight wobble disrupted Love's controls.

"Port-side rotor stability compromised," Green said.

"Diagnostics?" she demanded.

"Possible shrapnel damage. Functioning at eighty percent efficiency."

"Maintain current speed," she instructed.

Love kept glancing at the cabin cam, biting her lip.

Love's focus sharpened as the skyline of the extraction point came into view. Just a few more klicks.

"Multiple bogeys incoming," Green warned. "Deploying countermeasures."

Love felt like time slowed down. One of the missiles exploded harmlessly in the cloud of chaff they had released. A second followed suit. The third grew closer, seemingly avoiding the dummy particles in its path as well as the flares they'd released in case these missiles were heat-seekers.

Love exhaled sharply as she attempted a last-minute maneuver to avoid the incoming threat. "Brace for impact!" she yelled.

The Osprey lurched, but somehow the hit wasn't as hard as she'd been expecting.

"The last missile hit one of our flares," Green explained. "We definitely took some shrapnel, but it's not as bad as it could have been."

Love noticed that the controls were dragging a bit to one side, and she wondered what the hell had happened.

"Damn. Looks like one of our missile pods is dangling from our bird," she said as she read the damage reports. "It's really messing with our aerodynamics."

Green grunted. "It would almost be better if it had been taken clean off."

Love agreed. She was going to be fighting with the controls until they landed. If they didn't have wounded patients in the back, she might have attempted to see if a shaking maneuver could cut the dang missile pod loose, but that was not in the cards.

"Scanning the surroundings," Williams said. "I can't see the launcher!"

"Searching sector, as well," Ford responded. "There! On the ridge at eleven o'clock!"

"Engage!"

The magrails spat fire once more. The enemy launcher erupted in a fireball.

"Launcher neutralized," Ford said.

"Good shot," Love replied. She coaxed the wounded aircraft forward. The extraction zone was within reach. "Hang in there, girl," she whispered to the Osprey, and for a split second she looked at Jack's picture taped to the dash.

*Keep us safe.*

"Lieutenant, patients are critical." Ito's voice carried a weight that Love felt deep in her chest.

Love tightened her grip on the yoke, eyes darting over the flickering console. The Osprey's engines roared in her ears.

Green pointed ahead. "Lieutenant, FOB Oteren in visual range."

"Inform them of our situation—request emergency landing clearance," she ordered.

"Comms down," Green said.

Love huffed. "Then we'll announce ourselves the old-fashioned way."

She activated the external lights, flashing an emergency pattern.

At the base, warning lights flashed on as crews scrambled into action.

"Prepare for landing—engines at minimum thrust," Love said.

"Landing gear deployed," Green confirmed.

The Osprey descended, smoke trailing from its damaged engines.

"Hold steady," Love whispered, easing the aircraft onto the pad.

With a thump and a screech of metal, they made contact. The Osprey lurched but settled, the engines winding down.

"Touchdown achieved," the AI stated.

"Medical teams inbound!" someone shouted from the cabin.

Ito wasted no time. "Let's move these patients!"

Love powered down the cockpit, removing her helmet. The air felt good. Damn good.

She stepped out, surveying the damage on the *Jack.* Her heart clenched at the sight of the hanging missile pod.

Chief Engineer White approached, wiping oil-streaked hands on his coveralls. "She's taken quite a beating, Lieutenant."

Love nodded. "Can you get her flight-ready?"

"Not anytime soon," White said. "She needs extensive repairs."

"Then prep another Osprey," Love replied. "I have missions to fly."

White hesitated. "With respect, you need rest. Your bird isn't the only one running on fumes."

Before she could retort, a voice cut through the din.

"Lieutenant Love, stand down!"

## Chapter 25:
## Euphoria

**Year 2097**
**RNS *Poseidon***
**Brig**

Dr. Malik Reza studied the biometric feeds with detached precision, noting every spike of adrenaline, every frantic twitch, and every pulse of neural overload cascading through the Zodark prisoner's nervous system. Zar'Qui strained violently against his restraints, a primal growl rumbling from deep within his throat, echoing off the sterile bulkheads.

Reza's finger hovered calmly over the Pyroxin-K controls, incrementally increasing the dosage. Not too quickly, not too sharply—just enough to keep Zar'Qui balanced precariously at the edge of agony. It required precision. Too much and he'd lose consciousness. Too little and he'd regain the mental clarity needed to resist further.

Across the table, Major Hale remained utterly composed, watching the prisoner's suffering with patient indifference.

"The pain can stop anytime, Zar'Qui," Hale reminded the alien firmly, but without malice. "You control that. Cooperate with me, and Dr. Reza will make it go away."

Zar'Qui's eyes were wild now, muscles flexing helplessly as phantom flames consumed his nerves. Yet still, he shook his head defiantly. "You…you gain nothing…from me…" he rasped, fighting for breath.

Hale leaned forward slightly, his voice gentle but firm. "You've already told me so much. Why stop now? Tell me, Zar'Qui—how do your fighters and bombers keep communicating despite our jamming? Answer me, and I promise, the pain stops."

Reza watched closely as Hale pressed, incrementally dialing the Pyroxin-K higher. Zar'Qui's biometric signals surged and then faltered; a fresh wave of agony washed over him. The alien groaned through clenched teeth, sweat dripping from his forehead onto the interrogation table.

"They—frequency hop!" Zar'Qui finally gasped, desperation overtaking pride. "Our comm systems…dynamic…frequency hopping. Your jamming can't—lock."

"Huh, frequency hopping?" Hale echoed thoughtfully, his voice calm but curious. "See, that wasn't so hard Zar'Qui, we're making progress. Let's talk more about this. You said your comms frequency hop. What are these frequencies exactly? And what kind encryption method is used to protect them?"

Zar'Qui's fists clenched again, stubbornness flashing through the pain. Reza saw it and responded immediately, raising the Pyroxin-K another careful increment. The Zodark screamed incessantly as the increased pain washed over his body, sweat dripping profusely off his body as he begged for the pain to stop, desperate for relief.

"Come on, don't do this to yourself, Zar'Qui. Just tell me the frequencies," Hale calmly repeated, unshaken by his pleas. "The encryption. Tell me more about it."

Zar'Qui writhed, chest heaving. "It's a high-energy band… artificial gamma spectrum… Republic—blind to it. We rotate the bands... rapid cycle... three-second intervals... beyond your capacity to track…"

Reza glanced toward the observation window. Major Daniel Voss stood behind the glass, rapidly noting Zar'Qui's words and speaking into a commlink. Beside him, Captain Ethan Chen leaned forward intently, tapping at his data pad, already cross-referencing the info against captured Zodark flight data streams.

"Very good. See, this isn't so hard. Now tell me about the encryption protocols," Hale pressed, voice slicing through Zar'Qui's agony. "Answer clearly."

Zar'Qui's resistance cracked once more, a hoarse sob breaking through. "Quantum-modulated… dual-phase encryption... synchronized with band hopping… changes every three seconds... impossible to predict or jam…"

Reza watched the biometric markers spike dangerously close to neural collapse. Without hesitation, he switched the flow of Pyroxin-K off. Zar'Qui sagged forward, shuddering violently, his breathing ragged and shallow.

*Now comes the carrot.*

Gently, Reza increased Neuroplex-4 in the ventilation, watching closely as the prisoner's tense muscles began to ease slightly. The alien's breathing steadied, his sobs fading into shallow gasps of relief. The euphoria was carefully timed—making cooperation seem even more rewarding.

"Good," Hale praised softly. "You've done well. See how cooperation can benefit us both?"

Zar'Qui nodded weakly, his three eyes unfocused, his body limp, receptive.

Behind the glass, Voss turned to Chen. Reza watched closely as Chen nodded emphatically, signaling verification. Voss looked toward the interrogation suite and gave a firm thumbs-up through the partition.

Reza allowed himself a small, satisfied breath. Hale had done his part expertly, extracting critical intelligence, while Chen's quick analysis confirmed its accuracy. Their methods, controversial or not, were undeniably effective.

Reza keyed his console's intercom. "Major Hale," he said evenly. "Captain Chen confirms the information as accurate. We've got everything we needed."

Hale straightened, allowing himself the slightest smile. "Well done, Zar'Qui," he said with quiet satisfaction. "You've helped more than you know."

Reza glanced at the alien, nearly unconscious from exhaustion. The prisoner had reached his limits. But they'd found their breakthrough—vital intel on Zodark communication methods. The Republic could finally adapt, neutralize the enemy's advantage, and begin dismantling the veil of secrecy protecting the Zodark fleet.

Today had been a very productive day.

# Chapter 26:
## Learning Curve

**Year 2097**
**RNS *Gallipoli***
**Intus Orbit**

Coop stood before the Reaper training pod. The simulator's entrance practically called to him, a portal into uncharted territory. He took a breath and stepped inside.

The cockpit enveloped him. Panels crowded the space, every surface covered with holographic knobs and buttons, data flowing on the side panels. Two large touchscreens dominated the HUD. They displayed an abundance of mission data, weapon statuses, and in-depth terrain scans.

He settled into the seat. The harness clicked into place around his shoulders. He touched controls, feeling the ridges and textures designed for a good grip. Unlike the Orion's smooth interfaces, the Reaper's controls wanted a firm hand. So he was told.

"Feeling cozy in there?" Bear's voice came over the pod's intercom system.

Coop put on his helmet. "Like a sardine in a can."

"At least sardines don't have to pilot these beasts," Phantom said.

The cockpit felt more like a tactical operations center. The traditional stick-and-throttle setup remained, but now it shared space with an array of holographic displays wrapping around him in a 180-degree arc. Tactical overlays floated at eye level. It showed real-time threat analysis and weapons status. The primary flight controls were augmented with neural response sensors measuring his reactions down to milliseconds.

Coop kept his mouth closed, but it wanted to open. He was in awe. Why weren't Orion pods this technologically advanced?

To his left, a holographic battlefield map rotated, terrain features and known enemy positions highlighted in pulsing red markers. Squad locations blinked in blue, their movements tracked. The right panel displayed detailed system diagnostics—not just for his Reaper, but for every drone in his squadron. Power levels, ammunition counts, and damage assessments scrolled in columns.

On the heads-up display, target acquisition boxes tracked multiple threats at the same time as predictive algorithms calculated optimal firing solutions. Environmental data streamed—wind speed, atmospheric pressure, gravitational variations—all feeding into the targeting computer.

Where old cockpits had simple radar screens, this station had sensors detecting energy signatures through solid matter. The electronic warfare suite alone occupied three separate displays, monitoring communications, scanning for cyber intrusions, and maintaining defensive countermeasures.

"I'm in awe, y'all," Bear said over the comms.

"Ditto," Coop replied.

Even the peripheral displays seemed alive with data— ammunition depletion rates, fuel consumption analytics, armor integrity, and countless other metrics that would no doubt take weeks to fully master.

He powered up the systems. The HUD sprang to life. Layers of data flooded the screens—velocity vectors arced across a virtual horizon, altitude readouts hovered at the periphery.

*This will take some getting used to.*

He gazed at the weapons display. Sixteen multipurpose smart missiles stood ready. Four antipersonnel cluster bombs and four fuel-air explosive bombs awaited deployment. The two .50-caliber magnetic railguns mounted in the wings showed full charge, and the blaster-mounted chin turret tracked with his inputs.

"That's some serious hardware," Ajax said.

"Enough to start a small war," Ninja replied.

"All units, prepare for simulation launch," an automated voice announced. "Raven, you're lead for this simulation. Good luck."

The canopy sealed shut. The screens changed, and Coop's Reaper was soaring above a desert. Golden dunes stretched far, their rippled surfaces covered by the shadows of towering rock formations.

"Visuals are crisp," Raven said.

Coop angled the Reaper into a descent. The controls were sensitive. He adjusted his grip, doing his best to balance finesse and control.

Ahead, enemy vehicles showed from behind the dunes. Some hovered while others tore across the sand on legs, leaving trails of dust.

"Targets acquired," Bear said.

Coop armed a smart missile. The targeting reticle locked onto a group of hovering crafts. He pressed the launch sequence, but the missile faltered, veering off course before detonating harmlessly in the sand.

"Nice shot," Raven teased, his own missile finding its mark and obliterating an enemy unit.

"Just warming up," Coop said.

Phantom and Ninja dove into the fray, executing tight maneuvers as they unleashed a storm of railgun fire. Explosions burst on the landscape.

Coop adjusted his approach. He lined up the magnetic railguns, aiming for a cluster of ground vehicles skittering across the dunes. He squeezed the trigger. The Reaper lurched, the rounds missing wide.

Frustration bubbled. The controls felt foreign—weird, actually. He toggled the sensitivity settings. Doubt was creeping in, clouding his focus.

"Having trouble, Coop?" Raven asked.

"Just getting a feel for her."

Ajax swooped past, his Reaper releasing a cluster bomb, scattering a convoy of enemy machines. "Incredible."

Coop's teammates navigated the sim with ease. They weaved through enemy fire. Again, easy. Like they belonged in one of these Reaper pods, while he felt out of sync with everything. Sluggish. Disconnected.

The old baseball wisdom rang in his head—when you get into a batting slump, it's like quicksand… the more you overthink it, the deeper you sink. The only way out is to trust your mechanics and keep swinging.

*I need to get out of my own way.*

An enemy hovercraft locked onto Coop. A warning alarm flashed across his HUD. He banked, deploying chaff countermeasures. The incoming fire diverted, but his maneuver threw him off course.

"Stay on your instruments," Bear said.

Coop steadied the Reaper. He took a deep breath, trying to center himself. *Focus.*

Scanning the terrain, he found a cluster of enemy units advancing toward a rocky outcrop. He armed a fuel-air explosive bomb, calculating the drop trajectory. As he approached, hesitation reared its ugly head.

*Did I miscalculate? Ballistic computer's not responding. No release solution. Where's my damn pickle cue?*

"Engage, Coop!" Phantom said.

The targeting system wasn't responding until—there. "Got it. Target acquired. Time to light this candle."

He released the bomb. It descended, detonating atop the simulated enemy position. A massive digital fireball erupted.

"Roger that, good tone," Ninja said.

A surge of pride welled up, but it was short-lived. Raven zipped by, dispatching multiple targets with ease.

Coop's hands felt heavy on the controls, the interface overwhelming. The layers of data on the HUD blurred, symbols and numbers melding into a scrambled mess.

*Not good*, Coop thought.

"Enemy reinforcements incoming," Ninja warned.

New targets appeared—larger, more aggressive machines with spiked exteriors and glowing energy cores.

"Time to punch our combat card," Bear said.

The team split formation, each pilot engaging multiple threats. Coop selected a smart missile, attempting to lock onto a swift-moving hovercraft. The targeting system struggled to maintain a fix.

"Come on, hold together," Coop muttered.

The lock engaged. He fired. The missile streaked toward the target but was intercepted by an enemy countermeasure, detonating prematurely.

"Not your day, is it?" Raven's tone was light, but it stung nonetheless.

Coop switched to the blaster-mounted chin turret—manual control. As an enemy craft charged across the desert, he unleashed a stream of energy bolts. The shots peppered the sand, failing to connect.

"Adjust your lead," Ajax said.

"I know," Coop replied.

An alert sounded—a target was locking onto him. He glanced at the defensive systems. The ECM suite could jam the incoming signal, but his mind raced, the options blending together.

"Coop, evasive action!" Ninja shouted.

He yanked the controls. The Reaper responded fast. The enemy fire grazed his wing, the simulation registering damage.

"You're hit," Phantom said.

"I can see that," Coop responded.

Coop's initial excitement had turned into a hellish uncertainty. Each mistake amplified his anxiety.

*Keep it together, man!* he told himself.

He sought out a new target—a grounded enemy vehicle with turret-mounted cannons—and lined up the magrails, accounting for distance and movement. As he prepared to fire, the controls again blended together.

*Why does this keep happening?*

"Coop, incoming at your eight o'clock," Bear said.

He barely reacted in time. The enemy fire skimmed past his canopy. He rolled the Reaper, but the maneuver was sloppy.

Coop cursed. Enemy fire had come close—too close. His heart hammered in his chest.

He tightened his hold on the yoke, the desert battlefield alive with explosions and return fire. He scanned the HUD, but the myriad of data blurred yet again. Sweat trickled down his temple.

An enemy hovercraft swooped below, its cannons raised toward the sky and blazing. Coop pulled back, trying to gain altitude a second too late. He fired the thrusters, banking hard to the right.

"Watch your tail, Coop!" Bear's voice crackled in his ear.

"I see it," he replied, though his eyes struggled to track the target.

Another volley of fire streaked past. He rolled again, this time narrowly avoiding a direct hit. The Reaper wobbled, and he fought to stabilize it. Every movement felt off, like he was one step behind.

Memories of his father's stern gaze flashed in his mind. The relentless training sessions, the criticism for every minor mistake.

"Precision, Blake. Discipline," his father's voice echoed.

He pushed the thoughts aside. *This isn't the time.*

An enemy drone locked onto him, the alarm blaring. Coop armed a smart missile. "Come on, come on," he urged.

The lock engaged. He fired. The missile streaked toward the drone, hitting it square on. The explosion lit up the sky.

"Nice shot!" Ajax called out.

Relief rushed over him. Still, there was no time to celebrate. Two more enemy units zeroed in. Coop dove low, skimming the desert floor. Sand kicked up around him, the landscape a haze.

He switched to the magnetic railguns and lined his sights up on a ground unit. This time, the Reaper responded like a dream. He fired, the projectile piercing the enemy vehicle and sending it spiraling.

"That's more like it," he told himself.

"Adjust formation, heading northwest," Raven said.

Coop followed, falling into position. They flew toward a heavily fortified enemy base. Turrets swiveled to meet them, unleashing hellfire.

"Evasive maneuvers!" Bear shouted.

Coop veered left. A turret locked onto him. He deployed flares, the bright decoys drawing away some of the fire. A few shots peppered his drone's armor.

His hands trembled as the pressure bore down on him. Each mistake loomed larger, his father's expectations a heavy blanket over him he just couldn't quite escape.

"You're dragging, Coop," Raven's voice came through his helmet.

"I'm on it," he said.

He armed a cluster bomb, targeting the base's defenses. As he initiated the release, doubt hit him. What if he miscalculated again?

"Trust yourself," he whispered.

He released the bomb. It arced before splitting midair, smaller explosives raining down. The turrets erupted in flames.

"Dropped it in their mailbox, Coop," Ninja said.

A hint of confidence sparked. Maybe he could turn this around.

"Regroup for final assault," Raven ordered.

They converged on the last cluster of enemy forces. Coop steadied his breathing, focusing. He synced his movements with the team, matching their pace. Red markers swarmed his HUD—twelve hostiles grouped in a defensive formation around their command vehicle, their cannons firing at the incoming threat.

"Run Finger-Five pattern," Raven said.

The squadron split into attack vector. Their blue markers formed a pentagonal assault pattern. Coop's Reaper slid into position, matching speed and altitude with Bear's craft on his port side. The targeting computer highlighted weak points on each enemy unit, calculating optimal strike zones.

He armed his final smart missile, the weapons status display showing four remaining FAE bombs and half a belt of railgun ammunition. The missile's targeting cone swept across his vision as the computer acquired multiple locks. His squadmates' weapons readouts synchronized with his own.

"Three… two… one… release," Raven said.

Coop's thumb squeezed the trigger. His missile launched alongside a volley from the entire squadron. The projectiles streaked through the simulated air. Impact timers counted down in milliseconds.

The first wave of missiles struck, detonating in a chain. Enemy armor failed under the assault, their status indicators dropping to zero. Coop toggled to his magrails. The targeting assist highlighted gaps in the enemies' armor. The combined fire from five Reapers tore through the remaining defenses, turning the hostile force into expanding balls of fire and debris.

Damage assessment data scrolled across his right display: twelve confirmed kills, zero survivors, mission objectives achieved. The simulation's terrain map updated, showing the cleared sector in pulsing green.

"Simulation complete," the automated voice said. "Mission success."

Coop patted the pod's ceiling. *I could get used to these things.* He powered down the systems, the cockpit dimming. The canopy lifted, and the training bay's lights flooded in.

Climbing out, the cool air hit his flushed face. The others were already gathering, helmets tucked under their arms.

"Good run, team," Raven said.

Coop walked toward the group, forcing a neutral expression. Raven caught his eye.

"You pulled through at the end," Raven offered.

"Thanks," Coop replied.

Raven gave a curt nod before walking past as Phantom exited his pod, casting a glance in Coop's direction.

*Was that irritation in Phantom's eyes?* Coop wondered.

Phantom said nothing.

Coop swallowed hard, a knot forming in his stomach. He replayed the simulation in his mind. The success felt hollow, earned by the others, but not by him.

As he made his way toward the lockers, Bear walked beside him. The older pilot adjusted his gear, leaning in slightly. "Not bad for your first go in a Reaper."

"Could've been better," Coop said.

Bear glanced around, making sure they were out of earshot. "Listen, I've heard whispers," he said, lowering his voice. "They put us on the Reapers because of vulnerabilities in our Orion fleet."

Coop halted, turning to face him. "What do you mean?"

"There's concern our Orions aren't as secure as we thought. Cyber threats, hacking potential—you know, like what happened before…but more extensive. The brass is pushing the Reapers to counter that."

*Oh, no. Not this again*, thought Coop. Bear and Raven were really going hard on this whole conspiracy theory.

Coop wasn't sure how to respond to his friend. "How widespread do you think it is?" he asked, opting to see just how far down the rabbit hole his friend had traveled.

Bear shrugged. "Hard to say. But if they're rushing us onto Reapers, it might be worse than they're letting on." Bear glanced over his shoulder and leaned in closer. "Listen, I've got contacts in intel. Two days ago, three Orion fighter drones went dark during routine patrols. No malfunctions, no damage reports. Just…disappeared."

Coop had no idea what to say to that. *Is it possible Bear is right this time?* he asked himself. Doubt crept in.

"I don't know…" Coop's voice trailed off.

"Me neither," said Bear. "But I do know that I'm going to keep my eyes and ears open…wide open."

**Chapter 27:**
**Valley of Doubt**

**Year 2097**
**Operation Shadowstrike**
**Intus**

On Coop's HUD, the night sky over Intus stretched ahead like frozen teardrops suspended in eternal black. Coop guided the drone through the upper atmosphere. The landscape below was a bunch of shadowed peaks.

Earlier, he'd been called to a hastily convened meeting aboard the *Gallipoli*. The rest of the Jolly Rogers Squadron had crowded into the command room.

Strike stood before them. "Operation Shadowstrike." A holomap of Intus materialized, focusing on a deep scar in the planet's surface.

"Lysenia Valley," Strike continued. "Our ground forces are pinned down here by Zodark infantry. We're their only support."

Coop studied the topography—sheer cliffs, narrow passes, dense vegetation that could conceal entire battalions.

"We deploy immediately," Strike ordered. "The valley's a death trap for the unprepared. I want a clean exfil— two klicks west of the hot zone. Three Ospreys are on standby for emergency dust-off. Our primary objective is air support, lighting up those Zodark bastards on the ground, carving an escape route for the good guys. You'll provide suppressing fire. Keep your eyes on those ridgelines; intel suggests they've got spotters in the high ground."

Strike laid out a three-phase extraction protocol. He emphasized coordinated air support and strategic choke points to funnel the enemy forces away from the evacuation corridor.

Back in the cockpit, Coop shook off the memory. He scanned the targeting feed—red icons blinked without solid locks. The Reaper's sensors probed the darkness, seeking threats hidden among the crags below. He adjusted his heading. The drone responded with a smooth tilt.

211

Each mission carried risks, but tonight felt different. The recent cyber infiltrations still wouldn't stop gnawing at the edges of his confidence.

"Maintain formation," Strike's voice crackled over the comms.

Coop adjusted his position, sliding into the designated flight path alongside Bear and Raven. The Reapers glided through the night.

"Lysenia Valley ahead," Strike reported. "Keep those Mark Ones peeled."

The terrain shifted below—a deep gorge carved into the planet's surface. Walls rose on either side. The valley was a natural chokepoint, perfect for an ambush.

Coop's HUD lit up with multiple contacts.

"Picking up movement," Bear said. "Heavy infantry, armored units. More than we expected."

Red markers swarmed the display, converging on Republic troops.

"Zodark forces mobilizing," Strike said. "Prepare to engage."

Coop brought up the targeting array. His hands hesitated over the controls. The memory of his own Orion incident still haunted him—the Zodark EW attack that had made him believe he'd accidentally struck allied forces. Those manufactured screams over the comms, the fake signatures on his display, the planted voices of commanders telling him he'd just killed his own people. It had all been an elaborate deception, designed to paralyze him with guilt midmission. He hadn't actually hit anyone that day, but the psychological damage had been done.

"Coop, you on those targets?" Strike's pitch was monotone.

"Working on it," Coop replied.

He tried to lock onto an enemy unit, but the reticle wavered, refusing to settle. His palms grew slick inside his gloves. With a sharp breath, he disengaged the targeting system. How could he be sure? What if these signatures were false? What if friendly forces were down there, and his systems were lying to him again, showing him what the Zodarks wanted him to see?

"Ground forces are exposed," Raven said. "We need suppressive fire."

Coop swallowed hard. The seconds slipped away, each one a missed opportunity. Below, Zodark soldiers advanced through the valley.

"Coop, engage now!" Strike shouted.

He fought against the paralyzing grip of doubt. *Focus. They need me.*

"What's the holdup?" Bear asked. "They're closing in."

A flare erupted on the ground—a signal from the pinned Republic unit. Their situation was growing worse.

"Coop!" Strike yelled. "Engage now!"

"I'm trying." Coop's voice sounded thin, even to himself.

Ajax's drone dove ahead, cannons blazing. "Suppressing fire," he said, strafing the enemy lines.

"Taking the west approach," Bear said, missiles streaking from his drone and erupting amidst the Zodark ranks.

"Coop, we need you in this fight!" Strike's tone came though like a bullet.

Below, explosions lit the valley, but the Zodarks pressed on. Anti-aircraft fire spewed upward, filling the sky. A burst detonated near Coop's wing, jolting him back into the moment.

"Incoming flak!" Ninja called out. "They're locking onto us!"

Phantom's drone surged forward. "Taking out their AA." He veered into a steep dive.

"Phantom, wait!" Raven said, but Phantom was already unleashing a torrent of missiles.

The ground defenses erupted in fire, but retaliatory shots peppered the heavens. A beam clipped Phantom's drone, severing a wing.

"Mayday! I've been hit!" Phantom's Reaper spiraled downward, smoke trailing.

"Phantom's down," Bear reported.

Strike's frustration crackled over the channel. "This is exactly what we can't afford. Stay focused!"

Coop's chest tightened. If he'd pulled the trigger when he'd had the chance, if he hadn't let his fears paralyze him, maybe Phantom's drone would still be in the air. His hesitation had cost them, and cost the Republic military loads of money.

*No time for self-pity.* Below, Republic ground forces were still pinned down, needing support.

"Multiple Zodark positions identified," Bear said. "Heavy concentrations at the valley mouth."

"Clear that escape route," Strike replied. "Our boys need a path to those Ospreys."

Something snapped in Coop. The thought of more lives at stake because of his inaction broke through his paralysis. His targeting system locked onto a Zodark heavy weapons placement.

"Engaging," he said, voice steady for the first time that night. The missile streaked from his Reaper, destroying the position in a flash of flames.

"Good hit," Strike said.

Bear's Reaper swooped low, magrail cannons blazing. "West ridge is clear. Moving to the next sector."

Coop found his rhythm, taking out target after target. His fears faded with each confirmed strike. The targeting system wasn't lying—these were real enemies, real threats to their people below.

Another target came into view. Coop's reticle settled on a Zodark heavy gunner position. No static in the display. No ghosting. The target lock pulsed. He squeezed the trigger, and his missile flew through the night, detonating. Before the smoke cleared, he moved to his next victim—a mortar team setting up on the ridge. Two more missiles, two more explosions.

"Armor column, northeast ridge," Bear informed.

Coop banked hard. He brought his Reaper's magrail cannon to bear. The rounds tore through the lead vehicle's armor, setting off a chain reaction that turned the entire column into an inferno. Ground troops scattered, making easy targets for Bear's follow-up strikes.

"Republic forces moving to extraction point," Strike said. "Ospreys touching down now."

Through Coop's tactical feed, Republic infantry sprinted across the valley floor in groups. A Zodark squad tried flanking them from a cave mouth. Raven painted the entire entrance with missile fire, collapsing it in a shower of rock.

"Hostile sniper team, west cliff face," Strike warned.

Coop rolled his drone. One burst from his cannon turned their position into a crater.

"Last group boarding now," Strike said. "Guard that departure corridor until birds are clear."

The Ospreys kicked up clouds of dust. Coop and his squadron formed a web around them, their drones eliminating any threat daring an approach. The valley lit up with continuous blasts as they cleared the escape route.

The transports lifted off, heavy with their cargo of rescued soldiers. Coop fell into escort formation, scanning for threats until the Ospreys disappeared into the safety of the upper atmosphere.

"Mission accomplished," Strike said. "Return to FOB Oteren."

The flight back held none of the earlier tension. After they landed, Coop's legs trembled as he stepped out of *Gallipoli*'s pod bay. Sweat had soaked through his flight suit. The demons still lurked in his head—but tonight he'd made them bleed.

Phantom stormed toward Coop, eyes blazing. "You think this is a game? I lost my drone because you froze up."

Coop stumbled back. "I'm sorry. I—"

"Sorry? Are you serious?" Phantom's fist clenched. "You're a liability."

*Clever. Like I haven't heard that one before.* "I understand, but—"

Bear stepped in, placing a firm hand on Phantom's chest. "Not the time or place."

"Get out of my way, Bear," Phantom said.

Bear didn't budge.

"Stand down." Strike's voice burst through the tension as he hurried in their direction. "All of you."

Phantom glared but backed off, muttering under his breath as he stalked away.

Strike's gaze locked onto Coop. "With me. Office. Now."

**Chapter 28:**
**Duty and Instinct**

**Year 2097**
**RNS *Gallipoli***
**Intus Orbit**

Combat medals and service commendations lined the walls in rows. The overhead lights reflected off Strike's brass nameplate: COMMANDER LANCE DANNING "STRIKE", SQUADRON COMMANDER, JOLLY ROGERS.

On a shelf behind Strike, an RNS *Gallipoli* model dominated a collection of handcrafted starfighters, infantry vehicles, and capital ships—Strike's off-duty passion project. Each miniature bore perfect paint lines and microscopic decals—the work of countless hours. Through the viewport behind his desk, Intus hung like a jewel, its atmosphere casting an emerald glow across the office.

Strike leaned against the edge of his desk, arms folded across his chest. "Explain yourself."

"Sir, I accept full responsibility for Phantom and—"

"That's not what I asked. A drone lost. All because you froze up out there. This isn't the time for half measures. We're lucky we didn't lose any of our troops down there. Damn lucky."

"Yes, sir," Coop replied.

Strike pushed off the desk, taking a step closer. "You want to tell me what's really going on?"

"Permission to speak freely, sir."

Strike gave a nod.

"I'm concerned about the electromagnetic spoofing, sir. The signal deception tactics—it's affecting our operations more than we're being told. I believe it's compromising our drones and putting lives at risk. The command link interference is increasing. We're seeing microsecond anomalies in target acquisition—indicators that enemy forces are injecting false signals into our systems. The Zodarks aren't trying to hack our drones—they're *tricking* them. Every sortie, they refine their spoofing patterns. They're mapping our signal behaviors and adjusting their decoys accordingly."

Strike's eyes flashed, just for a moment. "You think Command isn't aware of the threats we face? We all are. We've had briefings on EW tactics, we've implemented countermeasures. We're on it, Coop."

"I believe they're aware, sir. But I also think the severity is being downplayed. We need more robust ECCM protocols, tighter beam control, maybe even hardened fallback frequencies."

"That's above your pay grade, Lieutenant." Strike's tone hardened. "Your job is to fly your drone and complete the mission. Who do you think you are? You're suddenly a subject matter expert in cyber-security? You are a drone pilot—leave it to the people who know a hell of a lot more about this than you do."

"With all due respect, sir, if our guidance systems are being spoofed mid-flight, every pilot out there is flying blind, and every soldier on the ground is exposed."

Strike took another step, now just a half a meter away. "I let you say your piece, but you are now way over the line here. This isn't your job, and you're treading on very dangerous ground."

Coop shifted. He had definitely overstepped. He lowered his head. "I'm just trying to prevent more casualties, sir," he said, speaking much more softly this time.

"And I'm trying to prevent you from getting grounded," Strike snapped. "Questioning orders, hesitating in combat—that's how people die."

Coop clenched his fists behind his back. "Understood, sir."

Strike narrowed his eyes. "Is it? Because from where I'm standing, you're causing some problems out there. If you can't follow orders without second-guessing, I'll have no choice but to pull you from active duty. You'd be shuffled off to a desk job faster than you can blink."

The thought of being benched hit him in the gut. "It won't happen again, sir."

"See that it doesn't." Strike circled back behind his desk. "The EW threat is real, and it's being handled. We have teams working around the clock to refine signal resilience and counter-deception routines."

"May I suggest a review of our drones' signal authentication layers, sir? Maybe push for a more adaptive filtering algorithm?" Coop asked.

Strike shot him a look. "Suggestion duly noted. Now, focus on your responsibilities."

"Understood."

Strike leaned forward, palms flat on the desk. "You're one of our best, Coop. Don't squander it by overstepping your bounds."

"I'm committed to the mission, sir."

"Then prove it. Next time you're in the cockpit, I expect you to perform without hesitation."

"Yes, sir."

Strike's gaze softened just a fraction. "And, Coop… if there's something else affecting your performance, now's the time to speak up."

"No excuses, sir. I'll be ready."

"See that you are. Dismissed."

Coop turned and headed toward the door. As his hand touched the panel, Strike's voice stopped him.

"And, Lieutenant?"

He glanced back. "Sir?"

"The Jolly Rogers have a reputation to maintain. Don't make me… ever again… reconsider your position here."

"Aye, sir."

"Good." Strike looked down at the datapads on his desk, the conversation evidently over.

Stepping into the corridor, Coop exhaled. He started down the passageway.

*The nerve of him*, Coop thought. *Acting like I'm a second-rate pilot.* He grimaced. *Thing is, he's right. I've been acting that way.*

He weaved through clusters of crew members, their conversations fading as he passed. Some gave him sidelong glances—news traveled fast aboard the *Gallipoli* when Phantom was involved. Ignoring them, he headed toward the pilots' quarters.

Bear intercepted him at a junction in the corridors. "How'd it go?"

"Fine," Coop replied.

"Doesn't look like it."

"Not now," Coop said, pushing past.

"Hey," Bear called after him. "We're all on the same side here."

Coop's shoulders tensed, his jaw clenching as he turned. His hands had balled into fists without him realizing it. "Are we? Because from where I stand, everyone's so busy following orders they can't see what's really happening."

"Watch it, Coop. That kind of talk—"

"What? Gets people killed? Or keeps them alive?"

Bear frowned. "What's that supposed to mean?"

"Nothing." Coop shook his head. "Just need some space."

He continued on, leaving Bear standing there. Reaching the barracks, Coop entered, kept his attention forward, and climbed up to his bunk. As usual, his gaze fell on the worn journal resting on the bed—the one passed down from Presley Paul Cooper. Reaching over, he picked it up, fingers tracing the faded cover.

Scrolling through, he stopped at a passage and read:

*June 15, 1944: Another dogfight over France today. Lost Bader and O'Connor. The Luftwaffe's getting desperate—using every trick in the book. Command keeps pushing us to press the advantage, but something feels off about their patterns. A pilot has to trust their instincts, even when the brass says otherwise.*

Coop reread the words. His great-great grandfather had faced similar doubts, similar struggles between duty and intuition. The next entry caught his eye:

*July 3, 1944: Took down three ME-109s over Normandy. That makes eleven confirmed kills. But it's not about the numbers—it's about keeping your men alive. Bailey wouldn't have made it if we'd followed standard engagement protocol. Sometimes you have to break formation to save lives. My Mustang might belong to Uncle Sam, but my conscience belongs to me.*

Below the entry was a faded sketch of his great-great grandfather's P-51, "Lucky Lady," complete with kill markers and the squadron insignia. The tech might have changed from propellers to computers, but the core truths of combat remained the same.

Closing the journal, he rested his hand on the cover. "You know what scares me most, Great-Gramps?" he said under his breath. "Not the Zodarks. Not even their EW attacks. It's the thought that one day, I might give an order that gets our own people killed because I can't tell what's real anymore."

He leaned back against the wall, staring at the ceiling. Images of Phantom's Reaper drone getting hit replayed in his mind.

"Coop."

Coop looked down. "Yeah?"

Raven stared up at him. "Got a minute?"

Coop shrugged. "Sure."

Raven climbed halfway up the ladder to Coop's top bunk, resting his elbows on the mattress. "Saw your confrontation with Phantom after the mission. Look, everyone's on edge. But we can't afford to be at each other's throats."

"Phantom's the one who got in my face. But I understand. Like everyone knows, I froze up. I let the team down."

"You're not the first to hesitate," Raven said. "But you need to move past it. Both you and I know the cybersecurity crap is worse than we probably can imagine, but still, out there, I would love to depend on you like I used to."

"Strike thinks I'm unfit for duty."

"He wants you to succeed. We all do. But you've got to get out of your head. Trust in the team, in the command."

Coop looked away.

"We're here for you. Don't shut us out," Raven said.

"All right." Coop tucked the journal under his pillow. "Thanks, Raven."

After Raven climbed down, Coop lay back, staring at the ceiling. Underneath it all, the Zodarks weren't just fighting a conventional war—they were attacking humanity's relationship with its own technology. Every drone pilot who hesitated, every moment of doubt, was a small victory for them. Coop understood now—his personal battle against uncertainty was just a microcosm of humanity's larger struggle. The enemy wanted them afraid of their own systems, paralyzed by doubt.

Tomorrow would be another mission, another chance to prove himself. And this time, he'd be ready. Not because Strike ordered it, not because of his great-great grandfather's legacy, but because his team needed him. The demons might still be there, but they didn't get to win. Not anymore.

**Chapter 29:**
**Orders Are Orders**

**Year 2097**
**FOB Oteren**
**Planet Intus**

Love blinked against the pale light seeping through the blinds. Her eyes struggled to focus. The sounds of the base filtered into her quarters—the distant thrum of machinery, muffled voices in the corridor, the occasional clatter of equipment. She pushed herself upright. The sheets slid off her shoulders.

*What time is it?* She looked at the digital clock mounted on the opposite wall. The numbers glowed 1300 hours. She rubbed her temples. The last thing she remembered was returning to Forward Operating Base Oteren, the adrenaline of the mission still coursing through her veins, and Commander Granger telling her to stand down and after a few seconds, letting her know she needed downtime.

She swung her legs over the edge of the bed, feet touching the floor. Her flight suit hung neatly on the back of a chair, boots lined up beneath it, laces loosened. *I don't even remember changing*, she thought. The exhaustion must have hit her like a freight train.

Pressing her palm against the wall sensor, she opened her closet compartment. She pulled out standard off-duty attire—olive drab T-shirt, tan cargo pants, and her low-quarter boots. The clothes were comfortable, casual but still regulation-appropriate for base. After changing out of her sleep clothes, she ran a hand through her hair, trying to look somewhat presentable.

A knock interrupted her thoughts.

"Come," she said.

The door opened. Commander Granger stepped inside. His uniform was impeccable. Every crease in place. "You're finally awake."

"Commander." Love stood straighter. A still-exhausted dizziness washed over her, but she masked it with a stoic expression.

Granger took a moment, assessing her. "I wanted to commend you on your bravery during the operation. You saved a lot of lives out there."

"Was just holding up my end." Praise felt hollow when there was still so much work to be done.

"Even so, you went above and beyond. The med team couldn't have evacuated those soldiers without you."

"If that's all, sir…"

"You need rest, Love."

A knot tightened in her chest. "Sir, I'm combat-ready. I need to be in the field. Sitting idle will only…" She decided not to finish the sentence. "I was performing my duties just fine."

"Orders are orders. Time for recovery."

"Recovery from what? Sitting around isn't helping anyone. I can help out there. I'm… fine."

"Enough," he said. "This isn't a discussion. You've been pushing yourself too hard. You're being sent to the new MWR facility they've built on Intus near Lodo Beach. It's a ninety-six-hour pass—pools, comfortable rooms, and all-you-can-eat buffet."

"Sir, with respect, my crew trusts me," Love protested. "They know I won't let anything happen to them."

"And that's precisely why you need a break," he said. "You're carrying too much weight on your shoulders." He stepped toward the door. "Take this time to regroup."

The door slid shut behind him, leaving her alone.

She rubbed her eyes, the grogginess refusing to lift. *I wouldn't be this tired if they hadn't forced me to stand down.*

Pacing the length of the quarters, she tried to shake off the restlessness coursing through her. Memories flooded back—the roar of engines, maneuvering through hostile territory, the relief on the faces of the wounded as they boarded her Osprey. That was where she belonged, not relaxing at some cushy MWR facility.

Granger's words echoed in her mind. *Orders are orders.*

She sat back on the edge of the bed. For a few long moments, the tick of the clock was the only sound. Each second seemed like it mocked her inactivity.

"Well, I guess I'd better get this over with," she told herself before giving in and packing an overnight bag.

The base was alive just outside her door—pilots walking out there, prepping for missions. In the hangar a ways away, mechanics no doubt fine-tuned engines, medics readying supplies. She just wanted to move something, do something. Fly. Protect. Help.

Instead, she marched her way over to the hangar, where instead of piloting an Osprey, she was forced to humble herself and sit in the back as a passenger. The lack of control was irritating to Love, but she reminded herself that this was the view that all the soldiers she picked up had every day.

Lieutenant Love had never been to Lodo Beach before. The sight of the shore was breathtaking, with its fine, light green sand and pristine waters that were so clear, she could see fish swimming fifteen feet below the surface. However, Love couldn't help but feel lost. Forced relaxation was unnatural to her.

The MWR facility reminded Love of advertisements she'd seen for beachside spas; the building was sleek and modern, minimalistic but somehow still inviting. She wanted to hate it, but it was one of the most visually appealing locations she'd ever traveled to.

She retreated inside, checking in and retrieving her room key. Love put her bag down and sat briefly on the bed, which was far more comfortable than the one she had been sleeping on back at FOB Oteren. The room was quiet—way too quiet. She couldn't hear anyone bustling about in the hallway; there was no sound of tools in the distance.

*Shoot, even the air conditioning in this place is practically silent,* she thought.

She lasted less than a minute before she decided to wander down the hall and see what she could find to distract herself. Following her nose toward the smell of food, Love happened upon an entertainment room.

*This is their idea of a good time?* she asked herself. A few Navy pilots and Army troopers were scattered about. One soldier read a book on a couch, looking like he was about to fall asleep. Two Navy officers played a game of chess, and a small group huddled around a holoscreen, half-heartedly watching a documentary.

Love decided that given the options, she should find an empty seat and settle in. The narrator's voice filled the room.

"The Primords' architectural achievements stand as a testament to their technological superiority." The camera panned across a cityscape of silver towers. "What would take human construction crews months to complete, Primord builder-drones accomplish in weeks."

The footage showed swarms of drones, each the size of a dinner plate, working in sync with one another. They moved like schools of fish as they deposited nano-enhanced building materials.

"Their residential structures are particularly remarkable," the narrator continued. "Self-healing metals combined with bioorganic compounds create living buildings that respond to environmental changes. Watch here as the exterior adjusts its molecular structure to deflect an incoming dust storm."

The cam zoomed in on a building's surface. It rippled like liquid. Its entire facade shifted to present a smoother profile against the wind.

"Their building techniques reflect this efficiency," the narrator explained as the camera followed a construction project. "Watch how their builder-drones communicate through entangled networks, allowing instantaneous coordination across vast distances. A single overseer can control thousands of units simultaneously."

The screen showed a massive structure taking shape, rising from the ground like a time-lapse flower blooming. Drones moved in boring patterns, weaving steel and glass and strange, gleaming materials Love had never seen before.

"Perhaps most impressive is their waste reclamation system," the narrator said. "Every structure is connected to a vast network of molecular recyclers. Nothing is wasted—everything from atmospheric moisture to organic matter is collected, processed, and repurposed."

The documentary displayed maintenance drones, barely visible to the naked eye. They drifted across surfaces like metallic flies, repairing and rebuilding.

"Yet despite their technological mastery, Primord social interactions remain formal and reserved by human standards. Their facial expressions are subtle, their gestures precise and economical. Where humans might embrace or shake hands, Primords acknowledge each other with slight inclines of the head or a raise of an arm."

The footage captured a Primord marketplace. Buyers selected products by scanning them through sensors worn on their wrists. Trade agreements were sealed through the exchange of small datapads containing encrypted data. Merchants displayed their goods on floating platforms adjusting their height and temperature for freshness. Children sat in learning alcoves, reading or watching people speak about market protocols either in person or through neural interfaces. Strangely, the kids seemed to like this, fascinated, soaking it all in. The entire space illuminated with bioluminescent indicators signaling product quality and availability to those who knew how to read them.

"Even their entertainment venues demonstrate their cultural values. These gathering spaces are designed to enhance intellectual exchange rather than emotional expression. Note the acoustic properties of these chambers, designed to carry whispered conversations with perfect clarity while dampening excessive volume."

Love leaned forward. The Primords' world was a study in control, every aspect engineered for maximum output. Yet there was beauty in their ways, everything streamlined, similar to their emotions.

The documentary continued, but Love's attention wandered. She couldn't help but compare their measured existence to the complexity of human combat operations. Plus, it was boring. Perhaps there was something to learn from the Primords' approach to life, their ability to accomplish so much with such careful control of resources and energy, but she needed to get out of there.

She made her way to the exit.

*How am I supposed to make it through ninety-six hours of this?* she wondered.

The fastest way she could think of to pass the time was to sleep, so she opted to return to her room and take a nap.

## Chapter 30
## When a Plan Comes Together

**RNS *Poseidon***
**Bridge Conference Room**

Commander Ripley Lee leaned back in his chair, arms folded, as Captain Ethan Chen concluded the intelligence briefing. Around the conference table aboard the *Poseidon*, the senior staff sat in tight silence, watching as lines of encrypted comms data scrolled across the tabletop display.

"…the frequency hopping method used by the Zodarks is more advanced than anything we've encountered before," Chen explained calmly, tapping a control to bring up a spectral mapping. "They're operating in what we're now calling the artificial high gamma band—a synthetic quantum spectrum Republic intelligence hadn't even identified until now."

"Gamma band?" Lieutenant Lucia Rodriguez echoed, brows tightening. "Captain, we don't even have the hardware to detect that range, let alone jam it."

Lieutenant Connor Rhom leaned forward. "That explains the drop-off we've seen in our EW effectiveness lately. We've been flooding traditional comms bands with jamming pulses, but if they're operating in a synthetic gamma band… we're not even hitting the right part of the spectrum."

Chen nodded. "Exactly. Their comms hops every three seconds across that high-energy spectrum, and each hop triggers a reinitialization of a quantum-modulated, dual-phase encryption protocol. Even if we detect one hop, by the time we try to jam it, they've already moved."

"Three seconds," Rodriguez commented. "That's slower than I'd expect for a high-tempo frequency hop system. Most Earth-based arrays operate in milliseconds specifically to avoid the possibility of being jammed unless you jam the entire spectrum. So why stretch it?"

Chen sat back in his chair as his eyes drifted skyward in thought. "Huh, that's a good question. This is just me spitballing here, but if I had to guess, I'd bet it has something to do with distance."

Rodriguez nodded. "Hmm, yeah that could make sense. On Earth—or even in orbital ops—signal latency is negligible. But out here, the tyranny of distance reigns supreme. In space operations, you'd have to account for propagation delay. This three-second interval you identified would allow time for a command signal to reach outlying fighters or bombers, be acknowledged, and maintain synchronization."

Chen reworked the schematic they had been looking at, then smiled. "If we assume they are using some kind of quantum architecture—entangled-pair relays or compressed state transmission—it would explain how they could hold coherence long enough to coordinate frequency hopping without dropping sync. This would help to explain why we haven't detected this until now or even knew to look for it."

Rodriguez picked up the thread. "You know, this lines up with a Republic naval study I read recently on the battle for Intus. It touched on this very subject. The report talked about a marked degradation in Zodark EW vulnerabilities about halfway through the engagement. When the conflict started, we were jamming them just like we always do—and then it changed, it stopped working."

"Oh wow. I think we might know why. They adapted, right under our noses," Rhom said flatly as he shook his head.

Major Voss nodded. "Exactly. Intelligence believes they switched to an alternate comms system mid-battle, or at least that's been our running theory. What the study couldn't identify was how, but the timing of it, that was clear and obvious. The data clearly showed as soon as our ships flooded the EM band, they shifted behavior—and their formations resumed the same level of coordination they had prior to the jamming."

Lee held a hand up to forestall further comments as he turned to face their Primord ally. "Captain Dharek, you've been quietly listening to our discussion. You've fought the Zodarks far longer than any of us. Does this track with what your forces have seen?" he asked.

Captain Dharek, seated at the far end of the table, folded his hands calmly. His gray-touched skin shimmered faintly in the overhead lighting. "Much of what you describe aligns with our experience, Commander," Dharek began in his usual, measured tone. "The Zodarks' comms behavior is coordinated, adaptive, almost instinctive. It is something the Primord Navy has faced for more than a century with mixed results. We recognized the patterns in how they communicate and coordinate their ships in battle early on. But this recent change is something we had not encountered before…at least not the mechanism by which it is currently happening."

He turned slightly to Chen. "High gamma bands were considered... unusable by our engineers. They considered it too unstable. Our engineers found them too risky and prone to feedback disruption which is catastrophic for sensor fusion. As a result, we deprioritized studying this further decades ago."

"Oh, so you never considered they could synthesize that spectrum, then?" asked Rodriguez.

"No, we did not," Dharek admitted. "A synthetic quantum channel operating at gamma thresholds was beyond what we thought possible at the time. Frankly, we lacked the data to prove otherwise, and our doctrine favored brute-force jamming. Flood the spectrum, blind both sides. It was crude, but it stalled their weapons targeting."

Chen nodded. "The blinding of both sides is what eventually drove us to specialize our EW capabilities so we could move away from that double-edge sword."

Dharek smiled faintly. "Agreed. It is a price we paid for our inadequacy in this area. I think it is also why we never made significant progress in reclaiming our lost systems. Until your people joined the alliance, we lacked the precision tools for surgical EW. You brought that."

Lee sighed audibly. He glanced at Voss, then at MacGregor. "I guess the question I have for the both of you is while all of this sounds great, is this just theory—nerd talk to explain away something we don't understand—or do we think we have something practical we can test? Is there something we can exploit during a fight to give us an edge we otherwise wouldn't have?"

"Commander, in intelligence work, facts are rare luxuries," Voss replied. "We almost never have all the variables. What we operate on—what we *live on*—are educated guesses, instinct, and pattern recognition. And in this case, the signals intel Captain Chen's team pulled from that captured Vulture lines up almost perfectly with what we extracted from the prisoner. Two independent sources, same conclusion. In our world, that's as close to certainty as we ever get. Now, whether we test it… that's a call only you can make, sir."

Chief Engineer Boyd MacGregor then added. "Sir, being realistic, we don't have the time or the kit to install a full gamma-band EW suite before we'll likely encounter a Zodark patrol unless we pull back to Captain Roberts's location. But that doesn't mean we're out of options."

Lee gave him a nod to continue.

"We've got modular access to our high-frequency arrays and about half a dozen spare low-yield signal processors. If my team reworks the modulation cycles and routes them through our secondary emitters. We normally use them for deep-space comms, but we might be able to spoof the synthetic gamma band just long enough to see if it trips something in their formation and verify this theory might work."

He glanced at Rodriguez. "Lucia, if we isolate the output to a tight forward arc, cut the bandwidth to avoid any bleed over, and crank the carrier signal to just below interference threshold… do you think it might be enough to screw with their comms to validate our theory?"

Rodriguez chewed her lip. "Maybe. It wouldn't jam them entirely, but it could scramble timing packets or desync their encrypted handshake protocols. It could throw their ships out of sync for a few seconds at a time."

Rhom smiled as he leaned in. "And that might be all we need. Even a five-second delay in Zodark reaction time is enough for our fire control solutions to land a clean hit."

MacGregor pointed at Rhom with his stylus. "Exactly. And if we reinforce that band with high-energy pulses on alternating cycles, we might trick their onboard systems into resetting. Force a hard reboot on their end."

Rodriguez frowned. "But we'll need to tune it in real-time. No preset cycle's going to hold—we'd be playing cat-and-mouse the whole time."

MacGregor shrugged. "That's your department. I'll give you a sandbox. You find the pulse shape that breaks their toys."

"Captain Dharek, if we test this theory and it proves true, will you join in writing a report with me to validate it?" Lee asked, hoping his Primord partner would back him up. "I think this would go a long way in identifying necessary changes to our electronic warfare strategies and equipment that'll likely prove invaluable in the next campaign."

Dharek considered the question, then nodded in agreement. "Yes, I will. Let's do this then—during our next operation, we are supposed to scout Sector 3 to see if the Zodarks have an outpost or some other support infrastructure in the area. If your reconnaissance force encounters a Zodark presence, you can test your theory to see if it proves true. If it does, send the signal and my battleships will join you, and we will do what we can to squash whatever force we encounter. Just remember, if Zodark reinforcements begin to arrive, we need to make sure we can extract ourselves from the fight. Our orders are clear—we are to scout and identify enemy forces. We are not to get locked into a pitch fight that might cost us ships."

Lee nodded; he knew the rules of engagement. While he understood them, it didn't mean he had to like them. "OK, then it's settled. We'll test our theory and see what happens. If we're lucky, we'll take a couple of ships out before reinforcements can arrive, and we'll have to bug out."

## Chapter 31:
## Micro-fissures

**Year 2097**
**FOB Oteren**
**Planet Intus**

Ford's hands froze on the maintenance panel as the diagnostic tool showed what two previous inspections had missed. The micro-fissures in the conversion actuator housing appeared as bright spiderwebs on his handheld scanner—hairline fractures spreading from stress points no one thought to check. He stared at the reading, running the test again to be sure.

*This can't be right,* Ford thought. *No way.* Thing was, it *was* right.

"Sweet mother of mechanics," he muttered, sliding out from under the nacelle housing. "Unbelievable."

Ford barely registered the activity in the hangar around him. Instead, his focus narrowed to the diagnostic readout, the implications hitting him like an knee to his midsection. Okay, not that bad, but indeed… bad. This wasn't just a maintenance oversight—it was a disaster waiting to happen—the kind ending with scattered wreckage and body bags.

"Jones!" Ford's voice resounded through the hangar. The younger mechanic's shoulders tensed before he turned around.

"Chief?"

Ford slammed the diagnostic tool onto the workbench. "Two separate maintenance cycles on this bird. Two! And nobody thought to check the secondary stress points on the conversion housing?"

Jones swallowed hard. "We followed the maintenance protocol, Chief. Every point on the checklist."

"The checklist," Ford said. "The checklist doesn't account for cumulative stress patterns from the recent flight operations. These fissures could have split mid-conversion.

You know what happens then? The nacelle tears off at two thousand meters up!"

The other mechanics stopped working, all eyes on the confrontation. Williams paused from his inventory check of the ammunition stores, his datapad no doubt forgotten in his hand. Even the Synths working on the adjacent Osprey halted their programmed routines, as if sensing the tension in the air. Well, sensing wasn't the correct word. More like… detecting, analyzing.

"This wasn't just missed once," Ford continued, grabbing a datapad and bringing up the schematics. "It was missed two times! By you, by him," he pointed to another mechanic who visibly flinched, "by everyone who touched this bird!"

Jones's face reddened. "With all due respect, sir, you signed off on those inspections too."

The hangar quieted. The muscles in Ford's jaw tightened, a vein pulsing at his temple. The accusation… no, the truth… hung in the air—undeniable and damning. He had indeed signed off. He'd reviewed the reports, checked the critical systems himself, and still missed what could have been a fatal flaw.

Ford opened his mouth to unleash another barrage, but stopped. He couldn't do this anymore, this anger, this hell he'd kept firing at his own crew, at other crews. He saw something in Jones's eyes, too—not insubordination, not lack of skill, not trying to skim, but exhaustion. The same exhaustion mirrored in every face watching him. The same exhaustion he felt in his own bones, the same exhaustion written all over Love's face after they landed after the last op.

He took a deep breath, stepping back from the precipice of rage. This wasn't working. Hadn't been working. The war. The endless maintenance cycles. The constant pressure. It wasn't just wearing on Love, on him—it was wearing on all of them.

Ford ran a hand over his face, feeling the stubble of too many hours without rest. When had he last slept? Forty hours ago? Longer?

"You're right," Ford said, his voice lower. The admission cost him something, but the payment felt necessary. "I signed off on it."

He turned to examine the diagnostic reading on the datapad again, giving himself a moment. The tension dropped a notch in the hangar.

"The fracture pattern is unusual," he continued, tone shifting to instructional rather than accusatory. "It propagates between the standard sensor points—that's why it didn't flag in automated tests."

Jones moved cautiously to look at the readings, as if approaching a wounded animal, one that might snap.

"Actually," Ford added, glancing at the mechanic, "your work on the hydraulic bypass last week was probably what prevented this from being worse. Good instincts replacing those seals when you did."

Jones blinked, probably at the unexpected praise. "Thank you, Chief."

Ford secured the access panel, mind on overdrive. The vibration pattern would have been subtle but distinctive during conversion—Love would have felt it while flying, while holding the controls. She should have reported it. The fact she didn't meant either she didn't notice... or she noticed and decided to fly anyway, or she noticed, and forgot to say anything. All of the above was no good.

"Finish the diagnostic sequence," he ordered while striding toward the hangar exit. "I want a complete replacement of the housing assembly. No patches."

"Chief?" Jones called after him. "Where are you going?"

Ford kept his pace. "To have a conversation with our pilot that should have happened two flights ago."

*She might need even more time off,* he realized.

## Chapter 32:
## Empty Cup

**Year 2097**
**FOB Oteren**
**Planet Intus**

Love bent over the small desk in her quarters, struggling to read a fictional novel. She flipped through pages without really absorbing the words. Love was not one for wistful romance novels or historical dramas—she usually read to gain information. A technical manual would have been much more familiar to her than the detective book she was attempting to pass the time with. This confinement, the prison of doing nothing, grated on her nerves. Being grounded felt like being caged.

She sighed and leaned back, looking out the window.

For some reason, the grouping of trees outside brought back a memory. She and Jack had been in their apartment in Colorado, boxes half-packed for the move to New Eden. They'd been reassigned. Coffee mingled in the air with the distant sounds of life beyond their window. Love stood by the glass pane, watching children play at a park across the street.

"It's so beautiful here," she said. "Don't want to leave."

Jack looked up from the couch, where he was sorting through a pile of holodiscs. "Second thoughts?"

She shook her head. "No. Just… appreciating what we're leaving behind."

He set the discs aside and joined her by the window. "Could always stay a bit longer. There's no rush. Just up and tell them we'll take the next ship out, or just run away and find a deserted island where you and I can make love in the sand and…"

Love snorted. "Oh, wouldn't you like that? You know we don't have a choice. Plus, humanity needs us out there."

"Sit down and relax with me. You've been going nonstop."

She turned away from the window, crossing her arms. "Every day counts, Jack. You said it yourself—time is a luxury we don't have."

"Whoa. Didn't mean to anger you. But, I said that? Well, if that's what I said, it comes from genius, so you gotta listen." He rested his hand on her shoulder. "Seriously, though. Naomi, you're wearing yourself thin. When was the last time you took a break… from anything? We've got time. Packing can wait. We can slow down and enjoy ourselves."

She stiffened. "We don't have time for breaks. Besides, I don't need one. Let's get our packing done, our extra things sold, and we'll have time to relax afterward."

"You'll find something else to do. Every ounce of time that's available, you take to do something else. You're not a machine. Pushing yourself like this isn't sustainable."

She pulled away. "There's nothing wrong with doing something. I don't like sitting on my ass, Jack. You know that. You married me because I get things done."

"That's not why I married you."

"OK, well, there's that love part, too, but still…"

"Plus the good looks." Jack winked. "And who wouldn't want to be with the best pilot in the Republic? It's sexy as hell."

"Let me do… what I want to do, when I want to do it."

"Usually do, Naomi," Jack replied. "Resting isn't doing nothing. It's necessary. You can't pour from an empty cup."

She scoffed, moving to the table where her comm device buzzed. "Maybe they have something for me," she said, tapping a message. "See? Someone at the base needs me before we go."

"Naomi, please," Jack said. "Just slow down for a moment. Listen to yourself."

Spinning around, she gave him a hard stare. "Why are you trying to hold me back?"

"I'm not. Just don't want to see you burn out."

"Well, it's not your decision to make," she said.

"I'm worried about you. That a crime?"

"Stop. Just stop," she shot back. "If I wanted a dad—"
She cut her words off. "I don't need you questioning my
choices."

"Wow, this escalated quickly. Was just making an
observation."

"More like a judgment. A criticism."

"For your health. Not because you make me mad or
anything. Just would be cool to relax together, that's all." Jack
looked away. "Well, fine. I won't bring it up again."

She grabbed her jacket with the urge to escape.
"Maybe you shouldn't." She headed for the door.

"Look, it's not that big of a deal. I'm sorry. Naomi…"

She was already gone, the door clicking shut behind
her. She walked as if in a hurry, not really caring where she
ended up. Only later, much later, had she realized what he'd
been trying to say.

Back in her quarters, the memory faded, leaving pain in
its wake. Love blinked away the sting in her eyes. "I'm sorry,"
she whispered aloud.

The stillness pushed on her once more, unbearable
now. She stood, shoving the unwanted novel to the side.
Needing space, she left her room, stepping into the hallway.

Naomi realized in that moment that this intense internal
drive had been around since way before she and Jack had ever
been together—probably some ineffective coping mechanism
she'd developed during her troubled childhood. It had
worked—sort of—until now.

Being forced to sit alone with her thoughts was almost
physically painful. There was so much hurt she'd shoved
down, deep into the recesses. Her grief over the loss of Jack
was only the tip of the iceberg, really. If anything, that was the
easiest distress for her to confront.

Love found herself sitting on a chair overlooking the
lake. She didn't really remember walking there, which
frightened her a bit.

*Why isn't my head in the game?* she asked herself. She
wondered if it might actually be a good idea to talk to
someone. That thought was fleeting.

*The lake is therapy enough,* she thought. And in that moment, with the waves crashing against the shore…it was.

## Chapter 33:
## Hit and Run

**Sector 3**
**Moon Kaelus, Zhoraan Orbit**
**Rass System**
**RNS *Poseidon***

Commander Lee cursed under his breath as the *Poseidon* shuddered violently from another hit. Turning to look at the damage control board, he saw lights flashing yellow across decks five and six in section two of the ship—the mid and upper crew decks. They weren't critical sections of the ship in terms of function, but each hit strained the vessel and damaged the outer armored hull.

Lee watched as the battle continued to unfold in front of them. Streaks of red tracers zipped across the blackness of space with each volley of magrails fired at the charging enemy vessels. Intermixed between volleys of magrail fire, the ship's triple-barreled turbo laser turrets joined the fray—their brief stabs of light briefly illuminating the darkness around the *Poseidon* before connecting with a Zodark vessel. Beams cut gashes across the enemy ship's armor.

"Helm, watch out for those destroyers—they're going to flank to our port side," warned Lee as he watched the Zodark destroyers maneuver while the enemy cruisers deployed their squadrons of Vultures and Glaives. "Evasive maneuver Delta-Two, engines to fifty percent."

Two hours and thirty-three minutes ago, Lee's reconnaissance force had exited FTL near the planet Zhoraan, a class II gas giant the Primords had nicknamed "The Pale Giant" on account of its light bluish-white coloring wrapped with a handful of soft, lavender bands. The planet itself wasn't the target of their reconnaissance—its moon, Kaelus, was.

At 5,900 kilometers in diameter, it was roughly thirty-six percent the size of Earth, with less than half its gravity. While its rocky surface wasn't ideal for colonizing in Lee's mind, its high concentrations of sulfur dioxide meant it was unbreathable for humans and its wild temperature swings fluctuating between -80°C to 45°C placed it squarely at the bottom of places he'd want to call home. But the reason this moon was on the list of places his recon force had been directed to scout was because of its strategic position in the system and its value as a mining colony.

What Lee hadn't expected when they exited FTL was the amount of orbital defense buoys and laser turrets attached to various rocks and asteroids that formed a loose orbital ring around the moon. Within half an hour of activating their full suite of sensors, they had identified a host of defensive works in orbit and on the surface. They had also found a series of mining operations on the surface, like the ones Primord intelligence had shared with them were likely slave camps, with forced labor working the mines.

*As if I didn't already have enough reasons to hate Zodarks*, Lee had thought.

"Sir, we're receiving a message from Captain Dharek letting us know he's received our report, and his ships are en route to our position," Rodriguez announced, bringing Lee's contemplations back to the present. "He said we should do our best to avoid getting pinned down until his ships arrive and they can save our bacon."

"Ha ha," Sato laughed. "Did he really say that?" Her amusement was infectious.

Rodriguez smirked as she nodded. "That dry sense of humor of yours is rubbing off on him."

Lee shook his head. The Primords weren't exactly known for their sense of humor. Sato and a few others had taken it upon themselves to try and introduce it to them. The jury had still been out as to whether they were picking up on the lesson until now.

"Very well, Lieutenant. All joking aside, tell him to hurry up," Lee replied. "We've kicked up quite the hornets' nest."

Lee turned to Rhom. "What's the status on the jamming?" he asked. "Can we tell if it's working yet?"

Rhom's face turned serious as his fingers danced across his workstation. "It's hard to say. We're trying, but as of right at this moment, I'm not showing a response one way or the other."

This wasn't the answer Lee was hoping for, but he realized it was what he had.

*We need more time to test this theory…*

"Sir, I'm receiving a message from the *Scimitar*," Sato announced. "Lieutenant Mikhailov says they took a hit to their vertical launch system—their missile systems are out of the action. No ETA on when or if they can be repaired."

Almost as if on cue, the *Poseidon* shook from another hit.

"Damn it, we needed their added missiles," Lee remarked.

He paused. "OK, Sato, tell Mikhailov to pull his ship back and slide into a position on our starboard side. We'll do our best to shield them from further hits until our Primord allies join the party," Lee ordered. The last thing he wanted to do was lose another ship on a reconnaissance mission. Captain Roberts was already on his case for sustaining more damage than he thought they should have.

Sato nodded grimly, passing along his instructions.

"Hold on! Executing maneuver Delta-Two—engines now at forty-eight percent," warned Lieutenant Reynolds as the ship turned hard to port. The bow rose by twelve degrees before leveling out. Lee gripped the sides of his chair as Reynolds executed the maneuver.

From the moment the Zodark patrol near Kaelus had begun their attack, it was clear given their approach vectors, speed, and the current flanking maneuvers as their force began to split into multiple groups that they were trying to box his force in. Lee was sure it was their intention to pin them down into a fight they couldn't easily extract themselves from, until reinforcements arrived and finished them off. Little did the Zodarks know, Lee had a surprise of his own—Captain Dharek and a squadron of five Primord battleships.

"Captain, enemy destroyers closing vector three-eight-one!" Lieutenant Rhom reported, his tone sharp. "You were right, Skipper—they're targeting our port side!"

Lee acknowledged. Inside, he felt a twinge of pride that he'd guessed correctly. He turned to glance at the tactical plot as it showed which guns would soon be able to fire as Reynolds leveled the ship.

Shortly after the attack got underway, the Zodark destroyers raced ahead of the main force of four cruisers in an obvious attempt to create a pincer move. While they attacked from one side, a separate group of corvettes had swung wide in the opposite direction before turning into Lee's flank while the cruisers attacked from the center. It was a brilliant move if they could make it work, but he wasn't about to sit idly by and let it happen.

"Helm, maintain engines at fifty percent. Alter our course zero-seven-eight," Lee ordered.

He turned to face Rhom. "TAO, bring the port side batteries to bear. Prepare for broadside engagement with primary and secondary turrets—make it count, Rhom," barked Lee. The tension on the bridge continued to increase the more the enemy surrounded them.

"Aye, sir! I'm on it!" responded Reynolds, banking the *Poseidon* sharply as the ship continued its evasive maneuvers.

Lee turned to Rodriguez, locking eyes with her. "I know Rhom's been trying our bag of tricks on these, but now it's up to you to see if you can make it work. Let's see if you can't generate a little chaos within the ranks for us."

Lieutenant Rodriguez gave a devilish smile as her fingers worked her station, activating her set of ad hoc jammers MacGregor had jerry-rigged. With any luck, they'd know soon enough if the information Major Voss's team had discovered would work.

While Rodriguez was readying the EW suite, the Zodark destroyers changed their angle of attack. They headed right for Lee's force as they fired a pair of plasma torpedoes, sending ten of the flaming darts of death toward his ships.

"Incoming torpedoes—bearing one-six-four—time to impact, one minute and forty-two seconds!" announced Ensign Baldry.

"Helm, evasive maneuvers! Rhom, engage those torpedoes before they convert to plasma!" shouted Lee. Reynolds kicked the engines into overdrive, thrusters firing in quick bursts as the *Poseidon* changed course again.

"Aye, sir! Interceptors away!" Rhom acknowledged. A pair of missiles flew toward each torpedo. "PDGs engaging in thirty seconds!"

*Let's hope the interceptors take 'em out,* Lee thought to himself as he whispered a silent prayer.

On the displays, the incoming torpedoes adjusted course, doing their best to evade the interceptors bearing down on them. As the tracks continued to close, one by one they began to merge. There was a flash, and then nothing. The twenty torpedoes had been reduced to seven. Then the point defense guns joined the party—spewing hundreds of 30mm exploding projectiles into the paths of the torpedoes before they could convert to plasma.

Two of the seven incoming plasma torpedoes blew apart when they flew into a curtain of exploding shells. A third and fourth torpedo exploded when a third volley of missile interceptors connected with them moments before they converted. The final three torpedoes still racing forward toward the *Poseidon* converted to plasma—the point defense guns' 30mm projectiles were too late to stop them.

Reynolds shouted something as Lee grabbed the sides of his chair. The ship executed a hard, twisting turn to their port side in a last-ditch effort to dodge the flaming arrows of death.

"All hands, brace for impact!" Lee shouted over the ship wide network as the time to impact reached zero.

The first torpedo missed—gliding meters beneath them. However, the second and third torpedo slammed into them—the ship shook violently as alarms blared and lights flickered.

Lee felt the deck pitch hard beneath his feet as sparks cascaded from overloaded circuits along the left side of the bridge. The lights flickered briefly from power fluctuations until emergency systems switched on, stabilizing power flows.

"Damage report!" Lee barked, steadying himself against his chair.

"Hull breach in section two, deck one—heavy damage reported in section two, decks three and four, lower gun deck—turbo lasers eight and ten are offline," Sato relayed.

"Acknowledged, stay on the repairs, Sato—and get those guns back. We gotta take those destroyers out before they pummel us with more torpedoes," responded Lee.

The *Poseidon* fired another volley of magrails.

"Sir!" Rhom called over the chaos. "It looks like the jamming is beginning to work. Those squadrons of fighters and bombers are showing evidence of confusion. They appear to be holding their positions and not attacking for some reason."

Lee turned to look at the tactical display to see what Rhom was talking about. Sure enough, as he studied it, he could see the Zodark fighters and bombers holding their positions. Usually when they approached Republic ships, they would break off into smaller attack groups of two to four fighters or bombers in coordinated attack patterns. It made it harder for Republic ships to track and engage them when they attacked from multiple different directions at the same time. Now they seemed to have gaggled together in a holding pattern, like they were waiting for something to happen.

"Rodriguez, send a message to all ships to focus their fire on those destroyers while their fighters are distracted. If we've got their comms jammed, I want us to capitalize on the confusion and take some of them out while we can," directed Lee.

Rhom acted swiftly as he shifted the focus of his gun crews to target the closest destroyer, firing at near pointblank range with the *Poseidon*'s primary and secondary turrets. His gunners expertly bracketed the vessel as volleys of penetrator slugs tore into the Zodark ship.

Explosions soon blossomed across the destroyer as slug after slug detonated deep within, igniting a series of secondary explosions within the ship, until the entire thing blew apart in a giant flash of flame and debris.

The crew cheered wildly as it broke apart, a moment of exhilaration Lee was all too happy to let them have.

*But something is missing...*, Lee couldn't help but think.

"Nice shooting, Rhom! Now score us another kill like that and get our Havocs in the fight," Lee directed. "We should have been hammering those destroyers with our missiles by now. Instead, we haven't fired a single volley. Get on it, Rhom!"

Lee shook his head in frustration before brushing it aside along with some of the lingering smoke the bridge's HVAC system still hadn't cleared. He hated the smell of scorched wiring and burnt polymer. It reminded him of the Battle of Intus, a memory he'd sooner forget.

He turned to face Sato, steadying himself before asking, "What's the status on those damage reports—any progress?"

She held up a hand, her eyes darting between the damage control overlays flashing across the left-side monitor. The 3D schematic of the *Poseidon* flashed with yellow warnings in a couple of sections of the ships. Those weren't his concern—the red pulsating warnings of hull breaches and continued atmospheric leakages in several areas of deck one were causing him to sweat.

Lee was about to repeat his question when he saw Sato's face contort. "Sir, damage control teams have the gun turrets on deck three operational. Turbo lasers eight and ten are back in the fight," she finally responded, her voice tight. "The Medbay's reporting twelve injured, two dead, and that's the good news. We still have a hull breach in section two, deck one—its partially contained, but the situation—"

"Whoa, back up, Sato. There is no 'partially contained' when you're leaking atmosphere," interrupted Lee, his voice cutting like a blade. "The breach is either contained or it's not—which is it?"

She hesitated for half a beat, then forced the words out. "Um, yes, sir—you're right. The damage control teams are reporting extensive damage across much of section two, deck one. The damage appears to be contained to the storage lockers, three, four, and five—the ones that experienced a sudden decompression event when that second torpedo hit us. It caused severe structural problems across multiple bulkheads connecting the corridors between sections one and two across the entire lower two decks of the ship. They are moving quickly to find the cracks still leaking atmosphere while continuing to evacuate everyone still on deck one and two. Casualties were high..." explained Sato before she glanced down, then met his eyes again. "They are still searching for survivors that might be trapped in workstations that automatically sealed when the hull was breached. As of now, we have nineteen spacers still unaccounted for."

Lee bit his lower lip as he listened to her bring him up to speed on the damage they'd taken and the likely loss of nineteen of his people—vented into the abyss without so much as a chance to save them. He breathed deeply, flexing his hands along his sides.

*We can mourn them later. Now is not the time.*

"Damn. I'm sorry, Sato," he said, trying to maintain his composure and stay focused. "Keep on it. We need those damage control teams moving. This fight isn't over yet, and it's going to be hard to stay in the fight if we're leaking atmosphere." Lee felt bad for snapping at her earlier. The sound of alarms and damage reports streaming in were smothering all but the loudest voices.

Lee had to suppress the urge to shout in anger over the loss of nineteen of his people. Instead, he turned to face his comms officer. "Rodriguez, whatever it is you're doing to jam the comms on those Zodark ships, keep doing it—it's working," he praised.

An instant later, he cursed, "Damn it, Rhom! Where are my freaking missiles? I still don't see a single Havoc on its way to a target. What the hell is going on?"

He'd barely finished speaking when a fresh tremor moved through the *Poseidon*'s spine as another salvo raked across her armored hull. The deck under Lee's boots vibrated from the hits, but no new alarms sounded—a good sign. The armor was taking a beating but holding.

Rhom was about to reply when he paused, then yelled at someone he had been talking to before turning back to Lee. "I'm sorry about that, Skipper. The computer processing unit that controls the Havoc missiles in the VLS pods was damaged shortly after we arrived in system. We didn't know about the damage at first as the missile interceptors fired just fine. It wasn't until we started sending firing solutions to the Havocs that we discovered there was a problem," Rhom calmly explained.

He took a swig of water before he continued. "Once we knew there was a problem with the Havocs, Commander MacGregor tasked one of his engineers to swap out the CPU controlling the missiles while they tried to figure out the problem later. Somehow, during the process of removing the CPUs, it caused a series of power surges that fried the other controllers tying the Havocs to the targeting computer."

Lee held a hand up. "Hold up, Rhom," he interjected. "I'm sure there's an interesting story to all of this, but right now, I just need to know if whatever was wrong is fixed. Do we have control of our anti-ship missiles or not?"

"Yes, sorry about that. I just spoke to Lieutenant Pierre from Engineering. We're back in action," Rhom confirmed. "We've got one hundred and sixty-eight anti-ship missiles ready to rock."

"Outstanding! Let's put them to use and capitalize on our disruption of Zodark comms before they're able to figure out what's happening," directed Lee. Rhom instantly went to work issuing orders to his missileers and gun crews.

With the battle around the *Poseidon* continuing to rage, the Zodark fighters and bombers appeared to finally be advancing toward Lee's ships. Rhom's missile and gun crews responded instantly—firing interceptors in one-second intervals toward the squadrons of Vultures and Glaives. Soon, the interceptors were being joined with a near-continuous firing of the larger Havoc anti-ship missiles toward the enemy destroyers still circling around for a second attack.

The void outside the *Poseidon* was alive with fury. Laser lances flared white-hot as they snapped past the external cameras, nearly invisible until they struck debris or burned into armor plating of an enemy vessel. With the distances between the Zodark fighters and bombers closing with the waves of missile interceptors, the *Poseidon*'s sixty thirty-millimeter point defense guns began firing, spewing hundreds of exploding projectiles toward the incoming threats. A curtain of flak detonations blossomed into brief artificial novas against the endless night—spheres of shrapnel ripping apart anything in their path.

Zodark missiles, torpedoes, Vultures and Glaives were being shredded as they flew into a wall of shrapnel and ball bearings. Seeing their comrades being wiped out, the second and third waves of Zodark fighters and bombers broke off their attack runs and veered out of harm's way.

"Sir, Primord vessels *Ek* and *Simsu* are seeing a change in the formation of those Zodark cruisers and corvettes. It's too early to tell, but it looks like the Zodarks might have found a way to reestablish communications or burn through our jamming," Rodriguez called out.

*Oh great.* Lee knew their improvised jamming trick wouldn't last forever. He was hoping it might have lasted a little longer during this attack. His goal was to prove this jamming theory could work and try to smash another Zodark supply base before having to withdraw back to Kita and hand over their prisoner.

"Thank you, Lieutenant. I guess it was inevitable they'd eventually figure out what we were doing. Send a message to the rest of our force to focus their firepower on this cruiser," Lee directed, then highlighted one of the three

Zodark cruisers he wanted them to destroy before they withdrew from the battle.

"Aye, Captain, sending coordinates and instructions now," Rodriguez confirmed.

While the orders were being sent, Lee watched on the right-hand monitor as the ship's video feed showed the *Poseidon*'s turbo laser and magrail turrets realigning toward the cruiser he'd highlighted. It was always impressive watching the massive barrels traversing toward the enemy as the targeting reticles flashed yellow, acquiring their targeting before turning red—target locked.

"Captain, primary guns and turbo lasers are ready to fire!" Rhom declared from his station, his voice raw but steady as he waited for the final order.

"The Primord ships, *Ek*, *Kulente*, and *Nyx* are standing by," announced Sato. She leaned in toward him and whispered, "Sir, after we take this cruiser out, we should extract ourselves from this fight before reinforcements arrive and pin us down. We accomplished what we needed to—the jamming works."

She was right of course, and he knew it. He just hated to leave a battlespace when he felt they could win. His reconnaissance force had scored some early victories—a pair of destroyers and a frigates. If they could take out one or more of these cruisers…

"Sir, guns are ready," Rhom repeated, still waiting for Lee to give the order.

Lee held his gaze on the monitor. The cameras magnified to their fullest still barely showing the trio of Zodark cruisers racing toward Lee's force.

"All ships, all guns—fire at will!" he finally ordered.

The port side guns of the *Poseidon* flashed as they fired—magrail slugs tearing into the void as they raced to cover the distance between the charging Zodark cruisers and Lee's force. Seconds after the primaries fired, the turbo lasers joined the fray, quickly followed by groups of four Havoc anti-ship missiles firing every couple of seconds.

The space between the two forces rapidly filled with volleys of magrail projectiles and Havoc anti-ship missiles bearing down on the enemy cruisers. The Zodarks fired next, sending volleys of plasma torpedoes as their squadrons of starfighters and bombers rejoined the battle. Lee's cruiser and the pair of frigates, *Cobalt* and *Thunderbolt*, unleashed a torrent of missile interceptors to race toward the torpedoes and enemy fighters and bombers. Meanwhile, the corvettes, *Horizon*, *Polaris*, and *Scimitar*, turned sharply to starboard, bringing to bear their compliment of 30mm point defense guns—a flak wall of exploding projectiles obliterated dozens of fighters and bombers before they could react.

Tiny flashes began popping across the armor of the Zodark cruiser Lee's ship had been targeting. Stabs of energy bursts from turbo lasers tore deep gouges into the armor of the enemy ship as the first volley of magrail slugs began to arrive. Several projectiles sailed harmlessly past the cruiser—missing the ship entirely. Then a pair of slugs careened into the weakened armor, penetrating into the guts of the ships before their warheads exploded within. Several of the Havoc missiles slipped past the cruiser's point defense guns. Some exploded against its armored hull. Others pierced it, burrowing into the vessel, the warhead ripping apart multiple decks within as geysers of flame and molten steel violently ejected through holes in the ship's armor.

Secondary explosions erupted within, brief spouts of flame spewing from holes and rips across the cruiser's battered hull. Lee was about to order the guns to shift fire to the next cruiser when a brilliant flash whited out the monitors. He briefly raised his hand to shield his eyes, the auto dimmer doing the job for him a moment later.

When the camera readjusted, the crew cheered and hollered excitedly. The ship had broken apart. The forward section was still careening toward them, although the rear section had broken into smaller sections, scattering in various directions as tiny flashes of electricity arced and remnants of atmosphere rapidly extinguished in the void of space.

"Switching to second targets," Rhom announced as the ship's guns resumed firing.

Rodriguez began relaying the new target when Sato's voice cut through the noise. "Sir, *Scimitar* and *Polaris* are reporting damage. *Polaris* took a direct hit from one of the cruisers; they've lost their primary weapons and targeting systems are down. *Scimitar* is reporting damage to their engines—they're falling out of formation."

"Sir, sensors are detecting multiple ships inbound," Lieutenant Reynolds announced. "It's the Primords! They're here." He paused. "We're receiving a message from Captain Dharek."

An image of the Primord captain aboard the *Ek* appeared on Lee's terminal next to his chair. "Commander, we were unexpectedly delayed. I hope you were able to conduct your test and obtained the data you needed because we need to get out of here ASAP!"

"We did. And yes, it works," Lee quickly confirmed before adding, "Affirmative on getting out of here. Do we have more Zodarks inbound to our position?"

Captain Dharek looked off screen for a second before returning to look at Lee. "We do. Looks to be a sizable force. ETA sixty seconds."

*Oh crap, that's quick,* he thought to himself.

"Great, well see if your ships can't draw some fire off ours while we spool up our FTL drives. Lee out." He disconnected the call and immediately ordered his ships to jump to the rally point and out of the area. One by one, acknowledgments rolled in.

Across the forward screen, the Republic and Primord warships began pivoting away from the tightening Zodark lines, laying down thick fields of covering fire as they disengaged.

The *Poseidon* shuddered again, a fresh wave of return fire lashing across her armor. Lee gritted his teeth, feeling the tension coil in his chest as Reynolds prepared the ship to FTL out of there. He watched as his ships jumped, vanishing before the next volley of lasers and plasma torpedoes could reach them. Seconds later, he felt his own ship surge forward, the stars elongated into lines as the *Poseidon* entered FTL, leaving the battlefield behind.

Lee allowed himself a small breath of relief once they were clear of the danger. They had survived another fight. And they had discovered a weakness in Zodark communications that might turn the tide in coming battles.

But first, they had to live long enough to exploit it.

**Chapter 34:**
**Locus of Control**

**RNS** *Poseidon*
**FTL Transit — Vector Toward Primord Space**

The bridge of the *Poseidon* buzzed with controlled activity as damage reports scrolled across Lee's display. Acrid smoke still lingered faintly in the air from the earlier hits, and the smell of scorched metal clung to every surface.

Lieutenant Rhom stepped up beside him, datapad in hand.

"Captain, preliminary casualty and damage reports," he said quietly, showing him the numbers but not daring to say them all out loud. "Across the fleet, we've sustained moderate damage: *Polaris* and *Scimitar* took the worst of it, but there were no vessels lost. Primord ships report manageable hits."

Lee took the pad, scanning the summarized data.

*Could have been worse*, he thought. *Should have been worse, given the odds.*

He exhaled slowly, feeling the fatigue settling into his bones. They'd walked a razor's edge—and somehow lived to tell the tale.

"Good work, Lieutenant. Pass along my personal thanks to the medical teams and damage control crews. They kept us in the fight."

Rhom nodded crisply. "Aye, sir."

Rodriguez turned from her station. "Captain, incoming secured transmission from Captain Roberts aboard the *Australia*. Priority level one."

Lee stood, then answered, "Send the call to my office. Sato, with me. Rhom, you've got the bridge until we're back."

Sato walked after him. "Are you sure you want me on the call?"

Lee sighed as they walked into his office. "Yeah, it's best for you to hear whatever it is he's going to say."

As Lee sat behind his desk, the monitor flashed showing the call had been transferred. He looked at Sato and then accepted the call. The screen flickered, then resolved into the stern, weathered face of Captain Eamon Roberts.

"Commander Lee, I understand you completed the final reconnaissance mission I assigned you," Roberts said without preamble. "Go ahead, report."

Lee sat a bit straighter as he collected his thoughts. "Yes sir. We just completed the final mission, and I wanted to report it was a success. You were right, the Zodarks were using the cover of Zhoraan's magnetosphere to disrupt long-range sensors and shield their activities on the moon Kaelus."

"Hot damn! I knew it," exclaimed Roberts excitedly as he slammed his hand against the desk he was sitting at. "This is great news, Lee! Tell me what you found."

Sato shot him a knowing smile, shaking her head at Roberts's predictability.

Lee nodded. "During our final reconnaissance mission in Sector 3, we were able to confirm the presence of Zodark activity near the moon Kaelus," he began. "At first, the magnetosphere caused some issues for our sensors, but as we got closer to the moon, we began to detect the presence of what appeared to be a fairly large mining operation. As we continued to approach, our sensors further confirmed the presence of planetside and orbital military facilities, orbital sensors, defensive works, and localized patrols consisting of orbital gun boats, Vulture starfighters, and a handful of corvettes.

"But sir, the real intelligence coup was the successful testing of a new electronic warfare protocol we developed with support from Major Voss's Det-5 exploitation team—"

"Wait, what? A new EW protocol?" interrupted Roberts, a hesitant look on his face.

"Yes, sir," Lee confirmed with a nod. "In fact, none of this would have been possible if you hadn't sent us that intelligence exploitation team after we captured that Zodark pilot. Their technical intelligence experts, in collaboration with their insanely good interrogation team, were able to identify a previously unknown Zodark communication system. We believe this is likely why our previous EW effectiveness had suddenly stopped being as successful as it had been during and following the Intus Campaign."

Roberts facial expression transformed in an instant, smiling broadly at the praise directed at him. He sat up a little straighter, nodding for Lee to continue. A bemused Sato smiled at him. Lee was still learning how to handle Roberts, and making sure he was given all the credit for anything good that happened was a surefire way to stay on the man's good side.

"If you'll recall, sir, Space Command conducted a post-Intus study to examine what went right and wrong during the campaign as part of the after-action review process. A key finding was a noticeable degradation in the effectiveness of our electronic warfare efforts compared to previous battles. At the time, no one was sure what happened or if something could be done about it. Captain Chen and Major Voss believe we have concrete proof of what happened and now have a solution that could restore our previous effectiveness. In fact, Major Voss is saying this could be one of the biggest intelligence finds of the war. I made sure he mentioned that this wouldn't have been possible if you hadn't made the call to bring in Det-5 following the capture our Zodark pilot. Major Voss did ask if we could return his team and the prisoner to Kita for further debriefing and study of the captured starfighter," explained Lee.

"Well done, Commander Lee," Roberts replied. "You have done an incredible job executing my reconnaissance plan for the Rass system. I'm glad to hear the intelligence team I sent you paid off. I took a lot of risk getting that team to you, and I look forward to reading this report from Major Voss before it's sent to Fleet Command. Now before I send you back to Kita, what is the status of your reconnaissance force and that of Captain Dharek and his QRF element?"

Lee sighed quietly to himself as he now prepared to deliver the bad news that he knew Roberts wasn't going to be happy about. Steeling himself, he dove in. "Ah, yes, sir. Well, I'm afraid our efforts to recon these areas haven't been without loss or damage. In fact, this last mission was by far the hardest of them. In terms of damages and casualties—I'll just get to it. The *Scimitar* lost nine crewmen when a torpedo tore through their forward weapon control center. The ship also sustained damage to their propulsion system that's going to require some time in the yard to fully repair.

"The *Polaris* took damage to their VLS system. One of the Havoc missiles detonated inside its cell—that unfortunately caused a hull breach, disabling half the ship's weapon systems. Twelve crewmen were lost when they were unfortunately vented during the hull breach. The ship is still flyable—we didn't have to abandon it—but it's pretty torn up and likewise is going to need some time in the shipyard before she'll be ready for action again."

The longer Lee spoke, the more Roberts's face turned from joyous to frustrated anger. Swallowing hard, Lee pressed on, knowing it was better to rip the band aid off and be done with it than delay the tongue-lashing he knew was coming.

"The *Poseidon* sustained damage during the engagement as well. We took two torpedo hits to decks one and two along the forward section of the ship. One of the torpedoes ripped a gash in our hull, just below the hangar deck—it vented storage lockers three, four, and five. It thoroughly destroyed most of our stored fabrication materials and many of our food supplies. We lost nineteen—spaced when the hull breached. We lost another eight more before damage control teams were able to regain control of the area.

"Commander MacGregor believes what caused the bulk of the damage was the angle of the torpedo hits. The first one tore through most of our armored hull. When the second one hit, the brunt of its explosive force punched through deck one and into parts of deck two. The sudden decompression event across the two decks caused multiple bulkheads to buckle, which led to further structure damage across other areas of decks one, two, and threatened to compromise parts of deck three—"

"Damn it to hell, Lee! I thought I had made it clear to you and the other ship captains to avoid direct combat with Zodark vessels at all costs for this exact reason!" interrupted

Roberts, his Irish tone sharp, his face beet red. "What's the total casualty count for your ship and the rest of your reconnaissance force?"

"The Primords lost sixteen KIA and forty-three wounded. My force lost forty-eight KIA and one hundred and nine wounded," Lee answered bluntly.

"So, what you are telling me, Commander, is two of *my* corvettes and a heavy cruiser, *yours,* are likely going to take more than a week or two of repairs before I'll have *my* ships back. On top of that, you lost forty-eight of *my* spacers and another one hundred and nine wounded. Is that correct? Is that what *you* cost me on this mission?" Roberts scolded, his tone cutting deep.

Lee opened his mouth to speak, then closed it when the words failed to materialize. Roberts's gaze continued to bore a hole through him as his superior officer waited for him to respond. "I suppose that is one way to look at it, sir."

"Oh really? And how else should I look at it, Commander?" countered Roberts coldly.

Lee wanted to reach across the video monitor to punch Roberts in the face, but he knew that kind of response would land him a court-martial and the loss of his command. Biting his tongue, Lee chose his words carefully. "Sir, your ships were damaged during a mission that uncovered a secret Zodark military base. The crew that was lost gave their lives to verify a potential way to jam enemy communications and targeting sensors—a success that will likely save the lives of countless thousands of Republic and Primord spacers and ground forces when the Rass campaign officially starts. It was a complete mission success that wouldn't have been possible without the courageous leadership of the task force commander, you—that's one way of looking at it."

Sato covered her mouth in shock. Her eyes went wide as they waited to hear what Roberts would say next.

"I suppose that is one way we could look at it," Roberts finally replied, his face softening just a bit. "Look, Lee—there is a reason I gave you guys a specific order to avoid enemy contact. I wasn't naïve enough to believe you guys would be able to scout these areas without detection—that was a given. But we lost a lot of ships during the Intus invasion. And those losses can't be easily replaced as our shipyards are limited in how many warships we can produce."

Roberts paused a second as he looked off screen, then returned his gaze back to Lee. "When Admiral Halsey assigned these Altairian-Human hybrid ships, she made it clear we needed to do our best to hold on to them. We're not supposed to lose them unnecessarily or damage them up so badly they'd be stuck in the yard for months when we need them in service. It's going to be a little while longer before these new warships begin arriving at scale. Losing the three of your ships for an unknown period of time is going to hurt."

Roberts tapped something off-screen, then returned his gaze to Lee. "OK, new orders: take your task force back to Primord space and the Kita Shipyard. I'll send a request for dock space and priority repair status. Your first order of business is to finish a report on this new equipment you tested and explain what's needed to upgrade your ship's EW equipment. We need to pass this newfound information on to the rest of the Fleet. We can't do anything about the crewmen we lost, but we can make sure their loss wasn't in vain."

Lee exhaled the breath he hadn't realized he'd been holding, then nodded sharply. "Understood, sir."

"Good," said Roberts. "Your second priority is transferring Major Voss, Det-5, and the Zodark prisoner to headquarters. Republic Intelligence is going to want squeeze this pilot to learn everything they can from him. We've captured him, now it's their turn to exploit him."

"Yes, sir."

Roberts' eyes narrowed slightly. "Be advised, Commander—this disruption tactic won't stay secret for long. You can bet Zodark high command will adapt—quickly, like they always do. What you found has a fleeting window of opportunity. Depending on how long your repairs will take, we might have a chance to exploit it. We'll see what Fleet HQ and the Primords want us to do."

"Understood, sir," Lee replied. "We'll do what we can to get repairs move quickly."

Roberts gave a tight nod. "I'm sure you will. Get your ships patched up. Get your EW upgraded. And get ready to hit them harder next time."

"Aye, sir," Lee said firmly.

"Roberts out."

The screen blanked and Lee slumped back in his chair, exhausted.

"That was tough. Guy's a real piece of work, Lee," Sato confided.

Lee shrugged. "We all answer to someone. Even Roberts."

"Yeah, well, not everyone has to be a dick about it," Sato replied as she stood. "I'll set a course to Kita and let the others know. Why don't you grab some rack time or shower or whatever. You should take some time to rest before we arrive. I've got this."

Lee smiled, nodding slowly. He knew she was right. Besides, he had forty-eight letters to write. "I'll be in my quarters. Let me know when we're approaching Kita. Oh, and Sato…thank you."

As she left his office, Lee wanted nothing more than to scream in anger and frustration at Roberts.

*Control what you can control*, he reminded himself, *and let go of what you can't.*

It was a phrase his father used to tell him. Lee found himself repeating it a lot lately. Maybe his dad was right. Maybe he should have stayed away from the military. Then again, if he had, who knew how things would have turned out in the battles he had fought.

*I guess we'll never know…*

## Chapter 35:
## Ready to Fly

**Year 2097**
**FOB Oteren**
**Planet Intus**

Inside his office, Granger took a seat behind his desk before motioning for Lieutenant Naomi Love to have a seat. She sat straight as a ramrod, hoping to demonstrate both her eagerness and her readiness to get back into the action.

"How are you holding up?" asked Granger, studying her face. "I mean, honestly."

"Never better. The off-time did wonders," she fibbed. While the sleep had been useful, all that time in her head had really gotten to her. If anything, she felt less mentally prepared for duty than before she'd left.

"Glad to hear it," Granger replied. He paused. "Are you sure you're all right?" he pressed.

"I am," she lied, her mind still a little off.

"Well, that's good, Lieutenant, because we've got a mission for you."

Immediately, her world grew brighter. "Absolutely."

"You're sure you're good to go?" Granger's voice betrayed his hesitation.

"Sir, with due respect, please trust my answer when I say I'm ready to fly."

He nodded. "Fair enough. It's another medevac operation. Urgent extraction."

"When do we depart?"

"Now."

She moved to her feet. "I'm ready."

"The mission details are uploading to your HUD in your Osprey."

"Understood." She headed for the door.

"Love," Granger called after her. "Fly safe."

She gave a quick nod and stepped back into the corridor. She focused on her strides, each one more confident than the last. "You're fine," she told herself. "Back in action. You're fine. Totally fine."

Inside the hangar, mechanics moved between ships. Fuel filled the air. *Jack*, her Osprey, stood at the center.

Ford read from a datapad near the ramp before he looked up at Love. "Lieutenant on deck!"

"At ease, Ford."

Green emerged from under a wing. "Ready to roll, Lieutenant?"

"Wouldn't miss it."

Lane, the gunner, climbed down from the turret. "Systems are prepped. She's in prime condition."

Love walked up the ramp. "Excellent work."

Inside, the medical team organized their equipment. They glanced up as she entered.

"Lieutenant Love," Ito greeted her. "Good to have you with us."

"Always a pleasure, Major. Everything set?"

Ito patted a portable med unit. "We're ready for anything."

Love moved to the cockpit. Controls beckoned, and she settled into her captain's chair. Screens illuminated.

Green joined her, running preflight checks. "All systems nominal."

"Flight plan received." She scanned the mission data. "Hot zone extraction. High stakes." *Just what the doctor ordered.*

"Just the way you like it."

"Yep." She glanced back toward the cabin. Medics secured equipment, Ford checked weapons, and Williams oversaw the loading.

Love put on her helmet and shut the visor. "Comm check," Love said into her helmet.

"Clear," came Green's response.

"Good to go," Williams echoed.

"All set back here," Ford added.

After sticking Jack's photo on the dash, she powered up the engines, kissed her fingers, and pressed her fingertips against Jack's face. "Control, this is *Jack* requesting departure clearance."

"Clearance granted. Safe travels, *Jack*."

"Copy that." Love grasped the controls. "All right, team, let's bring them home."

**Chapter 36:**
**Edge of Darkness**

**Year 2097**
**FOB Oteren**
**Planet Intus**

The Osprey lifted, rising above the base. Clouds parted as they ascended, the darkening sky embracing them.

"ETA to extraction point?" Love asked.

"Fifteen minutes," Green replied.

"Close by." She adjusted their course. Terrain data streamed across the HUD. Enemy positions, marked in red, dotted the map. The tactical overlay showed at least three Zodark heavy weapon emplacements. Infantry signatures swarmed between hardened positions, their movements hinting at a coordinated push toward Echo Company's position. Love studied the terrain mapping—the ridgelines gave minimal cover for their approach, and the enemy's anti-aircraft batteries had firing angles from their elevated positions.

"Expecting resistance," Green noted.

"Understood."

Ford's voice chimed in. "Gunners are ready. Med team is standing by."

"Keep sharp."

"How's our pilot doing up there?" Ford asked. There was concern in his voice, more so than she liked.

"Couldn't be better," Love responded.

"Glad to have you back," Williams said.

"Glad to be here."

The landscape below changed to rocky terrain. Smoke trails indicated conflict ahead. The valley below had become a war-torn hellscape. Artillery had glassed huge swaths of ground, leaving crystallized craters. Through breaks in the smoke came flashes of heavy weapons fire. Burning vehicles dotted the landscape, their armor still glowing red-hot from direct hits. The air was thick with particulate matter, creating a hazy dome over the battlefield that their sensors struggled to penetrate.

"Visual on combat zone," Green said.

Love narrowed her gaze. "Stand by for hard break."

"Standing by."

Anti-aircraft fire arced upward. Love banked hard, maneuvering through the onslaught. The Osprey responded well, thanks to Williams and Ford's maintenance.

"Hang on back there," she called out.

"All good," Williams said.

"You good?" Ford asked Love.

Love made a face. "I'm good."

Through the cockpit holowindow, bolts sliced through the murk. Love punched the Osprey through a wall of ground-based defense fire. The hull vibrated around her. Warning indicators flashed across her holo as she kept the ship's nose down, hugging the terrain.

"Taking fire from multiple vectors," Green said, swiping through defensive holograms. "Missile launch, three o'clock!"

Love rolled hard port. The Osprey's gravitational compensators worked hard as she wove between the rocky outcrops. Below, weapons fire strobed through the valley where Echo Company had been pinned down for the last six hours, according to the mission report. The designated LZ was a narrow strip of flat ground, currently being churned up by artillery fire.

The LZ was barely wider than the Osprey. There was wreckage on one side and a sheer rock face on the other. Impact craters pockmarked the approach, and pieces of shattered combat vehicles created an obstacle course. Their sensors showed a horrible picture—unstable ground from repeated artillery strikes, dangerous debris, and limited space to move. Not great. A direct hit had left a still-burning APC blocking the landing area, forcing them to come in at an angle that would expose their port side to enemy fire.

"Echo Actual, this is Wolfpack Lead," she said. "Visual on your position. Multiple hostiles, marking your LZ as hot. Stand by for immediate medevac."

Through her enhanced visor display, she could make out the scattered forms of the infantry squad, using broken barriers as cover. Their return fire was sporadic—they were running low on charges. An energy blast impacted twenty meters from their position. It threw debris upward.

"Copy, Wolfpack Lead," a voice radioed back. "We've got three critical. Can't hold this position much longer."

Love could feel that her head wasn't in the game the way that it usually was. Her thoughts drifted. She wondered if she had made the wrong call telling Granger she was ready to return to duty. She had taken the prescribed break, but somehow found herself thinking of all the dark emotions she had never processed, going way, way back. Maybe she should have gone to talk to someone after all.

*Stay focused!* she thought.

Love dropped the ship's nose further to prepare for the hot extraction. "Thirty seconds out. Pop markers on my mark. Bringing her down."

Ford's tone boomed through Love's helmet. "Taking up overwatch, laying down suppression."

Love steered the craft. She compensated for the scarred earth as she brought the Osprey down. The deck vibrated beneath her boots while Ford and Williams opened up with the heavy guns.

"Starboard battery engaged!" Ford said through the open channel as his turret lit up the ridgeline. "Multiple hostiles, eleven o'clock!"

"Port side covered," Williams responded, his gun thundering through the hull. "Keeping their heads down!"

The ship's targeting system showed threats across Love's visor in red markers. She held steady, bleeding off speed, feeling every minute adjustment through the stick. Beside her, Green monitored their hull integrity, calling out damage reports.

"Taking hits on the stern plating," Green said, reading data from the damage control console. "Hull stress at acceptable levels, but we can't stay exposed too long."

Love eased the thrusters as landing struts made contact. Dust and debris whirled around the viewports. The ship settled with a shudder.

"Solid ground contact," Love said. "Ramp down. Let's get our people home."

"Move, move, move!" Major Ito directed as the medics deployed.

Love tracked the evacuation unfolding on the external feeds. Echo Company had been pushed back to their final defensive line, using the broken remains of their defense perimeter as cover. Zodark assault teams were advancing in triangle formations, their heavy armor deflecting most of the return fire. To the north, their sensors picked up energy signatures of Zodark units moving into position. The Republic ground forces were running out of time—and options. Reports from the ground told her that the incoming casualties she was about to pick up were in critical condition.

Love glanced at the monitor for the back. Her medics sprinted from the ramp, kits clutched under their arms. The first casualty came in supported between two corpsmen—a soldier with most of his left leg missing below the knee. It looked like he'd lost a lot of blood before someone had applied a tourniquet—even on her small video feed, Love could see that he was pale as a ghost and nearly unconscious.

Another patient was brought on with multiple shrapnel wounds and severe plasma burns to their torso. A third was unconscious, and judging by the amount of blood on their head, they'd suffered severe head trauma.

While Major Ito and her team went to work, red dots closed in from the north. Ford and Williams maintained their suppressing fire, but the enemy was getting bolder.

"We need immediate dust-off," Ito said over the comms. "This one won't make it if we don't get him to surgery now."

Love nodded. "Echo Actual, confirm all casualties loaded. We're taking increasingly heavy fire."

"Wolfpack Lead, this is Echo Actual. All critical casualties aboard. Three walking wounded still crossing to your position. Fifteen seconds to complete load-up. We'll provide covering fire from our position."

On Love's tactical display, the last three soldiers limped toward the ramp. The look of one of them reminded her of a man her mother had brought over once when she was a child—the shouting had caused her to hide in her closet for the evening. She could feel the same fear and rage welling up inside of her.

*Not now!* she told herself.

"Incoming hostiles," Green said. "Multiple Zodark signatures, moving fast from the ridgeline."

Love blinked hard, forcing herself to focus. "Noted." She prepped for immediate ascent. She didn't have time for these dark thoughts—not now. Not with lives depending on her.

The ship's sensors screamed as blaster bolts from Zodark weapons started impacting their hull. Williams and Ford returned fire.

"Two Zodarks down!" Ford said. "But more incoming—they're trying to flank us!"

"All patients secured," Ito confirmed from the med bay. "Three walking wounded aboard!"

"Retracting ramp," Ford said, the hydraulics whining as the ramp sealed.

Love's head swam again, but she gritted her teeth. Each breath was a battle as she fought to stay focused. The cockpit seemed to shrink around her, displays blurring, then sharpening with each pulse of her racing heart. She could hear the medical team working behind her. The thought of failing them, of succumbing to weakness at this very moment, was worse than any enemy fire. "Stay with me," she whispered to herself, forcing her breathing to steady, forcing her hands to remain firm on the controls.

"Time to fly." She punched the thrusters. The Osprey lurched upward as enemy fire intensified. A direct hit rocked the ship. Klaxons blared.

"Port stabilizer taking damage," Green said, working on the damage control panel. "Compensating!"

Love rolled the ship hard to starboard, avoiding another volley of fire. Cold sweat beaded on her forehead. She pushed the Osprey higher despite the damaged stabilizer.

"Course set for base," Green said, plotting their escape vector. "We've got enough altitude. They can't touch us now."

The ship leveled out. Enemy fire fell away below them. Love released a shaky breath. Her hands trembled slightly on the controls. She'd done it. They were clear.

The realization that her lack of focus had nearly cost them their lives hit her hard. She cleared her throat. "Good work, everyone."

"Patients stabilizing," Ito reported from the bay. "We've got them."

"Glad to hear it," Love said, silently thankful her momentary lapse hadn't been worse. The base was growing larger on their forward screens.

Despite it all, she was back where she belonged. She'd proven—to herself most of all—that she could do this. Still, the thought lingered—*Why am I struggling all of a sudden? What is it that is making it so hard to keep my head where it belongs?* The image of the ship spiraling down, of all those wounded soldiers in the back trusting her with their lives, of Green unable to take control in time…

She pushed the thoughts away. Still, they clung like sticky gum—a reminder that next time she might not be so lucky.

## Chapter 37:
## Burden of Command



**Stavros Naval Shipyard-Helios Forge**
**Kita System**

Commander Ripley Lee stood alone on the observation deck, enjoying a silent moment.

The observation room was a thing of beauty—a wide, curved viewing panel stretched across the chamber like a cathedral window, framed by matte-black support struts and traced with faint Primord glyphs etched into polished obsidian walls. The floor beneath his boots was dark stone, flecked with silver veins that glinted under the soft underfloor lights. There were no consoles, no people…just the view, and silence.

With his eyes fixed on the stars beyond, Lee stood with his shoulders squared but heavy with the burden of command.

His ship, the *Poseidon*, floated in the distance, still tethered to its service gantry. The gashes to her hull were being sealed like a cauterized wound before they could be covered with new armored plating. In other areas along her hull, she bore the scars and scorched marks of her last engagement, each a story of triumph over her enemies.

While the final gashes were healed, a trio of maintenance drones worked along her forward spine, their plasma torches casting flickering blue reflections across the sleek, checkered gray-and-black exterior paint scheme of her upgraded sensor mast. Beneath her, a spiderweb of gantries, tugs, and power lines fed into her flank, like a skilled trauma surgeon reconnecting the arteries to a body after surgery.

His ship was nearly whole again, but Lee wasn't so sure he felt the same.

The battle near Kaelus had cost him twenty-seven crewmen. Nineteen of them had vented in an instant when the torpedoes hit. More had died afterward from burns, blunt trauma, and corridors that failed to seal. When Lee walked the decks of his ship after arriving in Kita, he could still hear the sounds of that battle echo in her halls, the screams of pain and agony from those hurt by the sudden arc of a power cable. The smell of burnt flesh, fried circuitry, and melted plastics still lingered long after the battle was over. And while the *Poseidon* had survived its brushes with death, Lee wasn't sure if part of him died with each close call, with each near miss.

Lee shook his head, pushing aside those thoughts before they went further. When he looked up, past the *Poseidon* and into the sprawling Stavros Naval Shipyard, he couldn't help but marvel at just how big this facility was. It was like a mechanical archipelago with clusters of massive skeletal shipyards connected to clusters of iron forges, factories, fabricators, and warehouses. All of this to support the war effort, a war Lee hoped the Republic could end.

Touching the glass, he activated a magnifier, zooming in to see a line of giant skeletal frames—capital ships, the informational icon told him. They were being assembled in groups, clusters of six warships, each cluster in various stages of completion.

*Thirty, maybe more,* Lee counted absently.

When his eyes returned to the *Poseidon,* he hoped the upgrades to her sensor pods and arrays that now included the recently discovered Gamma bands would restore the Republic's EW edge they'd once had. What Major Voss's people had uncovered could prove to be game-changing, if the Republic and Primords could discover a way to use it at scale before the Zodarks found yet another way to defeat it.

Lee recalled the conversation he had had with Lieutenant Rodriguez the other day when he was inspecting the repairs on the *Poseidon*. She'd told him the engineers had finalized the gamma-band spoofers and would have final calibrations before the end of the week. Lee just hoped the ship would be ready by the time Captain Roberts arrived in a couple of days.

He exhaled slowly, the weight in his chest tightening again. The image of Captain Roberts's red face replayed in his head. The scolding. The condescension. The inability of this old, crusty spacer to trust his people to do their jobs was grating. One of these days, Lee was going to have to confront him about it.

Lee looked at the *Poseidon* before tapping the glass with a knuckle. "Next time… we hit them harder," he said, his voice barely above a whisper.

He turned and left, making his way back into the station, where the rest of his crew was staying while the final repairs were completed.
*******


**Later that Evening**

The scent of roasted beans drifted through the air, faint but grounding. It mixed with the antiseptic tang of the repair bays and the distant hum of industrial compressors—a smell and soundscape only a naval yard could offer. Commander Ripley Lee stood in line, debating whether he actually wanted the coffee or just the moment of stillness the place provided.

This coffee shop was a new addition to the Stavros Naval Shipyard. Apparently, the Primords had realized that they could make some serious money off the Republic-wide vice of caffeine consumption. Lee saw the occasional Primord sitting there, but he wasn't sure if they were actually interested in the java or if they just had business with people from the Republic.

Lee continued the slow march forward until he realized that Lieutenant Rhom was there. He sat alone at a side table, near a viewport, half-slouched, staring into an empty mug as if it held the answer to a question he hadn't dared ask aloud.

Lee didn't hesitate. He ordered two coffees—black, standard issue—and made his way over. "Room for one more?"

Rhom blinked. He hadn't even noticed him coming. "Y-yes, sir. Of course."

Lee slid into the seat across from him, setting one cup down with a quiet clink. "No ranks right now—just two men who walked away from a bad day."

Rhom looked down. "Some of them didn't walk away. Because of me."

Lee didn't speak at first. He just wrapped his hands around the mug and let the warmth seep into his fingers.

Rhom finally broke the silence. "They were trying to fix the dorsal capacitor relay—Deck Seven. I gave the order. Manual override. We didn't have time to wait for the systems to recycle."

"And they died when the auxiliary breaker failed and exploded," Lee finished, nodding.

Rhom's eyes widened, and his cheeks flushed a bit.

"I read the damage report," Lee said quietly. "I had to, not to assign blame or anything. I read it because I needed to understand what happened. Just like you."

Rhom swallowed, throat tight. "If I'd waited ten more seconds—"

"They'd still be dead, Rhom," Lee interrupted gently. "And the forward batteries would've stayed offline at a critical time during that assault. We almost certainly would have lost the whole port side gun batteries. God, we probably would have lost the ship."

Rhom said nothing.

"It was a tough call, but you made a choice," Lee said. "The kind every officer hopes they'll never have to make, but knows one day they will. You traded lives to save lives. That's the job."

"It doesn't feel like a trade," Rhom muttered. "Feels like theft."

Lee stared into the swirling dark of his drink. "Yeah. It does."

The silence that followed wasn't awkward—it was familiar. Heavy, but shared.

"I used to think if I just got good enough—fast enough, smart enough—I could save them all," Rhom said. "That if I trained harder, drilled deeper, calculated better, no one would have to die under my command."

Lee's lips curved—not a smile, exactly, but something close. "You still believe that?"

"I… I want to."

"You're not alone," Lee said, his voice low. "I used to carry every name like it was carved into my skin. Twenty-seven lost. Nineteen of them gone in the first hit. You know how long it takes to suffocate in the vacuum of space? Less time than it takes to say goodbye."

Rhom winced. "So how do you do it, sir? How do you keep going?"

Lee looked at him fully, the weight behind his eyes not hidden but held. "You remember their names. You learn from what went wrong. Then you honor them by not letting the guilt bury you."

He leaned forward. "And here's the thing they don't teach you at the Academy. Sometimes the only way you can help someone else is by giving them the advice you needed to hear yourself."

Rhom met his gaze. "You mean like right now?"

Lee gave a slow nod. "Exactly like now."

A beat passed.

"Thank you, sir," Rhom said, more grounded than before. "I didn't know how badly I needed this."

Lee tapped his mug gently against Rhom's. "Neither did I."

They sat a while longer, the stars turning beyond the viewport, silent witnesses to a war that still raged—but for now, they held.

## Chapter 38:
### Codeword Athena

**Three Days Later**
**Republic Liaison Wing, Skjarnhold Command**
*Valdrakar, Primordia, Kita System*

"Admiral Chester Bailey, it is an honor to welcome you to Skjarnhold," offered Admiral Elvak Torsen as he welcomed the Republic Fleet Admiral.

Admiral Bailey smiled warmly, "The pleasure is mine, Admiral Torsen. Thank you again for hosting this meeting. We have much to discuss."

The Primord admiral nodded as he guided the Republic entourage into the briefing room. Rear Admiral Fran McKee was with Bailey for this one, and Primord Chief of Naval Operations, Admiral Dhorsar and Admiral Velmiran, the Head of Primord Naval Intelligence, were already waiting for them.

As Bailey made his way toward the table, he was drawn to the activity happening beyond the glass wall. Given the numerous spatial maps denoting different star systems and activities happening within them, Bailey guessed the room was an operations center.

After the required niceties were exchanged, Admiral Torsen began, "Admiral Bailey, I wanted to take a moment to commend your forces. Your people have proven to be capable fighters, despite only becoming a space-faring population a short time ago."

Bailey reflected on the fact that Torsen's people had been at war for more than a hundred years and wondered if the Republic had the stomach for that kind of fight. Sure, Earthers were adept combatants, but they typically liked to go in hard and fast and end the conflict as swiftly as possible.

"I appreciate your kind words, Admiral Torsen, but you and I both know that you didn't bring me here for compliments. What can I help with?" he asked.

Torsen seemed amused, although very little had changed in his expression. "You Earthers are quite direct," he replied. "It is a bit shocking for our Primord culture, but also, somewhat appreciated. I suppose we can just move to the part where I get to the point."

Admiral Dhorsar tapped a code into the table in front of him, and a drawer opened. Inside was a datapad, which Admiral Torsen used to project a 3-D holographic image above the table. Admiral Bailey squinted, unsure of what he was looking at.

*Is that a rock with spikes on it?* he wondered, intrigued.

"This is Varnak Outpost," explained Admiral Velmiran. "Due to its location in an asteroid field and the numerous countersurveillance measures employed by the Zodarks, it was very difficult spot to find. However, recent intelligence has led us to believe that this location is being used to stage Zodark ships and supplies for what our intelligence service believes is a potential attack on Intus. Further, we have calculated that the section of the Varnak outpost where the reactor core is located would be most vulnerable to kinetic strikes."

Admiral Torsen leaned forward. "Our ships do not have magrail technology, as you know. Republic warships do, and have proven to be incredibly effective against Zodark vessels and defensive platforms. Destroying this outpost is a high priority. We would like to request the assistance of your newly acquired Altairian-Human hybrid heavy cruisers for this operation."

Admiral Dhorsar chimed in. "The weapons aboard the *Poseidon, Oceanus, Thunder, Argo, Atlantis, and Stockholm* are the most advanced magnetic railguns in your navy. If they could participate in this operation, assist us in destroying this outpost—it could greatly aid us in removing one more obstacle before our joint invasion to retake the system from the Zodark Empire."

Admiral Bailey leaned back and stroked his chin. The Primords were direct as well, even if they took a little longer to get there. Unfortunately, the Republic didn't have a lot of ships to spare, not until the Altairians shipyards began steady deliveries of them. He looked over at Admiral Fran McKee, who shrugged.

"Well, I would love to help, but our resources are stretched a bit thin at the moment, and if I'm being honest, this looks like a bit of a suicide mission," Bailey said.

Admiral Velmiran nodded. "Without any additional information, you would be correct. However, we have been scouting this location for a long time, and we have uncovered a regularly scheduled supply convoy that travels from this location here," he explained, pulling up an appropriate star map to demonstrate his point. "We plan to interdict this group of ships, and then through the use of some electronic trickery, we are going to use the captured the IFF codes from this convoy and spoof the Zodark sensors approaching the outpost. This will allow us to trick them long enough for our ships to reach this point here." On the visuals of Varnak Outpost, a gap in the asteroid field appeared. "We believe that if we use the recent breakthrough in Gamma band jamming and have some help from your electronic warfare frigates, we can trick the Zodarks into believing our raiding force is their supply convoy, or at least deceive them long for our ships to get in close and attack."

Bailey smiled as he listened, nodding slowly as he played it out in his head. "Wow. That's genius, really. I have to admit; that is an audacious plan."

He turned to McKee. "Fran, I know we're tight on ships. Do we have any resources you can provide for this effort?"

"Well, Captain Eamon Roberts does have a small squadron of vessels working with Captain Yrithael, the Primord Commander of the Rass Expeditionary Force," Admiral McKee explained. "I know he wouldn't be happy about losing part of his force to go participate in a raid like this, but it sounds like those may be the only appropriate Republic ships we can spare."

Bailey chuckled. Even at his level, Roberts had gained a reputation as a somewhat salty character. However, he was also known to come through in a pinch, and his results were what kept him moving up the ladder.

"Admiral Torsen, I may have to do some serious convincing, but I will get you your ships," said Bailey.
*******

**Three Days Later**
**Neptune Briefing Room, Sub-Level 4**
**Republic Embassy – Naval Liaison Office**
**Valdrakar, Primordia**
**Kita System**

The doors to the Neptune Briefing Room sealed with a magnetic hiss behind the last admiral to enter.

This wasn't a standard ops update.

The lights were low, the room windowless, and the air scrubbers hummed with the quiet constancy of a sealed environment two floors below ground. No aides. No Primord observers. Just the Republic's top naval officers—senior ship captains, fleet staff, and the sharp-eyed flag officers who had come to dictate the next phase of the war.

A crimson SAP code strip glowed in the top right corner of the main display, along with a scrolling warning: ACCESS RESTRICTED — PROGRAM ATHENA SIGMA — NO EXTERNAL DISTRIBUTION.

Brigadier General Aimes Burke stood at the head of the room, his expression a chiseled stone mask. The soft overhead lighting cast a faint gleam over the matte-black polymer of his ocular implant—his left eye had lost decades ago during the Great AI War, long before the Republic had been born from the ashes.

He wore a service uniform with no combat tabs, no overt identifiers. There was only a single silver star on each shoulder and the black-and-steel shoulder flash of ISA— Intelligence Support Activities. To those who knew, that was enough.

Around the table sat Fleet Admiral Chester Bailey, cold-eyed and contemplative. Rear Admiral Fran McKee appeared stern as ever, arms folded as she watched the rotating 3-D map on the main screen. Captain Eamon Roberts looked more annoyed than curious. And a half-dozen other senior captains and ship commanders were present, Commander Lee among them.

"Let's get to it," Burke began, voice steady, low. "This briefing is classified Top Secret. All contents fall under the Athena Sigma SAP. Anything you hear or see today does not leave this room without codeword clearance. Violation is a court-martial and lifetime blacklisting from service. Understood?"

Everyone nodded or murmured assent.

Burke tapped a remote. The lights dimmed further, and the central display activated—an angular sector map of the Rass system, colored in high-contrast vectors and red-tagged overlays.

"This is Varnak Outpost," Burke said, a red icon pulsing within a distorted asteroid field near the Thorian Divide. "The designation comes from the Primords, who've identified it as a forward staging outpost for Zodark fleet operations in this region. To date, we've confirmed its existence through multiple intelligence channels, and the Primords are preparing an assault on the facility."

He paused, turning to face the room fully.

"This isn't a rumor. This is real."

Another tap brought up a series of sensor overlays and distorted telemetry feeds—glimpses of comms pings, faint power signatures, and vague thermal blooms inside a belt of frozen asteroids.

"Our confirmation comes from multiple sources," Burke explained. "The technical exploitation of a captured Zodark *Vulture*-class fighter provided intel, which was then verified after we secured a pair of *Glaive* bombers and a corvette seized during cleanup operations in Intus."

Another feed popped up—schematics of the IFF unit, transmission burst charts, and modulation frequencies. "Captain Chen's TechInt team, in coordination with ISA signals specialists, identified a layered quantum-encrypted IFF system used by Zodark ships during fleet maneuvers and docking approaches."

A soft murmur went through the group.

"These codes update dynamically, synced across their command net, but in the case of the corvette, the cycle was briefly isolated," Burke continued. "We now believe we can replicate the signal for short-term use—enough to enter the approach corridor to Varnak Outpost without being auto-flagged."

He looked at Admiral McKee. "We're still working on whether it can bypass the mines," he noted.

She nodded once, her expression unreadable.

"Major Voss and his Det-5 team's interrogations provided confirmation of a hardened outpost operating as a fleet coordination hub. A Zodark POW confirmed what we suspected—that Varnak is the command and logistics node for the enemy's planned offensive against Intus."

Burke tapped once more.

"Covert long-range sensor sweeps have also confirmed our intel. Quiet bursts. Magnetic shadows. Someone out there is moving large amounts of fuel, ordnance, and personnel—right through that corridor. But Varnak Outpost might not just be a staging area. Based on the way these logistics patterns behave, we suspect it could also be a transfer point for something else…something we haven't identified."

Burke's tone grew colder.

"There's a weight to the traffic flow. Not just weapons and fuel. But ships, transports—lots and lots of them are moving through this location. Regularly."

He stepped back, the map shrinking again to show the wider Rass system.

"That's what we know. The Primords are assembling a strike package to put an end to this. They've identified a weakness they believe can be exploited to destroy the outpost, and have asked us to provide direct kinetic support—specifically, our heavy cruisers with the upgraded magrail batteries. This is why we're here."

Burke turned to Bailey and McKee.

"That's it for my portion of the brief. Command decisions are yours."

He stepped to the side, sitting opposite McKee, as the display continued to rotate slowly—Varnak Outpost blinking like a red heartbeat in the void.

McKee stood, then walked to the head of the room. "Thank you, General Burke. That was informative and exactly what we needed." She cleared her voice, nodding to Bailey, who seemed to give her a signal. "Everyone except Captain Roberts and Commander Lee, please vacate the room. You are free to return to your duties. Oh, and remember, you are not to discuss the contents of this briefing with anyone— understood?"

A chorus of "yes, ma'am" rose from the room. One by one, everyone vacated until only Roberts, Lee, Bailey, McKee, and Burke remained.

Once the room was empty, McKee handed Roberts and Lee each a datapad. "These datapads contains your orders and the details of the raid Burke shared with us. I'll give you a few minutes to read them over. These do *not* leave the room. Before we leave, I want you to know this is a critical mission for the Republic. Your command, Roberts, and the actions it has taken during the Rass expedition has earned a lot of goodwill for the Republic with the Primords. Thank you both, and do us proud with this mission."

With nothing more to be said, McKee and Burke exited, leaving Roberts and Lee to wonder what they had just been voluntold for.

**Chapter 39:**
**Digital Hunt**

**Year 2097**
**Operation Cyber Wraith**
**Intus**

The AS-90 Reaper's cockpit thrummed around Coop as he guided the pod through Intus's skies. Below, emerald jungles went on for kilometers—a sight he never tired of. Mountain ranges rose into the clouds, their snowcapped peaks bright across the horizon. Rivers glinted, snaking through the tropical forests and cascading into lakes mirroring the midday sun.

He glanced to his right. Raven's Reaper kept a tight formation. Ahead, Bear's fighter cut through the air. To his left, Lucky's craft dipped slightly, adjusting for a sudden gust. Behind, the rest of the squadron fanned out—Ninja, Ajax, and the others. In the front, Strike. Phantom lingered at the edge of the formation.

"Eyes sharp, people," Strike's voice came through. "When it looks this good, that's exactly when it isn't. Maintaining angels ten point six."

Coop scanned his instrument panel. The sensors swept over the landscape, feeding streams of data. His attention moved between the monitors showing the world outside his drone and the blinking indicators inside his pod. A moment later, a blip displayed on the tactical holo—an anomaly on the edge of his screen.

"Picking up something unusual at grid sector eight-one," Coop said. He shoved down the panic attempting to crawl up his throat. *Calm, Coop. Trust the instruments. Reapers are hardened against electronic warfare*, he told himself. *Just be steady. Don't overreact.*

"Confirming anomaly," Raven replied. "Signals are irregular."

Operation Cyber Wraith had started not long ago in the mess hall, then in a secret conversation behind mechanics' equipment in the hangar bay. For a few days, Coop, Bear, or Raven would casually mention anomalous power signatures to other pilots over coffee, and Raven would drop databytes about irregularities to Strike during training sims. Anything to get the squadron leader to at least consider a mission to locate their biggest obstacle—Zodark electronic warfare attacks. Coop, Bear, and Raven never pushed. They just planted seeds. After all, you didn't push someone like Strike—you let him connect the dots himself.

Now, staring at his scanner, Coop's pulse quickened. The energy patterns were totally nuts—rapid oscillations between terahertz bands, displacement signatures that shouldn't exist in nature, and resonance patterns screaming artificial manipulation. Classic signs of a major cyber-warfare hub.

Apparently, without his knowledge, intel had been tracking these signatures for a while, watching them ghost through the networks. But this… this was the source. It had to be. The readings showed pulses of dark energy precisely matching the frequency gaps in Republic defense grids. Someone was probing for weaknesses, testing backdoors.

Coop suppressed a smile. Whatever Strike's reasons for finally listening and green-lighting this mission, whatever intel had finally convinced Command, none of that mattered now.

They might have just found their target.

"Strike, we've got anomalies consistent with Zodark cyber activity," Coop reported.

"Jolly Rogers, stay on my wing signatures," Strike's voice crackled through the squadron frequency. "No holes in this formation. Dropping to angels three."

Coop adjusted the Reaper's trajectory, homing in on the signals. As they drew closer, the anomalies multiplied.

"These readings are too concentrated," Coop mused aloud.

"Agreed," Raven said. "Feels like a setup."

"Possible decoys," Coop said. "They want us to bite."

"Phantom, loop around and scan from the east," Strike commanded. "Ninja, cover the west flank."

As the squadron shifted positions, Coop manipulated the controls. He overlaid thermal imaging, seeking any hidden threats. Just then, a spike in the sensors caught his attention.

"Incoming energy surge," Coop said.

Without hesitation, he veered port. A split second later, the space he'd vacated sizzled with laser fire streaking upward from concealed ground units.

"Triple-A lit up! Grid sector seven!" Bear said. "Ground batteries tracking!"

"Those signatures were bait," Coop replied. "They masked their defense grid."

"All wings, execute scatter protocol," Strike ordered. "Break on my mark… mark!"

The airspace lit up like a supernova. Energy weapons and projectile trails flew across the sky. Coop yanked his Reaper into a high-g vertical. He rolled out at apex, running a quick tactical sweep.

"Phantom, ground-to-air projectile on your tail! Break right, break right!" Bear said.

"Roger that," Phantom replied. "Executing Scissor Two defense. Fox Three deployed."

Coop scanned the terrain below. Camouflaged emplacements blended into the greenery. Identifying the patterns, he began marking targets.

"Uploading coordinates of enemy positions," Coop said.

"Coordinates received," Raven confirmed. "Preparing countermeasures."

"Bear, form up on me," Coop said. "We'll draw their fire while Raven and Lucky flank from the sides."

"Copy that," Bear responded, his Reaper sliding into position.

They dove toward the source of the heaviest fire. Ground units intensified their assault, lasers cutting through the air. Coop weaved through the barrage, the Reaper's engines roaring in his pod's speaker system.

"Now!" Coop said.

Raven and Lucky swooped in from opposite sides, unleashing volleys neutralizing the enemy emplacements. Explosions blossomed below, sending plumes of smoke skyward.

"Targets eliminated," Raven reported.

"Good work," Strike said.

"Save the victory roll, Coop," Phantom cut in. "Triple-A emplacements still reading hot but quiet. Don't get complacent. Stay above four point five. They're waiting for a shot."

"Roger that," Coop replied. "Keeping sensors hot, maintaining combat awareness."

The squadron regrouped, their sensors detecting stronger anomaly readings deeper in enemy territory.

"Those ground batteries were picket defense," Ninja said. "SAM sites are screening something valuable."

"Concur on assessment," Coop replied. "Request permission to push past their perimeter."

"Jolly Rogers, maintain combat spread," Strike commanded. "Advance on my mark. Keep above their engagement ceiling. No heroes today."

As they advanced, the landscape began to change. The jungles gave way to cliffs and waterfalls. Mist hung in the air. Amidst the natural beauty, hostiles lurked.

"Heavy interference at heading zero-two-two," Ajax transmitted. "All frequencies degraded."

"Multiple signal spikes on scope. Looking like a trap setup." Coop checked his display.

"Options?" Phantom asked.

"Drop to backup systems," Coop responded. "Run dark, visual flight rules."

"Bold move," Bear said.

Coop grinned. "Sometimes old-school gets it done."

"Negative on dropping systems," Strike said. "I know you're thinking it's safer from cyberattacks this close to their hub, but we need those sensors. We go in blind, we're dead. Stay tight, trust your training."

The squadron threaded through narrow canyons. Coop's eyes locked onto the terrain ahead as the Reaper sliced through the thinning mist. The cliffs parted, revealing a sight that made his pulse quicken. At first, he thought it was a trick of the light—a glint among the sea of green. In the next instant, the shapes solidified.

"Check fire," Coop said. "Got structure at coordinates zero-one-niner. How the hell was this not on our preflight intel?"

"Confirming visual on target," Raven responded. "Artificial construct against terrain features."

"Target matches Zodark architecture signatures," Bear transmitted. "Looks like we've found ourselves a Zodark hangout."

"All wings holding at angels two point four," Strike ordered. "Maintain orbital pattern while we gather intel."

There, amongst the canopy, stood a large structure. Its geometric design clashed with the surrounding wilderness. Electric fences encircled the perimeter, sparks of energy dancing along the lines. Guard towers rose throughout.

"There it is," Coop said. "The Zodark cyber ops center. That's gotta be it."

He adjusted his HUD, zooming in on the building. Massive antennas jutted into the sky from its rooftop. Lines of runes etched across the exterior pulsed. Spherical devices hovered above the ground, emitting waves no doubt warping the air around them.

"Check out those antennas," Lucky said, her voice full of awe. "They're not just for communication. Could be part of a larger network."

"Those runes," Raven added. "I've seen similar patterns in intel reports. Energy conduits, maybe amplifying their systems."

"There's more," Coop continued. "Those emitters are causing localized signal disruptions. Explains the anomalies we've been chasing."

Bear's tone came through the radio. "Multiple signatures consistent with network warfare facility. This is their command-and-control center, no doubt."

"Or it's another wild-goose chase," Coop replied.

"Uploading visuals and sensor data now," Phantom said. "See for yourselves."

Silence followed as the squadron reviewed the feed. The images left little room for doubt.

Strike's voice broke through. "Assessment?"

One quick look and Coop could tell Phantom was right. "Structural analysis confirms Zodark command-and-control center. Triple-layer defensive perimeter, heavy electronic countermeasures. This is our primary source for all sector interference."

Raven spoke up. "Analysis checks out. This place is significant."

Ajax sounded uneasy. "Defenses look heavy. We're deep in enemy territory."

"All the more reason to relay this intel ASAP," Coop said.

"Good work identifying the target," Strike replied.

Bear asked, "How do we get this information back to Command with those disruptors active?"

The disruptors would block standard transmissions. They needed a workaround.

"We can deploy a stealth relay drone," Coop said. "Program it to skirt the disruptor field and transmit once clear."

"Risky," Ninja replied. "But it's our best shot."

Coop took a deep breath. "I'll handle the deployment. The rest of you maintain a perimeter. We can't afford to draw attention."

"Negative, Coop," Strike said. "Delegate the task."

For a moment, Coop bristled at the order until he recognized the underlying trust in Strike's words. After all those careful conversations about anomalous signals, those breadcrumbs he'd dropped to get this mission approved—Strike was acknowledging his real value. Now wasn't the time to play hero with a drone drop—his skills were needed to monitor any changes in the facility's defenses. Strike wasn't sidelining him. He was maximizing the team's effectiveness.

"Understood," Coop replied. "Raven."

"Consider it done."

"That relay needs to drop below their sensor grid to transmit," Coop said. "Angels zero point nine, max."

"Copy that," Raven replied. "Going low."

Coop tensed. It put Raven right in the kill zone of their ground defenses, but the interference from the facility meant the relay had to get under their electronic warfare bubble to punch through.

"All wings, maintain overwatch," Strike ordered. "Keep those defense batteries suppressed."

Raven's Reaper peeled away, descending in a controlled dive. Ground fire immediately intensified, tracking his approach.

"Multiple targeting locks," Raven reported. "Deploying countermeasures."

The air filled with streaks of laser fire as Raven weaved through the barrage. At point nine kilometers, he released the relay drone. "Package away. Beginning egress."

The tiny relay drone dropped lower, skating beneath the electronic warfare bubble. Their displays sputtered as it began transmitting.

"Data upload at sixty percent," Raven said. "Taking heavy fire—" His transmission cut off as a laser burst caught his right wing, sending the Reaper into a spin.

"Raven, status!" Strike ordered.

"Controls sluggish but responding. Relay at ninety percent—"

Another burst of fire erupted from the facility. The relay drone exploded, but not before a confirmation flashed across Coop's screen.

"Data transmitted," Coop confirmed. "Command has the package."

"Ajax, taking hits!" The transmission burst into static before momentarily clearing. "Primary systems failing—"

Seconds later, Ajax's Reaper disintegrated under Zodark fire.

"Multiple sensor anomalies," Coop said. "We're getting feedback. Need immediate egress."

"Negative on evac," Phantom replied. "I say hold position until—"

"My scope's swimming," Ninja cut in. "Getting ghost signatures everywhere."

"All units, check instruments," Strike commanded.

"Strike, recommend immediate withdrawal," Coop said. "These readings match known Zodark system crash patterns. They could be spoofing us again."

"Stow that paranoia, Coop," Phantom snapped. "Just electromagnetic interference from—" His transmission turned into static as his Reaper's navigation system failed. The craft spiraled downward, vanishing into the jungle canopy in a flash of fire.

"Lost all flight controls!" Ninja's voice burst over the channel. "Can't maintain—" Another explosion lit up the sky.

"Three birds down," Coop reported. "They're reaching into our systems. We stay here any longer, we lose the whole squadron."

"All units, exfil route Charlie," Strike ordered. "Get us back to FOB Oteren. Now."

As they climbed away from the facility, Coop's instruments continued to fluctuate. They'd gotten the intel out, but at a cost bigger than what Coop wanted to admit. Three Reapers destroyed—and that wasn't just about losing advanced hardware. If the Zodarks recovered even fragments of those drones…

"Command's going to love the after-action on this one," Bear said as they accelerated toward friendly airspace.

"The Reapers were supposed to be unhackable," Coop replied. "But if they get their hands on those wrecks—especially at their primary electronic warfare hub—they might find a way in. One vulnerability, that's all they need."

"You think they can crack them?" Bear asked.

"These aren't standard drones. The Reapers have our most advanced cyber-defense systems. But that facility down there?" Strike said. "It's their primary EW hub for a reason. If anyone can find a weakness in the Reapers' architecture, it's them."

"So this mission could end up giving them more than we got," Bear said.

"Maybe," Strike replied. "But right now, we focus on getting this intel back to Command. Let them know the risks. They need to know both what we found—and what we left behind."

"Strike, that facility will go mobile the moment they confirm we've transmitted data," Coop said. "Window's closing fast."

"Agreed," Strike replied. "Already coding the priority flash to Command. Those displacement readings match exactly what's been hitting our defense grids."

"They'll have evacuation protocols in motion," Raven added, his damaged Reaper struggling to maintain formation. "Facility that size, they can't relocate quickly, but—"

"Twenty-four hours, max," Bear said. "Then we lose them."

"Less," Coop replied. "Those energy spikes we recorded? They're already spinning up their transport systems." And those Reapers they'd lost. Yes, always a risk when flying over enemy territory, but right here, right in the hands of the electronic warfare facility—none of it sat well with him.

The squadron pushed their remaining Reapers to maximum thrust, racing toward FOB Oteren. They all knew what came next—immediate debrief, rapid mission planning, and a full strike package within the hour. They'd found the hornets' nest. Now they had to hit it before the hornets scattered, especially before the enemy took full advantage of the downed Reapers.

"Command's already scrambling strike teams," Strike said. "The moment we land, we're rolling into assault prep."

Coop checked his tactical display as the facility dropped off sensor range. Three ships down, but they'd accomplished what weeks, maybe a month, of careful intelligence gathering couldn't—they'd found the source of the Zodark cyberattacks. This time, they'd make sure it was permanently neutralized.

The real fight was just beginning. And they'd be back before that facility could disassemble and disappear.

## Chapter 40:
## Ion Fire

**Year 2097**
**Operation Blackout**
**Intus**

Reapers were supposed to be hardened against EW attacks—their encrypted networks and triple-redundant firewalls were one of the most advanced in the Republic's arsenal. Still, the Zodarks had torn through those defenses like they were outdated software, just as they'd done to the Orion starfighters. Three ships lost today, their comms links corrupted in seconds.

The Zodark facility was the bleeding edge of Zodark cyber warfare. The way they'd spoofed secure systems, manipulated pathways that should've been locked tight… it was beyond anything they'd encountered. They couldn't let the Zodarks keep this capability. Finding the enemy electronic warfare facility wasn't enough—they needed to reduce it to atoms, and fast. Every minute it remained operational was another minute the enemy could exploit the destroyed Reapers, find new backdoors, new ways to turn Republic tech against itself.

It'd been ten minutes since Coop exited his drone pod and hurried to one of RNS *Gallipoli*'s briefing rooms. At the front, Strike stood tall as tactical displays came to life behind him.

"Before us is a critical operation," Strike said. "As many of you are aware, our objective is the cyber installation located deep in the jungles of Intus. Intel designates this as Operation Blackout. Mission parameters—neutralization of a Zodark cyber warfare installation."

The image of the facility hovered midair—a complex veiled by foliage. Memories of his earlier reconnaissance flashed through his mind: the thick canopy, the hidden emplacements, the sense of something monumental lurking beneath the surface.

"Thanks to Jolly Rogers' recent intel," Strike continued, glancing briefly at Coop, "we've pinpointed the facility. While its surface structure appears minimal, our penetrating scans show it extends several levels underground. We've mapped the entire complex and identified its structural weaknesses—both above and below ground."

The tactical holos shifted, zooming in on the facility's layout. Layers of underground structures unfolded, revealing corridors, control rooms, and defense points.

"Here"—Strike pointed to a section highlighted in red—"are the automated turrets. Surveillance systems are marked in blue. These are their primary defenses."

Raven raised a hand. "What about their communication arrays?"

"Disrupted," Strike replied. "Their capacity to call for reinforcements is limited, but not eliminated. We have a narrow window before they can restore full functionality after the limited strikes we conducted. Intel suggests there are still Vultures active on this planet. We don't have exact numbers, but stay alert—we need to be ready for potential engagement with their fighters at any time."

Coop studied the displays before him, noting the positions of the turrets and possible blind spots.

Bear spoke up. "Any intel on ground troops?"

"Minimal presence," Strike said. "Our focus is on disabling their cyber operations."

Another pilot shifted in her seat. "Are there vulnerabilities we can exploit in their surveillance?"

Coop spoke up. "During the recon mission, I noticed gaps in their sensor coverage along the eastern perimeter. The dense forest interferes with their equipment."

Strike nodded. "Exactly. Terrain is on our side. Now, this facility is the linchpin in their cyberattacks. Taking it down will cripple their ability to interfere with our operations. It's imperative we succeed."

The thought of grounding the Zodarks' capabilities made Coop feel dang good. He knew firsthand the havoc their cyber assaults had wrought.

"Coop, you'll lead a covert team designated Alpha," Strike said.

"Understood," Coop replied.

"Alpha Team will consist of Lucky, Bear, Ninja, Phantom, Raven, and Ajax, with Coop as lead." Strike looked at each pilot. "You were selected for your specific combat specialties. Each of you is mission-critical for this operation."

Phantom's eyes narrowed slightly, but he gave a nod.

Strike pressed on his own chest. "I'll command the main squadron. We'll create a diversion, drawing enemy fire and attention away from Coop's team."

The map displayed the planned flight paths—Strike's squadron would approach from the north, sweeping over the jungle-covered hills to draw attention, while Coop's team would use the mountainous terrain to the west as cover. The vectors were calculated to make Strike's group appear as the primary threat while Coop's team slipped in through their blind spots. Looking at the approach routes, Coop knew Strike's group would be exactly where the Zodarks would expect an attack to come from—and that was the point.

"While we engage from the north," Strike explained, indicating the route, "Coop's team will infiltrate from the west."

"What kind of resistance should we expect on approach?" Ajax asked.

"Anticipate heavy anti-air defenses once we're detected," Strike replied. "That's why surprise is essential. More than we saw during recon. They're upping their defenses as we speak. This is high-risk. But the payoff is significant. Disabling this facility will turn the tide, and afterwards, they cannot slow us down."

As the briefing wound down, Strike opened the floor. "Any final questions?" There was a brief moment of pause. "Good. Dismissed."

After dismissal, the pilots cleared the briefing room. Coop assembled his strike team in the port-side tactical alcove.

"Circle up for final brief." Coop's team formed a tight perimeter around him. "Launch sequence from bay four at FOB Oteren, 1600 hours. Maintain emissions control until drop point Delta. Questions on ingress?"

Bear's hand went up. "ROE for weapons free?"

"Strictly defensive posture unless compromised. Stealth is priority one until we're in range," Coop said.

"Weather report shows heavy canopy interference," Raven reported. "Navigation concerns?"

"Updated terrain mapping has no doubt been loaded to your crafts. Stay on prescribed flight paths," Coop said. "Phantom, you're on point. Ajax, sweep and clear our six. Lucky and Ninja, you're running interference if we meet resistance. Bear, Raven—you're with me on the primary objective."

Coop glanced back toward the briefing room, where Strike was deep in discussion with other officers. For all their clashes, he recognized the burden of command Strike carried.

Returning his focus to his team, a surge of confidence washed over Coop. "Any doubts, now's the time to voice them."

Silence met his words. Determined faces looked back at him.

"All right," Coop said. "Let's gear up. We launch in thirty."

They dispersed, each heading to prepare for the operation. Coop stayed a moment, taking in the bustling activity around him before he left and suited up, and made his way to the pod bay. There, his Reaper drone cockpit awaited.

Running a hand along the pod's surface, he felt a connection—a melding of pilot and machine. Climbing into the control pod, he began preflight checks, systems whirring to life under his command.

Displays flashed on. Data streams aligned. He calibrated the stealth systems for top-notch performance, and then he waited—he didn't know how long—until the faces of his team appeared on the comms interface, each signaling readiness.

"All systems green," Raven reported.

"Stealth modules active," Ninja added.

Bear's voice came through with a hint of eagerness. "Let's light this candle."

Coop smiled. "Hold tight. Strike, this is Coop. We're ready for launch sequence. What's your status?"

"My squadron is wheels up in three mikes. Begin your launch on my mark… mark."

"Copy that. Alpha Team, executing launch sequence."

The bay doors parted. Intus's late-afternoon sky shone back through Coop's screen. Deep oranges and purples spread out over the horizon. One by one, their Reapers glided out into the humid air, their stealth coating swallowing the dying sunlight.

Coop led them along the designated vector, keeping them low enough to blend with the terrain but high enough to maintain tactical awareness. Through his interface, target coordinates overlaid the landscape ahead. Somewhere beneath that green blanket, the Zodark facility waited.

"Maintain formation," he instructed. "Trust your instruments through the canopy interference."

The jungle rose to meet them as they descended to nap-of-the-earth flight level. Heat signatures from native wildlife scattered at their approach, though their stealth systems made sure they remained impervious to both organic and electronic detection.

"Terrain mapping engaged," Raven confirmed.

"Approaching waypoint," Ajax said.

Coop's sensors scanned for any signs of detection. So far, all was clear.

"Eyes on scan," he reminded them. "Party's about to start."

As they flew through narrow gaps and over treetops, the stealth systems continued to mask their presence.

"Visual on the facility," Phantom reported.

"Form up and follow vector three-one-one-zero," Coop said.

They soared over the jungle. The comms crackled with Strike's update. "Enemy activity detected eight klicks out. Stay low and maintain radio silence."

Coop adjusted altitude, skimming just above the treetops. The first blip appeared on his threat display.

"Anti-air radar pinging us," Ninja whispered over the channel.

"Countermeasures active," Coop replied. "Prepare for evasive action."

Missile alerts screamed through their systems. Coop banked hard right as a fiery trail streaked past. Explosions erupted around them, the sky filled with shrapnel.

"Deploying decoys," Raven said. Metallic pods shot from his drone, confusing enemy sensors.

"Phantom, flank left and target their missile arrays," Coop ordered.

"On it," Phantom replied, veering away.

Bear unleashed a barrage of suppressive fire, the drone's railguns tearing through foliage and striking concealed emplacements.

"Good hit," Coop said. "Keep pushing forward."

They weaved through a hailstorm of artillery. The installation was just up ahead, its structure bristling with weaponry. Seconds later, the scene shattered as a brilliant blue-white beam lanced through the sky.

"Ion cannon, three o'clock!" Phantom's warning blasted through the comm.

The beam caught Ajax's Reaper dead center. The drone's systems flared brilliant white before going dark, its frame tumbling lifelessly into the jungle below. The impact triggered a massive explosion, sending a fireball racing above the canopy.

"Ajax is down! Evasive maneuvers!" Coop ordered, yanking his controls hard port.

"What the hell?" Bear's voice boomed through. "Deltas were supposed to have neutralized all ion emplacements during the initial push."

"Obviously they missed one," Phantom replied, his Reaper diving beneath another azure blast.

"Cut the chatter. Focus on—" Coop's voice was cut short as another beam sliced through the air.

Lucky's desperate "Mayday! May—" ended in static as her Reaper took a direct hit. The drone's core overloaded. A blinding flash burst in the sky before the wreckage spiraled earthward, leaving a trail of burning debris over the landscape below.

"Coop," Strike said. "That cannon needs to go dark now. It'll tear our main force apart when we make our run."

"Copy that. Bear, Phantom—covering fire. Raven, Ninja—with me. We're taking that battery out."

The remaining Reapers split formation, weaving through the intensifying barrage of ion fire. Their threat indicators screamed as the cannon's targeting system locked onto them repeatedly.

A new blast nearly clipped Coop's wing. His interface brightened with multiple warnings across his field of vision— the ion cannon was cycling up for another shot, and this time, his Reaper was dead center in its firing solution.

WARNING: ION SIGNATURE SPIKE

TARGET LOCK DETECTED

COUNTERMEASURES INEFFECTIVE

The alerts flooded his drone pod's displays as the targeting system's warning indicators shifted from yellow to blood red. His HUD projected the ion cannon's power signature, a rapidly climbing curve that could only mean one thing—it was about to fire.

## Chapter 41:
## Cyber Strike

**Year 2097**
**Operation Blackout**
**Intus**

A blinding glow radiated from the ion cannon's barrel. The weapon stood atop a jagged outcrop, its spires jutting into the sky like twisted fingers reaching for destruction. It was positioned one klick west of their primary target. Energy sparked around it, the air shimmering with raw power.

Time slowed. Every detail sharpened—the whir of his pod's displays, the beads of sweat forming on Coop's brow, the rapid thump of his heartbeat echoing in his ears.

"That thing's about to light us up," Raven said.

"Visual acquired," Ninja added. "Coordinates locked."

Coop's eyed the controls. "Full assault—everything we've got."

He armed all weapon systems. The Reaper's HUD shifted, targeting reticles aligning over the ion cannon. The weapon loomed larger as they closed in, its surface pulsing with circuits of red light.

"On my mark," Coop said. The ion cannon's energy peaks spiked dangerously high on his display.

The cannon pivoted, its colossal barrel tracking directly toward Coop's drone. The weapon system's lock was absolute—hunter and hunted, with Coop squarely in its sights.

"Three... two... one... mark!"

Missiles burst from their Reapers in unison. Coop's drone unleashed a salvo of multipurpose smart missiles, spiraling toward the target. Raven and Ninja mirrored his actions, the sky filling with streaks of white contrails converging on the ion cannon.

The ground defenses roared to life. Flak exploded around them, fiery blasts tearing through the sky. Coop jerked the controls, weaving through the hell. Shrapnel pinged off his Reaper's armor.

"Incoming fire, adjust trajectory," Ninja reported.

"Stay on course," Coop replied. He pushed the drone harder.

The missiles closed the distance. Explosions rippled across the ion cannon's surface.

Coop wasn't satisfied. "Magrails, focus fire on the exposed sections. Aim for critical points."

They shifted their aim. The Reapers' .50-caliber magnetic railguns spat tungsten rounds. The projectiles slammed into the ion cannon's vulnerabilities, piercing through the weakened armor.

Sparks erupted. The cannon's glow flickered, its energy buildup stuttering.

"She's weakening!" Ninja shouted.

The ion cannon retaliated. A beam of incandescent energy lanced outward, skimming past Coop's drone. The sheer force rattled his craft, warning alarms blaring.

Coop gritted his teeth. "We end this now."

He armed the antipersonnel cluster bombs. "Deploying cluster munitions on my signal."

"Ready," Ninja confirmed.

"Aligned," Raven said.

"Release!"

The bombs dropped, descending like a swarm of meteors. Midair, they burst open, scattering smaller explosives over the target. The ion cannon disappeared in a cascade of fire and smoke as multiple detonations engulfed it.

A shock wave rippled outward, catching Coop's drone and rocking it violently. He fought the controls, stabilizing the craft.

"Direct hit," Ninja said.

"Target neutralized," Raven confirmed.

Through the dissipating smoke, the ion cannon's remains smoldered—a twisted wreckage where a formidable weapon had once stood.

Coop exhaled, tension easing from his shoulders. "Good work, team."

Before they could regroup, Strike's tone came through the comm. "All units, this is Strike. We're under heavy fire—unexpected ground batteries causing us to scramble. Request immediate support!"

Coop scanned the northern horizon. Distant flashes indicated intense combat. "Strike, this is Coop. Ion cannon neutralized. Moving to assist."

Coop's tactical display showed Strike's position—a kilometer northeast of the main facility where the terrain dropped into a ravine. Their sister squadron was caught between the facility's outer defense ring and previously undetected gun emplacements hidden in the cliff faces.

"Make it quick," Strike responded. "They've got more firepower than anticipated. We need those batteries taken out."

Bear and Phantom joined formation as they sped toward Strike's coordinates.

"Zodarks are desperate to protect that installation," Bear commented.

"Or buying time to evacuate," Phantom said.

Approaching the combat zone, they witnessed the ferocity of the engagement. Enemy emplacements dotted the landscape, spewing tracer fire skyward. Strike's squadron weaved through the onslaught, their maneuvers tight but strained.

"Target the nearest battery," Coop directed. "Bear, provide suppressive fire. Phantom, find us an opening."

"Copy that," Bear replied, his drone unleashing a hail of railgun fire.

Phantom veered left, scanning for weaknesses. "There's a gap in their coverage on the western flank."

"Raven, Ninja, follow Phantom. We'll split their focus," Coop ordered.

They broke off, moving to encircle the enemy positions. Ground fire intensified.

Coop armed his blaster-mounted chin turret, sending shots into the enemy's ranks. Eruptions dotted the terrain as the emplacements suffered.

"Battery two is disabled," Raven reported.

"Good. Keep up the pressure," Coop said.

A sudden jolt shuddered through his drone. "Alert: system anomaly detected," the onboard AI reported.

"Cyber intrusion detected," Ninja said. "They're trying to hijack our controls."

Coop's display flickered, vital readings pinwheeled through warning thresholds. He forced calm while swiftly working over the controls. "Engage manual override. Isolate critical systems."

He remembered the cyberattacks from previous missions. This was a new level of aggression. "They're getting smarter."

From their position above the western approach, massive transmission arrays protruded from the facility's third tier, their dishes tracking his squadron's movements. Beyond them, the facility's main structure descended into a mountainside like an inverted pyramid, each subterranean level marked by ventilation shafts and reinforced access points.

"Lost targeting systems," Phantom said.

"Stay unpredictable," Coop instructed. "We're zero-loss critical in this AO."

Coop rerouted power and severed compromised links. The drone's systems stabilized, but the threat persisted.

"Systems nominal," Raven transmitted. "Still taking active probes."

"That cyber facility stays up any longer, we're dead in the water," Coop said. "All units, weapons free."

"Strike to Coop, we're taking heavy fire. Cannot maintain current position."

"Copy that. Cyber assault's got us by the throat. Moving to neutralize source."

"Roger that, Coop," Strike replied. "Execute primary. Return to phase one. We'll keep them busy."

"All units, form up tactical," Coop commanded. "We're going straight down their gullet."

The Reapers rocketed through the canopy gaps, their stealth coating rippling against streams of data interference.

Below, the cyber ops center dominated the valley floor—a sprawling titanium fortress sunk deep into the terrain. Multiple reinforced tiers descended into the earth, each ringed with particle beam arrays and processors. The facility's surface structure was just the tip as intelligence suggested at least six subterranean levels packed with server farms and electronic warfare suites.

"Defenses are layered deep, Lead," Ninja said.

"Then we peel 'em back," Coop responded. "Target acquired—comms arrays at bearing zero-three-one-zero. Taking out their eyes."

Multiple missile trails lit up the afternoon sky. The arrays erupted in cascading detonations, shearing transmission dishes and scattering superheated metal across the compound.

"Target degraded," Raven called out. "Cyber footprint dropping to sixty percent."

"Push the advantage. All units, weapons free on secondary targets."

The air ignited with streams of blaster fire, ground defense batteries tracking their movement. Reaper units jinked and rolled, their tactical systems screaming proximity warnings as they dove through the mesh of anti-aircraft fire.

"Bear, light up those triple-A positions," Coop ordered. "Clear us a corridor."

"Solid copy." Bear's Reaper banked hard, its railguns spitting hypervelocity rounds in controlled bursts. Ground emplacements erupted in chains of secondary explosions, creating momentary gaps in the defensive screen.

"Coop, Phantom here. I've got a clean vector on their primary entrance. Request permission to deliver payload."

"Negative, too hot. You'll never clear the blast radius solo."

"With respect, Coop—if we time the FAE drop with their defensive reset, we can collapse their whole infrastructure. Window's closing."

Coop's tactical display highlighted multiple incoming bogies, launching from camouflaged hangars beneath the canopy. "Clock's ticking. All units, new contacts, bearing one-four-niner."

The concealed hangars were built into the valley walls, rising to attack altitude. Coop's squadron held the height advantage, but the Vultures were between them and the facility's vulnerable central core. Below, the target area for Phantom's bomb run—a heavily armored ventilation hub—was barely visible through the forest canopy.

"Time to dance," Bear said.

"Execute your run, Phantom. Raven, Ninja—you're on intercept. Keep those fighters off his tail. Rest of us will suppress ground fire."

The team split. Coop led his element low, their weapons systems cycling to close-range engagement mode. The jungle canopy erupted with blaster fire as hidden defense turrets revealed their positions.

"Winchester on missiles," Ninja reported.

"Switch to magrails. Maintain suppressive fire. Phantom, what's your status?"

"Final approach. Thirty seconds to release point."

Coop's threat warning suddenly screamed. "Multiple missile locks! Break, break, break!"

An enemy fighter locked onto Phantom. Coop reacted instantly, swinging his drone behind the Reaper to intercept. He unleashed the blaster-mounted chin turret, tearing through the Vulture's armor and sending it spiraling down.

"Thanks," Phantom said.

"Just keep going," Coop replied.

"Break, break!" Bear yelled.

The squadron scattered as lasers streaked through their formation. A Vulture fighter dropped on Raven's backside, its cannons spitting death.

"I've got him," Coop called, rolling his Reaper inverted. His targeting system locked, and he unleashed a burst from his railguns. The rounds shredded the Vulture's port engine, sending it into a death dive.

Two more enemy fighters came from above. Bear caught one in a crossfire, his shots punching through its cockpit. The second jinked hard, nearly ramming Ninja's drone before Raven's shots cut it in half.

"Three bandits, coming in hot!" Raven warned.

The Vultures split into a claw formation, their targeting systems painting the Reapers with active locks. Coop's threat detector screamed as multiple missile signatures launched. "Chaff, chaff, chaff!"

The squadron deployed countermeasures, filling the air with a cloud of electronic interference. Two hostile projectiles lost track, corkscrewing harmlessly into the jungle. The third stayed locked on Ninja.

"I can't shake it!" Ninja's Reaper veered hard, scraping the treetops.

Bear flew in behind the missile. "Hold course." His railgun burst caught the missile midflight, detonating it safely.

The Vultures regrouped, pressing their attack. Energy weapons fire crisscrossed the sky as the fighters engaged. Coop's Reaper twisted through the barrage, his targeting computer tracking the lead fighter.

"Ninja, left break. Bear, push right. Let's box them in."

The squadron executed the maneuver well. Two Vultures fell into the trap, shot down in a blaze of glory. Their armor collapsed under the combined assault, armor splitting open as railgun rounds found their marks.

The lead Vulture pilot was good—really good. He snap-rolled away from Coop's initial burst, retaliating with a spray of laser fire that nearly clipped one of Phantom's engines.

"This one's mine," Coop growled. He pushed his drone, matching the Vulture turn for turn. The enemy pilot weaved. Coop waited for his moment, leading his target just right.

His finger squeezed the trigger. The blaster-mounted chin turret spoke, its rounds catching the Vulture at the perfect angle. The fighter's reactor core breached, turning it into a ball of flames.

Through the roiling aftermath, Coop tracked the remaining Vultures breaking contact, their engine signatures diminishing as they fled southeast.

"Window's closing," Phantom reported. "Their defenses are cycling back online."

"Phantom, you still have that FAE package?" Coop asked.

"Armed and ready. About ready to drop."

"Continue your run. Everyone else, defensive screen. Nothing touches him."

Phantom's Reaper dove closer to the facility. The remaining squad members formed up, their sensors sweeping for threats.

"Approaching release point," Phantom called out.

"Wait for my mark." Coop watched the targeting solution crystallize. "Three… two… one… execute!"

"Deploying fuel-air explosive bombs," Phantom announced.

"Pull up now!" Coop ordered.

They ascended sharply. The bombs impacted milliseconds later. For a heartbeat, silence reigned.

Then, the FAE detonation ignited the valley like a miniature sun. The initial blast peeled away the facility's surface structures, but the real devastation plunged deeper. The pressure wave hammered down through ventilation shafts and access tunnels, creating a cascading collapse that crushed level after subterranean level. Processors shattered. Armor-reinforced server vaults crumpled like paper. The facility's power core breached, adding its own explosion to the inferno.

"Direct hit," Phantom confirmed. Relief tinged his voice.

"Enemy systems off-line," Ninja reported. "My prediction, ain't gonna be no more cyberattacks."

Strike's voice broke through the comm. "Excellent work. Their ground fire is weakening. Let's mop up."

Coop allowed himself a small smile. "You heard the commander. Let's finish this."

They regrouped, turning their attention to the remaining enemy forces. With their primary defenses destroyed, the Zodarks' resistance faltered.

Bear chuckled. "Their ground troops are on the run now."

"Don't get cocky," Coop warned. "Stay focused."

The squadron pressed their attack in perfect sync. Coordinated strafe runs shredded enemy positions, their railguns systematically silencing one emplacement after another. The Zodark ground forces, caught in the open during their advance, were cut down by perfect shots.

"Area secured," Raven declared.

"All units, return to base," Strike commanded. "Mission accomplished."

As they ascended through the atmosphere, the burning remnants of the facility faded below. The sky cleared. An hour later, the dense canopy parted, showing FOB Oteren's camouflaged hangar complex carved into the woodlands. Massive doors rolled aside, spilling light onto the approach path. The Reapers entered in sequence, their engines powering down as they settled onto their designated bays. Ground crews swarmed from their ready positions, connecting power lines and beginning immediate post-mission checks on the battle-worn drones.

On RNS *Gallipoli*, Coop exited the control pod, stretching muscles stiff from the interface. The pod room buzzed with post-mission energy, adrenaline still coursing through the squadron.

Strike approached, maintaining his usual composure despite the pride glinting in his eyes. "Well executed, Coop."

"Couldn't have done it without the team," Coop said.

Bear ambled over, fatigue failing to suppress his grin. "You still owe us those drinks."

"Since when?" Coop asked.

Bear's grin widened. "Since now."

Coop shook his head. "Making up rules as you go, huh?"

"Just buy us some drinks, Coop."

"Fine, when I get the chance."

Phantom fell into step beside Coop. "Nice lead."

The unexpected compliment from Phantom nearly made Coop stumble. "Thanks."

Phantom nodded and strode ahead, disappearing through the pod chamber doors.

As they made their way to the debriefing, Coop felt the mission tension beginning to ease. They'd delivered a crushing blow to Zodark's cyber operations—one that would cripple or completely halt their capabilities on Intus. Finally, Coop could breathe again.

# Chapter 42:
## Behind Enemy Lines

**RNS *Poseidon***
**Thorian Divide**
**Border Zone Intus-Rass/TD-7**

Commander Ripley Lee watched the *Poseidon*'s main tactical display as they continued to inch closer to their objective. The screen was usually populated with a host of data, but not today. Instead, the sensor data was showing nothing solid, nothing certain as they continued their silent approach toward the asteroid belt.

How the Primords had found the place was a mystery to Lee. The fact that they had was a testament to their persistence. The loss of corvettes and frigates mapping the Rass system had risen sharply in preparation for its eventual invasion.

When the joint Primord-Republic fleet had emerged from FTL an hour earlier, every warship in the task force had gone to silent running protocols the moment they'd entered normal space. Comms were tight beam ship-to-ship only, while engines burned cool to mimic a Zodark transport. Leading their force was a quartet of specially equipped Republic electronic warfare frigates, working overtime to project the false signature of a routine Zodark supply convoy on a regularly scheduled supply run approaching the asteroid field on their way to the Varnak outpost.

For months, following the discovery of this outpost, the Primords had been surveilling it to determine how ships were approaching and leaving it. Eventually, they had uncovered a pattern. Twice a week, a supply convoy arrived at the same jump location and then transited their way through a narrow path in the asteroid belt. With a little luck and incredible skill, the Primords had located where the Zodark convoy was originating from before it landed near the Varnak outpost. When the mission was officially a go, the supply convoy had been intercepted and destroyed, leaving the task force Lee was part of a small window of opportunity to spoof the Zodarks into thinking they were the regularly scheduled convoy and not an enemy force sneaking up on them.

The attack force had been broken down into two sections. Lee would lead the Republic ships armed with the heavier hitting magnetic railguns that would be necessary to demolish the outpost's command center and its power core. The second element would be led by Captain Dharek, the Primord commander aboard the *Ek* whose ships would provide Lee's vessels with the covering fire needed to effectively destroy the outpost. Until the Zodarks adjusted the armor of their ships and outposts, they continued to remain vulnerable to the kinetic impacts of the Republic's large-caliber magnetic railguns.

Truth be told, this was the part of the mission Lee was most uncertain about. The Zodarks had cleverly hidden this outpost amidst the clutter of an asteroid field. It made detecting it almost impossible unless you knew where to look. Approaching it was just as deadly. Nestled between massive chunks of floating rocks, the outpost used the terrain like a shield—limiting approach angles and cloaking itself behind a curtain of natural interference. It gave them the advantage of concealment and time. Any direct assault would be funneled through predictable lanes, turning attackers into fish in a barrel.

"Approaching visual resolution on the target," Lieutenant Reynolds reported.

The center monitor refined its image as the *Poseidon's* passive optical cameras locked on. Outpost Varnak emerged from the darkness—an angular mass of alloy and armor grafted into a hollowed-out asteroid spine, spanning several kilometers end-to-end. The station bristled with comm arrays, fixed weapons platforms, storage facilities, and fuel depots.

The camera tracked movement flaring along its docking spines, bulk freighters and gunboats maneuvering between mooring arms and shuttle bays blinking with activity.

Beyond it, a luminous haze flickered, an orbital minefield unlike any Lee had encountered.

"Bringing up minefield telemetry," Baldry muttered at the sensor console.

On screen, the outer defense perimeter appeared like a curtain of dying stars. The mines shimmered with faint blue coronas, each one a self-contained weapon platform. A single narrow corridor threaded through them, just wide enough for ships to pass one at a time, like threading a needle in full combat gear.

"Check passive scanners for pattern variances or cloaked nodes. Let's not miss anything," Lee ordered. He knew the limitations of using passive scanners, but he hated the idea of going in blind like they were right now.

Ensign Baldry nodded, running silent queries through the *Poseidon*'s sensor suite. "They're not just passive mines, sir. These are active—adaptive. Pattern spacing shifts slightly every ninety seconds. There's an AI core somewhere managing the entire field, likely in the command center on the outpost. Every mine appears to be exchanging telemetry data with its neighbors, forming a distributed detection net."

He paused, then added, "Deviate even slightly from the corridor, and the net wakes up."

Sato leaned forward from her command chair, reviewing the tactical overlay. "According to the Primords, these are Tier-IV antimatter warheads—designed to shear armored hulls in half. Each unit's sensor range overlaps with the next, and their spectral range is wide—thermal, gravimetric, even neutrino scattering."

Lee raised an eyebrow. "Huh, they're sniffing for quantum signatures?"

"Yes," she confirmed, zooming in. "If one mine spots something off—wrong emission decay, wrong IFF ping, it'll light up the grid and mark us. From there, everything with a gun in a hundred thousand klicks will know we're here."

Rodriguez glanced up from the comms station. "Sir, Zodark chatter is holding steady. Mostly internal traffic, dockmaster handoffs, logistics cycling. No indication they've noticed us. Our spoofed IFF is blending with the standard supply pattern. But barely," she added. "Their comm net is multi-layered—synthetic phase encoding that shifts by harmonic signature. If we get a single timestamp wrong, we'll trip their filters."

Lee moved between stations, watching the task force's formation on the left auxiliary screen. They were playing a deadly game of mimicry, gliding silently through the void like party crashers in a stolen costume. Their emissions, thermal trails, and IFF signals, all artificially generated by the four EW frigates leading them in, were spoofing the Zodark sensors into believing they were the regularly scheduled Zodark convoy.

"How close are we to the detection line?" Lee asked.

"Four hundred klicks and closing, but it's a guess, an estimate, not an exact science," Reynolds replied. "We just received a message from Captain Dharek. He confirms we're to proceed in."

Lee nodded. "Transmit our final signal burst to synchronize the fleet. Tight beam only."

"Transmission sent," Rodriguez confirmed. "Still holding ghost signature across all bands."

Before Lee could answer, a sharp beep interrupted him.

Rodriguez leaned in, face tightening. "Sir… we've got a spike. Signal density just increased across the Zodark comm layer. They're coordinating something."

On the screen, formations began to shift. Eighteen Zodark vessels—cruisers, destroyers, and battleships, rippled into focus as the sensor model updated. Their vectors adjusted slightly, orbiting like silent executioners around the outpost.

Rhom stared at the display. "I'm showing another twelve capital ships on the other side of the asteroid belt. That's a full strike armada they're amassing."

Lee didn't flinch. "Wow, this really is their forward staging base."

Sato frowned. "If they detect us and trap us in this corridor, they'll have us dead to rights before we can even turn around."

Lee watched the battlefield tighten like a noose.

"Well, we're not here to turn around," he said. "We finish what we came to do."

Lee watched their ships continue to move closer. They were almost in position, almost ready to attack. "Signal Captain Dharek—reconfirm our assault vector. Let him know our forward elements are nearing full visual on the target. Once the corridor opens and we have clean line-of-sight, we go weapons free."

Rodriguez gave a silent nod and passed the message to the Primord flagship. No further words were needed.

Lee turned back to the display. The task force continued its slow crawl through the field, threading the final hundred kilometers of the corridor. Every ship's hull shimmered faintly under the influence of Zodark-simulated IFF fields and null-signature drives. They were ghosts wearing enemy masks, gliding inches from oblivion.

And then—there it was. The final bend of the corridor flared open on the screen. A thin curtain of tumbling rock drifted aside, revealing the station's central spine in full, beautiful display.

Lee excitedly exclaimed, "This is it, people! We're here. Go active with our sensors. Rhom, get us a weapons lock and engage with all weapons now!"

The bridge erupted in a flurry of activity and orders as the ship came alive.

One by one, the other ships reported the same—*Bolt*, *Thunder*, *Oceanus*, *Ek*, and *Vrallin's Spear*. They had visual. Clean angles. Direct targeting lines.

The enemy had still not reacted to them.

"They haven't seen us yet," Baldry whispered as the ship continued to come alive, weapons activating, sensors sweeping the area.

Rhom's knuckles whitened on his console. "Enemy sensors active…weapon systems charging…"

Rodriguez's voice came like a blade. "Zodark net just spiked. They're sounding the alarms."

Lee turned to Sato. She gave a single, sharp nod.

"All ships, stand by to fire."

The moment the alarm klaxon lit red on the display, Lee was already shouting.

"Open fire—all ships, fire at will!"

The *Poseidon*'s hull shuddered as the forward magrail batteries spat two-ton slugs into the black, each one streaking through the void like silent red daggers. Turbolaser emplacements cycled up behind them, launching pulses of searing light at the exposed ridge of the Zodark outpost.

"Rodriguez, tell the Primords it's go time!"

Before she could answer, the Primord comm node flared to life. Captain Dharek's voice came across the channel, calm, ironbound, and resolute.

"Primord fleet—execute strike pattern Fyr'Vass. Fire."

Across the tactical screen, the three Primord battleships emerged from the asteroid veil like predatory beasts, weapon ports blooming with energy. A symphony of green and violet arcs lit the darkness as their plasma lances carved wide, spiraling trails through space, converging on the central spine of Outpost Varnak.

"Targets locked," Rhom shouted. "Direct line on the station's reactor housing. Engaging now!"

One by one, the rest of Lee's formation joined in: the *Dagger* and *Vigilant* unleashing salvos of long-range antiship missiles, the heavy cruisers *Oceanus* and *Thunder* hammering away with sustained magrail volleys. Trails of glowing projectiles sliced through the void, weaving around the drifting rocks that still half-obscured the battlefield.

Outpost Varnak answered with everything it had.

Bright motes of defensive fire erupted from its outer decks. Rotary flak shells burst in overlapping cones. Point defense lasers stitched brilliant lines across the dark, trying to catch the incoming swarm of projectiles. The twin Zodark cruisers flanking the mine corridor fired full broadsides— torpedoes and plasma bolts hurling outward in retaliation.

"Incoming! High-velocity plasma spread from the port cruiser!" Baldry yelled.

"Brace!" Lee called out. The *Poseidon* shuddered violently as a near-miss plasma bolt skimmed along their port armor, warping plates but not breaching.

"Return fire! Target that cruiser's main batteries. Suppress it!"

The forward batteries realigned. Two kinetic salvos and a barrage of missile fire answered the threat, slamming into the Zodark ship's midsection and driving it back into a roll.

The corridor between the fleets had become a meat grinder of blinding light and explosive death. Each second felt like a lifetime.

"Captain," Sato called from her station, her voice hard. "Republic missiles are tracking true. Primord lances converging on the target point. If they hit that reactor node—"

Lee didn't blink. "Then we cripple this outpost. Keep firing."

On the main screen, the center of Outpost Varnak grew larger, its shielding compromised, its flanks ablaze.

*Just a few seconds more...* Lee thought.

On the tactical overlay, one of the Primord cruisers, *Valmir's Blade,* angled to port, trying to reposition along the outpost's outer rim. But the movement pushed her too far from the protective fire arc of the formation, leaving her exposed.

"Three Zodark cruisers emerging from the asteroid flank," Rhom called out. "Bearing thirty-seven by six."

Lee watched as bright lances of violet light shot across the black. The lead Zodark cruiser fired in paired bursts. Plasma torpedoes followed, cutting across space like burning stars.

The first plasma strike slammed into *Valmir's Blade* amidships, boiling armor and venting atmosphere in a glowing wash of fire and steel. The second hit shredded through the rear third of her hull. Moments later, a third torpedo struck true, right as twin Zodark lasers carved deep into the weakened structure.

*Valmir's Blade* ruptured in a flash of molten fury. Her superstructure split, and her starboard engine nacelle spun free, trailing a spiral of debris and fire. Compartments tore apart like shredded paper. For one long, frozen second, the glowing wreckage floated silently.

Then it came apart completely.

"*Valmir's Blade* is gone," Sato said quietly, voice hard.

A split second later, the Zodark outpost joined the fight.

"Outpost is powering its dorsal arrays. Multiple plasma ports opening!" Baldry warned.

The enormous installation lit up like a star, its surface bristling with concentrated laser emitters and plasma launchers. A coordinated barrage tore through the dark. Focused fire aimed at *Kjorhaln's Wrath*, one of the Primords' heavy battleships.

The Primord vessel was hammered. Lasers cut across her hull in a crisscrossing pattern, severing antennae, sensor fins, and armor panels. Plasma torpedoes followed, slamming into her flank and igniting several sections along her mid-deck. Explosions flared along her spine as power cells ruptured, but the *Wrath* didn't stop.

"She's holding," Rhom said, stunned.

"*Kjorhaln's Wrath* returning fire," Sato called out.

The Primord dreadnought answered with a blistering full spread of anti-ship missiles, followed by sweeping laser blasts from her forward emitters. The missiles launched in tight clusters, streaking between asteroids as their engines flared.

The nearest Zodark cruiser attempted to veer away, but it was too late. Three missiles found their mark, exploding in sequence across the enemy vessel's prow and ventral hull. The detonations engulfed the forward third of the cruiser in white-hot flame. Then came the *Wrath*'s laser barrage, slicing across the enemy hull like a scalpel made of fire.

The Zodark ship lost control. Its port wing sheared off, venting burning plasma, and the rest of the cruiser tumbled into the asteroid field where it shattered against a drifting rock the size of a small city.

"Confirmed kill," Rhom said, voice taut.

Lee's fists clenched on the armrest. "That's one. Let's make it count."

"Primary turrets. Stand by for coordinated salvo," Lee ordered, his voice tight. "Target the reactor shield structure. Let's bring this bastard down."

Aboard the *Poseidon*, the deck vibrated with each magrail turret cycle as the ship's three heavy batteries aligned, sleek, armored barrels adjusting micro degrees as fire control finalized the trajectory. Beside them, *Oceanus* and *Thunder* shifted into parallel firing positions, forming a deadly triangle against the outpost.

"Targets locked," Rhom reported. "All Republic heavies green to fire."

"Let's crack it open. All ships… fire."

The *Poseidon's* forward batteries unleashed first. Two magrail slugs per turret screamed into the void, the high-velocity rounds burning red-hot as friction ionized what particles remained in their wake. A half-second later, *Oceanus* and *Thunder* followed suit, their salvos converging on the same target zone: the armored segment of the outpost protecting its central reactors.

The first impacts staggered along the station's outer hull; superheated armor panels shattered like brittle glass. The second wave punched deeper, blowing apart defensive guns and sensor nodes along the dorsal ridge. Dozens of point-defense turrets ceased firing, their control linkages and power conduits vaporized by the kinetic force.

"Direct hits!" Rodriguez shouted. "We've crippled their upper defense grid!"

"*Thunder* reports hull scoring but still in the fight," Sato added. "*Oceanus* holding formation. Two guns still hot."

The outpost convulsed with secondary explosions. Bright-orange fireballs burst from within the structure—one bloom, then another, lighting up the interior with flashes of molten metal and ruptured plasma lines. Yet the central reactor shielding held firm…blackened, dented, gouged, but not breached.

"They're not dead yet," Lee muttered.

From the asteroid field's far edge, Zodark vessels surged into view—cruisers and destroyers, their formation tightening as they fanned out to encircle the attackers. At least three battleships powered up plasma launchers, their arcs shifting to bracket the Republic and Primord ships in crossfire.

"Sir," Reynolds called from navigation, "enemy fleet is moving to flank us. They're trying to pin us inside the corridor."

"They want to trap us in here," Rhom added grimly. "Hold us down until reinforcements arrive and box us in."

"They won't get the chance," Lee growled. "All Republic heavies, maintain fire. That core's going to crack. We'll get our kill shot before they close the net."

The magrail guns roared again. Another synchronized volley tore through the outpost's scarred flank, and this time, the kinetic strike punched deep into the armored core. Fire vented from a breach in the primary shield ring, licking the edges of the central chamber.

Inside the *Poseidon*, the lights flickered as the capacitors fed another round into the coils.

"Let's finish it," Lee said, eyes fixed on the expanding rupture on the tactical map.

The *Poseidon's* CIC was a storm of focused chaos: crew shouting updates, alarms pulsing red across multiple stations, and the tactical map alive with threat vectors shifting by the second.

"EW frigates in position," Rhom reported. "GhostNet protocols live. They're blanketing the Zodark targeting grid with distortion pulses."

Lee gripped the rail beside his chair as the *Poseidon* rocked under the impact of a glancing laser strike. The starboard side lit up like a blowtorch had been dragged across its surface, showering superheated sparks across the outer armor. The deck rumbled, not from a breach, but from systems compensating for the kinetic stress.

"Damage to section one turbolaser turrets," MacGregor called from engineering. "We're rerouting power to lateral arrays."

On the forward tactical screen, the battle surged and twisted like a living thing. The Zodarks, previously fluid in their coordination, were now tangled in their own confusion. Several ships had drifted out of formation—some overcorrected, others fired at phantom signatures projected by the Republic EW frigates. Static-laced signals washed across Zodark fleet comms, their formations blurring as if trying to fight through a strobe light.

"*Poseidon*'s jammers are hitting them hard," Rodriguez confirmed, watching a trio of destroyers attempt to reorient. "Their C2 net's degrading—multiple ships are blind, reacting slowly."

"Good," Lee said flatly. "Keep them guessing."

Another beam lanced across their bow, striking the forward shielding node. The entire ship groaned, vibrations rolling through the deck like distant thunder. Behind the impact zone, armored plating scorched and buckled, but held.

"Maintain pressure!" Lee shouted. "Gunners, stay on that core!"

To port, a Zodark battleship moved to intercept the Primord right flank, plasma torpedoes building charge along its belly mounts. It never got the chance.

Twin Primord battleships, *Vrallin's Spear* and *Eskor*, broke from the inner asteroid ring in a pincer maneuver, their sleek silver hulls glinting in the flashes of battle. They opened fire simultaneously, one volley of searing blue lasers and a full spread of anti-ship missiles screaming through space.

The lasers carved through the Zodark vessel's outer hull, slicing off a third of its upper decks. A second later, the missile swarm struck, six warheads detonating across the spine of the ship. The entire midsection of the battleship crumpled inward as internal plasma reservoirs ruptured in a chain reaction.

The Zodark vessel disappeared in a silent inferno, its core going critical in a wash of blinding white light. Fragments of its armored plating scattered through the asteroid belt like burning leaves in a storm.

Cheers broke out across the *Poseidon's* bridge, quickly silenced as Lee raised a hand.

"Focus. We're not out yet."

He glanced at the main display. The outpost's defenses were still crumbling, and the enemy fleet, though disorganized, was regrouping. But now, the Republic and Primord ships had momentum. A narrow window had opened.

They just had to punch through before it slammed shut.

<h1 style="text-align:center">Chapter 43:<br>Open Fire</h1>

**RNS *Poseidon***
**Thorian Divide**
**Border Zone Intus-Rass/TD-7**

A sudden flare of light off the port side yanked Lee's eyes from the main tactical display.

"Contact loss, Primord frigate *Veydras*!" shouted Ensign Baldry. "It crossed the minefield perimeter!"

Lee's head snapped toward the viewport display just in time to see the *Veydras* vanish in a sphere of blinding plasma. One second, it was adjusting formation to swing wide of the outer ring; the next, a dozen anti-ship mines lit off in a chain-reaction blast that swallowed the sleek, curved vessel in an expanding blossom of blue-white energy. Chunks of burning hull and venting atmosphere spiraled outward, tumbling through the asteroid field like broken bones in the void.

"Dear god…" Sato murmured.

"Another one just lit up," Rhom said grimly, tapping his screen. "Zodark mines are on full autonomous trigger. No time for human error out here."

Before Lee could respond, a sharp vibration rolled through the deck.

"Direct hit!" Rodriguez barked. "That was the *Cobalt*!"

Lee spun to the left-side monitor, eyes locking on the feed of the Republic frigate. The *Cobalt* was limping, its dorsal engine nacelle gutted by a plasma strike, the starboard hull scorched and venting coolant in a swirling spiral. A second barrage of plasma torpedoes streaked toward it, greenish bolts glowing like coiled serpents in the dark.

"She's going to be finished if she doesn't get cover," Rhom warned.

"Not on my watch." Lee slapped the armrest. "Helm, bring us between the *Cobalt* and those bastards. Starboard five degrees, pitch down ten. Put us in the way."

"Aye, sir! Executing maneuver!"

The *Poseidon* groaned as her inertial dampeners struggled to keep pace with the sudden course change. From the tactical view, the ship's thick armored frame slid laterally across the battlespace, placing itself between the wounded *Cobalt* and the incoming fire. One torpedo struck the *Poseidon's* forward plating with a thunderous ripple, spitting fire across the armor and knocking out one of the secondary point-defense arrays, but the ship continued to hold firm.

"Damage to decks two and three, forward port section," reported Sato, her voice tight. "No breach. Systems compensating."

Lee exhaled slowly, jaw set. "Stay with the *Cobalt*. Keep her behind our hull shadow."

He keyed his mic, linking to Captain Dharek's ship. "*Poseidon* has assumed overwatch of a wounded Republic asset. Continuing suppression of the outpost. Requesting update—"

The response came almost immediately, Dharek's voice sharp and strained. "Commander Lee, I need you to redirect your firepower immediately. We have a Zodark battleship approaching from vector three seven two, its attempting to break through our flank. One of my capital ships, the *Vrallin's Spear*, is taking concentrated fire. It's not going to hold without support."

Lee frowned. His gaze drifted to the main screen where the *Poseidon's* primary batteries continued hammering the Zodark outpost, chunks of superstructure now peeling from its surface like shrapnel under pressure. They were so close…

He hesitated. Just a moment.

"Send targeting data," Lee replied flatly.

Data spiked onto the tactical overlay. The Zodark battleship Dharek identified loomed like a monolith, its heavy plasma batteries turning the void into a killing field aimed straight at the Primord line.

Lee clenched his teeth. "Helm, hold firing solution on the outpost. But load all remaining Havoc missiles and redirect to Dharek's target. Full spread."

"Aye, sir. Missiles locked and launching in three…"

He watched the display as a ripple of white-hot streaks launched from the *Poseidon*'s VLS cells. A dozen Havoc anti-ship missiles knifed through space, slipping past floating debris and burning wreckage as they arced toward the Zodark warship.

Lee didn't speak. He didn't need to.

His silence said it all.

*******

## Primord Battleship *Ek*
## Thorian Divide – Forward Assault Element

Captain Dharek stood rigid at the forward command deck, his jaw set like carved stone. The bridge of the *Ek* shimmered with real-time tactical overlays projected from the ceiling and floor alike, casting violet and indigo reflections across the sleek obsidian plating and matte white walls.

He watched, unblinking, as the *Torshal,* his third-line frigate, veered hard starboard to interdict the Zodark battleship closing on *Vrallin's Spear*, a Primord dreadnought already under concentrated fire. The *Torshal*'s final salvo of antiship missiles lanced into the void—beautiful, disciplined, perfectly timed.

It never reached its mark.

A heartbeat later, the minefield awoke.

Twelve antimatter mines flared in unison, an orchestrated detonation that vaporized the *Torshal* in a flash of radiant blue fury. Fragments of its reinforced frame spun end over end through space, caught in the residual wake of charged energy and disintegrated hull plating. The scream of its loss echoed through the ship's AI-linked battle network, a shiver in the mental undercurrent that every Primord officer could feel in their bones.

Dharek's throat tightened. "Another soul reclaimed by the void."

He turned his gaze to the secondary display, where *Vrallin's Spear* was now being gutted by beam-laced plasma fire from the encroaching Zodark warship. Its armor had collapsed under the relentless barrage. Entire decks were now exposed to vacuum, structural latticework glowing with venting plasma and residual reactor heat.

"Captain, our starboard formation is folding," warned his second-in-command, Commander Saelith. "If the *Poseidon* does not engage, we risk losing the flank entirely."

Dharek narrowed his gaze toward the Republic heavy cruiser on the tactical display. A spread of Republic missiles arced toward the Zodark battleship. A good strike. Accurate, deadly. But that was all.

The *Poseidon*'s magrail turrets and turbolasers remained fixed on the outpost, still pounding its superstructure with ruthless precision. Lee hadn't shifted his primary batteries as ordered…not even slightly.

Dharek's jaw tightened. "He heard my request. He acknowledged it. But his fire remains fixed on the station."

Commander Saelith glanced up from her console. "You did more than request, Captain. You issued a directive."

"Yes," Dharek said bitterly. "And he has not obeyed it."

On the display, *Vrallin's Spear* took another direct plasma hit to its midline. Its spine buckled. Atmosphere vented in geysers of white frost and jagged debris. Internal reactors began to fail-safe, cascading into cold shutdown.

"She will not survive the next volley."

Dharek took one step forward, his voice low and edged with fury. "I gave him command of the advance. Not license to ignore orders."

He watched in silence, fists trembling at his sides, as another Primord vessel died in fire, and the Republic's mightiest warship did nothing but stand watch. Focused. Relentless. And blind to anything else.

Captain Dharek gritted his teeth as he watched *Vrallin's Spear* being torn apart under the withering fire of the Zodark battleship. Great sheets of ablative armor peeled away from her flanks like slagged bark, plasma torpedoes punching through her portside hull and carving molten channels across multiple decks. Chunks of the battleship's dorsal plating drifted off into the void, tumbling and glowing red-hot.

"Helm, order the *Sulvaar* to reposition!" Dharek barked, stepping forward. "Put her between us and the enemy vessel. I don't care how close she has to get. If she can draw fire long enough, *Vrallin's Spear* might still survive this."

The helmsman relayed the order without hesitation. On the tactical display, the *Sulvaar*, sleek and dagger-shaped, broke from her current vector and banked hard toward the incoming Zodark ship, engines flaring with cold blue fire. She was older, her composite armor already pitted from earlier engagements, but she moved with the speed and precision of a ship that knew her duty.

Across the bridge, Commander Saelith muttered, "She won't hold for long."

"She won't need to," Dharek replied grimly, just as a cascade of new sensor alarms flashed across the forward hololith.

"Massive power spike—inside the outpost!" shouted Saelith. "Reactor core breach!"

The space beyond the asteroid belt lit up in a single, violent flash.

Varnak Outpost reactor detonated, a sunburst of white-blue flame tearing through the inner structure of the logistics station. A seismic shockwave of expanding debris surged outward, vaporizing nearby Zodark transports and crumpling scaffolding and dock arms like paper. Several fuel silos erupted in secondary blasts, sending spirals of orange and green flame spinning through the darkness.

The explosion tore a jagged swath through the asteroid belt. Massive fragments of the outpost's armored hull hurtled away, tumbling in slow arcs, trailing sparks and leaking glowing reactor plasma like arterial blood.

More than a handful of Zodark ships caught too close to the explosion were torn open or shoved violently off course when their hulls were smashed by flying debris. One enemy frigate blew apart when one of the asteroids drifted off course and plowed into it.

Dharek raised a hand as he squinted at the glare. Even filtered through the display monitor, the brightness was blinding.

"Report," he said calmly, regaining his footing as the deck trembled slightly from a pressure shock of another laser hit across the portside of the ship, proximity alarms adding to the chaos as debris drifted toward them.

Saelith stared at the pulsing red icon where the outpost had been. "Varnak is gone... vaporized. We've crippled their logistical hub. Their coordination grid is down, weapon systems and the mines are offline. No additional command signals are broadcasting from the debris."

Dharek stared at the carnage for a long moment, jaw clenched behind his pale lips.

The outpost's reactor core had ignited in a blinding detonation, flaring like a newborn star against the dark void. The blast had been incredible as it rolled outward in a shockwave of white-hot debris and vaporized metal, swallowing several Zodark transports clustered nearby. What he found most incredible was the series of secondary explosions that followed as stockpiled munitions and volatile fuel reserves, anchored to outlying asteroids, lit off in quick succession. In all the battles he had fought, he had never seen something like it.

With the destruction of the outpost, the Republic cruisers wasted no time shifting their guns to targets of opportunity. The *Poseidon, Oceanus,* and *Thunder* swept their batteries across the remnants of the staging complex, raking now silent weapon emplacements and munitions bunkers with railgun fire and turbo lasers, permanently silencing what few defensive platforms had survived the initial strike. Their firepower carved deep gouges through the outpost's remaining superstructure, leaving no survivors, no chance for regrouping.

But Dharek's gaze had already shifted to the far edge of the battlefield, where things were unraveling.

A violent bloom of plasma erupted near the *Sulvaar*.

"Impact!" one of Dharek's bridge officers cried out. "The *Sulvaar* struck a mine. Her stern section is venting, multiple decks compromised!"

The cruiser shuddered on the tactical display, trailing pieces of its shattered aft section as it veered off course, wounded and drifting.

Before Dharek could issue a stabilizing order, a second Zodark battleship powered through the debris cloud, its hull blackened by earlier strikes, but its guns very much alive.

*Vrallin's Spear*, his center-right anchor, had already been battered by the first Zodark warship. Now, under fire from two flanks, it began to buckle under the pressure.

"*Poseidon* still hasn't committed," his sensor officer said bitterly.

Dharek's nostrils flared. On-screen, *Poseidon* finally began pivoting into a flanking angle, magrail turrets and turbo lasers now focused on the first Zodark battleship he had flagged. Their impacts lanced across the enemy hull—effective, yes—but too little, too late.

*Vrallin's Spear* was caught in the storm of a brutal crossfire between two enemy battleships now. A concentrated volley of plasma torpedoes hammered its starboard midsection, rupturing its reactor containment lines. The explosion tore the ship apart from within, ripping a gaping hole through her central decks. Her spine fractured. A final internal detonation blasted through her upper hull, sending spirals of debris into the field.

Dharek's hands curled into fists at his side.

"Damn it. That's two."

The *Ek* rocked gently underfoot, still absorbing glancing blows from retreating Zodark skirmishers. He forced himself to look away from the ruined silhouette of *Vrallin's Spear*.

He didn't shout. Didn't bark. His voice, when it came, was calm, iron-clad with fury.

"Signal all forces—break contact. Retreat to Rally Point Zhurin. We've accomplished our mission. It's time to leave."

The communications officer hesitated only briefly. "Yes, Captain."

The Primord task force began their withdrawal, battered but not broken, leaving behind the smoldering remains of Varnak Outpost and too many of their own dead.
*******

**RNS *Poseidon***
**Thorian Divide, Border Zone Intus-Rass / TD-7**

The *Poseidon*'s bridge buzzed with strained focus as tension clung to the recycled air. The order to withdraw had just come through. Lee didn't speak for a beat, watching the tactical overlay as debris scattered in the aftermath of the outpost's detonation.

"Rodriguez," he said, keeping his voice even, "confirm Captain Dharek's withdrawal order. Priority to damaged vessels."

She nodded, already keying the tight beam across the Republic and Primord channels. "Confirmed. They're pulling out now."

Sato leaned over the primary console, eyes narrowed. "*Cobalt*'s jump drive is online—barely. *Scimitar* reports minor drive fluctuations, but they can make the jump."

One by one, the ships winked out of the battlespace, streaking into the void with brief flashes of FTL transition. Across the field, a battered Primord cruiser rolled limply before correcting course, its engines flaring as it leapt away from the growing Zodark encirclement.

Lee watched as the *Poseidon*'s sensors tracked enemy vessels repositioning, tightening their formation like a closing vice.

"Helm," he called out, "hold us for ten more seconds, no more. Get ready to punch us out the second the last Republic and Primord signature clears."

Another moment passed. The final friendly ship vanished from the board.

"All ships accounted for," Rhom confirmed.

Lee didn't hesitate. "Jump."

The *Poseidon*'s drives surged, pushing them into the blinding tunnel of FTL before the Zodarks could slam the door shut behind them.

The bridge of the *Poseidon* was subdued, systems stabilizing as the ship completed its transition to FTL. Ambient displays pulsed with diagnostic updates, and crew voices murmured over internal comms as they assessed damage across the fleet.

Lee stood near the systems console, reviewing the cascade of data scrolling across the surface. Reports showed heat scoring along the port hull, several forward batteries offline, and life support fluctuations on deck three for some reason.

Looking to a report that just came in from the *Cobalt*, Lee could see they had sustained damage that would once again necessitate more time in the shipyard—something he knew Captain Roberts was *not* going to be happy about.

"Commander," Sato's voice came gently from behind.

"Go ahead," Lee said without turning, eyes still on the cascading flood of post-action damage reports.

Sato hesitated. "It's about the *Vrallin's Spear*."

Lee's jaw flexed, but he didn't look up. "I know, Dharek flagged us. He wanted us to shift fire and screen his battleship."

"You saw the request?" Her voice was tighter now, uncertain.

He nodded once. "I did. I made a call to continue firing on the outpost. Rhom engaged the battleship with a volley of Havocs. I couldn't afford to split our guns. The outpost was our primary objective."

There was a pause before she spoke again. "The Havoc missiles hit, but shouldn't we have maneuvered to cover the *Vrallin*?"

Lee slowly exhaled, setting the datapad down. "Sato, the outpost was the objective. The Primords' job was to keep the Zodarks off our backs while we took it down. They did their job, and we did ours."

"I know. I get it…but the *Vrallin* didn't make it," Sato finally said. "The Zodarks got her, right at the end. Right before Dharek issued the order to fall back."

Lee didn't respond.

She swallowed hard, then asked quietly, "Did we mess up? Could we have done something differently?"

The silence between them stretched as Lee thought about it. This was probably a decision that would stay with him for some time. He knew he had made the right call, but that didn't make it any easier.

"I had hoped we would have had more time," he finally said, his voice quiet, brittle. "Dharek knew the mission. Knew the window we had to work within. We had to get in, smash the outpost, and get out before Zodark reinforcement could arrive and box us in."

"I know. You are probably right," Sato replied, not accusing, just sad. "Maybe if we could have shifted some of our weapons or repositioned our ship…we could have saved them."

Lee turned slowly to face her, the exhaustion behind his eyes heavier now. "Could have, would have, should have. What do you want me to say? That if I had shifted our weapons fire, the *Vrallin* would still be here? You don't know that. And the outpost *was* the objective."

"I get it. That's not what I was saying."

"Oh yeah? Sure seems that way to me," Lee shot back angrily, regretting it the moment he said it.

The air between them felt heavy. Neither wanted to speak. Meanwhile, the bridge hummed with soft operational chatter, oblivious to the storm quietly gathering in their corner.

Lee finally spoke, breaking the tension. "Sometimes, command decisions are about tradeoffs," he muttered softly. "I made one. I thought it was the right one."

"I know. You always think it's the right one," Sato replied, softer now, not cruel. "Sometimes the right decision isn't always the right decision."

Lee's hands fell to his sides, defeated. "You might be right. Dharek won't forget this."

"True, but neither should we."

**Chapter 44:**
**The Right Call**

**RNS *Poseidon***
**Rally Point Theta-9, Outer Rass Vector**

The moment the distortion from FTL faded, the stars snapped back into clarity as the ship returned to normal space. This was the second and final jump for the task force as they returned to their mobile command center and supply depot. Frankly, Lee was surprised that the Zodarks hadn't found it yet, but was glad they hadn't.

As the *Poseidon* continued to decelerate, her hull groaning from the battle damage from the recent fight. One by one, the rest of the task force dropped in around the Primord battleship the *Ek*, the task force flagship. Like the *Poseidon,* many of them sustained damage during the battle, but it was the Primords who had lost ships this time around.

Ahead, a screen of Republic and Primord support ships drifted into position as the damaged ships approached their mobile base. Lee watched as docking arms extended, and docking tugs guided in the most heavily damaged ship. A half-dozen corvettes and frigates extended a protective perimeter around the returning warriors.

On the bridge, a heavy silence lingered among the crew until Lieutenant Rodriguez announced, "Sir, incoming transmission from the Primords. It's on a secure command channel. Would you like me to patch it through to your station or to the conference room?"

Lee straightened in his seat, feeling the tension rise as he stood. "Put it through to the conference. Sato, with me. Rhom, you have the bridge."

"This should be interesting," commented Sato as they made their way to the conference room adjacent to the bridge.

Lee shrugged. He knew there would be a post mission brief at some point, though he had hoped it might have happened after they had time to write up their after action reports.

Sitting at the conference table, he nodded to Sato who connected the call for them. On the screen was Captain Yrithael, the Primord task force commander for the Rass expedition. Seated beside him was Captain Roberts, Lee's boss, who looked his typically grim self, though Lee thought there was a trace of satisfaction in his eyes.

A second later, the image of Captain Dharek appeared along with his deputy, then a third screen appeared. This last image was of Captain Sornvek, the Primord commander for the reconnaissance force tapped with identifying various targets across the Rass system.

"Excellent, it seems we have everyone," Yrithael greeted. "I want to congratulate everyone on a mission success. This was a critical victory for our side and a disastrous defeat for the Zodarks."

"Yes, but what it was not without loss," commented Dharek, his eyes staring daggers at Lee.

"Yes, well, not all victories are without loss," Roberts chimed in. It was obvious he could see the frustration between Dharek and Lee.

Yrithael raised his hand as if to silence further commentary. "Losing vessels under ones command, Dharek, is never easy. One can fight a hundred battles and not lose a ship and then lose several ships in a couple of hours. The Gods give life, and they can take it. It is understandable to be angry over the loss of ships under your command. Your job was to screen for the Republic ships to give them time for their kinetic weapons to destroy the outpost reactor core. You did that, and Commander Lee's ships succeeded in destroying the outpost, and not minute too late."

The image bearing Captain Sornvek came into focus as he joined the conversation. "One of my scouts observing the attack on the Varnak outpost reported not one, but three separate Zodark forces arriving less than five minutes after your force left the area, Dharek. Had your force taken minutes longer to destroy the outpost. You would have all been trapped and summarily destroyed.

"Instead, you managed to escape with the majority of your force intact and able to fight another day. I now want to draw your attention to this location here," Captain Sornvek brought up an image of sector-8, a quadrant of the Rass system labeled the Middle Reach Ice Fields. "Now that we have mapped sector-2 and -3, and destroyed the Varnak outpost. We have another area of concern we have to explore and map before we the invasion of Rass can begin—"

Yrithael cut in before he could speak further. "Thank you, Captain Sornvek for this information. Let us wait to discuss the sector-8 until we are in a secure place together."

The Primord commander nodded, deferring to Yrithael. "Captain Dharek, Commander Lee, with the completion of your mission you both are ordered to return to Stavros to get your ships repaired and your crews rested. You will report to Skjarnhold Command where you will be briefed by Admiral Velmiran of your next mission."

"Yes, sir," Dharek replied. "How soon do you want my squadron to depart?"

"You'll depart in twenty-four hours," Yrithael confirmed before turning to Roberts.

"Commander Lee, the ships under your command look to be ready to go," Captain Roberts said in his gruff manner. "Why don't you go ahead and depart now and report to Admiral McKee upon your arrival. I'll be returning to Primordia for consultation with the admiral in a couple of days. We'll speak further upon my arrival."

The meeting ended a few minutes later after some additional questioning. The entire time, Lee felt like Dharek still held him responsible for the loss of the *Vrallin.* They had a mission to accomplish, and each of them had their own part in it. Still, the loss of so many souls weighed heavy on Lee. It was a weight that continued to grow the longer this war dragged on.

As the meeting came to an end. Sato got up and left, not saying a word. He knew she was mad at him, mad that he didn't at least reposition the Poseidon to shield the Primord ship. *It was my call—not yours...* he told himself.

Leaving the conference room, he told Sato she had the bridge for the remainder of the day. He was going to check on the wounded in the Medbay, grab a bite to eat, and then rack out for as long as he could. His mind was burnt. He needed to rest and he needed to be ready for whatever was waiting for him they arrived in Kita.

## Chapter 45:
## Quiet Confessions

**Year 2097**
**FOB Oteren**
**Planet Intus**

The AT-70C Osprey touched down in the hangar bay, its landing gear kissing the tarmac. Love lowered the ramp, releasing a wave of medics, who rushed out of the cabin, their stretcher-bearers filling the space while their shouts filled the air. Love unbuckled her harness.

Green stood at the cockpit's threshold, helmet tucked under his arm. His gaze lingered on her. "Lieutenant, you coming?"

"Later," she replied, eyes steady on the cockpit viewport. "I'll see you soon."

He hesitated, then gave a slight nod. "All right." Turning, he joined Williams and Ford as they exited the aircraft. The clamor subsided as the last footsteps faded, leaving the Osprey enveloped in stillness.

Alone, Love's gaze drifted to the photograph taped beside the instrument panel. Jack's smile met her, unchanging yet distant. She reached out, fingertips just above the worn edges. Confusion crossed her mind as she remembered something. It wasn't long ago—maybe a week or two—that she'd thought she had brought this picture into her quarters. However, she'd just remembered she'd done the same thing as she did now—hovering her fingers over the photo and deciding to let it remain stuck to the dash.

She recalled standing in her quarters the next morning, searching for the picture that wasn't there. Why had she believed otherwise? The realization settled like a brick in her stomach. The long hours, the stimulants—they were eroding more than exhaustion could explain.

Weariness crashed over her, heavier than any she'd felt before. The relentless pace, the missions stacked back-to-back—had they become her way of avoiding the unavoidable?

Her eyes stayed on Jack's image. Lines she hadn't noticed before etched his face, or perhaps her memory added them now.

"What am I doing, Jack?" she asked. "Running myself into the ground like this… it's not helping anyone, is it?"

Her hand dropped to her lap. "I'm forgetting things—important things. I'm tired all of the time, pushing myself too far. Always. Nearly cost us today."

A yawn overtook her, pulling at muscles she hadn't realized were sore. "I thought keeping busy would fill the void. But it's just a distraction. A dangerous one." She leaned back in the seat. "These people rely on me, and I'm letting them down."

Her gaze returned to the photo. "You'd tell me to slow down, wouldn't you? Always the voice of reason."

Love walked out of the cockpit, through the troop bay, and down the ramp. The hangar's overhead lights made her squint as she rounded the Osprey's stern. She stopped at the ship's hull, where she'd crossed out the name "Genesis" with a red streak and crudely painted "Jack" beside it… how long ago? She crossed her arms.

"You kept me safe again today," she whispered, palm resting against the metal. "Remember Prospect Lake? That perfect summer day when we had a rare day off from flight training?"

The memory came over her—sunlight dancing on ripples, Jack's arms around her waist as they waded into the cool water. His laughter echoing across Memorial Park when she splashed him. The warmth of his chest against her back as they lay on their beach towels, his fingers intertwined with hers.

"You held me while I dozed off by the shore." Her voice cracked. "Said it was the most peaceful you'd seen me." She pressed her forehead against the Osprey. "I miss that peace. Miss you showing me how to find it."

She sighed. "I've been running myself ragged, thinking if I stay busy enough…" She swallowed. "I know, you just heard me whining about this a second ago. But you'd want me whole, right? Not this damn shell I've become."

She pushed off the ship. "I think it's time I talked to someone. Really talked, Jack. Doctor what's-her-face has been offering, and I keep brushing her off. Ford's looks, they tell me he's bothered by my lack of sleep, my exhaustion. OK, doctor what's-her-face only offered once, but it was an offer nonetheless." She squared her shoulders. "Can't be much of a pilot if I'm falling apart."

Boots on metal rang through the hangar. Love turned to see Chief Brian Ford striding toward her. "Lieutenant Love, I think we should talk."

She knew exactly what this talk would be about. "Sure. Over chow?"

## Chapter 46:
## Beyond the Pod

**Year 2097**
**RNS *Gallipoli***
**Intus Orbit**

Coop leaned back, balancing his chair on two legs, and surveyed the busy mess hall. The Jolly Rogers Squadron filled the space with conversation. Trays clattered, and the scent of steaming chili mixed with the aroma of fresh bread. Bear sat to Coop's left, motioning wildly as he recounted their daring maneuvers during Operation Blackout.

"And when that ion cannon lit up, I thought we were toast," Bear said. "But Coop here swoops in like some kind of hero out of an old vid and takes it out in one shot."

"That's not even close to how it went," Coop replied.

"Then how'd it go… Ace?" Bear asked Coop.

Raven shook his head, sitting across the table. "You're going to give Coop a bigger head than he already has. Ego much?"

Coop smirked, tipping his chair forward. "Can't help it if I'm just that good. Just runs in my line, I guess."

"Sure." Bear slapped the back of Coop's chair. "Modest as ever."

Plates emptied and stories flowed, each pilot adding their own flair to the mission's retelling. A rare ease settled over Coop, the adrenaline of the mission replaced by a warm camaraderie.

Raven leaned in with a mischievous glint in his eye. "Did you see Strike's face after the mission when—"

A shadow fell over the table. Coop glanced up to see Phantom, Ninja, and Lucky standing there, trays in hand. Phantom's gaze was unreadable, his posture stiff.

"Mind if we join you?" Ninja asked.

"Only if you promise not to ruin the mood," Bear said, his eyes on Phantom.

Lucky slid into the chair beside Raven. "Can't make any promises."

Phantom sat, his attention on the untouched food before him. An awkward silence hung in the air.

Ninja cleared his throat. "Listen, Coop… about the mission…"

"What about it?" Coop asked.

"Just wanted to say thanks. Your leadership out there—well, it kept us all in one piece. Well, most of us. You did damn good, is all I'm saying."

Coop gave a nod. "It wasn't me, really. We've got a hell of a squadron. The Jolly Rogers… well, I can't say enough about us. Couldn't have found a better home."

Lucky nudged Phantom's arm. "Right, Phantom? Coop kicked butt out there."

"Like he said, we all did." Phantom continued to stare at his tray, then finally looked up. "I think you did good, though, Coop." He stabbed his food and took a bite of his meal.

Raven hid a smirk behind his cup. Bear's eyes darted between Coop and Phantom.

Coop feigned shock. "Did Phantom just praise me? Say it again. Do it. Say something nice to me, one more time. I gotta get it out of you."

Ninja laughed. "Stop egging him on, Coop. You might not get another compliment if you don't quiet down about it."

Phantom's lips twitched. "Just calling it like I see it."

"Well, I'll take what I can get," Coop replied. "Maybe next time you'll even crack a smile."

"Let's not get ahead of ourselves," Phantom said.

Bear swallowed a bite. "I bet we can make it happen."

Lucky joined in. "I'd pay good money to see that."

Phantom shook his head. "You guys are relentless." He tried to hide a smile.

Coop seized the moment. "See? There it is! A smile. Knew you had it in you."

"Miracles do happen," Raven said.

Phantom's facade softened just a touch. "Don't make me regret it."

"Too late," Bear said. "We're witnesses now."

Laughter erupted around the table. The earlier tension melted away.

Ninja pointed a fork at Phantom. "Next thing we know, you'll be telling jokes."

"Don't push your luck," Phantom replied.

"I'll settle for a knock-knock joke," Coop said.

Phantom stopped chewing. "Fine. Knock, knock."

Coop played along. "Who's there?"

"Interrupting pilot."

"Interrup—"

"Mission briefing in thirty minutes," Phantom said.

A collective groan sounded. Raven checked his watch. "He's right, you know."

Bear sighed. "Trust Phantom to bring us back to reality."

The mess hall doors slid open. Commander Strike stood at the entrance, scanning the room like a targeting system. Conversations hushed. Utensils paused midair.

Strike's eyes locked onto Coop. "Coop, I need to see you in my office. Now."

Coop's grip tightened on his fork. *Now? I'm eating*, he thought. *Why do I have to keep seeing this guy in his office?* He pushed his chair back, the legs scraping against the metal floor.

"Looks like someone's in demand," Bear said.

Raven smirked. "Try not to have too much fun."

"Yeah, blast of a time," Coop said.

He rose from the table, leaving the half-eaten meal behind. As he walked toward Strike, the squadron's gazes fell on him. Strike turned, leading the way out of the mess hall without another word.

Coop followed a step behind, matching Strike's brisk pace down the corridor.

*Another stroll to the principal's office. What's this about?* he wondered. *Every meeting with Strike feels like a debriefing and a dressing-down rolled into one.*

They approached a junction where a maintenance crew worked on a flickering panel. Strike navigated around them without slowing, and Coop sidestepped a toolbox left in the walkway.

*Does he ever relax?* he thought, noting the rigid set of Strike's shoulders. Memories of previous encounters surfaced—the critiques, the stern lectures, the occasional nod of approval that always felt earned the hard way.

When they reached Strike's office, the door opened at their approach. Inside, Strike gestured toward a chair, like always. "Have a seat."

Coop settled into the chair, back straight. Strike took his place behind the desk, fingers steepled.

"I've reviewed the after-action reports," Strike said.

*What did I do wrong this time?* Coop braced himself.

"Your performance during Operation Blackout was commendable."

Coop blinked. "Thank you, sir."

"Your quick thinking neutralized critical threats. You demonstrated initiative and an understanding of enemy tactics."

Coop nodded, uncertain where this was leading.

Strike rested his elbows on his desktop. "The Zodarks might be dormant right now, but I've got a feeling they're cooking up new cyber warfare tactics. We need to stay ahead of them."

"Like decryption breakers?" Coop asked.

"Among other things. The silence worries me—means they're developing something big. I want you heading up our preventive measures."

Coop's eyebrows lifted. "Me?"

"Yes. I'm assigning you as lead instructor for cyber defense training. Three days a week, starting very soon. Get our pilots and techs up to speed."

"Training? I've never—"

"You'll do fine. Sometimes the best teachers are the ones who learned it in the field, not the classroom. Besides, you can't spend all your time in a pod and behind a screen."

"Sir, with all due respect—you do realize that Raven is the one who is the subject matter expert when it comes to cyber defense, right?" asked Coop.

Strike smiled. "Of course, he is," he replied. "But you need to get better in this area, and what better way to improve your knowledge than by forcing you to teach it?"

Coop suppressed a laugh. *That does sound about par for the course with the military*, he thought.

"Can I at least bring Raven into this to help guide me?" Coop asked.

"Sure, I'll let you have Raven as a tutor," Strike replied. Coop was surprised by how easily he had just made that accommodation without any pushback.

"Thank you, sir," said Coop. "I'll make it work."

"Ensure that everyone understands the protocols. We can't afford breaches." Strike stood, signaling the meeting's conclusion. "We launch the initiative immediately. Keep me updated on your progress."

Coop rose from his chair. "Understood."

As Coop exited the office, his mind spun with plans—training drills, simulation scenarios, ways to outsmart the Zodark cyber-warfare attackers. He'd not only teach, he'd learn. In truth, Raven knew the most about EW, and Coop was simply along for the ride.

He passed the maintenance crew again, the hiss of their tools barely registering. The echoes of Strike's words resonated louder.

Reaching the mess hall entrance, he halted. The laughter and clatter inside beckoned, but his new role stressed him out a little. He didn't know why, it just did. Maybe the added responsibility bugged him, or the extra time spent teaching would give him less sleep.

"Time to get to work," Coop decided, turning away from the mess hall. He headed toward the squadron quarters, intent on gathering his thoughts and outlining the training program.

**Chapter 47:**
**Honor Among Heroes**

**Year 2097**
**FOB Oteren**
**Planet Intus**

Love stood near the back of the assembly hall. Soft
conversations filled the air. The hall stretched wide and long,
its walls decorated with flags of the Republic. The grand hall
was packed to capacity, rows upon rows of uniforms
stretching back into the shadows.

She adjusted the collar of her own uniform. To her left,
Ford leaned against a pillar, his gaze fixed on the stage. The
other day, she had a great conversation with him over dinner,
him sharing his concerns about her running herself ragged,
and she agreeing to fix that issue. Williams and Green chatted
quietly nearby, while Ford flipped through a small notebook,
ever the meticulous notetaker.

As Love moved closer to the front, a few soldiers
caught her eye. A young corporal with a bandaged arm gave
her a nod—she remembered airlifting him out of a hot zone
days ago. Another, a sergeant with a new prosthetic leg, stood
and offered a respectful salute. Heat flushed her cheeks, but
she returned the gesture with a humble nod.

The murmurs quieted as Commander Granger strode
onto the stage. He approached the podium while holding a
datapad. "Soldiers of FOB Oteren, we've faced challenges that
tested us to our core. Today, we honor a few among us who
showed remarkable courage during our recent operations."

Love felt every eye shift toward her. She focused on
Granger, his words pulling her back to the medevac
missions—each one a race against time, under fire, navigating
storms both literal and figurative.

"Lieutenant Love piloted her Osprey through enemy
fire and treacherous weather to extract wounded comrades,"
Granger continued. "On multiple occasions, she and her crew
placed themselves between danger and those in need."

A ripple went through the crowd. Love spotted Ford giving a slight smile.

"Lieutenant Naomi Love, come forward," Granger said.

Love took a deep breath and walked down the middle aisle toward the stage. Nerves washed through her, this somehow more difficult than flying through a bedlam of Zodark anti-aircraft fire. After she ascended the stairs, she stood beside Granger, her hands cupped in front of her, her hair in a tight bun.

Granger held the Flying Cross Medal and pinned the medal onto her uniform. He then presented the Bronze Star with Valor, adding it beside the first.

"Well done," Granger said in a soft voice.

"Thank you, sir."

Those in the hall applauded. She turned to face the audience—a sea of faces, some familiar, many not. The clapping echoed, filling the vast space. When it subsided, Granger leaned in, his voice meant only for her ears. "You've shown extraordinary courage. But remember to take care of yourself—and those around you. Find that balance. It's not easy, but it's there."

Her heart quickened. The truth in his words hit home, stirring something deep within. She thought of the sleepless nights, the relentless push forward. "Understood," she whispered. "I'm doing my best."

"I know." Granger grinned before stepping away.

Love approached the microphone, the heaviness of the medals tangible against her chest. "Thank you. I'm honored to receive these awards, but I wear them for all of us—for every soldier, every medic, every crew member who puts themselves on the line. Most of all, I couldn't have done this without Lieutenant Caleb Green, Lance Corporal Tyrell Williams, and someone who has kept me going for the last year, Chief Brian Ford.

"I've pushed hard, sometimes too hard," Love said into the mic. "I realize now the importance of taking care of ourselves so we can continue to take care of each other. I promise to find that balance. And maybe together we'll face whatever comes our way. We're stronger as a team than we could ever be alone."

She stepped back from the podium to applause once more, but this time it felt different—more personal, more connected.

As Love walked off the stage and down the aisle toward the back of the hall, Chief Ford met her. "You deserved this more than anyone."

"Can't believe they actually gave us one, let alone two medals," Love said.

"Us?"

Love rolled her eyes. "Since when could I have done any of this without you? These are as much yours as they are mine."

"Didn't you say you didn't need one? Because I distinctively remember after Coop got some medals, you played it off real cool and all."

They took a seat in the back, Commander Granger coming to the podium again to give out more awards.

"I don't know what I said, but still, doesn't matter. I got one… well, now two… who cares."

"Well, I kinda care," Ford said. "Makes the uniform look a bit more flashy, you know?"

"Oh, you want to be important?" Love joked in a hushed voice.

"I am important. Probably the most important," Ford said, clearly fibbing.

"Well, honestly, Ford. You are to me and my crew."

"I'm what?"

"Very important."

"Now who's trying to be flashy?" Ford said.

"Just stating facts, Chief. Just stating facts."

**Chapter 48:**
**Clear Skies**

**Year 2097**
**Operation Heliport Echo**
**FOB Oteren**
**Planet Intus**

Flight preparations had become second nature after all these years. As she secured the last buckle on her flight vest, Lieutenant Naomi Love took a moment to appreciate how different everything felt today. Last night's deep sleep and the morning's brisk walk had felt good, energizing even. The frenetic haze clouding her mind just days ago seemed distant now.

Green sat beside her, flipping switches and monitoring the instrument panel. His hair peeked out from under his helmet. Behind them, Williams double-checked the ammunition on the port-side gun. At the starboard gunner station, Ford went through his preflight checklist.

Reaching forward, Love touched the photo of Jack stuck to the dash. "Hey, Ford, how was mentoring some fresh recruits this morning?"

"Threw them into the deep end with some engine diagnostics," Ford said.

"Brave man," she replied. "How'd they handle it?"

"Not too shabby," Ford said. "Took a bit longer than I'd like, but you know what they say—slow and steady wins the race."

"You're patient with them. Good to hear."

"Teaching's got me rethinking a few things," Ford responded. "Turns out, slowing down has its perks."

"Well, don't slow down too much. We might start mistaking you for a Synth."

"I'll keep that in mind."

She nodded. "Seriously, though, good work. They're lucky to have you."

"Thanks, Lieutenant."

Leaving the cockpit momentarily, she made her way to the troop bay. The med techs were securing their equipment, conversation filling the space. Major Ito stood nearby, taking in every detail.

"All right, everyone," Love said as the med techs turned their attention to her. "This might look straightforward on the tactical display, but experience tells us different. Your priority is maintaining constant contact. The moment something feels off, you'll hear it—either from me or Major Ito. Questions?"

"Hey, Lieutenant," Abbot said, rubbing his eyes, not quite hiding his exhaustion, "tell me there's a bed with my name on it after this."

Love almost smiled. Almost. "How about we focus on getting back in one piece first?"

"What she means," Ito cut in, leaning against the bulkhead, "is stop thinking about your pillow and keep your head in the game."

"We wouldn't dream of screwing up." Huff double-checked his equipment. The dark circles under his eyes matched everyone else's on the med team.

"Just…" Love hesitated, choosing her words carefully. "Watch each other's backs out there. One team, one mission. And for God's sake, speak up if something doesn't feel right. I mean it."

She headed back to the cockpit, taking her seat. The controls felt natural under her hands, each switch and dial exactly where it should be.

"Diagnostics report full capability, ma'am. Bird's ready," Green said from the copilot seat.

"Solid copy," Love said. "Tower, Wolfpack Actual requesting clearance for dust-off, over."

"Wolfpack Actual, Tower. You're cleared hot. LZ is yours. Winds zero-two at six knots. Check your corners and fly safe, over."

"Roger that, Tower. Wolfpack Actual going vertical. Breaking ground."

She brought the Osprey into the air and eased the throttle forward. As they ascended, the base shrank below them, the landscape unfolding in all directions.

"Beautiful day," Green said.

"It is." Love scanned the horizon. The sky ahead stretched clear toward Heliport Echo.

Ford's voice came over the intercom. "Starboard gun is all set."

"Roger," Love said. "Let's keep everything running smooth."

Williams chimed in from the port side. "Locked and loaded over here."

"Good to hear."

The Osprey leveled off, cruising toward their destination. Love gifted herself a moment to simply breathe. For the first time in a long time, she was calm, collected.

She glanced at Jack's photo again, a silent acknowledgment. Turning her focus back to the sky ahead, Love guided the aircraft with confidence. Whatever awaited at Heliport Echo, she'd face it with Jack, and the rest of the crew… all by her side.

# Chapter 49:
## The Stage is Set

**Republic Embassy, Naval Liaison Office**
**Valdrakar, Primordia**
**Kita System**

When Lee returned to Primordia, he hadn't realized it was autumn. That was one of the oddities of serving aboard a starship; you didn't experience seasons. That was always a strange thing to get used when he returned planetside. It felt good, though, seeing the changes in the trees. Lee knew the crew was enjoying the time off to explore Valdrakar and the surrounding hills and the nearby mountains. Snow had even started falling at higher elevation. He wished he had been able to give his crew more time off, but duty called, and once their ship had finalized a few minor repairs, they were back in rotation for another mission.

As he continued to walk toward the Republic Naval Liaison Office, which was located on part of the embassy grounds, Lee smiled as he passed fellow Earthers. Some were dressed in duty uniforms, some in more formal attire, like he was. Occasionally, he'd spot some in civilian clothes,

*They must be off duty or on R&R.*

This part of Valdrakar was quickly becoming known as Little Earth, given the numbers of Republic military, government, and civilians taking up residence there. The Primords, for their part, were gracious hosts, welcoming in every facet and conceivable way. Thankfully, at least as far as Lee had learned, the Republic was doing its best to make sure its people were respectful, and did not abuse the hospitality and kindness shown to them through rowdy or abusive behavior. Lee wondered how that perception would hold up should large numbers of Republic soldiers become stationed here.

The walk to the embassy grounds from the hotel he had been quartered in since his arrival wasn't far, just a few city blocks. However, it was enough time for him to enjoy the fall weather and the changes it brought. Valdrakar in this season reminded him strongly of his upbringing in Wyoming. The air was crisp, cool, but not biting, and carried with it that smell of fresh-turned soil and the faint sweetness of drying corn stalks. It was like an old memory coming to life, of happier times.

Ahead of him was the main road that ran parallel to the embassy grounds, which reminded him of visits he'd made with his grandparents to Cantigny Park. Every summer, he'd spent several weeks with them in Wheaton, Illinois, and the Cantigny grounds had always struck him as a place of grandeur and wonder. McCormick, the original owner of the park, must have made a lot of money in the spice trade to afford such stately and well-manicured surroundings. Similarly, the Primords clearly took great pride in maintaining their properties.

The building that house the diplomatic mission and the attached naval liaison office didn't look like much from the outside, but that was the whole purpose—appear like nothing special, meanwhile, hidden within its walls and beneath the ground was an entirely different world.

As Lee approached the security checkpoint to enter the grounds, he pulled out his credentials. Lee presented them to the guards, who scanned his identification cards while his biometrics were verified. While Lee was not privy to the location of the various cameras that grabbed images of his face and iris, he knew the system would have collected his data before he even approached the guards. With the formalities completed, the Republic guards waved him in.

Lee walked into a facility with a simple innocuous sign that read "Naval Liaison Office." He made his way to the receptionist, signed in and was given a security badge that would allow him access throughout the building.

"Good morning, Commander Lee," a young ensign offered. "I was told to inform you upon your arrival to report to Captain Roberts' office. It's on the second floor, room 209T."

Lee smiled at the instructions, affixing the security badge to his uniform. "Thank you. I'm on my way."

He had come to learn that the second floor of the building was set aside for transients—officers and senior enlisted who needed a temporary office to work from when not aboard their warships. Technically, if Lee was going to be planetside for any length of time, he could request one himself.

When he reached the elevator, the door opened, and a couple of officers exited before he walked on. When he reached his floor, he was greeted with the smell of fresh coffee. Following his nose to the breakroom, Lee found a fresh pot on the hot plate and some nearby cups. After using his bank card to deposit a few credits into the community java fund, he helped himself to a fresh cup.

*Now I'm ready for whatever Roberts has for me*, he thought as he savored the hot liquid.

Walking down the hall, he eventually came to room 209T. He knocked, but no one was inside. Lee was about to leave when he noticed a note in the center of desk addressed to him:

*Lee, find me in Briefing Room S3.*
*--Roberts*

"Short and to the point, as always," Lee observed.

Lee made his way once again to the lift, descending in silence. This time, he was traveling a few levels down, to the subterranean floors.

The doors opened with a soft chime, and Lee emerged into a clean, angular corrido lined with low-level command personnel and inset terminals humming with encrypted data feeds. Everyone moved with purpose. There was no small talk, no wasted motion.

Lee followed the illuminated markers to Briefing Room S3. The door slid open, revealing Captain Roberts standing near the head of the table, arms crossed, flanked by two unfamiliar officers and a Primord aide reviewing an orange-colored datapad, denoting the device as Top Secret. A holo-projector in the center of the table displayed a slowly rotating sector map of the Rass system.

Roberts looked up. "Commander Lee," he said without preamble. "Good. Take a seat. You're going to want to hear this."

Lee took his seat without a word, his eyes drawn instinctively to the hologram in the center of the table. The map of the Rass system rotated slowly, certain regions overlaid with tactical annotations and faded red outlines. One quadrant—Sector-8—was highlighted in a muted amber glow, its borders pulsing faintly.

Roberts didn't waste time.

"You're heading back out," he began. "New orders came down last night. Joint operation. High-priority recon."

Lee raised an eyebrow. "Another raid?"

"No," Roberts said flatly. "This time, we're not sending you in to break anything—at least not yet. This is about finding something."

He gestured toward the amber-highlighted section on the holo. "Sector-8—the Middle Reach Ice Fields. It's a narrow corridor that stretches between our current forward line and the Alfheim front. Primord territory—at least it used to be."

Lee leaned forward slightly. The Middle Reach had been marked on every recon map he'd seen since arriving in the system—but only as a vague, shaded region with minimal intel.

"We've sent scouts in before—Republic and Primord," Roberts continued. "None of them came back. Not a whisper. And the ones that did send fragments of data and unusable telemetry…"

He tapped the console, bringing up a distorted video clip. The screen flickered. A forward sensor feed showed jagged, mountainous ice fields drifting silently in a dimly lit void. Frozen monoliths the size of city blocks spun in slow rotation, caught in the region's gravitational churn. Static crept across the screen—then a burst of chaotic movement.

A voice shouted. There was a blinding flash. And then it all went black.

The feed ended.

"That's the last transmission we got from a Primord scout ship," Roberts said grimly. "That was nineteen days ago."

Lee nodded once, slowly. "So, this is what, a ghost hunt?"

Roberts didn't smile. "No. This is a needle-in-a-graveyard search for whatever the hell's out there. Look, Primord Intelligence believes something big might be brewing out there. Varnak Outpost was just a piece of the puzzle. We still don't have a clear picture of what the Zodarks are up to in Rass, and Republic Intelligence is hesitant to issue a green light to Halsey to launch the invasion in that system."

Lee's brow furrowed as he listened. "Understood. Varnak did seem like it was part of something bigger," he remarked. "There was too much there—too many storage facilities and warehouses to just be a staging ground or refueling point. It seemed more like a transfer point—supplies coming in and then being moved to somewhere else."

"Yes, exactly!" one of the Primords interjected. "We read that in your post-battle report and had already come to the same conclusion."

Lee had never heard a Primord so excited.

After a brief awkward pause, the Primord continued, "Pardon my interruption. We briefly met following your return from Varnak. My name is Captain Sornvek; I work for Admiral Velmiran, Head of Primord Intelligence. I am the one leading the reconnaissance efforts in the Rass and Alfheim systems. We have reason to believe the Zodarks—and possibly the Orbots— are using the region to mask something big. I have been charged by Admiral Velmiran to figure out what it is. To that end, we are putting together a joint task force, an expedition if you will, to investigate this region once and for all."

"Ah, I see. And who is going to lead this expedition?" Lee asked, though he had a sneaking suspicion of who it might be and was already bracing for it.

This time it was Roberts who acted first, tapping the interface again. A new holo-image shimmered into view— Captain Dharek, with a permanently stern expression on his face—eyes hard, jaw set.

Lee hadn't spoken to Captain Dharek since they returned from the Varnak raid. Truthfully, he hadn't expected to.

"This is a Primord Intelligence operation," Captain Sornvek explained. "Captain Dharek will lead the expedition with a contingent of Primord ships. Captain Roberts was gracious enough to lend us you, Commander Lee, to serve as his second-in-command, and operational commander of the Republic ships participating."

"So that this is clear, Lee—we're not in command this time," Roberts echoed. "This is Captain Dharek's task force. You'll serve as his second, backing him up. But this is a Primord Intelligence operation, and they are taking point on this one. The Republic is there to support this mission, not to lead it."

Lee didn't respond immediately. He caught the hint; this was about being a team player and knowing his role.

Roberts must have noticed his hesitation. "Lee, I've read the post-Varnak reports from both sides. You made the right call—you stayed focused on the outpost. That decision also cost Dharek a battleship. He's obviously not happy with how things turned out, and given what I read in the report, he's likely taken it personally. You don't have that luxury.

"I'm not interested in how you two feel about each other," he said bluntly. "The brass on both sides here doesn't care either. You're professionals. You both got the job done at Varnak, and that's why you two are being paired up, to do it again."

Sornvek added, "Dharek's frustration is understandable, Commander. He's also wrong if he holds a grudge. I've spoken to him about it, and he knows you were following orders. He may not like it, he may not agree with it, but he knows you had a job to do, and you did it—he respects that."

"Commander, your force departs in forty-eight hours," Roberts finished. "Briefing materials will be uploaded to the secure terminal aboard the *Poseidon*. Get your crew prepped and your head clear. There's something out there, Lee… and I have a feeling it doesn't want to be found."

Lee sat motionless for a moment, eyes fixed on the slow rotation of the sector map. Sector 8 pulsed in amber, a shadowy gulf at the edge of the known. Ice fields, magnetic storms, vanished patrols—it was everything a seasoned commander should dread.

And now it was his next battlefield.

He gave a slow nod. "I'll have the *Poseidon* ready. Whatever is out there, we'll find it."

Roberts studied him for a beat, then leaned back slightly in his chair. "Good. And Lee—just so we're clear, this isn't Varnak. There's no reactor to hit, no weak spot to exploit. This is the kind of mission where you bring everything you've got and still come back with more questions than answers. So, keep your instincts sharp. And your ego out of Dharek's way."

That last part landed with more weight than Lee liked, but he didn't flinch.

"I understand," he said. It wasn't a protest. Just a fact.

Roberts gave a short nod. "Dismissed."

Lee stood, turned, and walked toward the door as it hissed open. The air outside the briefing room felt colder somehow, like the temperature had dropped while he was inside.

*Forty-eight hours.*

He was going back into the dark—and this time, not even the stars could be trusted.

*******

### From the Authors

Brandon and I hope you've enjoyed this book. If you'd like to preorder book three of the Battles of the Republic series and continue this action-packed military sci-fi series, please visit Amazon.

If you would like to stay up to date on new releases and receive emails about any special pricing deals we may make available, please sign up for our email distribution list. Simply go to https://www.frontlinepublishinginc.com/ and sign up.

As a bonus, if you sign up for our mailing list, you will receive a dossier for the Rise of the Republic Series. It contains artwork of the ships we've written about, as well as their pertinent stats. It will really help make the series come to life for you as you continue reading.

As independent authors, reviews are very important to us and make a huge difference to other prospective readers. If you enjoyed this book, we humbly ask you to write up a positive review on Amazon and Goodreads. We sincerely appreciate each person that takes the time to write one.

We have really valued connecting with our readers via social media, especially on our Facebook page https://www.facebook.com/RosoneandWatson/. Sometimes we ask for help from our readers as we write future books—we love to draw upon all your different areas of expertise. We also have a group of beta readers who get to look at the books before they are officially published and help us fine-tune last-minute adjustments. If you would like to be a part of this team, please go to our author website, https://www.frontlinepublishinginc.com/, and send us a message through the "Contact" tab.

# Abbreviation Key

| | |
|---|---|
| AA | Anti-aircraft |
| AI | Artificial Intelligence |
| AO | Area of Operation |
| ASAP | As soon as possible |
| BDA | Battle Damage Assessment |
| BP | Blood Pressure |
| CAS | Close-air Support |
| CHU | Containerized Housing Unit |
| CIC | Combat Information Center |
| CMO | Civil-Military Operation |
| COMSEC | Communications Security |
| CPR | Cardiopulmonary Resuscitation |
| CPT | Captain |
| DZ | Drop Zone |
| ECCM | Electronic Counter-countermeasures |
| ECM | Electronic Countermeasures |
| EENT | End of Evening Nautical Twilight |
| EMCON | Emission Control |
| ETA | Estimated Time of Arrival |
| EWO | Electronic Warfare Officer |
| EVA | Extra-vehicular Activity |
| FOB | Forward Operating Base |
| IFF | Identification Friend or Foe |
| FAE | Fuel-Air Explosives |
| FLIR | Forward-Looking Infrared |
| FTL | Faster-than-light |
| HUD | Heads-up Display |
| JAG | Judge Advocate General's Corps |
| JATM | Joint Advanced Tactical Missile |
| KIA | Killed in Action |
| LIDAR | Light Detection and Ranging |
| LT | Lieutenant |
| LZ | Landing Zone |
| MRE | Meals Ready-to-Eat |
| OPFOR | Opposing Forces |
| QRF | Quick Reaction Force |

| | |
|---|---|
| R & D | Research and Development |
| REDCON | Readiness Condition |
| RNS | Republic Naval Ship |
| RON | Remain Over Night |
| RPG | Rocket-propelled Grenade |
| RTB | Return to Base |
| SAM | Surface-to-Air Missiles |
| SEAD | Suppression and Destruction of Enemy Air Defenses |
| SIGINT | Signals Intelligence |
| SW | Sand and Water |
| UV | Ultraviolet |
| VTOL | Vertical Takeoff and Landing |
| WFJ | Wideband Frequency Jamming |
| XO | Executive Officer |

**THE END**